D0206513

Other Books in the
Blackbird Sisters Mystery Series

How to Murder a Millionaire
Dead Girls Don't Wear Diamonds
Some Like It Lethal
Cross Your Heart and Hope to Die
Have Your Cake and Kill Him Too
A Crazy Little Thing Called Death
Murder Melts in Your Mouth
No Way to Kill a Lady
Little Black Book of Murder
A Little Night Murder

Novellas in the
Blackbird Sisters Mystery Series

Slay Belles
Mick Abruzzo's Story

continued . . .

Murder Melts in Your Mouth

"Hilarious repartee and zany characters move the story along.... Martin is an outstanding mystery author."
— *Library Journal* (Starred Review)

"The long-awaited reunion between the sisters and their parents will satisfy longtime fans." — *Publishers Weekly*

A Crazy Little Thing Called Death

"A window on a moneyed world that the author skewers and spotlights with equal fun."
— *San Antonio Express-News*

"Why can't the perfect little black dress serve for interviewing benefit hostesses and dodging bullets? Of course [it] can, darling. The proof's right here."— *Pittsburgh Magazine*

Have Your Cake and Kill Him Too

"Martin, a master of one-liners and witty repartee, mixes the zany lives of the Blackbird family with posh Main Line Philadelphia society and comes up with another winning mystery." — *Library Journal* (Starred Review)

"Charming and funny." — *Publishers Weekly*

"Fabulous ... peppered with witty dialogue, oddball characters, and a clever plot ... delightful."
— *Romantic Times* (4 Stars)

Cross Your Heart and Hope to Die

"Nora Blackbird has humor, haute couture, and sexual heat." — Harley Jane Kozak, author of *Keeper of the Moon*

"A laugh-out-loud comic mystery as outrageous as a pink chinchilla coat." — *Booklist*

"The right mix of humor ... but like the best writers in this subgenre, Martin keeps the story grounded in reality."
— *South Florida Sun-Sentinel*

"A blend of fashion-forward romance and witty suspense.... Martin's wicked tongue-in-cheek satire will appeal to fans of Jennifer Crusie ... and Janet Evanovich."
— *Publishers Weekly*

LITTLE BLACK BOOK OF MURDER

A BLACKBIRD SISTERS MYSTERY

Nancy Martin

AN OBSIDIAN MYSTERY

OBSIDIAN
Published by the Penguin Group
Penguin Group (USA) LLC, 375 Hudson Street,
New York, New York 10014

USA | Canada | UK | Ireland | Australia | New Zealand | India | South Africa | China
penguin.com
A Penguin Random House Company

Published by Obsidian, an imprint of New American Library, a division of Penguin Group (USA) LLC. Previously published in an Obsidian hardcover edition.

First Obsidian Mass Market Printing, August 2014

ISBN 978-0-451-41526-4

Printed in the United States of America
10 9 8 7 6 5 4 3 2 1

For my Great Friend, Ramona

AUTHOR THANKS

I owe many thanks to friends and family who helped in the creation of this book. Jennifer Nedrow Wilkerson is Noah's virtual surrogate mom. Dennis Marsilli and Kurt Schazott offered excellent law-enforcement information. (I have taken some liberties—sorry, gentlemen!)

Jorge Ramirez and Elizabeth Regner are even more charming in person than I have portrayed them here. Thank you for your donation, Jorge!

Sharon Redfern very kindly suggested Filly Vanilli.

Thomas Christopher taste-tested Ralphie so I didn't have to. Thank you, Tom!

The team at NAL is the best in the biz, especially my longtime editor, Ellen Edwards. Thank you! And of course the rowdy crew at the Jane Rotrosen Agency—particularly Christina Hogrebe and the irrepressible Meg Ruley— are my champions.

Meghan Graham in Tasmania—crikey!—was a great help in providing some details from Down Under. Thank you, honey. And I owe a decent lunch with Diet Coke to my writer buds, Lila Shaara, Rebecca Drake, Kathryn Miller Haines, Heather Benedict Terrell and Kathleen George. Where would we be without one another?

Chapter 1

"The only time a woman is truly helpless," said my sister Libby as she sailed into the musty lobby of the old theater, "is when her nail polish is wet. Even then, she should be able to pull a trigger. I read that somewhere."

I had asked her for help regarding my new boss.

"I can't shoot my editor," I said as we skulked past the closed refreshment stand and into the back of the dark and empty auditorium. "As satisfying as that might feel, the long-range consequences would interfere with my social schedule. Which is still my job, and I need to keep it."

Libby arranged herself in a back-row seat like a contented hen settling on a nest of warm eggs, an impression heightened when she pulled off a scarf to reveal a T-shirt under her velour tracksuit. In sequins, the shirt said, HAUTE CHIC. She tossed her scarf over the adjacent empty seat. "Why are you asking me, Nora? I'd suffocate in a humdrum work environment! My inner goddess needs freedom to flourish. I get hives just thinking about punching a time clock. Darn it, I wish I'd thought to bring some popcorn."

Our sister Emma plunked herself down next to me and immediately propped her muddy riding boots on the seat back in front of her. "The sign in the lobby said stage mothers are supposed to stay out of the theater."

"I am not a stage mother," Libby snapped. "I am a powerful life force guiding my children to a brighter destiny. I pull them into the turbulent current of life with my own indomitable momentum."

Emma said, "Just a guess, but have you added to your collection of nutball self-help books lately?"

Libby blithely ignored that shot. She had dragged her fourteen-year-old twins, Harcourt and Hilton, to an audition for something I still wasn't clear about. Then, instead of lunch, she had insisted the three of us sneak into the back row to watch. Onstage, a couple of shady characters muttered beside the velvet curtains, which had been pulled open to reveal an empty space with a battered piano on one side. The piano player appeared to noodle one-handed on the keyboard while dozing off from boredom with his chin propped in his other hand. From some distant place, we could also hear the high-pitched buzz of a preteen mob that had been corralled like a herd of wildebeests eager to break into a stampede.

Libby dug into her handbag in search of a restorative snack. "Those stage-mother rules don't apply to me. I made it clear my sons should be first to audition this afternoon, so we'll be in and out as soon as the director gets started. Meanwhile, we can solve Nora's workplace issue."

If Libby could solve a workplace issue, it certainly wouldn't be because she had ever held down a formal job in her entire life. Like me, she had grown up on the Old Money accumulated by our entrepreneurial Blackbird relatives who came to America early and amassed an enviable fortune by investing in railroads and safety pins. There were no parcel-tying shopkeepers in our ancestry, Mama often said. Blackbirds had always allowed their money to do the work, and she made darn sure her daughters had none of the skills that might threaten that dubious family record. We had enjoyed all the luxuries money could buy until our parents went broke and ran off with the meager remains of our trust funds. They now applied themselves to perfecting their samba skills in South American dance halls while my sisters and I learned to navigate the real world.

My younger sister, Emma, had actually worked for a living since she was old enough to put a boot into a stirrup, so I turned to her and said, "How do I handle an obnoxious boss?"

"I suppose you've ruled out sexual favors," Emma said.

"That's not funny. I need a solution from this century, please."

"I was only kidding." Emma slumped down in her seat as if sliding farther into the funk she'd been fighting for months. "Why the hell are we here? I could use some food."

I had arranged a reconciliation lunch for my squabbling sisters, and it had taken all of my powers of peacemaking persuasion to get Emma to show up at all. At Libby's last-minute request, we had changed plans and met in front of a venerable Bucks County theater mostly used for amateur productions of Neil Simon plays and the occasional high school talent show.

Emma had appeared wearing an expression of sisterly resentment. Tall and lean and more perfectly proportioned than Miss Alabama, she might have been mistaken for a beauty queen except for her dirty boots, breeches and the mud-spattered shirt that said she'd been exercising someone's expensive horses somewhere nearby. Her short hair was mashed on the sides as if by a helmet and still managed to look chic. But the scowl on her otherwise flawless forehead told me that she and

Libby hadn't forgiven each other for harsh words snapped a few months ago when Emma gave birth and handed over her illegitimate baby to the child's very married father.

Both of my sisters were still pretending the other was invisible.

Therefore, sitting between them, I was the recipient of their undivided attention.

To me, Emma said, "What's so wrong about your boss?"

"Maybe the problem isn't your boss at all," Libby said as if Emma had not spoken. She focused intently on thumbing a stick of gum out of its packet. "Maybe it's you."

"I *know* it's me," I said, unable to hide my exasperation. "Look, I was hired to be a society columnist—to attend parties and report about charitable giving. That's where my skills are—parties! And I'm good at it."

"So what's the big deal?" Emma picked a hunk of mud off the side of one boot.

"Newspapers are failing all over the country, and half the staff of the *Intelligencer* has been laid off. We're putting out every edition on a shoestring. Because my salary is so low, I'll be the last to get a pink slip. Meanwhile, the new editor seems to think I'm a real reporter who should be capable of writing real news."

"That's a good sign." Libby handed me one of her two sticks of gum and kept the other for herself. "He must like your work."

"He likes that I'm cheap," I clarified, passing my share of the gum to Emma, who took it.

Emma said, "Is this Crocodile Dundee, the Australian guy?"

Libby sat up eagerly. "That man with the cute accent? Oh, I saw him on television, talking about the future of journalism. He's very handsome, Nora. The ex-surfer whose father is that bossy media mogul in Australia?"

"That's him. Thing is, I'm not suited to surfing with the crocodiles. He's asking me to be something I'm not."

"You're a reporter," Emma said. "So, report. Except instead of noticing flower arrangements, you gotta decide which gangbanger robbed the liquor store. Not much different."

"I'm not covering any gangs, thank heavens, but I'm floundering. I don't have the right skills."

My cell phone gave a jingle to tell me I was getting another text message. The phone had already gone off half a dozen times since I left my house. I glanced at the screen and held it up as Exhibit A. "See? He's texting me right now. Probably to ask when I'll be sending my column. Trouble is, I haven't had time to *write* the damn thing because he's also got me working on celebrity profiles!"

"That's what he considers real reporting?" Emma said. "Celebrity profiles? What, he hasn't heard of any flying saucer stories he could send you on?"

"Oh!" Libby cried. "Nora, I meant to tell you how much I loved your series on the *Real Housewives of the Main Line.* That one who owns five hundred pairs of shoes and keeps them organized by color? What an inspiration she is. How do I meet her?"

"Within five minutes of meeting her, Libby, you'd want to stab yourself in the eye with a stiletto."

"But it was a great article! All the girls down at the Pink Windowbox were talking about it." Libby set her handbag on the sticky floor, thought better of it, then put it on the seat beside her. "Here's my suggestion, Nora. Make a list of all your best accomplishments. Write them on slips of colored paper, and keep them in an old jewelry box—you know, the kind with the pop-up ballerina and the mirror inside? And every time you start feeling blue or inadequate, open your box and read one. You'll feel better, trust me."

"I'm not sure I want to be reminded that my best accomplishment is a story about a woman with five hundred pairs of shoes."

"It was better than you think," Libby insisted. "It made me want to buy shoes while also feeling morally superior. That's an accomplishment."

"People smarter than you are out of work right now," Emma pointed out, dropping her gum wrapper on the floor.

I picked up her wrapper and crumpled it in my hand. "Yes, I should be happy I have a job in the first place. It's just—I don't know how much longer I can keep making it up as I go along."

Libby said, "What other celebrities are you profiling?"

"The big one is Swain Starr, the fashion designer who retired. I started pestering him a few weeks ago, and he finally agreed to give me some interviews."

Libby lit up. "I love his clothes! And he makes plus sizes, thank heavens, and in colors other than black. Do all designers think fat girls are in mourning for their thin selves?"

"Who she's writing about is not the point," Emma snapped. "The point is Nora's overwhelmed."

"I'm not dense," Libby said without turning her head to acknowledge Emma's presence. "I'm completely sympathetic to your problem, Nora. You're in crisis. We should *all* learn to give and accept support in a crisis."

"I'm plenty supportive." Emma popped the gum into her mouth and started to chomp with enough force to break a molar. "But it doesn't do any good for her to wallow in self-pity."

"I need to be proactive," I agreed. "So tell me what to do, Em."

"Well, you can't resign. If you give up your salary, you'll lose your house for sure. After that last ice storm in January, Blackbird Farm looks more dilapidated than ever."

"Some of the gutters were damaged. I have to save up for the repairs."

"Go into business for yourself," Libby said. "Like me."

We turned to her, surprised to hear her news. I said, "You're in business?"

Emma snorted. "Are you selling sex toys again?"

"For your information," Libby said to me, "I am representing my children now. Specifically, the twins."

In recent years, Libby's teenage twin sons had developed unspeakable hobbies—I had the enormous jars of dead snakes and rodents in my cellar to prove it—and last I'd heard, they were lobbying to take a summer science course that required the purchase of a human cadaver. They had spent the winter eagerly shoveling sidewalks to earn enough money to buy one. They still spoke in their secret language of twins, and their conversations often sounded like a couple of bloodthirsty assassins planning mayhem in code.

So I assumed the worst and said, "You mean you're representing them in court? Shouldn't you hire a real lawyer, Libby?"

"They're not in trouble, silly. They've expressed an interest in the entertainment industry. And you know I leap at indulging their creative process."

"What kind of entertainment?" Emma asked. "Jumping motorcycles across canyons? Shooting apples off each other's heads? I presume whatever it is, there are deadly weapons involved?"

"I'll have you know," Libby said severely, "that all my

children have excellent karma of the soul. Their creativity responds to positive stimulation, that's all, not mean-spirited influences."

I intervened before Emma could throw a wad of chewing gum. "What kind of entertaining do the twins want to do?"

"I think they should start with modeling. Then acting, of course. But I want to keep them open to musical ventures, too. That Justin Bieber is so adorable. I could just eat him with a spoon."

Muttering a rude word, Emma sank down in her seat.

"The twins might especially thrive in the rock-and-roll scene," Libby said. "Most famous music stars can't carry a tune in a bucket, you know. There are machines that tweak your voice now. And instruments practically play themselves. Anybody can be a star. It just takes relentless representation to get ahead in the business. That's where I come in. What better, more determined business partner can a child have than a loving parent? And nobody can outshine me when it comes to determination."

Emma and I exchanged a look while Libby continued to rhapsodize.

"I was back doing some restoration work for the museums, but painting isn't very satisfying for me anymore. I'm too spontaneous to spend hours in a hermetically sealed laboratory. I need energy pulsing around me! If my own life has reached the period when things have slowed down a bit—well, it's a mother's job to turn her attention to making her children's lives as fulfilling as possible, right? Why work myself into a tizzy of disappointment and frustration when I can usefully turn my energies to something positive?"

I said, "Things fell through on your date last week?"

She heaved a wavering sigh. "We had a nice dinner, and I invited him back to my house for cappuccino, but when we got there, I had a zillion carpenter ants swarming all over my living room. Nothing like a huge black swarm of hideous bugs to suck the magic out of a romantic evening. It was horrible. A nightmare. But," she said, perking up, "I remembered that I have better things on my horizon. A few weeks ago, I went to a free seminar at the Holiday Inn. I didn't figure out I was in the wrong room until I was thoroughly entranced by the workshop. It was a tutorial for mothers of talented offspring. Immediately, I was inspired! Why should somebody else's pimply kid get all the attention when mine are perfectly capable?"

"Capable of what?" Emma asked under her breath. "Homicide?"

"The twins have oodles of potential," Libby said to me. "We just have to tease out the most marketable skills. Porter says every TV producer in the world is on the lookout for twins these days. Twins are very hot in sitcoms."

"Porter?" I asked cautiously.

"Sitcoms," Emma repeated, "Don't you think they're better suited to the horror genre?"

Steadily ignoring Emma, Libby said, "I've turned an important corner, Nora. By facilitating my children's reaching for the stars, I'll attain my own fulfillment, see? If the twins make it to Hollywood, I will have done my best as a mother, and that's reward enough in life."

"Who's Porter?"

"The young man who runs the seminars. He's accepted the twins into his exclusive program."

"He's some kind of a talent scout?"

"Well, first he scouts, then he nurtures. He represented that little girl who played a baby vampire on a cable show, and then she was hired for that movie with Meryl Streep. He's very successful. Of course, he's far too young for me," she added in a rush.

"Libby," I said, putting my arm around her plump

shoulders, "there are plenty of nice men in the world, and someday you're going to meet the right one. A man who's put off by a few insects isn't worth your—"

"It wasn't just a few bugs," she said, her voice catching on a sniffle. Her eyes pooled with tremulous tears. "It was about two million. That's what Perry the bug man said this morning when he made an emergency trip to my house. Fortunately, he d-didn't charge me the weekend rate, which is d-double the astronomical fee I actually paid. He says I'm such a good repeat customer that I d-deserve a d-discount."

I handed her my handkerchief in the nick of time. Libby burst into tears and sobbed her heart out. Nobody wept like Libby—gushing tears, heaving bosom and howling sobs that turned heads up onstage.

The man with the clipboard came to the apron and raised one hand to his forehead to squint out into the dark theater. "Ladies? You're not supposed to be here."

Emma called back, "We came to see our nephews."

"This is a closed audition. And anyway, we don't start for an hour. You have to leave."

Libby emerged from my handkerchief looking as radiant as a saint fresh out of Lourdes. "An hour?" She checked her watch. "That gives me enough time for a manicure. I think I saw a nail salon on the corner."

When we were out in the lobby again, Libby handed over my sodden handkerchief. "A manicure or maybe an herbal body wrap. I want to look my best for the high school graduation in a few weeks. There's a chance Rawlins will be honored with an award or two, and since I may be asked to pose for posterity with him, I want to look wonderful. I've been dieting, too, but it doesn't seem to be working."

I asked, "Libby, what happened to your theory that dieting is a weapon of oppression against women?"

"Theories come and go, but photographs are forever," she replied.

She went off to her body wrap, and Emma and I went out to her truck. While she drove me to the event I had to attend, I checked my phone messages.

"Well?" Emma asked. "Is your boss putting on more pressure?"

"Yes." I tucked my phone back into my bag without responding to the demanding texts. "He wants everything done yesterday."

"Fake it till you make it, Nora."

"I'm trying," I said. "But maybe I should research some night classes. I don't want to fail. I want to do a great job. I want to knock my editor's socks off."

"Be careful what you wish for," Emma said. "First it's his socks; then it's his pants."

I turned to look at my sister. Behind the wheel of her truck, she looked as composed as ever. Good-humored, even. And sober, which was the important thing. I hoped she hadn't started drinking again.

But her good humor was deceiving. Just two months earlier, on Christmas Day, Emma had given birth to an eight-pound baby boy who was immediately whisked off by his new parents—Emma's married lover and his new wife. The newlyweds were enjoying their infant son, we heard, while Emma tried hard to pretend she had no memory of delivering a love child. Her body showed no signs of having experienced childbirth except—if it were possible—even more perk to her already faultless breasts. The condition of her mind, though, might be another story.

Having suffered two still-painful miscarriages myself, I had some unexplored feelings on the subject, too, but I said, "Have you had your postpartum checkup?"

"Don't start," she warned.

"I just want to be sure you're taking care of yourself."

"I'm fine," Emma snapped. "And as far as I know, the baby's fine, too. We're both fine, peachy keen, in the pink, perfectly healthy. You can lay off the sisterly concern. I'm back to normal."

"Of course you're fine," I said. "Libby popped out all five of her babies like Life Savers. But the estrogen aftermath was another story. If your hormones are anything like hers, any second you could be making an emergency landing at the Crazytown airport."

"I'm *fine*," Emma insisted. "I'm strength training at a gym. And I'm back to work."

"Oh, really? At Paddy's barn? Does he have some promising jumpers this spring?"

"He's not using me full-time, so I picked up some hours as an exercise rider to take up the slack. And to build some muscle."

At once I knew she was disappointed not to be on the big Grand Prix jumpers. Emma needed to prove herself all over again, I guessed, before the owners of valuable animals boosted her into their saddles. "You're working as an exercise rider? You mean racehorses?"

"Just morning breezes on the less valuable livestock. I know a trainer at the track. He's the one who gave me the job."

"How do you know him?"

"Around. Look, I'm supposed to get him a Filly Vanilli for his kid. How do I find one of those?"

Aware that she was changing the subject, I relented and asked, "What's a Filly Vanilli?"

"A toy. Or a music box. A music box that's *in* a toy. It's a horse thingie you hang on the side of a crib, and the horse sings songs in this goofy voice and puts the kid to sleep."

"Sounds cute."

"Yeah, except you can't find them anywhere. They're, like, impossible to buy."

"And you need to find one for this trainer who gave you a job?"

"Right. Where can I get one?"

"I have no idea. This trainer. Are you dating him?"

"Hell, no. He's old and cranky from lack of sleep with this new kid at home."

"Are you dating anyone right now?"

"If you must know," she said, exasperated, "I'm seeing Jay, the kid who washes dishes at the Rusty Sabre."

"Why him?"

"Why not?"

There was something in her tone that made me suspect she was telling more lies than Pinocchio. Since the death of her husband in a car accident, Emma seemed hell-bent on sleeping with every man who struck her fancy. And her fancy had gotten quite a workout before she landed in a maternity ward. Men who could ride fast, party hard and climb into bed without any fear of commitment were the ones she preferred. Since her pregnancy, though, I hadn't heard about any new exploits.

I said, "Em—"

"Don't worry about me, Sis. The biggest problem I have is finding a damn Filly Vanilli."

But I did worry. On the chance Emma's hormones were not as stable as she wanted me to believe, however, I decided not to risk further discussion about her personal life.

The three of us—Libby and Emma and I—had all survived the loss of our husbands. We had each coped with widowhood differently. I had to trust that Emma was on a path that would get her somewhere good in the end.

The sun glinted on the Delaware River to our right as we swooped around the curves and over the hills of the two-lane road that led north from New Hope. We passed my home, Blackbird Farm, and kept going.

I said, "Why don't you come for dinner tonight?"

"Can't. I've got a date." Before I could decide if I should ask why she recently had plenty of excuses not to visit us, Emma switched subjects again. "How's Mick?"

I barely held back a sigh of dismay at the mention of Michael Abruzzo, tickler of my fancy, man of my dreams, the love of my life, who had dodged his prison sentence for racketeering when facility overcrowding had gotten him reassigned to house arrest. For the last few months, he had been trapped at home with an electronic monitor. Which I was happy about. Really.

"He's frustrated," I replied. "Most of the time, he paces like a caged animal."

Emma glanced my way. "How bad is it?"

"The conditions of his parole are that he can't really run his business the way he wants to. He can't deal with things in person. So he's on the phone. A lot."

"He's more the hands-on type than the phone-it-in type."

"Yes," I said. "He's definitely hands-on."

She heard my change of tone and laughed. "Oh, I get it. His hands are on you, huh? He jumps you every chance he gets? Plenty of funny business going on in your bedroom?"

"Not just the bedroom. We've always had a very satisfying—well, lately it's been rather more than I can . . ."

"Don't sugarcoat for my benefit." Emma was amused. "He's bored, so he wants a lot of nooky? Anytime, day or night? And you're—what? Exhausted? Or out of creative ideas?"

"He's always had big appetites," I admitted. "Sometimes I have a little trouble . . . keeping up."

"Take your vitamins, Sis." Emma was laughing at me again. "How's the baby-making going?"

"No results yet." I tried to keep my tone upbeat.

She glanced my way. "Time to see a specialist?"

"Not yet." The subject was a touchy one, and for fear I'd bust into blubbers, I said, "I'll tell Michael you said hello."

"Don't bother," she replied, pulling to the gates of Starr's Landing.

An impressive pair of ornamental brick pillars was flanked by white split rail fences on either side and centered with a set of elaborate gates whose wrought-iron curlicues formed the letter *S* entwined in the middle. The owners of a Transylvania castle could barricade themselves against peasants attacking with pitchforks and blazing firebrands with less of a barrier.

I dug out my invitation and gave Emma the access code. When the security gate opened, Emma pulled through. Her old truck didn't quite match the expensive automobiles parked along the curved lane, but Emma didn't notice.

She whistled as she got her first look at the state-of-the-art farm. "Hey, this place looks like Disneyland."

"I've seen every pristine acre, even behind the scenes," I said. "The owners showed me the hydroponic tanks and the perfect baby chicks. The whole farm is everything you'd expect from a fashion designer who gets the urge to go back to the land. It's a work of art."

Today I had been invited back to Starr's Landing for the great unveiling. Swain Starr eventually wanted the world to see what he had accomplished, but first he had invited a few important friends and the eager press. Swain had promised he'd donate to a local farmers' co-op if other guests pledged, too. It was a nice gesture, but not exactly world-class philanthropy. His primary reason

for throwing the party was to show off. I had to find a
way to make it seem otherwise in the newspaper.

"Want to join the party?" I asked my sister.

"For champagne punch and petits fours?" Emma extended her pinky finger and waggled it contemptuously.
"You know that's not my kind of scene."

No, it certainly wasn't. Beer and pizza were more her
style. So I waved good-bye to Emma and walked into the
party.

Our diminutive host greeted his guests in front of the
barn, looking like an absurdly handsome miniature cowboy in perfectly faded jeans and a tailored chambray
shirt. By his bronzed face, his signature gray hair, his
crinkly blue eyes, anyone who had opened a fashion
magazine in several decades would have instantly recognized him and known he was a billionaire fashion baron,
not a humble Pennsylvania farmer. In person, though,
Swain Starr stood about half as tall as people imagined.
Even wearing his red cowboy boots with heels, he barely
came up to my chin. He was less hardy than people
imagined from his photos, too. He had the tentative walk
of a more elderly man not quite confident in his balance.

He gave me three air kisses—producing runway shows
in Paris had left its mark, even though he was retired—
and pulled me by the hand through the paddock gate.

"Nora, you look beautiful."

"Why, thank you." I performed a pirouette to show
off my dress. "Recognize it?"

"Should I?"

"It's from your collection. Of course, it's from twenty
years ago. No wonder you forget. How many dresses
have you designed over the years?"

"Thousands." He smiled, pleased by my gesture of
homage. "Surely this wasn't something you wore as a
child?"

I had pulled out of my closet a seductively simple Swain Starr party dress made of cotton damask printed with pink cabbage roses and tulips. Ladylike, even demure. Sleeveless, piped with pink satin and with a light cashmere sweater in a matching pink—it suited my fair coloring and dark auburn hair as well as the occasion. And I had already noticed that the farm had been decorated with huge tubs of pink tulips exactly like those on my dress. Of course, we were smack in the middle of tulip season, so I had made an educated guess.

When I started working for the newspaper and needed the right clothes to attend the many black-tie and formal events on the charity circuit, I had climbed the attic stairs and dug into the trunks my grandmother Blackbird left behind. Her extensive collection of haute couture—gathered over many years and dozens of trips to the ateliers of world-class designers—suited me very well, and I embraced the vintage couture as my "look."

I didn't want to make Swain feel old by mentioning my grandmother had been his client, so I said, "It's a family piece. Do you still like it?"

"It's a classic," he said proudly. "And it looks positively new on you."

I thanked him, and together we turned to gaze across the landscape spread before us.

"What do you think, Nora?" Swain asked. "Have I created one more masterpiece?"

He had certainly taken a few dozen acres of Bucks County farmland and turned them into a bucolic paradise complete with a weathervane on top of the red barn and a picturesque flock of white ducks paddling across a perfect little pond dappled with lily pads. Half a dozen black-and-white cows grazed in a lush pasture alongside a woolly little burro that would have made the perfect character in a children's picture book.

Hoping to muscle his way to the forefront of the Farm-to-Table movement, Starr promised old-fashioned agrarian methods blended with the latest scientific advancements in breeding and cultivation, all while nurturing personal relationships with the local food community. By the look of things, he was certainly working hard at reaching his goal.

Not by making much personal sacrifice, however. I had seen a contingent of local laborers troop through the security gate every day to bring the animals, install the solar panels on the barn roof and get the first crops into the ground. Swain had watched them from the porch of his spectacular, newly built home, which stood on the hillside overlooking the rural paradise. The house was a meld of Shaker-style simplicity and ultramodern glass and steel construction with a view of pasture, barn and river out front and a steep cliffside panorama out back. It was a home befitting a king of fashion. I couldn't guess how many millions it cost to build.

"It's all marvelous," I said.

He waved his hand to indicate the animals. "The vegetables are my wife's specialty. I'm focusing on meat. In addition to the dairy cows, I plan on having at least a hundred producing sows by fall. All kept in sanitary conditions or roaming the pastures. My lovely wife will hold me to that promise."

At the mention of her loveliness, Swain's wife materialized beside us.

"Hello, Nora."

I recognized her breathy voice and turned. Zephyr Starr. Her wholesome American face was probably pasted on billboards from Japan to Paris and every continent in between, but once more it entranced me. Clear eyes, flawless skin. Straight blond hair braided to look as if the farmer's daughter had stopped at a chic salon. Perhaps thirty years old now, the former supermodel could pass for a teenager in forgiving light. A physically perfect specimen for displaying every kind of clothing from bathing suits to haute couture, Zephyr must have been accustomed to taking the breath away from everyone she met. Today, dressed in simple, yet cunningly cut skinny pants with a close-fitting, iconic white T-shirt that showed off youthful breasts and a tiny waist, she looked anything but casual. Her own beauty was accessory enough to make her magnificent.

I attempted to be as friendly as she had been. "Hi, Zephyr. The farm looks wonderful."

"Yes, it does. Thank you for coming."

During my interviews with her husband, Zephyr had floated in and out of range, alighting on a chair only when Swain finally begged her to join us. He asked her to move to a different chair so the light from the windows illuminated her skin in a way he admired. Looking so gorgeous that I had trouble concentrating on her words, she had spoken very briefly about herself when I asked—only giving up the kind of superficial information I could read in any press release—but when she'd talked about the farm she and her husband envisioned, she had grown emotional. She wept over the conditions of chickens kept on commercial farms, and she spoke passionately about growing vegetables without pesticides. So she wasn't just a shallow beauty. Her husband was very proud of her, I could see. They were the picture of marital happiness.

She wound one of her graceful long arms through Swain's and bestowed her world-famous smile upon him. "Darling, our best hope has come true. We have our first ripe tomato on the vine. Would you like to help me pick it to show everyone? Or can I pour you a lemonade first?"

He patted her slim hand and shot a smile at me. "She takes good care of me, see? Will you excuse us, Nora?"

"Of course. Enjoy your day."

They moved away—the tall, stunning young woman and the proud-as-a-peacock man who was shorter and older than she. He leaned on her arm, as if needing her strength. I almost shook my head with puzzlement. There must have been a forty-year difference in their ages, yet they seemed devoted to each other.

I had known Swain's first wife—a good mother, a smart conversationalist with plenty of brains and personality, plus a fair amount of sex appeal even in her midsixties—so it was hard to make peace with his having left the woman who had stood shoulder to shoulder with him as he built his career and family.

Zephyr was beautiful. No—beyond beautiful. And almost geisha-like in her attention to her older husband. Maybe that combination of wifely attributes was more important to a man of Swain's years than loyalty and history.

Why had she bothered to marry him, though? Had their passion for growing organic food truly brought them together? Or was it some alchemy I didn't quite grasp? Stranger unions had happened, I supposed.

I turned to admire my surroundings again—the true purpose of today's event. A white party tent stood next to the modest strawberry patch, and beautifully dressed guests milled around with crystal champagne flutes in their hands. Tables had been dressed with enamel pitchers stuffed with more pink tulips.

I began to make my usual party rounds among the guests. It was the kind of thing I did several times a week—exchanging pleasantries with familiar faces and introducing myself to people I didn't know. I had grown up among the Old Money set, and from my years in the

Junior League before my husband died, I knew a wide circle of friends from the arts and medical communities, too. I also had contacts in the fashion crowd, so I was called over to chat with many small clutches of guests.

After saying a few hellos and promising lunches with friends, I bumped into my nephew, Libby's oldest son, Rawlins.

"Rawlins, what on earth are you doing here?" I gave him an exuberant hug.

"Hey, Aunt Nora."

I could have sworn Libby's teenage son had grown since I'd seen him a week ago. During the past year, he'd gradually shed all the jewelry he had worn pierced through his ears and face, and along with the hardware, he'd also lost most of his hostile attitude—except where his mother was concerned, and I had to admit that if Libby had been my mother, I might have felt occasionally hostile, too.

Today Rawlins looked surprisingly relaxed and adult in khaki pants and his trusty navy sport coat over his usual T-shirt. He had brushed his dark hair, and his Blackbird blue eyes were clear and direct as he smiled at me. He gave me a kiss on the cheek.

"How on earth did you get invited to this event?" I asked.

"Someone I know invited me. I'm not sticking around long." He was making a good show of sophistication, but I saw hints of teenage unease in his body language.

"Someone from the neighborhood?"

"Yeah," he admitted, without sharing more details about his current love life.

"I could use a ride home. Look for me before you go? I'll stow away in your trunk if you want to keep me out of sight."

He grinned. "I'll look for you."

I couldn't resist giving him a little elbow. "Are you on an official date? Or just girl watching? There are some very pretty young ladies here. Zephyr isn't the only one worth a second look." ·

He blushed so deeply even his ears turned red, a likely indication he was waiting for a girl to come back to him. But he said, "Uh."

With a laugh, I said, "I won't insist on an introduction to your latest. I have to get back to work. Come for dinner sometime soon? Michael would enjoy seeing you."

Another flicker of shy pleasure showed on his face. "That'd be great. Thanks. Don't work too hard, Aunt Nora. Have fun."

But the next notable person I came upon wasn't any fun at all. He was none other than my new editor.

Gus Hardwicke was leaning on a fence, studying the crowd with an air of being highly entertained by what he saw. He had a glass of champagne in one hand and a slight, perhaps condescending smile on his mouth. He wore dark sunglasses, so I couldn't see his eyes.

"Nora Blackbird," he said to me, his smirk broadening. "Do you always dress like you're going to a garden party?"

Chapter 2

I gathered my composure. "This is a garden party, Mr. Hardwicke. I try to be suitably dressed when I represent my employer."

He remained leaning against the fence, but he took off his sunglasses and gave me a long perusal, brows raised over piercing green eyes. I couldn't tell what he was thinking, except I got the fleeting impression that the new editor-in-chief of the *Philadelphia Intelligencer* had decided I was a tasty hors d'oeuvre fresh off the barbie.

I must have bristled.

"I'm not criticizing," he said, continuing to examine me over the rim of his champagne flute. "Far from it. In fact, where I come from, we'd call you a smoke show."

"A—?"

So far, every time I'd encountered him, Gus Hardwicke had managed to get me off balance and keep me there. He did it, I knew, because he recognized I was too polite to fight back. He took advantage of my good manners.

Tartly, I said, "Is that a compliment in Australia?"

"Smokin' hot? Of course it's a compliment."

Hardwicke wore a sharp jacket—probably Ermenegildo Zegna, if I had to guess, very expensive, but worn casually over jeans and a button-down shirt. He was very much the hip Aussie.

He said, "I just looked in on an invention called an eco-toilet—earth-friendly, I'm told. There was a sign inside, 'If it's yellow, let it mellow. If it's brown, flush it down.' Can you tell me what that means, precisely? I can't imagine."

I was fairly certain he was taunting me, and I wasn't falling into the trap. "I haven't the faintest notion. Some organic-living policy, perhaps?"

"Perhaps." Still eyeing me with a calculating smile, he said, "You were very brave to choose those shoes, knowing you were going to be around cows."

"The trick to cows is keeping your distance," I said, and returned my attention to the party. At least, when I wasn't looking at him, I could pretend he wasn't ogling me. "Don't you have cows in the land Down Under?"

"Sheep. We have sheep in Australia. Last I was there, anyway." He stopped a passing waiter and scooped a glass of champagne off the silver tray. He handed the glass to me. "Drink up, luv. The bubbly's a bloody good drop."

In my short career as a journalist, I had never been called "luv" by a superior. But the *Philadelphia Intelligencer* had been in a state of flux since the death of its owner, a retired tycoon who had treated the newspaper like one of his many expensive hobbies—with lax management and only periodic supervision. Now the new owners were taking a firmer hand. They had hired a new editor—Gus, once a slacker surfer who became a brash, journalistic buccaneer who cut his teeth on less-reputable Australian newspapers owned by his family before escaping to Canada after a rumored scandal that his powerful father had hushed up. Finding immediate work in Canadian tabloids, he sold scads of papers by reporting on drunken television stars who misplaced their underwear and politicians with the instincts of rutting bonobos. I heard he paid vast sums of money for the unsavory photographic proof.

In short, he sold newspapers in an era when other editors couldn't.

Under his cutthroat regime, the staff of the *Intelligencer* lived in fear for their jobs. He had laid off half the journalists during his first week. Some of the remaining reporters claimed concern for their professional ethics. So far, only one reporter had left with his head held high, but there was more rumbling in the lunchroom—rumbling and posturing, if the truth be told.

Me, I simply hoped I could continue to receive my meager paycheck. Standing beside our merciless new editor, I felt my palms begin to sweat.

So I sipped champagne to summon my courage and said, "May I ask why you're here, Mr. Hardwicke? Is it to supervise me? Is my work not up to snuff?"

He gave me another unsettling look with eyebrows raised. "Do I give the impression I'm snuffling your work, Nora?"

"I realize this is the first important profile I've been asked to write, but it's going well. After he finally agreed to be interviewed, Swain met with me twice this week. He's been very forthcoming—"

"Relax, luv. I'm not checking up on you. I was invited to this—what do you call it, a hoedown?—by Starr himself. Even in Australia we know a fashion designer or two, so how could I refuse? He throws a good bash, doesn't he? Do you know anything about farms?"

"As a matter of fact, I grew up on a farm. I still live there. It's just down the road a few miles."

Hardwicke turned and blinked at me. "Well, bugger me. I hardly pictured you spending your off-hours tending lambs with a crook in your hand."

"I don't tend anything. It was a working farm back

during the Revolution, and my grandfather raised Hereford cattle—more as a hobby than anything else. Now that the farm is mine, though, we struggle to keep the grass mowed. But I love it." Without understanding why I wanted to say it, I added, "I feel rooted there."

For two hundred years, Blackbird Farm had stood alongside the Delaware River, not far from where George Washington climbed into a small boat and crossed those icy waters. I had been raised on the property, spent my childhood climbing the trees and looking for pollywogs in the feeder creek. I read Nancy Drew and *Wuthering Heights* in the loft of the barn. Even when my husband's drug addiction had been at its worst, I had come to the old place to walk in the woods to clear my head. I still loved it even though these days the farm was looking a little worse for lack of maintenance.

"To tell the truth," I went on cautiously, "Swain came calling and offered to buy Blackbird Farm for this project. That's how I met him in the first place. Maybe I should have taken him up on it."

"Why didn't you?"

How much does one tell the boss? After a moment, I said, "My family doesn't have much left these days, unless you count names in history books. Except for Blackbird Farm. So I'd like to hang on to it as long as possible. Maybe someday bring it back to its old glory." Although that day was looking more and more distant. "So I turned down Swain's offer. Frankly, he wasn't as excited to buy the place after he took a closer look. It was more cost-effective for him to build new. Looks as if he made the right choice."

"I hear he built this farm for his wife."

"Second wife," I said. "Zephyr. She was a model."

He grinned. "Yes, Zephyr, the supermodel discovered in something you Americans call a . . . hillbilly holler? I have seen her photos. Lovely girl, no offense to present company."

"No offense taken. She's gorgeous. Like the rest of the world, I'm surprised she stopped modeling. She must have years left in her career."

"True love," Hardwicke said. "It makes people do stupid things. She's the one who's the nut for organic farming, I hear. And she made her husband retire to pursue it."

"I don't think she had to twist his arm much," I said.

"You can lead a horse to water? Well, maybe." He signaled a passing waiter, who instantly offered him another glass of champagne, which he accepted without a thank-you. "What have you learned about Zephyr?"

"The focus of my profile has been her husband."

"Nora, Nora," Hardwicke chided. "Eye on the ball, please. Readers want to know the dirtiest dirt about Swain, and that means Zephyr. Why did he dump his wife? Did he retire from a billion-dollar career for Zephyr? What's her magic? Youth? Sex? That's a cliché. Check the bottles in the refrigerator and medicine chest. See what they keep in the night table, too. Heroin? Rope so the beautiful supermodel can tie up her old hubby and give him enemas while watching donkey porn? That's the kind of thing I want to know."

"I—I don't think I can do that."

I must have turned pale, because he peered closer. "You're a sensitive little sheila, aren't you? I'm trying to boost your skills, luv. Make you a tall poppy, the head of the class. So your job is this: Find Starr's soft underbelly and slash it open."

I had a feeling he was taunting me with the sheila bit. But pushing me to invade someone's privacy truly felt like a bridge too far. I said, "I'm not really the slashing type."

"But you want to keep your byline," he said with an unpleasant smile. "So start drilling down. See what you can really learn about Zephyr and Starr. How does a twentysomething stunner fall for a short, old bloke like Starr?"

"He might be short and old, but he's charismatic."

Hardwicke laughed. "Trust me, charisma is not what that relationship is about. That's the kind of info I want you digging up. That, and more."

How much more could there possibly be? I wondered.

He speared me with a sharp, sideways glance. "While you're at it, find out why Starr left fashion. He didn't retire from a billion-dollar trade because his new wife asked nicely. There's more to the story."

"He's not going to tell me," I said.

"You know his family, right? His ex? His children?"

"Ye-es," I said slowly.

"You're the expert in the rich and powerful. Supposedly the girl who knows all about Philadelphia high society? Make use of your contacts. Didn't I recently hear you were the one who introduced the future mayor to his first financial backers? I'm just the boy from Melbourne who swept the floors of the print shop to earn my lunch, so I must rely on you." He gave me a grin to show he was joking about the lunch part. He'd grown up in the lap of Australian luxury. Even I knew his father's yacht could almost be mistaken for a destroyer. He said, "Why don't you introduce me around? Show me what you've got. Maybe I'll have some ideas of what wounds to poke."

The story had gotten around that I had introduced an up-and-coming politician to some moneyed friends. There was a soupçon of truth to that, but it had been blown out of proportion. As far as I had seen, there were no million-dollar checks written on the spot, despite rumors to the contrary. "Mr. Hardwicke—"

"Call me Gus," he commanded, grabbing my hand and placing it in the crook of his arm. "At least, while we're off the sheep station."

I don't know why I hesitated to use his given name. Gus Hardwicke was only a few years older than me. It should have been natural. But he was my boss. Not to mention a reasonably attractive man—with thick reddish hair and a ruddy outdoorsy complexion and freckles. Appealing freckles. And he had a tendency to use his sparkling green eyes to bore intimately into whomever he was speaking to. He had a tall, confident body that he maintained—so I heard around the office—by daily trips to the gym where he soundly defeated all comers in ruthless racquetball. His arm was a powerful knot of muscle.

He trapped my hand in that strong arm and pulled me to the receiving line. "Come on, Nora. Introduce me to the blue bloods. I need to add some names to my little black book."

Although I didn't like being put in the position of demonstrating my familiarity with the many influential guests, I did know the Starr family quite well, and I made introductions. Gus released me to shake their hands.

Starr's first two sons and one daughter from his first marriage stood along the fence. Taller than their father, they were all tanned and attractive. And successful. The older ones—Jacob and Eli and Suzette—worked for Starr Industries, and the two spouses were very glamorous, too. I shook their hands and gave Jacob a hug. He had gone to school with my sister Libby.

Suzette was the only family member to give me a half-hearted handshake. Despite our spending a semester abroad together in college, she had been one of my late husband's friends, and she had never forgiven me, I think, for Todd's death. She warmed up to Gus Hardwicke when he flirted with her, however.

He laid the Aussie routine on very thick, and I let him misbehave for a minute or two, then slipped my hand around his arm again. "Let's meet Suzette's younger brother, shall we?"

Gus hesitated. I knew he wanted to spend more time with Suzette. She was very pretty and beautifully dressed in her father's latest designs, and she was probably a bazillionaire, if it was money that turned him on.

But I gave his arm a meaningful squeeze. Obediently, Gus said good-bye to Suzette, and we moved down along the fence.

"What was that for?" he muttered.

"Suzette is gay," I said in a low voice that matched his. I released his arm. "And her brothers enjoy watching men make fools of themselves over her. So I'm sparing you from becoming a family anecdote."

Gus laughed, unrepentant. "You really do know everyone, don't you?"

"Not everyone," I said, annoyed all over again at being cast in the role of his trusty native scout. "But I spent several months traveling around China with Suzette, so I know her better than most."

"China?"

"A school thing. I took Chinese in college. She ate nothing but oranges the whole time."

"Crikey, I'm glad I came," he said. "This afternoon is even more informative than I'd hoped."

"Would you like to meet the youngest son?"

"Is he anybody important?"

"Actually, Porky—er, Porter Starr is the only one of Swain's children who managed to strike off on his own and make a career outside the family. He became a child actor with a popular TV show."

"Porky?"

I felt myself turn pink. "That was a slip of the tongue."

"I can hardly wait to meet him."

We came upon the youngest Starr son leaning against a fence, under an oak tree. The short, rather chunky young man wore a small-brimmed fedora cocked over one eye with more suave panache than he could quite carry off. He held a kitten while talking with a young woman in a pretty dress with a very short skirt. Just as we approached, the young woman threw her drink in Porky's face and snatched the kitten from his grasp.

He laughed, and she stalked away.

Gus handed over his handkerchief. "Looks like you're a mite damp, mate. What did you say to her?"

Porky took the handkerchief with a cocky grin. "I asked her about pussies."

Without removing his hat, he mopped his face while I made introductions.

I read Gus's mind. Porky Starr didn't look like his father except for his short stature. Instead, he was the spitting image of his mother's family—the piggy little Rattigan face with a flat, upturned nose, wide cheeks and little porcine eyes. Porky's looks had worked in his favor as a kid—he was almost cute back then—and he'd gone off to Hollywood and fame in the sitcom world. He had outgrown his cuteness, though, and I assumed he was still trying to live down the nickname that had probably started when he was still in the cradle.

It wasn't until I was shaking his sweaty hand that I made the connection.

Porter. This was Libby's mentor in the world of child entertainment.

"Right," Porky said when I brought up my sister. He used one wrist to swipe his nose. "Her boys have a lot of potential. Hollander and Hyatt, right?"

"Harcourt and Hilton," I said.

"Yeah, yeah. Twins are very hot right now, yo."

The *yo* almost made me laugh. He was the wrong social class to be talking like a streetwise rapper.

Porky Starr had none of the Starr confidence his siblings naturally exuded. None of their innate friendliness, either. He had dressed for the occasion in stovepipe jeans and a too-tight T-shirt that advertised a long-forgotten rock concert I was willing to bet he hadn't attended. His impatient manner said he couldn't wait to be rid of me.

"So you're managing talent?" Gus asked, ignoring Porky's dismissive behavior. "You're an agent?"

"Not an agent," Porky corrected. "I put the right people together. You know, matching opportunities."

"Is that lucrative?"

Porky wasn't offended by the blunt question. "I conduct seminars—educational events for young people with big dreams."

"Seminars. You mean classes? How to behave in front of a camera, that kind of thing? You charge for that?"

"I get finder's fees when dreams come true."

"Kickbacks, right?"

"People value something more if they pay for it."

"Nothing in life is free, yo," Gus agreed cheerfully.

"Right you are." Porky looked past us again in hopes of spotting more entertaining guests to talk to.

Gus said, "Is your business regulated in any way?"

The question acted like an electric shock on Porky. He jumped, then frowned at Gus as if trying to remember who he was and why he should be tolerated. "Many reputable businesses function on a handshake and a promise."

"Yes, but—"

"Excuse me."

"It's been a pleasure," Gus said to Porky's back as he stalked away.

I said, "Well, I guess we won't be invited to stay for dinner."

"Unless somebody mistakes him for a pork chop. No wonder you called him Porky!"

"Hush. He'll hear you."

"I'm sure that name won't come as a surprise. What's his story? I don't think his television show made it to Australia."

"It was a silly program, anyway. A family comedy that lasted only two seasons. He played the young son who cracked age-inappropriate sex jokes. He's more memorable for crashing one Maserati into three more parked at a California car dealership—the most expensive car crash in history. The video was all over the Internet. Rumor has it, Porky lost everything he made in television in that crash. He still doesn't drive much."

"Did he go by Porky in Hollywood?"

"It's probably impossible to dodge it, don't you think?" Feeling embarrassed that I'd slipped with Porky's name, I said, "Look, I should get back to work."

"I'll tag along," Gus said, strolling with me as I pulled out my notebook.

I snapped a few photos for my column, inviting bystanders to pose for the pictures. Everyone was smiling, enjoying the lovely spring afternoon. We bumped into a well-known wine dealer, and I introduced Gus. The dealer's wife engaged Gus in a laughing conversation while the dealer took me aside and thanked me for hooking him up with the chair of a hospital auxiliary. A mutually beneficial relationship had sprung up between them, and the upshot was that he had been chosen to supply a variety of fine—and expensive—wine for an upcoming tasting.

"You really do know everybody," Gus said after we said good-byes and moved on. He sounded surprised. "What about the farm folk?"

I looked around and saw whom he meant. Many of the guests were dressed more simply than the fashionistas. Jeans and sweaters to ward off the spring chill. A preponderance of rubber barn boots and hiking sandals. They were clustered together near the paddock, seriously discussing the animals. I guessed most of them were the "locavores"—farmers, restaurant owners, chefs and eager foodies who advocated eating local foods, in season.

"Let's go meet some of them," I said to Gus.

I was right. We introduced ourselves to a portly, smiling man who turned out to be the manager of the local farmers' market. His enthusiasm showed in his spirited pitch for the farmers' cooperative in New Hope.

But I heard a familiar voice nearby and turned to recognize a popular Philadelphia restaurant owner, Tommy Rattigan. As usual, Tommy wore overalls—one buckle undone—over a thermal shirt and with acid green kitchen clogs. He seemed to be trying hard to establish his clothing choices as a kind of trademark look while he worked to make himself into a celebrity chef. He caught my eye and raised a glass to me.

I took that as a positive signal and excused myself to go to him. Gus followed.

"Tommy's sister, Marybeth, was married to Swain Starr," I explained to Gus while he shook Tommy's thick hand. I decided not to go into Tommy's wealthy upbringing, or ask why he felt compelled to attend today's event, since his sister's divorce from our host was still raw, by all accounts. Wearing his clogs and his overalls, Tommy obviously preferred to play down his moneyed roots—and probably his connection to Swain's previous marriage. So I said merely, "Tommy's new restaurant is getting a lot of attention."

"We're all about meat," Tommy said, leaping to the

opportunity to pitch his latest culinary venture. "Charcuterie in the winter, lamb in the spring—we'll be doing seasonal features. Popularity-wise, it's going to be big."

"Wait." Gus snapped his fingers. "I know about you. You come from the Howie's Hotties family!"

Tommy's expression hardened with resentment. "Uh, yes, Howard Rattigan, my grandfather, built his reputation making hot dogs."

Tommy was underselling his family's success. His family had, in fact, made millions of hot dogs before selling its name to a giant food consortium that paid the Rattigans a fortune for the right to use their name and the logo of Howie's Hotties—a dancing sausage that ended his little hopping routine by flinging himself into the waiting arms of a voluptuous bun for a decidedly sensual snuggle.

"Yes!" said Gus with enthusiasm. "Howie even looked like a pig!"

Tommy flushed. The family resemblance was apparent in him, too—the snoutish nose, the deep-set eyes that disappeared into his fleshy pink face in little squiggles.

"It was great marketing," Gus said to me. "Like the chicken bloke who looked like a chicken? Howie looked just like his product! And what a marvelous American success story. He started out as a pig farmer, then pushed a cart around Philadelphia and gradually made a mint selling hot dogs."

"Hot dogs are a form of charcuterie," Tommy said seriously. "I've been the beneficiary of my grandfather's financial windfall, but also philosophy-wise. I've adopted his conviction that the best cuts of meat make the best meals. I'm establishing my own brand, separate from Howie's Hotties. My restaurants will be much more high-end."

Gus was grinning with delight. "What do they say

about sausage? That nobody wants to watch how it's made?"

To rescue Tommy from embarrassment, I said, "When he opened his new restaurant, Tommy was a huge hit with his winter-foraging menu."

Gus looked politely mystified.

"To enhance our meats, I'm becoming an urban forager," Tommy explained. "Just last week, I found wild fennel in a Burger King parking lot. I used it in a memorable pasta."

Gus belatedly tried to subdue himself. "I'm sorry I missed it. Fennel's one of my favorites."

In case Gus was teasing, I said quickly, "Will the Starrs let you go foraging on this farm?"

"Maybe. But my interest here is pigs."

"Pigs," I said.

"Yes, Swain and I are spearheading a movement to breed a totally new variety of swine. Very lean, but tender. And fed on whatever grows naturally around here, so flavor-wise, the meat will be uniquely regional. We think the breed is going to revolutionize pork. It will put us on the food map."

So that explained Tommy's presence at the party. Despite his sister's divorce, Tommy was a partner of Swain's now. I felt a tug of sympathy for poor Tommy—trying so hard to become a celebrity chef when perhaps his talents and solemn personality weren't up to the challenge. His food, it was reported, was perfectly nice. But "nice" wasn't enough to revolutionize anything.

Gus looked a little pink from all the champagne as he lifted his glass. *"Vive la révolution!"*

That was all the encouragement Tommy needed. He launched into a discourse on pigs that might have baffled a genetic biologist. Gus endeavored to appear fascinated, but I wondered if he was experiencing one of those moments when foreign visitors marvel at the eccentricities of Americans whose interests reach almost fanatical heights.

When his lecture wound down, Tommy said seriously to Gus, "We're becoming part of the artisanal butchery movement."

"How on earth does one butcher an animal," Gus inquired, "in an artisanal way?"

"The same as any other kind of art," Tommy assured him. "Precision, respect paid to the living creature as well as presenting an excellent final product—that's what it is. How do you feel about pork?"

"I can hardly face the morning without a bit of bacon."

Tommy's eyes took on the fevered gleam of a zealot. "Then you should consider attending our artisanal butchering for the Farm-to-Table gala on Friday. We'll be demonstrating how to use every part of the pig. Snout to tail. Pig tails are the latest food trend, you know. They're going to be bigger than chicken wings. We fry them, add a dash of sauce—which will change according to our daily foraging. Yes, we expect our pig tails will blow away gourmands."

I could sense Gus's growing amusement and decided to sidetrack the conversation to avert a social disaster. "Tommy, I didn't realize you and Swain were in a partnership."

"That's what it is," Tommy said sharply. "A partnership. Foundation-wise, the stock of the swine he's raising here started with my grandfather's work. You can see for yourself—the results are superior to anything else in the world."

Tommy pointed toward the nearest fence where eight perfectly immaculate young piglets emerged from behind their large mother and made a mad dash for a trough. They looked adorable to me, but I couldn't see any difference between Swain's fancy breeding stock and your average pig at a county fair, except perhaps their unique coloring—brownish gray with leopardlike spots running down their backs. Seeing the piglets coming near, Tommy hustled over to give them an even closer inspection.

Just as a silver Mercedes zoomed up the driveway and rocked to a stop in front of me.

The party went deathly quiet.

When the driver's-side door of the Mercedes opened, I understood why all the guests were stunned into silence. The petite person who stepped out of the vehicle was none other than Swain Starr's first wife.

Clearly, uninvited.

Marybeth Rattigan Starr launched herself toward the first friendly face she spotted—me. She took purposeful strides, shoulders square and a determined smile frozen in place. She had the Rattigan pinkness, too—along with the piggy nose she had learned to camouflage with makeup so that she looked more like a sexy cherub than a pig.

She headed straight for me. "Nora! I haven't seen you in ages! Are you enjoying the party, dear?"

"Marybeth," I managed to say. "What a surprise."

"No kidding," she said as she hugged me close and breathed whiskey fumes all over me. "You're not the only one who's surprised."

In her hand, she carried a short-barreled antique musket.

Trying to remain calm, I said lightly, "If you're here to frighten your ex-husband, let me get out of the way first, will you?"

She laughed in a hard voice. "Don't worry. My marksmanship is pretty good."

Trying to maintain a cheery expression, I said, "Are you going to make a scene?"

"Stick around and watch."

With that, she spun toward her husband, who was warily pushing through the crowd to reach his ex-wife.

Marybeth exploded. "You son of a bitch!" Her voice carried over the heads of a hundred people. "Do you really think I'm going to let you get away with this?"

"Please, Marybeth, let's be reasonable—"

"Reasonable? You're stealing decades of my family's hard work. I want what's mine! Where's the pig?"

"Darling—"

"Still walking funny, Swain?" she asked nastily. "Let's see if I can make it even funnier."

Marybeth shouldered the musket. The crowd around us gasped. But nobody ran, nobody screamed. Everyone fell silent—frightened, yes, but also full of horrified anticipation.

Over the resulting quiet, Marybeth shouted, "My grandfather bred that boar through years and years of careful planning. And I've spent a decade refining the breed. If you think you can snatch him from us just as you walk away from thirty-five years of marriage, you weren't paying attention, you asshole. Where is he? Where's our pig?"

Swain tried to sound placating. "He went missing. You know that."

"Bullshit! You're hiding him!"

He put his hands out as if to stop Marybeth from firing the weapon. "I've told you over and over—"

"Pigs just don't fall off trucks and disappear," Marybeth snapped from behind the musket. "You're hiding a valuable animal so you can cash in on my family one more time."

A tiny noise came from behind me. I sneaked a cautious glance over my shoulder in time to see Zephyr come out of the barn with a single, somewhat gnarled tomato cradled in her hand. Looking like a tall, graceful angel in the sunlight, she drew every eye.

Marybeth's face turned scarlet, and her thinly controlled composure cracked. She swung the weapon away from Swain and took aim past my shoulder at Zephyr.

The whole crowd recognized her change of heart. Everyone surged away, shrieking in panic. Some threw themselves to the ground—others bolted for the parked cars. Swain Starr shouted.

Marybeth pulled the trigger.

But in the split second before the gun went off, Gus Hardwicke made a flying leap out of the crowd. He knocked the musket from her hands and tackled her to the ground.

I felt something deadly whistle past my ear and go harmlessly across the pasture.

Damn, I thought.

Now I owed my life to Gus Hardwicke.

Chapter 3

Nobody was hurt. The family shooed us away. The guests obediently headed for their cars, all sorry the party had ended on such a sour note, yet giddy they'd witnessed what could have become a newsworthy incident.

Except, Swain assured everyone, "There's no need to call the police. It was a misunderstanding. Nothing to worry about."

Gus drove me home in his convertible. "I should have let that nutter shoot Zephyr. What a headline!"

"Marybeth is not crazy," I said firmly. "She might have been angry, but she isn't crazy. She's an agricultural geneticist—a very serious one."

"We could have had a news event on our hands if I hadn't lost my head and wrestled her into the dirt."

"Yes, it's too bad we lost out on a mass shooting."

He laughed. "I'm having a bit of fun, and you know it. We were all lucky."

I did my best to control my trembling hands. Maybe nobody had been hurt, but it had been a close call. Although it pained me to do it, I said, "Look, I appreciate what you did back there. It wasn't luck. If you hadn't stopped Marybeth, she might have missed her target and hit me instead."

Gus threw me a grin. "Did I save your pretty neck, Nora?"

"Yes, I think you did. And I—well, thank you."

He laughed. "I was hoping to see an old-fashioned American-girl fight between Marybeth and Zephyr. Some hair pulling, at the very least. She'd been drinking, you know. I smelled it when we were rolling around in the dust together."

"Marybeth does have a temper," I said. I remembered how Gus had lingered on the ground with her—and how her arms seemed to find purchase on parts of his body that would normally be off-limits. Maybe her temper wasn't the only hot part of Marybeth.

"And what did she say about Swain walking funny?" Gus asked.

"I don't know what she meant."

"That story isn't over," Gus predicted. "Starr might be starting a new life down on the farm, but he hasn't dealt with his first family properly yet, has he? What do you think? Money problems?"

"There's so much money in the family, it's hard to imagine they need to fight over it. The Rattigans have hot dog money. And Swain made his own fortune."

"Something has them all stirred up," Gus said with delight.

"You mean besides Swain dumping his supportive wife after four children? For one of the most beautiful women in the world?"

Gus groaned. "I'll be bored to death if this story ends up being about jealous wives."

Me, too, I thought.

I watched the passing scenery, thinking about what we'd just witnessed. "Did you hear the other thing Marybeth said? I get the impression Swain and Marybeth's brother have gone into a partnership to raise some unusual variety of pig—a pig that Marybeth bred. But something must have gone wrong."

"Too bad she couldn't breed some of the pig out of her own son. What happened to Porky? He didn't stick around for the shooting."

"Stop calling him Porky," I said. The pig jokes were an easy habit to fall into where the Rattigans were concerned. I fervently hoped I didn't slip again and call Porter by his awful nickname to his face. To Gus, I said, "Marybeth said something about wanting the breeding stock back."

"But the pig disappeared," Gus said.

"That seems to be Swain's side of the story."

"What do you think? Is he telling the truth?"

"Why would he lie?"

Gus had a rollicking laugh. "Do you always assume people tell the truth?"

I sent him a frown.

"Nothing insulting intended," he assured me. "You'll have to see what you can find out, that's all. Not about pigs. Who cares about livestock? It's Zephyr who's going to be the marketable headline in all this, you'll see."

I pointed out the turn, and Gus pulled into the lane of Blackbird Farm. The once-austere house sat back a considerable distance from the road. If you drove past fast enough, you still got the impression of baronial splendor. But our private lane curved around the grove of oak trees in the front, following the line of the pasture fence, and brought guests around to the back of the house where the truth became clear. The broken windows of the solarium gave the impression of an old man who'd lost half his teeth, and the rest of the house looked like a ramshackle pile of fieldstone and slate.

Emma's herd of Shetland ponies chased us along the pasture fence, but I don't think they were enough of a distraction to hide the condition of my home.

A couple of cars were parked on the gravel driveway

between the house and the barn. One of them was a jacked-up muscle car with a pastel paint job—a sure sign the infamous Michael Abruzzo was in residence. The other was a plain sedan.

Gus Hardwicke got out of his side of the convertible in time to be greeted by Ralphie, the pet pig that was supposed to be our Christmas dinner but had ended up becoming our guard dog instead. He refused to stay penned and happily roamed the farm at will. Michael had devoted a few weeks to teaching him the perimeter of the property, but Ralphie spent most of his time mooning around the back door, waiting for Michael to come out and play.

Gus said, "What is it with you Yanks and pigs?"

I said, "He's just a pet."

"A cocker spaniel is a pet," Gus said as Ralphie snuffled his legs. "Does he bite?"

I went over and scratched Ralphie's bristly back. He had gained another fifty pounds over the winter and now stood as tall as one of Emma's Shetland ponies. Lately I had begun to wonder if he had a hormone imbalance and might grow to the size of a hippopotamus. I said, "He won't bite. You just have to show him who's boss."

"How?" For the first time, Gus looked as if his ever-ready confidence was shaken. He backed up against his car.

For a moment, I almost liked Gus Hardwicke.

"Move over, Ralphie." I gave the pig a shove, which had no effect. In fact, Ralphie crowded Gus against the car and determinedly rooted his snout into Gus's crotch.

Gus yelped and climbed like a crab onto the hood of his convertible.

Michael came out onto the back porch and let out a piercing whistle.

Ralphie quit bullying Gus and gave a happy snort before trotting toward the house. Michael had been eating an apple, and he tossed the remains of it to his pig. Ralphie caught it in the air and retreated to the shade of a tree to savor his treat. After maraschino cherries, he loved apples best.

I hadn't planned on inviting Gus to stay. But at Michael's appearance, his newsman's instincts kicked in, and he headed for the porch almost as fast as Ralphie had.

One of Michael's employees, a member of his ever-changing posse, came out of the kitchen. He stepped off the porch, clutching a bloody towel to his face as if he'd been beaten with a baseball bat. He limped, too. Gus did a double take and probably assumed the worst.

When the battered wiseguy reached me in the driveway, I asked, "What happened?"

"We were trying to fix your furnace," he said through swollen lips, adding some foul words that began with *f.* "A lever kicked back and hit me in the kisser. You should sell this heap, lady, before somebody gets killed from flushing a toilet!"

He climbed into his car and made a hasty exit.

Lately, Michael had been enlisting his mob hoodlums to help him with a few home repairs. So far, the results were mixed. Bracing myself to face one more household disaster, I headed for the porch.

Usually, Michael took pains to avoid meeting my friends. This time he hadn't performed his usual vanishing act. By the time I reached them, Michael was impassively shaking Gus's hand.

"G'day. Quite a place you've got here," Gus was saying in a cheerful tone, pretending he hadn't just witnessed the swift retreat of a bloodied man. "I expect a long-forgotten minor royal to lean out a window any minute. Do you have housemaids and a stuffy butler? Footmen to polish your shoes at night?"

"It's just us," I said when Michael made no effort to respond. "The last butler packed up a century ago."

"I can see why Swain Starr passed it up. You could use a handyman."

Gus cast a glance toward the neglected barn, the overgrown orchard and my still-unplanted vegetable garden. Then he stood back and let his gaze rove up the house, across the drooping gutters to the roof that sagged even lower than it had last fall. The chimneys had lost a few bricks over the winter. The fieldstone walls looked magnificent, though, and the old windows had the gentle ripple of very old glass. The place looked as if Ben Franklin might stroll out the door to fly his kite in the back pasture.

But instead of historical figures, it was Michael Abruzzo on the porch. Michael, the son of New Jersey's last remaining crime boss—and a dangerous-looking customer all on his own—didn't quite fit the picture. No hayseed with a rake, he looked every inch a mobster's heir apparent. He was very tall—six foot four—and had a face that had endured more than a few prison-yard brawls. His shoulders were powerful enough to suggest he'd emerged from those brawls the undisputed winner. His heavy-lidded eyes gave the impression he didn't like strangers.

While Gus looked him over, Michael kept silent, his face a mask that usually intimidated lesser men.

I went up the steps and slipped my arm around him. "Hi."

"Hey." He accepted my kiss, conscious that Gus was watching us. "How'd it go?"

"It was interesting," I said. "Anything new here?"

"Rawlins stopped by, looking for you." Michael was fond of Libby's oldest son. If anything, his influence had helped ease Rawlins out of his teenage rebellion. I thought we were through that period, but I read something subtle in Michael's expression.

I said, "I saw him at the party. He was going to give me a lift home."

"He said he looked for you before he left but figured you'd come home already. I told him you'd get a ride with somebody else."

I had told Michael I'd find my way home without needing a taxi service. "Was Rawlins okay?"

"He had a new pal in the car. Funny-looking kid wearing a stupid hat. Said his name was Porter something."

"Porter Starr?" I was surprised. "That's Swain Starr's youngest son. I didn't realize he was Rawlins's friend." I frowned. What was my nephew doing with Porky?

Michael shrugged. We'd discuss it later, in other words—when we were alone.

But Gus had a big grin on his face, as if he had no intention of leaving. He said, "You missed some excitement. I saved your enchanting lady friend from certain death."

Michael glanced sharply at me.

"It's true," I admitted. "Marybeth Starr got a little excited. She was waving around a musket and it went off. Revolutionary era, I'd guess. I think her father was a collector. It looked authentic."

"I don't care about the gun. What the hell was she doing shooting at you?"

"She wasn't aiming for me. She was—well, it doesn't matter. It's over now, and nobody will press any charges, so—"

"These parties of yours are supposed to be high class."

Gus tucked his hands into his pockets and rocked on his heels. "The higher the class, the more exclusive the weaponry. That's my take on it, mate. Say, I love old houses. Mind if I come inside? Take a look around?"

Although Michael maintained his menacing silence that said a firm *no*, I could hardly refuse. If it hadn't been for Gus, I might have been in an ambulance right now.

I opened the door and Gus followed me through, saying gregariously, "So, are you two married, or what, precisely? I've heard the workplace gossip, and nobody is quite sure of the situation."

"Is it anyone's business?" I asked. I pulled off my sweater and dropped it over a kitchen chair, then tried to tame my hair into something less windblown.

"Not in the least," Gus replied cheerfully. "And I'm a vulgar sod to ask. But then, everybody knows vulgarity runs in my family. I'm just curious. No wedding rings, I see, although that diamond on your finger looks as if it belongs in Ripley's, Nora."

"It's very pretty, isn't it?" I said.

I felt married to Michael—that was the main thing. We had exchanged a quirky set of vows on a beach in front of my family, in a ceremony cribbed from one of my mother's dubiously mystical texts, and that was enough for me. Michael was still pushing for a trip to a church, just a quiet ceremony before God with his local priest officiating and a license from the Commonwealth of Pennsylvania. But that seemed like overkill to me.

Besides, the women in my family were afflicted with the Blackbird curse. Our husbands tended to die and leave us widows. I hoped that if I didn't exactly marry Michael according to law, maybe he'd dodge the curse. Meanwhile, we had committed to each other until death did us part, and we'd both meant it. That was going to have to be enough for now.

Michael closed the door.

"Coffee, anyone?" I asked.

"Tea would be better, actually, but I have yet to meet a Yank who can make a decent cuppa." Gus stopped still and looked around. "This place is a cozy sort of derelict, isn't it?"

My house tended to elicit such reactions. The cavernous kitchen boasted cabinetry with a fine old patina polished by generations of housemaids, more antiques than a junkyard and an Aga stove that hunkered in the corner like a sullen dragon, sometimes even smoking just a little.

I was relieved to see Michael had recently mopped up the puddle that gathered in the middle of the floor at the most mysterious and inconvenient times. Nothing sent me into orbit like that damned puddle.

Gus strolled around the kitchen, glancing up into the rafters where a collection of antique kitchen utensils was hard to separate from a collection of assorted weapons left behind by war-mongering patriots who visited the farm on their way to nearby battlefields. "Are you expecting an invasion?"

"Only by mice."

He pointed upward. "Is that a sword?"

"Technically, it's a saber. Rumor goes, Lafayette left it behind when he came to pay a social call. We can't prove the story, of course. I should probably try selling it."

Gus took a peek into the butler's pantry. "You could, but there goes family loyalty. Of course, you might switch families, couldn't you?"

Gus turned around and smiled, inviting Michael to speak.

Michael leaned against the counter and folded his arms over his chest.

Before Gus could push further into the touchy subject of crime families, I said, "Yes, I'll keep the saber. I'm sentimental."

Gus's cell phone chirped. He took it out of his pocket and glanced at the screen. "This is a call I've been expecting. Mind if I step outside and take it?"

Without waiting for a response, he went out the back door.

I said to Michael, "You're trying to scare him."

He looked surprised. "What did I do?"

"I don't know, but you're doing it."

"Did he really save your life?"

"If not mine, somebody's." I pulled my wallet out of my handbag and gave him a ten-dollar bill.

"What's this for?" he asked, his face softening with fondness now that Gus was outside.

"I borrowed it this morning while you were still asleep. I grabbed it off the dresser. I didn't want to leave the house without any cash." I folded the bill into his hand. "It's our entire fortune at the moment, so hang on to it. Wait—what's this?"

His left thumb was wrapped up in a makeshift bandage. He said, "I hit it trying to fix the furnace. No big deal."

I unwrapped his thumb and took a look. His thumb might turn a little blue, but there was no permanent damage. I gave it a kiss. "Thanks for trying. Your friend looked a lot worse."

"He'll recover." Michael pocketed the money and reached to rearrange a strand of my windblown hair. "We'll get through this, you know. The bank account won't stay empty much longer."

Being penniless wasn't much fun, I had to admit. The winter had been one long struggle to make ends meet. It felt as if we were just one household catastrophe away from total fiscal meltdown. And unlike Michael, I didn't see any relief in sight.

At least, not from my end. What he was up to, I couldn't guess. He was keeping secrets again.

With a glance over his shoulder to make sure Gus was still occupied, Michael pulled me out of the kitchen and into the privacy of the scullery. "Who the hell is this guy, anyway?" he asked when we were alone.

"Gus Hardwicke. My new editor."

"I thought you said your editor was old."

"I said no such thing."

"With a name like Gus, I figured he had a beard and arthritis."

"Well, he's not old at all."

"I can see that. What'd he do? Leave his kangaroo back at the party?" Michael said. "He wants to do more than edit you."

"Don't be silly." I slipped into his arms and gave him a kiss on the mouth.

He pulled me closer and met my lips with more oomph than before, but when we parted, he said, "He called you enchanting. I don't like the way he looks at you, either."

I touched his cheek. "He's my boss. He doesn't look at me."

Michael used one hand to tip the scullery door closed and turn the lock. "The hell he doesn't."

I gave Michael a warmer, lingering kiss to prove my point, then said softly, "I suppose I should like it when you get jealous."

"I get jealous every time you walk out the door." Smiling, and with a flickering light in his blue eyes, he backed me against the porcelain sink and pinned me there. With both hands, he began easing the folds of the damask Swain Starr skirt up my thighs. "How well do you know him?"

"Hardly at all. Usually, he ignores me, but today he showed up and—are you really feeling jealous?" I smiled up at him.

"At the moment, I'm feeling something else."

I laughed a little, allowing Michael to unfasten the

buttons at the back of my dress. In the last couple of months, I'd gotten used to his spontaneous advances. He was frustrated in the house and directed his excess energy into frequent amorous interludes that often left me limp. I had learned that if I indulged in a postcoital nap, though, I was just inviting even more lovemaking. It had become an endless cycle. Nice most of the time—exhilarating, even—but exhausting.

In another moment, Michael was easing the bodice down around my waist. He was quick and sure with the clasp on the front of my bra, too. I leaned back and let him get away with it—watching his eyes and smiling. "Michael—what do you think you're doing?"

"If you can't figure it out, I'm doing it wrong."

"You're acting like a caveman. We can't—no, hang on a minute." I tried to fend off his roving hands—not very firmly. "Stop. Gus will see us through the windows."

"Ralphie will keep him on the porch." Michael hiked my skirt up higher and started to ease my panties down. His hands were warm, and his voice was barely a whisper in my ear. "I missed you this morning."

When Michael thrust his way into my world, a refined part of my upbringing blew away like a leaf borne on a hot summer wind. Up until then, I had been a good girl all my life. Right out of college, I married my husband, Todd, who was the kind of man my family expected me to settle down with. He'd been finishing med school, intending to be a researcher who specialized in transplants, and we thought we'd have a peaceful life together. We went sailing and bought antiques and took trips to Paris, holding hands on the airplane. But cocaine came along. Drugs drove Todd to his eventual death and me beyond what I thought was the limit of my strength.

Now? Now I knew life was short. And I didn't want to waste a minute of it.

Michael and I shared stormy emotions and a lot of laughter and physical cravings that sometimes felt wanton, but our relationship had become anchored in the knowledge that we weren't going anywhere without each other. Maybe it was strange that I trusted a convicted criminal over any number of yacht-hopping potential husbands from my own world. I knew he wasn't going to ruin his life with drugs, though, or take me down with him.

Even though he'd been the one to initiate a lot of sexual congress lately, I was the one who unsnapped his jeans. The afternoon had been long and trying, and I wanted to be wrapped up in the man I loved.

He pulled back, laughter in his gaze. "Are we really doing this?"

"Yes," I said. "Yes."

Emily Post, forgive me. Other people didn't understand why we were together. But being with Michael felt like thumbing my nose at all the constraints—the people of my so-called social class, the rules, the strangling and antiquated edicts of civility, the tired idea of what a family ought to be. His criminal past worried me sometimes, but he had won my trust. I wrapped my arms around his shoulders and held on tight. He knew exactly how to coax me to the brink of life. Even when he turned me around and I braced both hands against the sink, I was laughing, loving. He made me close my eyes and gasp. Made me forget myself. Made me feel as if I had the power to be something strong and willful and complete. He was hot inside me, a life force too strong to doubt.

It was over in minutes. I came first, barely holding back the cry in my throat as the spasms racked me, and Michael climaxed seconds later. When we could breathe again, he tugged my skirt back down, smoothed it, pulled me around against his chest and kissed me—gentler this time, one hand in my hair.

"You like it, don't you?" he murmured against my mouth. "On the edge with me."

"Yes," I whispered back. "I love you."

He bumped his forehead against mine and looked into my eyes. "Me, I'm feeling kinda enchanted."

I laughed. He didn't have the poetry of a more-educated man, but he knew when to use the right words.

We kissed again, long and gently, murmuring the magic words a few more times.

When he tried to help me put my clothes right again, I pushed his hands away. "Here, let me do that." I tried to refasten my bra, but it was tight. I rolled my eyes. "I've put on a couple pounds. Too much pasta."

He smiled. "If there's one good thing that comes out of being broke, this is it."

I let him cup my breasts for a second, then snapped my bra. "You won't say that if I outgrow all my working clothes. Button me up?"

I turned around so he could fasten my dress.

"We won't be broke forever," he said, dropping a kiss on my neck. He hugged me from behind, and I leaned against him, eyes closed for another moment to absorb his strength. If all the people at Starr's party had felt false and posturing to me, this was what I needed most—honest love and something else that calmed my soul.

In a while, Michael opened the door. He went out into the hallway first. I tottered past him into the powder room. In the mirror, my cheeks were glowing.

When I emerged from the powder room, Gus had come back into the house. He pocketed his cell phone.

Michael was reaching for his car keys.

Gus said to him, "I heard you're under house arrest."

"You heard right." Michael grabbed his leather jacket off the peg by the door.

"You making a break for it, mate?" Gus asked jovially.

Michael said, "Parole appointment."

I came up behind Michael and said, "We need milk."

He turned and gave me a last kiss. He winked. "See you later."

"Put Ralphie in the barn before you go?"

"He won't stay there."

I handed Michael another apple. "Give him some incentive."

Michael tossed the apple up and caught it, then turned to Gus. He surveyed our guest, clearly debating whether or not to encourage his departure. Gus merely smiled at him, holding his ground. At last, Michael gave a grunt and went out the door. When he was gone, Gus turned to me.

"Well, well," he said. "A cool customer, isn't he? Not what I expected."

I didn't ask what he expected. "That's why you brought me home, isn't it? To get a look at him."

"Can you blame me? He's a newsman's Holy Grail. Mick Abruzzo, Mafia Prince, the stuff of screaming three-inch headlines. I've heard what he's done, the crimes he's been convicted for. And the things he's apparently gotten away with. He hardly seems your type."

"My type?"

Gus laughed uneasily. "I didn't expect a good girl like you to go for—never mind. I'm just going to dig this hole deeper, aren't I? I'm sure the two of you have long, romantic discussions about John Donne and Schopenhauer."

"He's smarter than you think."

"I hear he's plenty smart." Gus stopped smiling. "I just wonder if you are."

"What does that mean?" I asked.

Gus suddenly wasn't my pushy, egotistical boss anymore. He had puzzled concern written on his face. "Are you safe in this house, Nora?"

"Safer than anywhere in the world."

Gus mustered another smile and straightened his shoulders. "In that case, I stand corrected. I'd better be going. My phone call came from the office. We're moving up your Starr article to Friday, the day of the Farm-to-Table event. You'll have a draft ready for me tonight? Just a draft, a little something I can sink my teeth into. If I see it, I'll be better able to point you in the right direction where Zephyr is concerned. I want our circulation numbers up, and that kind of article will do it."

"I'll e-mail you this evening," I said with more confidence than I was feeling.

He gave me a longer look, assessing something. Then he nodded shortly. "Good. Then I'll see you in my office bright and early Monday. Say—seven?"

"Sunday and Monday are my days off."

"Not this week." With a jaunty salute, he took his leave. "Remember, you owe me your life now."

I wanted Ralphie to run him down and stomp him into the grass, but Gus hotfooted it to his car unscathed.

Alone, I wobbled over to one of the kitchen chairs and sat. I held very still, thinking.

The new twist in my career wasn't my only worry.

Michael had left almost an hour earlier than usual for his parole appointment, and he'd gone off happily. I hadn't asked him where he was going, because Gus was in the room. If I were honest with myself, I'd admit I might not have asked him even if we'd been alone.

While his father, the infamous Big Frankie Abruzzo, was serving time in prison, Michael had told me he was devoting himself to dismantling the Abruzzo crime family's gambling empire. Two of Michael's three brothers were also incarcerated and temporarily out of the way. The oldest brother, Little Frankie, was presumed dead, and nobody seemed sorry about his disappearance. While they were all safely out of the picture, Michael was dealing with furious former partners who used every technique in the criminal repertoire to get around his edicts. It had gotten bad enough that we sometimes had the protection of an Abruzzo family roadblock at the bottom of the lane, and Michael kept a rotating number of cell phones to ensure that his communications were not overheard by his many enemies . . . or by law enforcement.

I knew he had good intentions. I also knew he was enjoying himself.

The way Todd had been drawn to drugs, Michael was pulled by some instinctive urge to rejoin his family in their illegal activities. He loved outsmarting the law, skirting the edges of criminality. Now he was trying to outsmart his own family, too. I hoped that was enough of an intellectual challenge for him.

Eventually, I worried he was going to do something truly bad—and get caught.

I heard a vehicle in the driveway, brakes squealing. I got up and took a peek out the window. Libby's minivan. She hopped out and left the door open, the engine running.

"It's me!" she sang as she burst into the kitchen. "You must have dropped your cell phone in Emma's truck. I passed her in town, and she gave it to me. Here you go. I can't stay. I've got Lucy and Max and the twins in the van, and the twins are in an instigating mood. My word, it's freezing in this house!"

"The furnace is on the fritz. Thanks for my phone. You're a lifesaver." I was always leaving my phone places

I shouldn't, and it made Michael nuts. "How did the audition go?"

She blew a gusty sigh. "It was hours and hours of little girls yelping that awful song from *Annie*! I'll never get it out of my head."

"Did the twins sing?"

"No," she said with a shade of relief.

"What did they do?"

"Well," Libby said, "they did magic tricks."

"That sounds like fun!" I remembered her wish that we should all be more supportive with one another, so I mustered some auntlike enthusiasm. "What kind of tricks?"

"First they made the director's car keys disappear."

"Oh."

"Then a twenty-dollar bill."

I could sense where this was going. "They reconjured everything, right?"

Libby beat a path to my refrigerator and opened it. "Do you have any of those yummy wine coolers? Or the fruit thingies with the vodka? Those are so refreshing."

"Libby, you're driving."

She sighed and closed the fridge. "It was just a passing impulse. Actually, I was hoping I might catch my son here. Have you seen Rawlins?"

"Yes, I bumped into him at a party at the Starr farm." I went over to the Aga stove and opened one of the vents to warm up the kitchen.

"Really?" Happily surprised, she forgot about needing a drink. "You mean, he was invited and everything?"

"Yes, of course he was invited. He looked terrific, by the way. Very grown-up, wearing a sport coat. But I lost track of him. Michael said he stopped here, before I got home."

"Why?" Libby's expression changed. "What was my son doing with That Man of Yours?"

"I don't know, Lib," I said, a little sharply. "If either of them was here at the moment, you could ask them."

She seemed to sense my annoyance. "Rawlins is being so secretive! And I can't find him half the time. He never answers his cell phone when I call. I assume he has a girlfriend, but does he bring her home to introduce me? No, he just spends every waking minute with her." She sighed again and slumped into one of my kitchen chairs. "He's probably embarrassed by his mother."

"That's not true."

"Maybe I should just go home and make a pitcher of margaritas and resign myself to watching that show on the BBC with Judi Dench playing a boring gray-haired divorcée. Spending every Saturday night with my children isn't the kind of action I was hoping I'd have at this stage of my—oh, never mind." Wistfully, she propped her chin in one hand, elbow on the table. "Do you have any chocolate? I know you keep a stash for emergencies."

"I'm fresh out." I patted her shoulder. "You're anything but boring, Lib."

"Rawlins is worrying me," my sister admitted.

"He looked fine. Better than fine. But when Michael said he stopped here with Porky—I mean, Porter Starr, I—"

Libby sat up. "He was with Porky? How nice." Her funk began to clear. "I don't need to be worried at all, do I?"

"Are they friends? How did that happen?"

"Oh, a few weeks ago after an appointment for the twins, I asked Rawlins to take Porky—that is, Porter, back to his mother's place. Porter had wrecked another car, you see, and needed a ride. Why didn't one of his parents teach that young man to drive properly, I wonder? I thought Rawlins could earn a few dollars by taking Porter where he needed to go. But that was ages ago.

I never thought they'd become friends. Pork—er, Porter is several years older, and much more sophisticated."

I decided not to debate the level of Porky Starr's sophistication.

I felt a certain loyalty to Rawlins. I didn't want to rat on him if he was simply being a high school senior, straining to get through his last semester of high school and bending a few rules along the way, so I simply said, "Don't worry about Rawlins. He's a nice kid. His head is screwed on straight—at least, most of the time. If he has a new girlfriend, that's a good sign, too, right? He's just got a little senioritis. Give him a break."

"That's the difference between you and me. You're too trusting." Libby got to her feet and headed for the door once more. "I have a mother's instincts."

I tried not to be hurt by her remark. She knew Michael and I had been trying to have a baby for a long time. But her wisecrack cut deep.

She prattled on. "If I didn't have a dog at home, there would be nobody at all to appreciate me."

"Max loves you to pieces. Lucy, too."

"Max is having second thoughts since I stopped breast-feeding. And Lucy's imaginary friend calls me the Wicked Witch of the West. She finger painted it on my bedroom door." Libby pulled herself together. "The twins need head shots, so I'm researching photographers. You know that glamour shots booth at the mall? Do you think they could do something to—I don't know—glamorize the twins a little?"

"Do they need to look glamorous?"

"It couldn't hurt. I thought I'd go first—to make sure it's quality photography." She touched her hair. "They also do lingerie photos for women. They pose you on red velvet cushions. Do your hair and makeup, too. I love being fussed over. Maybe someday I'll have a man in my life who'd enjoy a few sensual photos of me."

I could imagine Libby posed on velvet in her best lingerie. With the gleam in her eye that was glimmering at that moment, she'd look like a king's mistress.

She shook herself out of her fantasy. "Well, I'll look into what Rawlins is up to. Bye-bye!"

"Good luck," I said, but she was already gone with a slam of the door that rattled the windows.

Under my feet, I heard the furnace give a plaintive moan. I almost ran after Libby and asked her to share that pitcher of margaritas.

Chapter 4

By the time Michael came home, I had changed into jeans, a warm sweater and my sheepskin-lined slippers. I had also put a load of delicates into the washer and spent a couple of hours at the kitchen table working on my profile of Swain Starr. The kitchen was the warmest room in the house, and I sat close to the stove. Michael walked in with his cell phone pressed to his ear and a modest bag of groceries in one arm.

He gave me a kiss on the top of my head and kept listening to his caller while he put the milk in the fridge. I knew he was doing family business, because his answers to all the questions were a monosyllabic "No."

"No," he said while I e-mailed the profile to my editor.

He flipped open a cookbook and started dinner with the phone still pinned to his shoulder, saying, "No."

He used his favorite knife and said, "No."

He slipped a pan under the broiler, and listened another minute before he finally said, "Okay, do it."

He terminated the call and tossed the phone onto the kitchen counter.

I finished reading e-mails and closed the program. "Something brewing in the underworld?"

"A feeble attempt to con me, but that's nothing new. It's insulting, though, guys thinking I'd fall for an old scam." Michael came to me and rested his hands absently on my shoulders. But I knew he was thinking. Deciding his next move? Calculating collateral damage? Or considering our dessert options?

In addition to initiating sex more frequently than was surely natural, Michael had been cooking like crazy during the last several months. Maybe it was boredom or a manifestation of how much he loved me, but he made enormous quantities of food two and three times a day. We may have been broke, but we certainly weren't missing any meals.

As I closed my ancient laptop, a fragrant steam began to surge out of the oven door. Michael grabbed a mitt and pulled the pan out from under the broiler. He got busy with the final preparations of the food, and I watched him. He worked with an economy of motion, but his thoughts were far away.

When he set a plate in front of me, I inhaled the mouthwatering scent of lemon sole and fresh asparagus. "Wow, fine dining," I said. "Can we afford this?"

"I splurged on a lemon. The asparagus came from Father Tom's garden. The fish was on sale."

On sale because it would go bad in another day or two?

As Michael sat down across from me, he caught my hesitation and laughed. "The fish is fine. I figured I'd better feed you something besides pasta."

Immediately, I felt contrite for having brought up my weight gain. I knew we were eating a lot of spaghetti because it was what we could afford. Why was inexpensive food so fattening? But I said, "Don't feel guilty about the pasta. I love that you do most of the cooking. I should have been more careful about portions, that's all. I'm sorry I said anything about it."

"You look great to me." He poured some wine into my glass and splashed a more sizable portion for himself. We were down to the last few bottles in the collection he

had amassed while studying wine with his usual acute
focus.

I lifted my glass. "Welcome to the world of the working poor."

"Yeah." He touched his glass to mine but didn't drink.
"I guess that's what you are now. And it's partly my
fault."

"Not even remotely. Unless—are things still bad with
Gas N Grub?"

I wasn't the only one with money trouble. After a
rogue employee embezzled from him while he was incarcerated last fall, Michael was struggling to keep his string
of gas stations afloat. He could have sold one to get our
heads above water, but selling real estate took time, and
the market was bad at the moment. Taking a loss on the
property seemed foolish in the long run. We had decided
to try living as frugally as we could manage and see what
happened.

He said, "I paid my employees last week. That's good
news. I don't know about next week, though."

"What can you do?"

"Raise the price of gasoline."

"Will that take care of your problem?"

He shrugged. "Until customers start looking for a
cheaper way to fill their tanks."

"So it's a short-term solution?"

"Very short," he agreed. He slugged some wine and
picked up his fork at last. "Tell me what happened at
your party this afternoon."

I toyed with an asparagus spear, aware that he had
changed the subject. "The party was lovely. Picturesque."

"How picturesque was the shooting?"

"Oh, that. Marybeth looked very well dressed with
her musket in hand. Of course, that doesn't mean she has
the right to go around shooting at his new wife, but—"

"Especially with you standing in the wrong place."

"Believe me, I'd have headed for the hills if I'd had any clue she was showing up with a gun." I twirled my fork. "Before she pulled the trigger, she was shouting about something, though. Her ex and her brother, Tommy, are partners in some kind of farming venture. They're raising pigs—high-end pork, probably for Tommy's restaurant. But one of the pigs important to the breeding went missing. A special pig her grandfather had bred."

"Who's her grandfather?"

"Howie Rattigan," I said. "Of Howie's Hotties fame."

"The hot dog guy?" Michael grinned with delight. "The old coot who looked like a pig? Did those TV commercials with the hog calling? Is he still alive?"

"No. And the family sold Howie's Hotties to a big food conglomerate for a lot of money. But they're still breeding hogs, I guess. Marybeth seemed very upset about the missing animal—as if this particular pig is extremely important, the family legacy, that kind of thing. She claims Swain has it, but he says it disappeared."

"Kinda hard to hide a pig. I mean, look at Ralphie. We try to keep him penned up, but he's not exactly—" Michael's face went still. "Wait. When did this important pig go missing?"

"I don't know." I let Michael think it over.

It took him less than a second. "You think Ralphie is the pig they're worried about?"

"That was my first thought. What are the chances a pig wandered onto Blackbird Farm around the time the Howie's Hotties pig disappeared?"

"Slim to none," he said, no longer amused.

"Maybe I'm wrong," I argued. "Nobody ever came looking for him, and surely they'd have put out a search party if he was as valuable as Marybeth was saying."

"Well, don't go telling anybody about Ralphie," Michael said. "He belongs here now."

"You're actually fond of a pig!" I said. "A misbehaving pig, in fact."

"A kindred soul." He smiled at me across the table. "I should have let him rough up your editor today."

I tried the asparagus. It tasted like springtime—a welcome flavor. Swallowing, I said, "The young man who came here today with Rawlins. The one with the hat. Did he see Ralphie?"

"Ralphie's kinda hard to miss. Why?"

"He was Pork—er, Porter Starr, Swain's youngest son. Marybeth's son, too. I don't know if he'd recognize Ralphie, since he doesn't seem to be involved in the farm side of things. He used to be on television, in a sitcom, as a child. Now he's a talent scout."

I told him about Libby and her plan to get her twins into the entertainment business.

Michael laughed again. "Anybody who thinks he can teach those twins anything must have some stones. But what's the talent scout doing with Rawlins?"

"Libby said Rawlins gave Porter a ride a few weeks back."

"They've been hanging out together ever since? What does Libby say about that?"

"You think they shouldn't be friends?"

He smiled again. "You always see the good side of people, Nora."

"I see flaws, too," I said at once. "But I choose to think the best of everyone."

Michael gave me a longer look, but his thoughts were elsewhere. He shook his head. "I didn't like something about the Starr kid. And Rawlins was acting shifty, too. They were up to something."

"Why do you say that?"

Michael concentrated on his plate as if trying to find a way to explain something. "Growing up? My delinquent brothers and me—we spent most of our time beating each other up or throwing blame so we could get ten minutes alone just to—I dunno, be alone, I guess. That friend Rawlins brought around had the look. Like he was trying to get away with something."

I forgot about Rawlins for a moment. Michael rarely talked about his childhood. "Your brothers sound . . . challenging."

"I hated them," Michael said without emotion. "They hated me more—the bastard half brother that Pop seemed to favor. Little Frankie and I fought like animals. It was good practice for prison, I guess." He caught himself and tried to brush off the memory. "I spent a lot of time with the family next door."

I knew Michael never had the kind of home life other people did. This new footnote in his life intrigued me. "What was that family like?"

"Fun. They collected all kinds of junk to play with—trash can lids for shields so we could pretend we were saving the planet from aliens, that kind of stuff. We shot a lot of basketball in the driveway, too. The parents were always laughing—not laughing at anybody's mistakes or weaknesses, but, you know, having a good time." His smile faded. "But I got into some trouble—broke Little Frankie's arm and went to a foster home for a while. When I got back, they had moved. Anyway," he said, firmly tucking his memories back down inside, "I guess I know shifty when I see it. Rawlins was uneasy. And the other kid had an agenda."

Michael's instincts for trouble were finely tuned. I hadn't realized how deeply into his childhood that particular instinct was rooted. My heart ached for the boy who'd had such a volatile youth, and I wondered what had happened to the other family who'd made a difference.

But he was finished talking about himself, I could see, so I said, "You think Rawlins is in trouble?"

"I dunno. How much trouble can a white-bread kid like him get into? Whatever it is, it'll all shake out soon enough."

"I have a problem of my own," I said on a sigh. "Gus wants me to dig up some dirt on Starr's wife, Zephyr."

For the last week, Michael had listened to me brainstorm my article, and he knew the story of the Starr marriage. His interest sharpened. "There's dirt on the model?"

"She seems perfectly nice to me. I mean, there are the usual rumors that she has done some drugs and partied with infamous people back when she was modeling, but I don't think that's what he has in mind."

"Zephyr's the one from West Virginia, right? I know a guy who's connected there."

"I need to find out why Starr gave up his career so abruptly. Gus seems to think it has to do with Zephyr."

"Playing Old MacDonald doesn't quite have the same luster as hobnobbing with beautiful girls, I suppose. Why do you think he retired?"

"To make his wife happy?" I ventured.

"Makes sense to me," Michael replied with a smile that turned his eyes very blue. He reached across the table to touch my face.

In the morning the house was colder than ever, so I wrapped up in two sweaters and made pancakes while Michael Skyped with his teenage daughter, Carrie, who was still serving in Afghanistan. Their standing video appointment wasn't always easy—they were going through a rough patch in their already tenuous relationship—but this time Michael closed his laptop with a smile.

After breakfast, we went down to the cellar to coax the furnace with a technique I remembered my grandfather using—a lever pushed here, a well-aimed kick there. The huge motor groaned and something gave a terrifying bang before it revved up again.

Michael laughed and gave me a high five. "Show me that trick one more time."

Upstairs, glad to have heat in the radiators again, we read the Sunday newspapers for a while. I looked through the advertising pages to see if I could find a Filly Vanilli toy for Emma. No luck. Not entirely playfully, Michael and I argued about the politics shouted on one of the morning pundit shows, and then Michael decided he'd go to Mass.

I hoped he wasn't going to seek absolution for something I didn't know about yet.

After he left, I pulled on my jacket and went outside to do some work in the garden. With the sun shining, it was almost warmer outside the house than inside. While I puttered, I thought about Rawlins. I hoped he wasn't getting into a bad friendship with Porky. I had helped him with his essays for his college applications, and I knew he was feeling restless these days.

I cut some of the dried hydrangeas off the bushes and arranged them in the big marble urn by the back porch. The urn had come from Europe when my grandparents returned from their honeymoon. My grandmother said she found it in a Paris flea market. All her life, she kept the urn full of something from the garden during every season, and since moving back to the farm, I tried to do the same. I wanted to make a home for Michael and me that included some gracious traditions.

Last night's asparagus had also gotten me thinking it would soon be time to get some veggies started in the garden. In the fall, I had spent a week putting the garden to bed, so the spring cleanup was going to be a snap. Ralphie sat in the grass, blinking in the sunshine as he watched me rake up the straw.

I said to him, "This garden is not going to be your buffet."

He gave me a happy grunt that sounded like a request to hurry it up and plant something juicy.

I was down on my knees in the dirt with a trowel when I saw a fat blacksnake.

It was sunning itself in the dark earth a few yards away. One second I saw it, and the next second I was standing on the porch, doing a dithery dance.

About that time, Emma's red pickup came rumbling up the drive. She was towing a horse trailer. She parked by the pony fence but came over when she saw me hugging myself on the porch. At her heel trotted her speckled spaniel, Toby.

"What's with you?" she asked.

"A snake." I pointed a shaky finger. "In the garden. A really big black one."

"Blacksnakes are good snakes."

"I don't care. I want it gone."

"Jeez, Nora. You live on a farm. Time to get over the snake thing." Emma strolled over to the garden and took a look. For all her tough talk, though, I noticed she didn't exactly stride confidently into the rows where I planned to plant lettuce. She kept her distance and peeked. A moment later, she came back, shaking her head. "You must have scared it away."

I sat down on the top step of the porch, and Toby licked my face with sympathy. Ralphie poked me with his snout. I said to him, "Thanks a lot, Ralphie. You could have earned your keep by killing that snake for me."

Ralphie gave a snort to say he didn't like snakes, either.

"Mick around?" Emma asked casually. She leaned down to scratch Ralphie between the ears. He gave a sigh of pleasure and leaned against her legs.

"Michael went to church." I pointed at her trailer. "Are you here to pick up ponies?"

"Nope, just dropping off a horse. And I got some extra work making livestock deliveries in the neighborhood, so this is a drive-by. I'm taking some heifers up the road."

By the sound of it, she was taking any work she could get. I admired her hustle. Like a child begging for a parent to hurry up, one of the young cows in the trailer gave a plaintive moo.

I said, "What horse are you dropping off?"

She grinned. "Your favorite. Mr. Twinkles."

I did like Emma's jumper, a splendid chestnut she hoped to ride in summer competitions. I said, "Is he healthy enough to jump this year?"

"I think so. But I can't afford to board him at Paddy Horgan's stable. Mind if he bunks here for a while?"

"The more, the merrier."

Toby and Ralphie followed us to the trailer and watched while Emma unfastened the tailgate and went inside to unload Mr. Twinkles. The nervous gelding hated riding in any vehicle, but he must have smelled familiar territory, because he came down the ramp in a rush and nuzzled my sweater.

"Hi, bad boy." I rubbed his neck and let him snuffle me.

Emma led Mr. Twinkles over to the paddock and turned him loose. He took off at a gallop and bucked with joy at being free again. Ralphie went to the fence and watched the horse with interest. Eventually, Mr. Twinkles cantered back and stuck his nose down to sniff the pig.

"Well, I've heard of dogs and goats keeping horses company," Emma said, "but never a pig. Ralphie will behave himself, right?"

"If he doesn't, we'll have ham for Easter."

Emma laughed. "I doubt it."

"Where are you off to now?"

She checked her watch. "I'm supposed to deliver these heifers to Starr's Landing. A guy I know owns a dairy farm, a good one, and he sold three heifers to Swain Starr for his fancy farm experiment. Anyway, I was actually hoping you might ride along this morning."

"Why me?"

She rolled her eyes. "Zephyr Starr was giving me the stink eye a week ago. Like I was there to hit on her antique of a husband. I mean, he could barely walk. If you're along, I won't have to deck her."

"Was he flirting with you?"

"No. In fact, he looked half sick. But the power of Viagra," Emma said, "gives some women exaggerated ideas about what their husbands can do. Can you come?"

"Sure." With the snake in my garden, I wasn't keen on going back to digging in the dirt. "Let me change my clothes and—"

"We're not invited to a party," Emma said. "I'm just delivering cows. With luck, nobody will see either one of us. I'll just turn 'em loose in a pasture and leave."

"Okay." I dusted the worst of the garden earth from my jeans. "Let's go."

In a few minutes, we were speeding up the road toward Starr's Landing in Emma's cluttered pickup. I'd had to shove aside an old coat and an extra shirt to sit on the passenger seat, and my feet got tangled in a couple of halters on the floor. I saw a six-pack cooler there, too. I had to put my feet on top of it. Toby sat on my lap with his head out the window, tongue lolling.

The Delaware River ran smoothly on our right. Fishing season hadn't started yet, but in a few weeks the river would be full of anglers wading out into the silvery water. With a pang of dismay, I realized Michael wouldn't be fishing this year. His house arrest forbade it.

To Emma, I said, "Having any luck finding that Filly Vanilli toy?"

She sighed. "I tried to wrestle one out of the arms of a scary grandma at Toys 'R' Us yesterday. It was the last one, too. I lost."

"Childbirth might have diminished your killer instinct. Anyway, you don't want to get arrested for assaulting a grandmother."

Emma rubbed her shoulder. "She had a really good right hook. But she made me more determined than ever. I gotta keep looking. It's a mission for me now. I'm like one of those navy SEALs—swift and deadly. The grandmas won't see me coming."

"Just don't hurt anybody. How was your date last night?"

"Date?"

"You said you had a date. Jay, the dishwasher."

"Oh yeah. It was nothing special. Tell me about Swain Starr's fancy party."

"It had a surprise ending."

I told her about Marybeth and her musket.

Emma laughed. "Those Rattigans have short fuses. Remember back when Tommy was in school? He broke all the windows in his kindergarten classroom. The ones he could reach, anyway."

"He's turned into a bore now. He hopes to become a celebrity chef, I think, but he was giving very dull lectures about food at the party."

"Marybeth had all the personality in that family. Was she really going to shoot Zephyr?"

"She was angry about something else when she arrived. But then Zephyr showed up, and instinct took over."

"Zephyr better watch her step."

"I bet she stays on the farm most of the time. She's committed to growing healthy, organic food, and Swain talks passionately about raising animals in a humane and organic way."

"Organic, huh?"

I heard derision in her tone and glanced at her. "You disapprove?"

"Hey, I'm as humane as the next person. Just—these new organic farmers crack me up. Organic fruits and vegetables have no more nutrients than any other kind."

"How would you know that? I've seen you pour beer on Corn Flakes."

"I can read a newspaper. Organic fanatics pretend everybody else uses poisons and toxins to grow their food."

"Big commercial farms do use pesticides, herbicides, fertilizers that get into groundwater and—"

"So wash your food before you eat it. Besides, everybody around here has been organic for two hundred years. Need fertilizer? You plow some manure into the ground."

"I think the organic movement is admirable."

"I think the people are sanctimonious," Emma shot back. "The way they act at the farmers' market in town on Wednesdays? It's like they've seen the Virgin Mary in a head of cabbage."

"You're in a mood today. What's up? I don't think losing out to a grandmother put that frown on your face."

Emma kept her eyes on the road, but her jaw tightened. "My mood's the same as always. Nothing new."

Emma had moved out of my house nearly two months ago. I knew she came to Blackbird Farm very early to feed her ponies. She arrived when Michael and I were still asleep, so I hardly ever saw her anymore. If she was galloping racehorses at five a.m., she wasn't enjoying much nightlife. Something had her usual schedule scrambled.

I said, "Giving up your baby can't have been as easy as you'd like us to believe, Em."

She blew an irritated sigh. "Can't I catch a break from you?"

"I'm just saying, you can talk about it if you want. I'm not upset about the way things turned out."

She glanced at me, then back at the road again. "I wanted you to have the baby, y'know."

"I know," I said, more steadily than I felt. "And we wanted to take him. But not if that meant losing you. Seeing your child with us would have been very painful for you. It would have driven you away from us, for sure. And I couldn't stand that."

She reached for a squished pack of cigarettes in the clutter between us.

I said, "But lately you've been staying away anyway."

Emma punched the lighter on the dashboard and waited for it to heat up. "Think I'm dodging you? Forget it. I'm just giving the two of you a honeymoon. You don't need me hanging around."

"It's a big house. Why don't you come home? We like it when you stay with us."

"Does Mick say that?"

"I know how he feels."

Emma didn't respond to that.

I changed the subject before she could get mad. "You're not the only one with problems. I've been thinking I should get a second job."

Emma knew all about the tax problem our parents had stuck me with when they hightailed it to South America. I still owed the lion's share of the two million they had skipped out on, and the problems of maintaining the farm had only escalated lately. There just wasn't enough income to support the outgo. She lit her cigarette. "A job doing what?"

"That's the problem. I'm not really trained to do anything. I could work in a bookstore, maybe. Or wait tables."

Emma laughed. "I can't see Mick letting you take orders down at the corner diner."

"It's honest work. And," I added, "he doesn't have to know."

She blew smoke and shot me a derisive glance. "Mick's got guys reporting to him all the way from Serbia. He'd learn about your waitress job before you poured your first cup of coffee."

"I have to do something. Are there any jobs in your world?"

"Mucking out stalls and hauling feed. Swain Starr has hired half the neighborhood to do that kind of work at his place. From what I hear, he and his ex-model wife aren't getting their hands dirty. You'd have to leave your Givenchy collection at home, though."

I considered her suggestion. "I'm ready to try just about anything. But maybe that's too far off the charts for me."

"Yeah, okay. I'll keep my ears open. Here we are," Emma said.

The lovely green pasture and white fence had been rolling along on our right for the better part of a mile. Emma eased on the brake at the barred gate. Across the road from the gate stood an old ferry landing, which had been restored to its original Revolutionary War appearance—a charmingly rustic landmark. A flock of Canada geese had taken up residence on the landing. They looked charming, too, but they were probably coating everything in goose poop.

Emma pulled her truck and trailer to the gate, and she pressed the intercom button.

We waited for a response.

After thirty seconds, Emma pressed the button again.

"They're expecting you, right?" I asked.

"Yeah." She planted her finger on the button and held it there.

No answer.

She laid her hand on the horn.

"Hang on a minute," I said. "For the party, I was given an access number, remember? Maybe it still works."

It took several tries before I remembered the combination of numbers correctly, but finally the automatic gate swung open. Emma drove through and headed down the lane. When we curved around a stand of hemlock trees, the picturesque barn came into view.

The farmyard looked exactly as it had for the party, minus the guests. Even the white tent remained. The trash cans hadn't been emptied. The bunting on the tables billowed in the breeze. It looked as if our hosts had walked away from the setting as soon as the guests departed. On the hillside overlooking the farm, the modern Shaker-style house looked magnificent in the morning sun.

The whole place was eerily quiet.

At the paddock fence, the cows and the burro lined up to watch our arrival. Even the sow with the piglets stood at attention.

Emma stopped in front of the barn, and we got out of the truck. Emma rolled down her window and told Toby to stay.

"Hello?" she called. Her voice echoed back at us.

The cows lowed, sounding plaintive. Emma walked over to the fence. She frowned. "These cows need to be milked."

"How can you tell?"

"Look. They're full." She pointed at the swollen udders. "They're also miserable. And that sow looks as if she doesn't have any water. Where the hell is the famously humane butthead who owns this place? How come he's not taking care of his animals?"

"The code on the gate must have kept out the workers. What can we do?"

Emma's annoyance gave way to purpose. She pointed. "See that hose? Fill up the water troughs. Then go pound on the door. Get Starr the hell out of bed. I'll see if I can figure out where the milking parlor is."

We split up. The cows eagerly followed Emma toward the barn.

I turned on the water. The pig began making agitated squeals and pushed against her fence, so I dragged the hose over to her pen and aimed the water at her trough. She drank thirstily.

But I forgot about the pig.

Inside her pen, half-covered in muck, lay a person.

The body was facedown and motionless in the mud, arms flung out. The mud was mixed with blood.

I dropped the hose and seized the fence railing to keep from collapsing to my knees.

"Swain?" I said.

Because that was who it was. I recognized his jeans, his fancy red boots, his tailored chambray shirt.

Overhead, the sun began spinning, the light blinding. The silence of the farm became so complete that I could hear my own blood rushing in my head.

"Swain," I said. My voice barely came out of my throat.

With shaking hands, I hauled myself over the fence and landed in the wet earth on the other side, scattering the startled piglets. I staggered over to him and stood for a horrible second, frozen with indecision. Swaying over his body, I knew that he was gone. Blood had pooled around him, soaking into the ground. The next moment, though, I knelt beside him and rolled him over. Hoping he was breathing. Hoping he was alive.

But his body was stiff, his face a muddy mask of death. His chest had been perforated—over and over. I reeled back from the horror of the wounds.

"Emma," I called—still too shaken to make myself heard. I gathered my wits and shouted, "Emma! Zephyr! *Emma!*"

I clapped one hand over my mouth to hold back a sob. He'd been stabbed through the chest many times. Now on his back, his eyes half open and cloudy, he stared at nothing.

Whoever had killed him—was that person still around? A murky surge of darkness flooded up around me, and I felt my knees give out again. In the next moment, I was kneeling in the mud beside him, fighting to stay conscious. I touched his arm. Rigid. And cold.

Which meant the killer had to be gone. Long gone.

My brain steadied. A pitchfork lay in the mud near the fence, tines up. I knew instantly it was the murder weapon. I could see gore on the tines. Someone had used it to stab Swain through his chest and had thrown it down afterward. With intensified concentration, I found myself focusing on everything else about the muddy pen—the better to block out the horror, maybe.

Three yards away lay a half-buried set of keys.

My vision sharpened. I knew those keys. I recognized the high school logo on the ring—it was the school my nephew Rawlins attended. And the second key on the ring was an old skeleton key.

To the back door of Blackbird Farm.

Rawlins had been here.

Behind me, I heard Emma calling. She came up to the fence and skidded to a stop. When she saw what lay on the ground beside me, she cursed.

"It's Swain," I said, still unable to get up. "He's been killed."

Emma cursed again, prayerfully this time. "Get out of there. Come on. Let's go. We could be in danger or—"

"He's been dead for hours."

Emma steadied herself on the fence, reassured that the killer wasn't still hanging around. "Did you call 911?"

"Not yet." I turned to look up at my sister. "I'm afraid to look for Zephyr."

Emma met my gaze, and her jaw hardened. "You think she's dead, too?"

"I'm afraid to look," I said again. "She must be in the house. She might be alive, though, and need help."

Emma yanked her phone from her pocket and tossed it to me. "I'll go in the house."

"Wait for the police."

"If somebody comes after me, they'd better be prepared for a fight."

"Be careful," I warned.

Her face grim, Emma ran up the hillside toward the house. I heard her calling Zephyr's name.

My hands were trembling so hard, I could barely hit the numbers on Emma's phone. I spoke to the dispatcher, answered her questions, but I must have hung up on her. I don't remember how, exactly, but I must have communicated that we needed the police.

One fact was very clear in my head.

I put the phone in my pocket and crawled over to Rawlins's keys.

I picked them up and slid them into the pocket of my jeans.

I'm not sure how long it took, but Emma came back. "Nobody's up there. The house is empty."

"The police are on their way. They'll need help getting through the gate."

"I'll go. You okay?"

I managed to nod.

"Wait over here," Emma suggested.

But I couldn't leave the body. It felt wrong to abandon him there. I knew Swain had been dead for some time, but it felt disrespectful to leave him alone. I remembered the night Todd was shot, the hours I spent at his side, knowing he could not survive, yet holding him, willing him to live. His last moments would forever be branded in my mind—along with the dreadful notion that I had failed him. I stayed for hours after his last breath, unable to tear myself away—perhaps arguing with myself until I reached a hazy conclusion about his life. It had not been wasted. His research had been important. His parents had loved him. His sister, too.

So I sat with Swain out of respect for his life.

But I could not stop myself from wondering about Rawlins. Had Rawlins come back after the party? Surely he had not been here at the moment Swain died.

Surely not.

Please, I said to a greater power. Please don't let Rawlins be mixed up in this.

Chapter 5

At Blackbird Farm, Michael was helping another one of his wiseguys into a car. The man was clutching his hand as if it pained him. Another household repair gone awry?

Michael came over to the truck.

"Where have you been?" he said, pulling me out of Emma's pickup almost before she had it stopped. "There's something going on up the road. Cops and an ambulance and everything. First I thought—I was afraid there was another shooting."

"I tried phoning you. We went to Starr's Landing. What happened here?"

"The furnace is out again. We tried your kick-start thing, but—never mind." By that time, Michael had seen the mud all over my jeans and recognized something in my face. His hands turned gentler on my shoulders. "What's wrong?"

"We've been with the police. Swain Starr has been murdered." I began to tremble again, and I felt myself losing control. "Stabbed with a pitchfork. He's dead, and I—we couldn't leave without answering a lot of questions. I phoned you from Emma's cell, but you didn't answer."

Emma leaned over from behind the wheel and spoke

tersely out the open door. "It's a long story, big guy. She needs a little TLC."

"Come inside, Em," I said.

Michael's arm tightened protectively around me.

Emma shook her head. "I'm going to help the neighbor who's taking Starr's animals to another farm. Go relax. Take it easy for the rest of the day."

Michael took me inside, sat me down on the library sofa, brought me a cup of tea and a piece of toast to settle my stomach. The house was stone cold again, so he threw another log on the fire and poked it until a warm flame jumped up. Then he sat on the coffee table in front of me while I nibbled the toast and told him the whole story.

"What do the cops think?" he asked when I'd explained the grisly afternoon.

"They didn't share any theories with me. Swain must have been killed last night. He was— his body was cold, and there was so much blood that I— I—"

Michael steadied me with hands on my knees. "You gonna be okay?"

"Getting there," I said with a smile that felt wan. "I just hope it wasn't Marybeth who killed her ex."

Michael looked grim. "You think she went back and took care of unfinished business? With a pitchfork?"

Although Marybeth had behaved in a reckless way at the party, my instinct was that she'd been prepared to make a scene yesterday, but not really hurt anyone. I said, "I can't imagine she'd do such a thing."

"But that's what the cops will think, right? She was taking potshots a few hours earlier."

"Trying to frighten Swain, that's all. That's a long way from stabbing him over and over." I had a sudden vision of Swain on his belly in the mud and realized he must have been crawling away, trying to escape, when he died. I shuddered again and tried to push the thought away. "The big question is where Zephyr has gotten to. What if she's hurt? Or someone took her away?"

"Or maybe she's the one who killed her husband and ran off."

"Why would she do that? He changed his life for her!" I shook my head. "And she's such a nice person—kind to animals, so attentive to her husband. No, I have to hope the whole thing was a kind of random break-in."

"In that case," Michael said grimly, "we better get some serious security around here." He took the empty plate from me and set it aside. "I don't think anybody'd sneak onto a rich guy's farm to steal an organic tomato and end up killing him by accident. On the same day his ex pulled a trigger? Coincidences like that don't happen, Nora."

"I guess you're right." I risked taking a sip of tea and was glad not to choke on the few dribbles that made it down my throat. "And Swain—whoever killed him left him in the pigpen—maybe hoping the animals would destroy evidence." My cup rattled dangerously in its saucer, and I set it down before the tea spilled. "I just can't imagine—I don't understand how people can be so awful."

"I know." Michael pulled a cashmere throw from the arm of a nearby chair. He wrapped it around me and kissed the top of my head. "It's one of the best things about you."

He settled beside me, and I leaned against him. When I could speak again, I said, "There's one more thing."

"Don't think about it anymore."

But I reached into the pocket of my jeans and fumbled for the set of keys I'd taken from the mud. Instinctively, Michael put out his hand, and I dropped the dirty keys into his palm.

He went very still.

"You recognize them?"

One-handed, he thumbed the skeleton key away from the others. "Not many houses use these anymore. And the high school emblem on the ring? These belong to Rawlins."

"Michael, I found them near Swain's body. On the ground, just a few feet away from him."

He closed his palm around the keys as if to hide them. "Oh hell."

"I don't know how the keys got there."

As if I had not spoken, Michael said, "I knew there was something fishy going on yesterday."

"But Rawlins came here during the party," I argued. "Swain was alive then. He was murdered much later. By that time, surely Rawlins wasn't anywhere near Starr's Landing."

"I thought you said Libby came here last night, asking for him."

I closed my eyes to shut out the possibilities. Last I'd heard, Rawlins hadn't come home at all, and Libby was still looking for him.

Michael sat back against the cushions and looked at me. "What did the cops say?"

"I told you. They didn't share their theory with me, but Swain must have—"

"I mean about the keys."

I met his gaze uncertainly.

His expression changed, going from concern to laser-like intensity in a heartbeat. "You didn't tell them, did you?"

"No. I took the keys. I didn't tell anyone, not even Em. I just—if Rawlins was at the farm last night . . ." My voice trailed off. I couldn't bring myself to complete the thought.

"It's okay." Michael put his hand on the back of my neck and squeezed. "You don't have to explain to me. But you'll need to get your story straight for the cops."

I winced at the thought of getting my story straight.

"The police will come looking for you, Nora. You found the body. They'll want to talk to you again when you're calm and thinking straight. You'll have another chance to tell them about finding the keys. But explaining why you took them—that's going to need some spin."

I felt my cheeks turn warm. For all my worry that Michael might be turning to the dark side, here I was the one who'd broken the law by removing evidence from a crime scene. Softly, I said, "I need to talk to Rawlins."

"Yeah, you do." He released me. "Just in case, use one of my cells."

He meant one of the telephones he used when he wanted to be sure law enforcement wasn't listening in. The thought of needing to be careful on behalf of dear Rawlins made me feel cold all over again. Michael brought me the phone and left me alone. I phoned Libby's house.

"I just heard the news," Libby exclaimed. "Emma says you discovered Swain Starr dead in a pigpen! And his new wife nowhere to be found!"

"It's a shock," I agreed.

"Emma said maybe Marybeth killed him. The Howie's Hotties heiress stabbed her husband? What a scandal. It'll be all over the national news any minute. Do you think they'll have to recall the hot dogs? I mean, the idea of a dead man being eaten by pigs is revolting."

"The pigs didn't eat anything," I said. "He was dead, but otherwise untouched."

"Maybe they ate Zephyr!"

"Don't be ridiculous, Libby."

I must have sounded undone, because she said contritely, "Are you okay? Did you faint?"

"Not this time," I said, rubbing my forehead, but grateful for her concern. "Libby, listen. Is Rawlins around? Did he come home?"

"That boy is pushing the limits! He didn't get home until the middle of the night."

"Can I talk to him?"

"He's still sleeping."

I looked at my watch. Nearly five in the evening. Demanding that Libby wake him up to talk to me was only going to arouse her suspicions, though, and suggesting that her son might be involved in a murder would certainly send my sister into an epic tailspin. Keeping her in the dark seemed like a good idea for the moment. I tried to sound casual. "Could you have him call me when he wakes up?"

"Sure," Libby said, clearly uninterested in what I might want to discuss with her son. "I have to go. I'm helping the twins memorize some lines for a mayonnaise commercial."

"A mayonnaise commercial?"

"It's just for practice. Bye-bye!"

Rawlins didn't call me back.

At the ungodly hour of five minutes to seven on Monday morning, I presented myself at Gus Hardwicke's office, determined not to look as if I had spent the night tossing and turning. I wore my trusty Calvin Klein pencil skirt with a crisp white shirt and a simple knee-length coat—my favorite shade of blue was making a comeback—with kitten-heeled Ferragamos and black hosiery, which I hoped made me look more professional than my tulip-printed party dress.

The Pendergast Building was nearly deserted until I

reached the floors where the *Intelligencer* was produced. There, the offices were a hive of activity. Normally, I arrived just as the rest of the staff was clearing out for the day, so I stepped off the elevator and was surprised by the noise and bustle of my coworkers.

I picked up the morning issue from the table beside the elevator door and scanned the headlines.

Fashion Designer Dead
Supermodel Missing

Not quite three inches tall, but definitely screaming. With the paper under my arm, I headed for the executive suite and steeled myself for another trying confrontation with my editor.

Gus's assistant—the latest young, attractive, unpaid intern from a local university—was just removing her coat and a red beret that gave her a jaunty look not matched by her dour expression. She tipped her head toward the office where we could both hear Gus shouting. She said with remarkable calm, "He's busy at the moment. He had three appointments before yours."

"Does he ever sleep?" I asked.

"I think he's a vampire, but not the sexy kind," she said in a tone that told me she wasn't planning on sticking around after her internship was up. "There's been a big celebrity murder, so he's all excited."

I guessed this savvy intern would find a good job as far away from the *Intelligencer* as she could manage.

The office door burst open, and Rick Mendenhall, the medical-desk editor and part-time book reviewer, came barreling out, his face flushed.

Gus shouted after him, "If I wanted a bloody bad story about tumors, I'd be running the *New England Journal of Medicine*! Bloody hell! Get me a story that will sell papers! Nobody cares about experimental treatments!"

Rick banged the outer door shut. Gus stalked out of the office and glared after him.

"Nobody cares about experimental treatments unless they have sick relatives," I said calmly.

Gus slapped his forehead. "So that's what's wrong with the newspaper business! We don't have enough dying subscribers!"

"Good morning," I replied, determined to remain composed. "Should I have brought you coffee? You seem a little sleepy."

He gave me a sour look. "Tea. I drink tea. Don't try jollying me this morning. Unless you're bringing a new headline on Swain Starr's murder. I hear you discovered the body."

"I did." Although he hadn't invited me, I preceded him into his office. "I am not bringing you any new headlines, however. As far as I know, there have been no developments in the case since I left Swain's house."

"Then you're behind the times." Gus followed me into his office and closed the door.

The office of the *Intelligencer*'s editor-in-chief was a domain I had entered only once before—on the day the newspaper's owner took me to meet my new boss, a man who had lasted in his job only a few more months. Today the office looked as if Gus also didn't intend to remain long, or else he traveled light. Gone were the diplomas and framed awards from civic organizations—the kind of decor that most executives hung to remind themselves of past glories. Instead, Gus had stripped down the office to its barest essentials. He used a tall desk without a chair, as if he were too energetic to sit. His open laptop sat on the desk, e-mail program blinking. A wooden boomerang decorated with tribal markings lay beside it, making me wonder if he sometimes threw it out of frustration. Large sheets of newsprint were tacked haphazardly on the walls, and someone had used a fat red marker to furiously sketch the next day's layout on the paper—the first sign that perhaps Gus didn't embrace technology the way nearly everyone else in the building did.

Large portions of the paper bore nothing but impatiently scrawled red question marks.

A Polaroid of a battered surfboard had been stuck to the wall with a pushpin. Otherwise, the room was bare. Windows overlooked the city and the Schuylkill River beyond. There was no chair for me to sit on.

Since there was no place to hang my coat, either, I kept it on.

I said, "Has Zephyr been found?"

Gus commenced to pace. He wore gray suit trousers and a white shirt with a silver tie. I didn't necessarily think of Australians as fashion-forward, but he looked good. He had already rolled up his sleeves to show the muscles of his tanned and freckled forearms. When he glanced my way, his eyes were narrow. "I'll ask the questions. How soon can you finish that profile of Starr?"

"I planned on the Friday deadline, but if you need it sooner, I can probably finish it in a couple of—"

"Hours?" Gus said.

With an effort, I suppressed a squeak of dismay.

"Two hours then," he said firmly. "We'll run it with the extended obit tomorrow. And I'll need a profile of Zephyr, too. With as much dirt as you can dig up on her between now and sundown. I'll get somebody else to find the usual research—my assistant can probably stop bitching about the unglamorous nature of her job long enough to assemble a few pages. Then you can add what you have and write it up."

"Forgive me," I said, "but printing a lot of dirt about

Zephyr while the poor girl is missing, perhaps hurt or even—God forbid—dead, seems a little heartless."

"Excellent," he snapped. "That's exactly what we want to do around here, Nora. Stir up people, make them want to run out every morning and buy a paper to see what outrageous thing we have to say on every subject."

"But—"

"Controversy! Excitement! That's what the *Intelligencer* is going to bring to the city of Philadelphia."

"I just don't think—"

He swung on me. "Have I offended your delicate sensibilities?"

"I'm uncomfortable," I said, "putting my name on anything salacious."

"Really?" He stopped pacing to stare at me. "You? The girl who has stand-up sex with her mobbed-up boyfriend in a kitchen closet?"

In the silence that stretched, I must have turned white and then six shades of purple, because Gus laughed rudely.

"Do you think I'm deaf?" he asked. "That's what you were doing, am I right? Or did my ears deceive me?"

"I—I—"

"You have a charming blush, Nora." He pulled a pair of eyeglasses from the desk, the better to further examine my humiliation. "I can see exactly why your knuckledragger has such a yen for you. You come off like the kind of girl who keeps her knees together. Pure as the driven snow. But you've drifted, haven't you? I bet he buys you sexy undies. If you wear any at all."

I spun around and faced the window. I tried to focus on the flat, calm surface of the distant river while blocking out the memory of what he must have heard.

He said, "I find this reckless side of you very

appealing—very appealing in an employee, that is. I want you to put it to work in your job."

"I think," I finally managed to say in a strained voice that trembled in time with my ker-thunking heart, "it might be best if I go write my letter of resignation, Mr. Hardwicke."

He laughed again. "I don't want your resignation. And, honestly, you don't really want to give it. You'd be stupid to abandon a paying job, and I know you're not stupid. Let me sweeten the pot. I am giving you a raise."

"A—?" At last, I could look at him. Although he sounded amused, he wasn't smiling. If I was uncomfortable before, I was on pins and needles now.

"You're officially on the fast track," he snapped. "I liked the notes you sent me over the weekend. They were very complete, only need a little sharpening of the poisoned pen. If you don't want your name on the byline, just say so. We'll make up a name, something clever, so people start guessing who you really are. That'll help sell papers, too."

"I'm uncomfortable," I began again.

"In case you haven't gotten the point yet, I like making people uncomfortable," he said. "It makes my pulse race, my heart sing. But to keep you working here, I'll increase your salary by ten percent."

"I just don't feel—"

"Twenty percent."

I couldn't respond. Mostly out of shame.

"Thirty percent," he said. "And not a penny more. I've seen your house, Nora. You can use a raise. Of course, the new cash won't kick in until your next paycheck, so you'll have to keep the haunted mansion standing for another couple of weeks, but maybe you can ask your gorilla to hold up the roof. He looks as if he could lift some deadweight. Must be all that practice burying his enemies late at night."

"You should be careful about Michael," I said.

"Is that a threat?" Gus asked on a disbelieving laugh.

"He can't be intimidated. Or manipulated."

"But you can," Gus said wisely. "Why do you think I brought you in here this morning instead of discussing it all at your home? I want you working for me, Nora. For a lot of reasons. Foremost among them is that you are connected. On Saturday you proved to me that you know the movers and shakers of this city like nobody else I've met. You're an insider, and I'm not. I need you—you, who can sneak into any hallowed hall on my behalf."

"I do not sneak," I said.

"No, you walk right through the front door. I see exactly what you're doing—using your friends and your reputation as an Old Money heiress to gain entrance into special places, to see special people. It may not feel like using them, but you are. You belong to the secret society, Nora. You're a long-standing member, in fact, a card-carrying Philadelphia aristocrat. For me, that makes you a golden goose."

"I don't like where this is going."

"Have you guessed?"

No, I hadn't guessed yet. I felt as if I had been ambushed. My face must have said so.

Gus smiled. "I want to start a little competition."

"What kind of competition?"

"With the police. Remember Watergate? It was the reporters who broke that case. And they sold a hell of a lot of newspapers while they did it. I think the *Intelligencer* can beat the police in solving the murder of Swain Starr."

"How?"

"You, Nora Blackbird, can walk into the workrooms of fashion designers and the living rooms of hot dog heiresses all over the city, and people treat you like their best mate. I've seen you do it. So I want you to figure out who murdered Swain Starr."

He went on. "You practically live in his backyard. And you know all the right things to say. People trust you. That makes you an ideal detective for this case. You will phone all your discoveries to me, and I—or someone on the staff—will write up your daily reports." His gaze glowed with ambition. "We'll stand this city on its ear with the story."

"What makes you think we could possibly—"

"Here's the latest on Zephyr," Gus said. "She was found in a very nice hotel suite last night. Not alone."

"She's alive," I said with relief.

"Very much so."

"What hotel?" I asked without thinking. "Who was she with?"

Gus's smile broadened as if I were a star pupil who had just blurted out a correct answer. "The cops won't say, bugger them. When you find the hotel, you'll get more answers. She managed to send her companion out the service entrance before anyone could identify him. But you're going to find out."

"I have no idea where to begin, and if you want the profile done by tomorrow—"

"I'll give you a break," he said. "I'll dust the mold off your profile of Swain myself. I'll take out a few commas and add some exclamation points. It'll run tomorrow under a byline other than your own, if that makes you less *uncomfortable*." He said the word with dripping sarcasm.

I said, "The hotel will have security tapes. They'll know who was in her room."

"See? You already know where to start."

Gus's cell phone jingled in his pocket. He took it out and looked at the screen. "Nick off now, Nora. I've got a newspaper to rescue. And you've got legwork to do."

"But—"

"Go," he said. "I expect your first results before noon."

Chapter 6

I fled Gus's office. The roomful of reporters turned to look at me, the latest staffer to get rough treatment from our esteemed editor. Before anyone could flag me down to ask sympathetic questions, I rushed to the elevator and rode it down to the street. The last thing I wanted was anyone else in the building to hear about the particulars of how Gus browbeat me into doing his bidding.

Who had killed Swain Starr? I hadn't a clue.

But I did know one thing nobody else did.

My nephew Rawlins had been at the Starr farm the night Swain was murdered.

I knew in my heart my nephew had not killed the fashion designer. Why would he do such a thing? But he had not phoned me back when I asked, which telegraphed to me that he was over his head in something bad.

Rawlins had his whole future ahead of him, and I dreaded the idea of how a murder investigation could jeopardize that.

So I walked to get my brain to function. On the crowded Monday morning sidewalks, I walked for blocks among the many people who were rushing to get to work. It was half an hour before I realized I needed a cup of coffee to help my brain function. I went into a coffee shop that was jammed with people who crouched over their laptops, doing whatever solitary business could be conducted while elbow to elbow with similarly occupied workers, each making a paper cup of astronomically expensive coffee last as long as possible. And while I tried to think of where to buy myself a bargain cup, I thought of someone I could talk to about the murder.

I hurried a few more blocks to Tommy Rattigan's restaurant. It wasn't open for breakfast, but the green-and-white-striped awning snapped cheerfully in the morning breeze. I stopped at the front door and peered inside. No lights, no customers. The door was locked. The discreetly painted sign on the door said the restaurant would open at eleven—hours away.

I tried using my cell phone first. I punched the numbers painted on the door, but a recorded message came on, instructing me about their reservation policy. I hung up, remembering something Michael had said once about restaurants—that someone was always around back, maybe stealing from the company refrigerator or helping himself to the cash register. I didn't believe that—not exactly—but I hoped someone was already working in the kitchen.

I walked around the block and into the alley behind the restaurant. The cobblestones underfoot nearly defeated my heels, but I carefully made my way past several trash bins and a couple of homeless people sleeping on a grate. At last, I found the employee entrance to Rattigan's. Two Mercedes had been left in front of a No Parking sign. One was small and silver, the other an older black station wagon.

Behind the expensive cars idled a rusted panel truck, a plume of blue smoke rising from its tailpipe. A padlock hung open on the truck's cargo door, as if the driver had just removed something from the truck and had taken it into the restaurant.

I tried the restaurant's door. It was unlocked.

I let myself into a back corridor. The white tile walls were immaculate, the floor very clean. I could hear a tinny radio playing—and voices raised in anger.

Bright lights blazed in the kitchen. On a long stainless steel counter were cases of produce and a large cardboard box stuffed with long baguettes of bread. Already, the fresh ingredients that went into the restaurant's famously organic menu had been delivered.

But the shouting voices drew me farther down the hallway.

I went around a corner and discovered myself in a prep area. I remembered Tommy's words about becoming part of the artisanal butchering movement, so I expected to walk in on some doomed animal destined for the restaurant's stove. Instead, I found several men in aprons, all steadily working at cutting open Styrofoam containers marked with the logo of a big-box store.

From the packages, they were grabbing hunks of meat. Steaks, chops, chicken parts.

They froze in their chores to look at me. Nobody said a word.

It didn't take Libby's mothering instincts to know what was happening. The restaurant was purchasing its meat not from local, organic farmers, but from a big national chain that offered cheaper prices.

"Uh, excuse me," I said. "Is Tommy around?"

One of the aproned men pointed silently down the hall.

I backpedaled into the hallway. Taking a few more steps, I located the office of the owner and executive chef. Tommy's name was painted on the glass door.

Through the glass, I was surprised to see him holding a woman who struggled in his arms. Red-faced, he gripped her tight to his chest, but she hit at his shoulders with her fists. Then I realized the woman was his sister— Marybeth Starr. On Saturday, she had come to her ex-husband's farm with fire in her eyes. Today, she was an emotional mess.

I gave a little cough to alert them to my presence.

Tommy had heard me, and he spoke to her urgently. Her struggles ended. More gently, he turned his sister away so he could look over her shoulder at me. He recognized my face and reacted with surprise. "Nora! What are you doing here?"

Marybeth pulled out of her brother's embrace and hastily wiped her eyes with a restaurant napkin.

"Excuse me," I said, conveying with my tone that I hadn't seen anything amiss. "Marybeth, I'm so sorry about Swain. It must be an awful shock for you."

"And you." Marybeth managed a teary, sympathetic smile. "I hear you were the one who found him."

"I only wish I had gotten to him sooner."

"They tell me he died horribly." She gave a hiccough, and her eyes overflowed again. She pressed the napkin to her face, and her voice sounded strangled. "Probably only hours after we saw him."

"I'm so sorry," I said again.

She nodded. "I'm very upset. You know better than anyone what it's like to lose your husband, Nora."

Of course I had to stay then. If I understood anything at all, it was the tornado of emotions that hit a woman in the hours after her husband died—especially a husband with whom she had a conflicted relationship.

"It was awful when Todd died a violent death," I admitted. "I'm sure you're in shock. And overwhelmed by a dozen different feelings."

Gratefully, Marybeth grabbed me up in a hug. She whispered, "You do understand."

When my husband was shot, I had been horrified as well as grief-stricken. And angry with him, too. The confusion of emotion had felt like a storm inside me. So I knew why Marybeth was so disjointed.

Tommy reached up to put a comforting hand on his sister's shoulder. "Have you had anything breakfast-wise, Nora? I was just going to ask Marybeth if I could make her some eggs."

My first thought was that a celebrity chef ought to be able to come up with something more exotic than scrambled eggs. Tommy's pedestrian suggestion also caused Marybeth to pull her shoulder out from under his touch. "Eggs are so boring. Anyway, I couldn't choke down a mouthful this morning."

I smiled at Tommy to ease the sting of her criticism. "Frankly, I'm not sure I could keep down any food, either. But coffee sounds wonderful. If you don't mind my intruding."

"You're not intruding," Marybeth answered for her brother. "I need my friends now."

I wouldn't have called myself a friend of Marybeth's, exactly, but if my experience as a grieving widow could help her through the next hour, I was willing to do whatever she wanted.

In his green kitchen clogs, Tommy led the way into the back of the darkened restaurant. Without food cooking in the kitchen, the rich scent of herbs floated to us from the main wall of the dining room—a two-story wall of rocks and tumbling water where the staff had carefully planted a variety of fragrant herbs that suffused the space with subtle but aromatic scents. From the center of the wall of herbs protruded the severed head of an enormous boar, complete with beaded eyes and sharp tusks. The wild pig appeared to survey the restaurant from on high.

Tommy found us a table near the espresso station. While he poured a generous handful of coffee beans into a handsome machine, Marybeth and I eased into chairs.

Over the whine of the coffee grinder, Marybeth said, "I don't know what happens next. I'm no longer Swain's next of kin, of course, so my role is uncertain."

"You've spoken with your children?"

"Yes, I talked to all of them this morning. They went immediately back to New York to attend to company business." When I looked surprised, she added, "There's nothing they can do here. Except look after me, and I have Tommy for that." She sent an unreadable look at her brother. "And the welfare of Starr Industries is, of course, important to preserve. Since Swain left the business so recently, his death may have an impact on the company. Suzette must fly to China right away to make sure holdings there are under control. It's going to be so hard on her to be away for the funeral, but Jacob and Eli will handle the arrangements."

"And Porter? Did he go to New York with his siblings?"

Marybeth blinked as if she'd completely forgotten about her youngest child. Then she teared up again and held her handkerchief to her nose as her face crumpled. "Porter's going to be so upset about his father's death."

"You haven't seen him yet?"

"He—he's been so busy starting up his Hollywood venture, you see."

What Hollywood venture could be more important than sharing comfort with his mother over the death of his father? But that was none of my business, so I said, "Have the police given you any indication of—well, besides the manner of Swain's death, did they have any ideas about how—I mean—"

She swallowed hard. "If you can believe it, I am—I

was their first suspect. They're asking a lot of imperti-
nent questions. They even asked Tommy for an alibi!"

From the coffee station, Tommy said, "I was foraging
near the naval shipyard."

Marybeth turned pink. "And I had a visitor."

Before she could say more, Tommy snapped, "I'm
sure Nora doesn't need to hear all the details of your
life."

"Of course not," I murmured. But I guessed Marybeth had had a lover spend the night in her home. Which
meant she had an alibi for the stabbing of her ex-
husband. Tommy, however? Had he gone foraging with
a companion who could vouch for him?

I tried to think of the questions a journalist might ask,
but everything seemed too tactless. I wondered about
Marybeth's marriage to Swain Starr. At first, he'd been
the impoverished one, the artist who dabbled in fashion.
A big injection of cash from his wife's family fortune had
sent him on his skyrocketing success. While he globe-
trotted, she had stayed home to raise the family and to
pursue her own scientific interests.

But Gus wouldn't care about all that. Gus wanted to
know how Swain had met and married Zephyr—
questions I couldn't bring myself to ask Marybeth.

Tommy set down two cups of fragrant coffee on the
table. "As long as you're here to keep Marybeth calm,
Nora, maybe I'll get back to the kitchen? With Swain
gone, I have to make some fast changes, supply-wise."

Marybeth sniffled into her handkerchief. "Tommy was
instrumental in getting some attention paid to Starr's
Landing. Interest in his food has been very high. Reservations are almost full for the next six weeks. You should
book a table now, Nora."

I was too broke to afford a trip to McDonald's, let
alone an evening at Tommy Rattigan's fine restaurant. I

couldn't help noticing Tommy looked surprised to hear about his full reservations book. I picked up my coffee cup to hide my own expression. "Tommy, you mentioned something about being partners with Swain."

Tommy folded his arms over his chest and frowned to himself. "The main thing I needed from Swain was the pork. We were launching a marketing program that was going to catapult the hog into the culinary stratosphere. I was going to use the meat to maybe earn a couple of stars for the restaurant."

"Your aspirations will have to wait, Tommy." Marybeth took a composed sip of steaming coffee. Her voice was steely. "*Our* hog began as a pet project of our grandfather, Nora. He raised his own stock for Howie's Hotties. After my divorce, I decided to continue his work. Once I had a prototype, I understood the three of us were going to begin operation that was mutually beneficial for all—"

"Nora doesn't need to hear that, either," Tommy snapped, sending her a stern glance. "Bottom line–wise, couldn't wait to taste the pork."

Marybeth took a sip of her coffee and winced at its flavor. "Tommy, do you have a little whiskey?"

"Isn't it too early in the morning for that, Mare?"

"My ex is *dead*, Tommy."

"But—"

"And your coffee is too strong for me."

"How about a little cream?"

"A little Jim Beam, please." Her voice was firm, but she didn't turn to look at him.

Clenching his teeth, Tommy went to the sideboard and opened a bottle of liquor. He brought it to the table and poured a sizable dollop into his sister's coffee cup. Replacing the cap, he said with a hint of a whine, "I planned my whole fall menu around that pork. Now my schedule is shot. The restaurant business is very competitive. It won't be easy working out another seasonal menu."

"Surely the piglets we saw on Saturday will be grown by fall?" I asked.

Tommy shook his head as he put the bottle back on the bar. "Those won't be nearly enough. And besides, they aren't the true breeding Marybeth worked on. They're only half-bred pigs. Swain promised he could raise a lot more for me." Pretending not to hear his sister's barely audible grumble of disagreement, he said, "That highfalutin French restaurant down the street went under because of supply issues like this. I have to move fast to avoid the same problem."

"Maybe Zephyr will take over the breeding program," I suggested.

Marybeth slugged her coffee and gave an unladylike snort. "Zephyr objected to the animals from the very beginning. She's into hydroponic tomatoes. And kale. Kale was her specialty. Now, really, who wants to eat kale? She probably thinks it will be a gold mine!" Marybeth didn't catch her brother's expression of consternation and kept going. "I still can't imagine what Swain saw in her. His midlife crisis was worse than I ever imagined."

I said, "Swain went ahead with raising animals without her approval? That doesn't seem like much of a partnership. Or a marriage."

"They didn't agree pig-wise," Tommy said. "In fact, they had a serious blowup over that issue. It's why Zephyr was pouting at the party. She had taken a stand about Swain advertising their meat production."

"I didn't notice her pouting."

"Believe me, she was angry. They had a big fight just as the guests were arriving."

"Hmm. What about the missing pig?"

Together, the siblings snapped their mouths shut. Their expressions reminded me of my niece, Lucy, when she was asked if she'd finished her homework before her favorite television show started.

"The pig you mentioned at the party," I said to Marybeth.

"What about it?"

"Well," I said, "you seemed to think Swain had done something he shouldn't have."

Marybeth shook her head firmly. "It was all a misunderstanding. There's no missing pig."

"But—"

Tommy said, "There *was* a pig, but it was—we think Swain sold it."

"Was it his to sell? I thought you said—"

"The prototype was definitely not his to sell." Marybeth sent another glare at her brother. "He shouldn't have had it in the first place. I think he was keeping it on the farm somewhere out of sight."

"I checked," Tommy said. "It wasn't there, Marybeth. Before the party, I looked everywhere."

"He wanted it too soon," Marybeth said. "The program wasn't ready. The two of you jumped the gun."

"My restaurant can't wait any longer." Tommy was still fuming, lost in his own problem. "I counted on Swain bringing me a finished product—animals I could use for my menu. Now I'll have to start all over again. He really left me in a bind, meat-wise. Finding another pork source will take considerable time that I don't have."

Tartly, Marybeth said to her brother, "I'm sure he didn't mean to inconvenience you when he died."

"Sorry, Mare." He bent to give her a perfunctory kiss. "I'm not thinking very straight this morning."

Neither of them was. They had tried not to argue in front of me, but they hadn't pulled it off. I assumed Marybeth was in shock, not to mention a little tipsy already. Tommy's single-minded focus on the future of his menu seemed misplaced on the morning after his former brother-in-law's death.

Michael had said I only saw the good in people. Now I found myself thinking these two were ugly and self-obsessed. And both of them were intent on helping me forget about the missing pig that Marybeth had gone to the farm to reclaim.

"Go back to work." Marybeth patted Tommy's hand as it rested on her shoulder. Or maybe he was pinching her into silence? "That's always been the best medicine. Our grandfather said that often, Nora. In fact, I should get moving, too. I'm sorry I broke in on you, Tommy. I just needed a quick cry, I guess." She took another slug of coffee and set the cup down in the saucer before getting to her feet.

In the back corridor, Tommy remembered to hug his sister, although without the appearance of affection. Once again, Tommy wasn't exactly Mr. Personality. He shook my hand to say good-bye. Marybeth and I went out into the alley together. I wanted to ask who her night visitor had been—her alibi. But I couldn't get past my own reticence.

"Thank you, Nora," Marybeth said when we were standing in the sunshine beside her silver Mercedes. She pulled a set of keys from her handbag. "You've always been a kind person."

"I'm happy to help in any way."

She studied me. "If the police come calling, I hope you'll make light of my—our little incident on Saturday. I don't know what came over me. Maybe I shouldn't have had my date with Jim Beam before I went to Starr's Landing. I thought I had handled the divorce perfectly well, but suddenly I had a gun in my hand and there was that silly Zephyr looking so—well, it was naughty of me to wave a gun around." She giggled.

I didn't know what to say. She hadn't been waving the musket. She had nearly killed me with it. And now she was giggling—a grown woman, giggling. Perhaps the whiskey in her coffee hadn't been her first of the day.

I said, "I know what you're going through, Marybeth. Not just your husband's death, but feeling angry with him at the time. I wished I had said something nice to my husband before he was shot, but before he left the house, we had a fight instead. That's always weighed heavily on me."

Marybeth concentrated on sorting through her keys to find the one for the car. "Yes, I know. I was furious with Swain. I still am. We all are, actually. All my children—well, except for Porter, who was never really— well, the rest of them are very angry about the condition he left the business in when he turned it over to them. And the old fool just underwent surgery to undo his vasectomy, can you believe it? At his age! To have more children hardly seems in the best interest of anyone, does it? I was delighted to hear he spent two weeks sitting on ice packs. But we'll all find our own ways to forgive him."

What was she telling me? That all of her children were angry enough to have killed their father? That any one of them could have? And what about the vasectomy reversal? What did that mean?

Suddenly she burst into tears.

I handed over my handkerchief and put a sheltering arm across her shoulders. "If you want to talk, Marybeth, you have my number, don't you?"

"Yes." She snuffled up her tears. "I'll definitely call. We have so much in common now."

As she drove away, I thought about drinkers and ex-spouses and wondered what in the world I had learned.

The siblings clearly wanted to divert me from asking about the missing pig. When her car squealed around the corner and disappeared, I thought about the moment when I'd come upon her in her brother's arms. I knew Tommy had wanted me to think that he'd been comforting his sister in her time of need.

But Marybeth had not been sad. She had been angry—and so had Tommy. They were still disagreeing about the missing pig. Tommy wanted it back to save his restaurant. And Marybeth? She wanted it back for herself, I guessed, for some other reason.

She hadn't been grieving at all for her ex-husband. Her blood was still boiling.

Chapter 7

I checked my watch. Nearly nine, still very early in the morning. I longed to be at home in my bed, catching a couple more hours of sleep. But Gus wanted an update, and I didn't have much to report except impressions.

I thought Marybeth hadn't been ready to give up her prototype pig. Tommy and Swain had rushed ahead with their plan and taken it from her—probably because Tommy's restaurant was in jeopardy. Zephyr objected to her husband's selling meat for consumption. And Swain Starr's family was angry about some business issue. Plus Marybeth seemed infuriated by her ex-husband's vasectomy surgery—and his apparent plan to have more children. All tidbits I didn't feel I could ethically reveal to my editor until I had proof—and perhaps not until I knew what it all meant.

The only fact I could obtain without jeopardizing my scruples was the identity of the man who had been found with Zephyr. So I hiked over to the Ritz-Carlton in the hopes of finding a friend of mine who worked behind the scenes in the hotel's hospitality department. If Zephyr had spent Saturday night at that hotel, I might be able to gossip among the staff to find out who her companion had been.

Unfortunately, my friend was out.

I walked down to one of the city's small, luxury boutique hotels and ran into Sammy Dumpleton, a local actor who supplemented his spotty theatrical income by waiting tables in the hotel's chic little café.

Sammy was removing his apron and readjusting his vintage bow tie—he had been among the first to adopt the "chic geek" style of eyeglasses, plaid vest and high-top sneakers—when he caught sight of me in the lobby. He crowed with delight. "Nora, darling! As soon as the stock market opens, this place clears out like somebody pulled a fire alarm in a whorehouse. Come have a cup of coffee with me and tell me all about scarves!"

"Scarves? Sammy, why on earth do you need a scarf?"

He gave me two kisses and looped his arm through mine to draw me to the center table. The rest of the café was deserted. Perhaps the opening bell of the stock market was the cause, but the prices on the menu might have scared off customers, too. The café was famous for serving forty-dollar scrambled eggs—topped with a dollop of caviar—which was why Sammy chose to work there. His hours were short, but his tips were enough to pay the rent on his tiny but exquisitely furnished riverside loft.

He sat me down and brought a carafe of coffee and an elegant basket of pastries—bite-sized muffins and croissants arranged on a snowy white napkin. He said, "These are on the house, darling. After nine, we just throw them away."

"If I even breathe any more carbs, I'll have to find a new wardrobe." Reluctantly, I pushed the basket away.

"Say no more! I am fighting a little flab myself." Which was a complete lie. Sammy dashed into the kitchen with the lightness of a woodland nymph and returned carrying a fruit plate and two forks. He slid into the chair opposite mine, handed me a fork and speared a perfect strawberry for himself.

Happily, he said, "I need to know about scarves because I'm playing Madame Arcati in *Blithe Spirit* at the Playhouse. She's a medium or a psychic or some such who brings down the house in the second act—in a totally arch Noël Coward style, of course. I'm far too young for the role, but it's going to be a kick. I want to be swishy, but elegant. Therefore, scarves. Share your wisdom, Nora."

"I have a collection of vintage Hermès," I said. "Come to the farm, or I'll bring them to you later this week. You can choose what you like."

"You're the best!" he cried. "But you'd better bring them, darling, if you don't mind. I can't set foot on a farm. Allergies. My nose runs like a faucet, very embarrassing. But speaking of tilling the fields, what's the lowdown on Swain Starr? The morning newspaper says you stumbled over the corpse!"

"I didn't actually stumble," I said. I told him the whole traumatic story.

When I finished, Sammy leaned conspiratorially close. "Can I tell you a secret?"

"Probably not," I said on a sigh. "I work for the *Intelligencer* now, you know."

He popped his eyes playfully wide. "I haven't bought an *Intelligencer* in years, but that exposé on *Real Housewives of the Main Line*? Too juicy to skip! I may have to break down and subscribe."

Good news for Gus, I thought. The sleaze was paying off. "Thanks. You're keeping me in a job," I said.

"Survival of the fittest ain't pretty," Sammy said. "Well, I can't resist telling you my secret. Guess where the police found Zephyr Starr, the soon-to-be-grieving widow, yesterday morn?"

"She was here?"

"Yep. Checked in around midnight, from what I hear in the break room." Sammy used one forefinger to solemnly cross his heart. "I saw the police escort her out about six."

"She was under arrest?"

"I didn't see any handcuffs."

"How did she look?"

"Not exactly devastated," he said with a coy smile. "In fact, she looked like she could go back on the runway anytime. She was strutting her stuff with the de rigueur sullen expression on her gorgeous face. I'd kill for those eyelashes of hers, though. Do you think they're real? But she was *barefoot*, darling. Barefoot! As if she'd gone back to her hillbilly roots."

"I heard she was with someone. Do you know anything about that?"

He refilled both our cups of coffee, keeping me in suspense. Finally, Sam dropped his voice and said, "I have a special relationship with Fred, the night security dude. He looked at the tapes with the police. And *he* says she was entertaining a very young gentleman. *Very* young, was Fred's impression."

"Did Fred mention anything about the man except his age?"

"He was wearing a hat. Like Frank Sinatra."

Porky, I thought at once. "Sammy, you're a gem."

He smiled. "Tell your friends."

I laughed. I had known Sammy since we played jacks together on a shuffleboard court at our parents' racquet club. Years later—a few months after my husband's death—we bumped into each other one night at a Rittenhouse Square restaurant where I'd gone to pick up some takeout, and he insisted on dragging me to a *Sound of Music* sing-along. That night in a packed movie theater turned out to be silly and wonderfully restorative for me, and I owed him a debt of gratitude for helping me when I was very low.

Like me, Sammy had come from a family that enjoyed a very high tax bracket, but he'd fallen a long way when his stodgy father rejected his flamboyant lifestyle. From the private schools, vacations in Switzerland and golf lessons with professional players of his younger days, he was now making his own way in the world, just as I was. Although perhaps with more panache. Waiting tables was a long way from Gstaad. I felt a rush of comradeship.

I thanked him for the fruit. "If you need something to go with the scarves, let me know. Take an allergy pill, and we could rummage through my grandmama's trunks for just the right outfit."

He squeezed my hand. "Darling, you're a treasure."

We chatted for a few more minutes. He wanted to know about my job and what charitable events I had attended lately. I asked him for more details about his work for the Playhouse, and he promised to send me a couple of tickets for a performance.

When he was summoned to deliver some room service orders, I sat at the table and tried to make a few notes to figure out what I had learned, and where I could go next.

My phone had been pinging at me the whole time I talked with Sammy. I checked the screen to see who had tried to reach me and saw that mostly it was people calling to invite me to parties or to benefits in the near future. I saw the name of one woman—a nervous Nellie who ran a local nonprofit—and I remembered she wanted me to drop in on their awards luncheon next week. I quickly texted back to assure her I planned to attend. Otherwise, she'd bug me all day. I'd take care of the other messages later.

But one missed call was the state police. I listened to that message right away. A deep voice asked me to stop by the barracks to clear up some details about the crime scene at Starr's Landing.

The phone rang in my hand, and the screen told me the incoming call was from Michael.

I answered, and because I was still thinking of Sammy and how he'd been rejected by his family, I said without preamble, "If we ever have children, we're always going to love them even if they turn out to be people we didn't expect."

"If?" Michael said. "Are you losing hope already?"

"No," I said, chastened. "No, not at all."

We had stopped talking about having a baby lately, but the subject had never been far from our thoughts. Now, though, it was becoming a painful subject, and we didn't discuss it much. Or even joke about it. Maybe I was too sensitive about my infertility.

"Good morning," Michael said, starting over. "Sounds as if you've already had a tough day."

"I'll vent later," I said, making an effort to sound cheery. "You know a few things about restaurants, right?"

"Does my sister's pizza shop count?"

"Of course," I said, although I knew the shop had already been busted once for money laundering, so maybe food was not the primary purpose of his sister's business. "A little while ago I saw something strange in a restaurant kitchen."

"A health department violation?"

"Not exactly. I was in Tommy Rattigan's place, where the menu claims all the meat comes from local farmers. But I surprised the kitchen staff opening packages — Styrofoam trays wrapped in plastic like the kind from the supermarket."

Michael laughed. "So what else is new? Restaurants cut corners to stay in business. Question is, did the packages legitimately come from a store, or were they stolen?"

"Stolen?"

"Little Frankie's first criminal act—that is, the first one he got caught for—was stealing steaks from the meat case at the Red Lion and reselling them out of the trunk of a car. Easy way to raise some beer money."

I remembered the padlocked truck in the alley behind the restaurant. It had been unmarked. Maybe Michael was right. He usually was, where crime was concerned. I remembered him telling me that high-end restaurants rarely laundered money anymore because most customers used credit cards. His sister's shop was a cash-only business. His speculation about possible crime going on when we dined out occasionally gave me indigestion.

He said, "Did they see you?"

"The men in the kitchen? Yes."

"Hmm. Well, let me know if you start to think somebody's following you around, okay? Could be, the guys in the kitchen are selling drugs, too. That's another typical restaurant scenario. I don't want you mixed up in some misunderstanding with idiots who panic and overreact."

"Okay," I said. "I played dumb, though, so I don't think I'm in any trouble. The good news is that I just got a raise today."

"Hey, that's great!"

I didn't want to mention the raise had come with strings attached. I said, "Did you call to wish me a good morning?"

"Not exactly. The police just stopped by."

"They left a message on my phone. They want me to talk to them about the crime scene."

"That wasn't why they were here."

I sat up straight, alarmed that Michael was being so closely monitored. "What's wrong?"

"They weren't looking for me this time. You know the car Rawlins has been driving? It's still registered in my name. And the cops found it abandoned out on a country road."

I felt my pulse skip with concern for Rawlins. "Abandoned?"

"Rawlins is okay. I called your sister already. She said he went off to school as usual this morning. She hadn't even noticed he came home without his car."

"Libby is heavily involved in the twins right now."

"Keeping them off the Most Wanted list, I hope."

I felt a sinking sensation in my chest. Half to myself, I said, "What in the world is going on with Rawlins?'

Michael said, "I'm maybe thinking he had a tiff with a girlfriend and walked away. Teen melodrama. Anyway, the cops need one of us to take a look at the car today and sign some papers. Since I'm stuck here, that leaves you. Do you mind?"

"Of course not. I'll sit down to answer their questions at the same time." I could telephone Gus that I'd discovered which hotel Zephyr had been found in. Then maybe I'd be free to go for the day. "I'm not making much headway here. I'll take the train. Maybe Libby will pick me up at the station."

"If she can't, call me back. I can arrange something else for you. Later on, I'll have one of my guys pick up the car. Listen," he said in a different tone, "you need to be careful."

He let a silence stretch, and I suddenly wondered if our phones were being tapped again. Was somebody investigating Michael? And he didn't want to say anything incriminating on the phone with me? Or was he more concerned about Rawlins than he let on? If I spoke to the police about the car Rawlins had abandoned, I had to be sure not to implicate him in anything illegal. After a moment, I said, "I will. Michael?"

"Yeah?"

I gathered up my handbag and headed for the door. "The keys?" If Rawlins had left the car somewhere out on a country road, what were his keys doing in Swain Starr's pigpen the morning I had discovered his dead body?

"I dunno," he said, guessing what I meant. "If the kid's got a problem, we need to get out ahead of it."

"Yes."

"Watch your step. Gotta run."

We hung up without ceremony, and thirty seconds later, my phone rang again. I assumed it was Michael calling back to say good-bye properly, so I said, "I love you."

Gus Hardwicke said, "So soon? Usually it takes women at least a month to fall for my charms."

"Oh, it's you," I said, embarrassed all over again.

"Don't disappoint me," he said. "You were expecting someone else?"

"Is there something I can do for you?" I asked tartly.

"What's the latest?"

"The latest? I've been out of your office for only a couple of hours."

"Plenty of time to dig up something good. What have you learned?"

"I know the name of the hotel where Zephyr stayed the night of her husband's murder."

"Which hotel was it?"

I told him.

Gus said, "Who was she with?"

"I don't know yet."

"It was a man?"

"Yes," I said uneasily. I wasn't sure how much of what Sammy had told me I should divulge. "A young man."

"How do you know?"

"A hotel employee saw him on video."

"What did he look like?"

"They couldn't see his face. He was wearing a hat."

"The piggy kid?" Gus said, making the same mental leap I had. "What did you call him? Porky?"

"I'm not positive it was him."

"What else have you got?"

I could have told Gus about Swain's vasectomy reversal, but that seemed like unimportant information, not to mention an indelicate subject. "I think—look, Marybeth was upset about a pig. The pig she mentioned at the party."

"Forget about her."

"The police seem to think she's the primary suspect."

"She's not interesting enough to sell papers. Next?"

Desperate to give him something that would make him happy, I said, "Nearly all of his children were angry with him at the time of his death."

"What for?"

"Some business thing. I don't know anything specific."

"With Starr's fashion company? That could mean big bucks. Okay," Gus said. "Find out what had them so pissed off."

"But—"

He hung up.

I glared at my phone. "You're welcome."

With my fears for Rawlins growing, I called Libby.

"Of course I'm available," she said when I told her about the police finding the abandoned car and how I needed to stop at the impound lot. She didn't seem disturbed by the idea of her son leaving a car in the middle of the night. She said, "Thank heavens you called. You can help me brainstorm for the twins. I need a branding strategy."

I hoped she didn't mean heating up an iron and burning a symbol into their backsides as if they could be let loose to roam the range. As far as I was concerned, the twins should not be left unsupervised.

An hour later, I stepped off the commuter train and climbed into her minivan.

She had little Max buckled into his car seat, sound asleep. Part of me wished I could be similarly snoozing.

Libby was dressed in one of her jogging outfits with a T-shirt underneath the velour jacket. The T-shirt said, IF ONLY MOSQUITOES SUCKED FAT INSTEAD OF BLOOD . . .

Libby had never jogged a day in her life, but she believed the tracksuits in her colorful collection were slimming and made her look energetic to any male person she might casually encounter during her day. Instead of running shoes, today she wore a cute pair of wedge heels with a peep toe that showed off a somewhat-chipped pink pedicure. A matching Bakelite bracelet on her wrist clanked against the steering wheel.

"You won't believe what it costs to bring a child up to performance level these days," she began as soon as I had buckled my seat belt. "There are elocution classes and movement workshops and readings and fittings and—"

"Fittings for what?" I asked. "Have the twins been cast in something already? Libby, that's amazing."

Amazing because I had never guessed my twin nephews were remotely interested in anything pertaining to show business. I had always assumed Harcourt and Hilton would end up either working as crime scene experts or serving time for some gruesome dismemberment. Even Michael was afraid to be alone in the same room with them.

"No, of course they haven't been cast yet," Libby said. "We're doing all the prepping, though. Training and whatnot. Their wardrobe is immensely important. Have you ever seen a child performer poorly dressed?"

Yes, as a matter of fact, I had. But I said, "What kind of wardrobe are you buying for them? Something from the Starr Collection?"

"Heavens, no. Porky hates those clothes. Too fuddy-duddy. I get the distinct impression Porky hated his father's guts, by the way. So I've hired a wardrobe consultant."

"Wait—how did you get the idea Porky and his father didn't get along?"

"He gets this look on his face when his father's name comes up. I've been a parent long enough to know what that expression means. It's a long-standing father-son feud, probably stemming from a psychological issue regarding the mother figure. Porky always felt unloved, so he left the family and broke out on his own, and now he doesn't even want to think about his father."

All of Libby's usual mumbo jumbo was based on the late-afternoon TV shows she watched and the pop psychology books she read so avidly while waiting for after-school ballet classes or swim practices to be over. She might be a crackpot most of the time, but now and then, she came up with observations that were spot-on. I remembered how Marybeth had spoken of her children, but Porky had been an afterthought.

"Anyway," she continued, "I've hired a wardrobe consultant. He's a young man with a shop in Manayunk, just around the corner from the studio where the classes take place. The shop is very vintage Hollywood with a little punk thrown in, cutting-edge fashion. And he stocks adorable things. I got a Hells Angels skullcap for Maximus."

I turned around to look at the baby, but Max was hatless. He had something in his hands that might have been a hat once. He had been chewing on it. I turned back around in my seat. "Is that where your bracelet came from?"

Libby took her hand off the wheel to wave her wrist. "This old thing? Why—well, yes, as a matter of fact. Why shouldn't I buy myself a bauble now and then? And Drake is not so much a salesman as a connoisseur of fine things. He appreciates a person's spirit and finds just the right accessories. His insight is an amazing gift. The twins, though, they're very difficult to brand."

I decided not to inquire about Drake. If Libby had already pegged him as potential boyfriend material, there was no stopping her. So I asked, "You're branding your children now?"

"It's a vital part of the child performer process. Should they be Michael J. Fox or Honey Boo Boo?"

"My bet is they don't want to be Honey Boo Boo," I said.

"Just an example. They're going to be their own brand, of course, but we're fine-tuning the concepts. I thought you and I could stop in a hair salon where I'm told they do great haircuts for boys. All of the Phillies baseball players get their hair done there."

I had seen the Phillies players, and none of them looked particularly well-groomed to me. Shaggy, unshaven and tobacco-spitting seemed to constitute their "brand."

"Libby," I said, "how many consultants have you hired? Do you think maybe it's a little early to be going overboard with this child star thing?"

"Child *performer*," she corrected. "We don't want to get ahead of ourselves. It's bad karma."

"Good thinking," I said. "Listen, it's not the twins I

wanted to talk to you about. What's going on with Rawlins?"

"That boy!" she cried. "He'll be the death of me. Well,
no, the twins will probably be the death of me, and I'll
end up pickled in my own refrigerator. But Rawlins—! I
thought we were finished with the problems he used to
bring home."

"What did he used to bring home?"

"He has no sense when it comes to choosing his
friends. It's been that way all his life. Even in kindergarten, he'd bring home one three-legged puppy after another. Do you remember the boy who set fire to my
living room rug?"

"I thought that was Harcourt."

"I mean the first time," Libby said. "And then there
was the kid who gave us lice. And the girl who released
the mutated frogs in our bathroom—"

"Wasn't that Hilton?"

"And the boy who started Rawlins on piercing his
ears. Not to mention his eyebrow and his nose and that
awful rivet he wore in his cheek for a while. That friend
ended up with his earlobes stretched down to his shoulders!" Libby frowned. "Although I hear he is playing in
a rock band now, and he's very successful. I wonder if it's
time Rawlins looked him up again? Maybe they need a
drummer."

I was having trouble keeping up with all the catastrophes in my sister's household. "Rawlins plays the drums?"

"How hard can it be?" she cried. "I'm trying to make
a future for my children, Nora. If I'm ever going to have
a life of my own, I need to make sure my offspring can
function without me. I want them to have all the advan-
tages and not be dependent for the rest of their lives.
They need skills and connections and—and—only then

can I become the fulfilled person I'm destined to be, a woman with a wonderful, full life."

"Lib, you're already a wonderful person, and you have a very full life. Didn't you just get reelected to be president of the Erotic Yoga Society?"

"Those losers," she muttered. "Now they want to start a hot yoga class. I thought that sounded very exciting until they told me it just meant turning up the thermostat. I get red in the face when I get hot, and it's very unbecoming. No, Nora, I need more challenges, more adventures, more meaningful relationships with people who can nurture my spirit. Even Drake says so."

"Uh-huh." With caution, I said, "You aren't pinning a lot of hope on this Drake person, are you? Because if he owns an accessory shop in Manayunk that helps young boys find their brand, chances are he's not really your type, Libby."

"What do you mean?"

"You have many talents," I said, "but your gaydar is terrible."

"You think Drake is gay?" Libby cried.

"He has insight into your spirit? Have you ever known a heterosexual man who has anything approaching spiritual insight, let alone Bakelite bracelets?"

"How can I be so *blind*? Oh—forget the twins. Let's go shopping."

Chapter 8

Libby pulled into a mini-mall parking lot, and we got out of her van. She unbuckled Maximus from his car seat, and he woke up happy. I took the baby from her arms as we walked into a boutique with a sexy red dress in the window. Inside, I realized all the dresses were red. The shop was decorated with hearts and little cherubs that floated along the ceiling. The expressions on their faces were a little unnerving, though. They reminded me of a horror movie about a demented, revenge-seeking puppet.

The shop's female owner fluttered over, wearing a red apron that depicted two breasts threatening to burst out of a corset, which set the tone for the establishment. She and Libby hit it off like soul sisters. I found a spot on the window seat with Max. From Libby's diaper bag, I pulled a container of cheddar-flavored Goldfish. I popped them into Max's eager mouth while Libby rushed over to the display racks and began loading the owner's arms with garments. Within minutes, Libby was trying on outfits in a dressing room.

She came out wearing an extremely tight red dress that made her look as if she were wrapped in bloody bandages. "What do you think?"

"It's definitely your color."

The shop owner nervously eyed the zipper, which looked as if it might explode any second and put somebody's eye out. "We can order—uh, other sizes. I'll go check the computer."

While she went off, Libby frowned at herself in the mirror. "I don't know why stores don't stock larger sizes all the time. The average American woman is a size sixteen, for heaven's sake. Nora, don't you think this would be nice for the right occasion?"

"It's very sexy," I said, still striving for diplomacy. "Did you get your carpenter ant situation fixed so your date wants another shot?"

She sighed, and her reflection drooped in the mirror. "Perry did a preliminary spray treatment. He's coming back tomorrow for another check. It's going to cost me a fortune, but who wants ants all over the place? Even the twins are grossed out, and that's saying something."

I remembered Perry Delbert from last winter. He was a local exterminator who looked like a big honey bear, except with smudged eyeglasses that kept sliding down his prominent nose. I had noticed he gazed at my sister with a particularly smitten look in his eyes, but Libby was blind to his infatuation. To her, he would always be the bug man.

My phone pinged in my handbag for the third time since Max and I had sat down, and I glanced at the screen. It was just another text message, this time from the editor of the online version of the *Intelligencer*. He asked which party video I wanted for tomorrow's edition, a question he'd already asked, and I'd answered. I texted him back as politely as I had the first time.

Libby checked the price tag hanging from the armpit of the red dress. "You're so much busier than before, Nora. What's going on? Still having a problem with your boss?"

"It's not just him," I said, sending the text. "The social season is heating up. The flower show always kicks off spring in a big way, so I've got a lot of big events on my calendar. And the Farm-to-Table Restaurant Gala is Friday."

She perked up. "That sounds like fun. Should I go?"

"I'll get you a ticket. Or tickets if you'd like to bring a date. It's supposed to be very elegant."

"I could wear this dress!" She perked up. "I'll get back to you about the number of tickets."

"Maybe I should invite Emma, too."

"She probably won't come. She's obsessed about Filly Vanilli."

"She told you about that?"

"Of course. She asked me to send a mass e-mail to my PTO friends to see if anyone had a used one. Filly Vanilli is very popular. I told her she'd probably have to find one on the black market for her friend's nephew."

"Nephew?" I said. "I thought she was trying to find one for her boss's new baby."

Libby shook her head. "I'm sure she said it was for a nephew of someone she met in line at the post office. But now she's insanely obsessed. She told me she ransacked a flea market yesterday because somebody said a dealer was hiding a couple of Filly Vanilli horses under the Beanie Babies."

"That doesn't sound like Em."

"Her hormones are still out of whack. If I thought it would help, I'd give her my collection of Cabbage Patch dolls. The twins cut most of them apart and burned the heads for a movie they made last Halloween, but I have a couple left."

"Libby," I said, trying to reel her back around to the important topic, "it's Rawlins I wanted to talk about."

Libby groaned and began flipping through red lingerie that was hanging on a rack by the window. "His friends are going to get him into trouble, aren't they?"

"He has perfectly good taste in friends," I said reasonably. "And that girl he was dating last summer? Shawna? Didn't she go to Harvard in September?"

"And they promptly broke up." Libby pulled out a silk teddy and gave it a critical scan.

"Who has he been seeing lately?"

"I assume he's been hanging out with his usual friends. Before Christmas, he was writing a science fiction graphic novel with two other boys. They draw the pictures, and he writes the story."

"And Porky Starr? The talent scout?"

Libby shook her head and put the teddy back. "It's the twins Porky has taken a wonderful interest in."

"But Rawlins took Porky home when his car was being worked on? And they've been together a couple of times since then?"

"What are you suggesting?"

"I'm not suggesting anything, Lib. I'm just concerned that Rawlins is hanging out with someone who might not be the best influence. For one thing, Porky's four or five years older than Rawlins."

Libby found a nightgown with spaghetti straps and a see-through décolletage. She went to the mirror and held it up against herself. "Rawlins has always needed a father figure."

Porter wasn't nearly old enough to be a father figure. I said, "What do they do together?"

"How should I know? Go to the malt shop? Skip stones on the river, maybe? What do boys do these days?" She hooked the spaghetti straps over her shoulders and squinted at her reflection.

"Well, I'm pretty sure they don't abandon their cars in the middle of the night."

Libby spotted the owner returning and hastily took off the nightgown. "Rawlins probably had engine trouble or something."

"Does he let other kids drive his car?"

"He'd better not. He knows my insurance doesn't cover that."

The owner returned and expressed sorrow that the red dress didn't come in a size sixteen. They retreated to the dressing room, where I could hear Libby lecturing the woman about size discrimination.

Max squawked at me. His language skills hadn't exactly grown over the winter, but I knew what he wanted. I pulled out three more Goldfish and held them out to him on my palm. He made a grab and stuffed his face with a broad, toothless smile of thanks. I ate a few Goldfish, too, with Max pushing them into my mouth. I used my handkerchief to swab some of the orange drool from his chin, and then we played peekaboo with each other. Max giggled with delight at the game. Like all of Libby's children, he had a happy heart. His lack of language skills seemed inconsequential. He'd talk when he needed to. I leaned over and gave him an impulsive kiss on his chubby cheek.

Libby paraded two more red dresses for me. Both were too small and better suited to younger women—women who didn't wear underwear. I refrained from saying so and hoped Libby saw for herself. She went back into the dressing room to put her clothes back on.

To the boutique owner, I said, "Do you carry any dresses by Swain Starr?"

"Oh, isn't it terrible that he died?"

"Just awful," I agreed. "Do you have any of his clothes?"

She shook her head. "In the store where I used to work, they carried all of his things. But that was years ago before the problems started."

"Problems?"

She bit her lip. "I probably shouldn't say more. Maybe the company will recover, right?"

"What do they need to recover from?"

"They used to be a great company to work with. But things have fallen apart in the last five years or so. Supply issues, mostly. They did great advertising, but the good clothes never made it to the retail level, or if they did, the fabrics often shrank, and returns became an issue. I heard Swain lost interest in running things, and his family had to learn everything from the ground up. I hope they get their act together. The Swain brand is very popular."

Libby came out and bought some panties, and we went outside to the minivan.

"Before we go to the car impound lot," Libby said, "would you mind if I stopped at the salon to make an appointment? If I'm going out Friday night to the Farm-to-Table gala, I might need a facial."

"Take your time," I said, barely stifling a yawn.

Libby pulled out of the parking lot and headed for town. "What's the matter? Aren't you getting enough sleep?"

"It was a short night last night," I admitted.

"Emma says . . ."

I thought it was a good sign that my sisters were speaking again. "What does Emma say?"

Libby shot her eyes sideways at me. "She says That Man of Yours is being rather demanding."

"He doesn't demand anything," I said. "He's . . . energetic, that's all."

"He's bored."

"A little," I admitted.

"Has he read the book?"

"Which book?"

"The book everybody's reading. About sex," Libby said. "Handcuffs and feathers and blindfolds and all the unusual things you can do. Is he—? Are you—?"

"Michael finds nothing playful about handcuffs. We're

not doing anything unusual, Libby, so wash out your brain, please."

"Well, that's disappointing," she said on a sigh. "I was hoping to get some new ideas."

"Why don't you just read the book?"

She groaned. "The twins found the last book I bought, and I don't want to go through *that* again."

When Libby parked and dashed into the salon, I stayed in the minivan with Max. We rolled down all the windows just an inch for fresh air, and I sang silly songs to him. But he fell asleep at once.

My phone jingled, and I checked the screen. *Gus Hardwicke.*

I answered. "Yes?"

"What have you got for me?"

"I heard another rumor that Porter Starr and his father don't get along."

"Boring."

"Swain's fashion business has been having management problems for the last five years. Maybe that's why he transferred the company to his children."

"It's hard to make readers give a toss about rich drones with money problems. What else?"

I thought I'd gotten some good information, but he still wasn't satisfied. "Nothing else yet."

"Zephyr. I need stuff about Zephyr," Gus said, and he hung up.

I leaned my head back against the headrest and tried to think of a way to learn more about Zephyr. But I suddenly felt very drowsy. In the backseat, Max gave a little snore, and soon I was dead to the world, too.

I jolted awake when Libby climbed back into the minivan.

"You were sleeping," she said, extending her foot at me, "so I got a pedicure. What do you think?"

I rubbed the crick in my neck and looked at her toes. Schiaparelli pink. "Nice," I said. "How long was I asleep?"

"An hour," she said. "I figured I'd give you an extra hour for ordinary sex tonight. Let's go get that car Rawlins left in the woods."

The township impound lot was located near the state police barracks. When Libby pulled in and parked, Max woke up and demanded his mother's attention. While she changed his diaper, I went looking for someone to talk to about the car. I could see the vehicle behind a chain-link fence.

A tall state trooper was coming out of the building. When he saw me at the fence, he came over, wearing his Mountie-style hat with the chin strap under his lower lip. "You're Nora Blackbird. You were at the Starr farm on Sunday."

"Yes, hello." I shook his hand. He had been the first trooper on the scene of Swain Starr's death, and I had answered his questions. His name badge was printed with his last name: RICCI. I said, "I hear you have more questions for me."

"Just a few. I didn't make the connection when we talked at the farm. You're living with Mick Abruzzo, aren't you? I spent a few shifts in a cruiser sitting in front of your driveway last winter. You brought me coffee."

Over the winter after Michael was released from prison, the state police had maintained a vigil at the bottom of my lane. We guessed they wanted to be sure he didn't sneak off Blackbird Farm and go on a one-man crime spree. A few times I worried the police were going to get frostbite while they watched the house.

"Yes, I did. I'm sorry I didn't recognize you on Sunday." To me, all the troopers looked the same in their hats.

He added, "I followed Mick to church a few times. I guess he found religion in the pokey?"

"He's introspective."

My response caused Trooper Ricci to laugh.

With a little more snap in my voice than I intended, I asked, "How is the investigation going?" Hastily, I clarified, "Into Swain Starr's death, I mean. Have you located his killer?"

"We're still gathering information." He glanced into the impound lot. "Maybe you can help us piece together what happened at the party on Saturday. But can I help you with something here first?"

"I came to claim my nephew's car."

"The Mustang? It's registered to Abruzzo, right?"

"Yes, but—well, yes. I'm told I need to sign some papers to get the car back?"

"Yeah, go inside and check with the clerk at the desk. I'll catch up with you after that."

I left him by the fence, but when I opened the door to go into the building, I glanced back and saw him thoughtfully studying the car.

Libby breezed into the building behind me, Max in her arms. By the time she had looked around and counted all the state troopers at their desks, the sparkle was back in her eyes. "Don't you love men in uniform?"

"Control yourself, Libby," I said to her in an undertone. The clerk had taken the papers and gone into one of the offices to consult with someone. I had hoped to slip in, sign the papers and get the right clearance to reclaim the car. But now I had a bad feeling about getting the vehicle released, and my sister throwing herself at the feet of every police officer in sight was only going to make us look more suspicious.

She handed Max to me and began rearranging her hair. "I need a date for the Farm-to-Table gala, don't I?"

"Libby—"

The clerk returned, looking more stern than friendly. But one glance at Max's cherubic face made her smile. "Aren't you a cutie-pie? I have three grandsons. Is this your little boy?"

"No, he's my nephew."

She tickled Max's tummy with her pen. "Would you step outside with me, please? We need you to verify the condition of the car."

We trooped outside where Ricci had the driver's-side door open on the Mustang.

I tried to sound cheerful. "Is everything all right?"

Ricci was sitting behind the wheel, frowning. "Where was this car found?"

The clerk looked at her papers. "On Sheffield Road."

"Not far from Blackbird Farm," I said.

Ricci said, "Not far from Starr's Landing, too, right? Sheffield runs through the woods behind both farms, doesn't it?"

"Yes. In the summer, I still ride my bicycle that way."

My summertime exercise routine didn't interest Ricci. He got out of the car and walked around it, his face studiously blank. He said, "Who was driving this vehicle the night it was abandoned?"

Libby had already noted the wedding ring on Ricci's hand, so her usual laserlike intensity was powered down. She piped up, "My son Rawlins. He bought the car last year."

Ricci came back to me, his demeanor less casual than before. "He bought the car from Abruzzo?"

"We haven't had time to change the registration," I said.

"How old is this Rawlins?"

"Seventeen," Libby said promptly. "He's usually very responsible."

"He is," I agreed. "Very responsible."

"So why did he leave the car?"

I said, "He had engine trouble."

But at the same time I spoke, Libby said, "He ran out of gas."

"Engine trouble," Ricci repeated, "or out of gas? Which is it?"

"We're not sure," I said with a feeble smile.

He nodded. "You have the keys?"

"I don't have them with me now," I said. "Michael told me he'd have one of his employees pick up the car later."

Libby began nattering. "Rawlins came home in the middle of the night all by himself. We really should have some kind of taxi service in this area. He could have called someone for a ride, but instead he walked home. He made himself a sandwich before he went to bed and—"

"Libby," I said, "why don't you go pay the impoundment fine? And I think Max needs a dry diaper."

I handed the baby back to her, and she said, "I just changed him!"

Ricci said to me, "Where is the Rawlins kid now?"

"He's in school, of course." I tried to look pleasant as I gave Libby a gentle shove toward her minivan. She went off, grumbling, with Max in her arms. "Why do you ask?"

"If the kid was out in the woods on Saturday night when Swain Starr was killed, maybe he saw something. We're going to want to talk to him."

"He didn't mention seeing anything," I said. "And he's usually quite observant."

"All the more reason to talk to him."

"Please don't pull him out of school," I said. "It would be very disruptive."

"A man's dead, Miss Blackbird. That's about as disruptive as it gets."

"Surely you have other people who can tell you what happened at Starr's Landing that night. Or at the party. Wouldn't you want to hear about that?"

"It helps to ask as many people as possible."

I took a chance and said, "Have you spoken with Swain's ex? Marybeth?"

"I didn't talk to her personally, no. The first wife, right? The one who was waving a rifle around earlier in the day?"

"It was a musket, actually."

"That wasn't the murder weapon, if that's what you're thinking."

"I know." Reminded about the condition of Swain's body when I found him, I felt another ripple of nausea.

Perhaps Ricci noticed I had turned pale, because he said, "Look, we want to talk to you about the party, what happened, what you saw. But maybe that can wait another day." He glanced toward the impound lot again. "For the record, the car was out of gas. You'll have to bring a gas can when you come back."

He was putting me off because he had a new lead, I realized, not because he had any concern for my health. He was hot on the idea that Rawlins had abandoned his car near the murder scene.

"Okay. You know where to find me," I said, and turned to the clerk, smiling as best I could in an effort not to show my concern for my nephew. "Are we finished? Are there more papers to sign?"

"You just need to make sure the vehicle hasn't been damaged while in impound."

I glanced into the car and saw nothing amiss. Rawlins kept it very clean. But there was a new scrape on the front bumper. I wasn't sure how long it had been damaged, though. While I walked around to the passenger side, Ricci and the clerk conferred with each other. I opened the passenger door, and something small and plastic fell out on the ground.

Instinctively, I bent to pick it up. A plastic cylinder.

It was a home pregnancy test. When I figured that out, I almost dropped it all over again.

Neither Ricci nor the clerk noticed me. They were busy reading the paperwork together and muttering.

"Everything okay?" Ricci asked.

I straightened up hastily. He was glowering at me with suspicion. Over the roof of the car, I said in a voice that sounded high and strained, "Everything looks fine to me. Uh—do you have any Filly Vanilli toys?"

"Huh?"

I addressed myself to the clerk. "I was just thinking if you have three grandsons, you might know where I can get a Filly Vanilli."

Ricci looked blank.

The clerk perked up as if I had mentioned winning lottery tickets. "Oh, they're adorable! I found one online. But I'm not giving it up for any price. My youngest grandson won't go to sleep unless his Filly Vanilli is playing. Check eBay. You might get lucky."

"Thanks!" I went around the car, hands shoved down in my pockets. "I'm obsessed with Filly Vanilli."

Humorless again, the clerk handed over the papers, and I signed above Michael's printed name.

When I was finished, Ricci had his notepad out. He said, "The kid Rawlins. What's his full name and address?"

Reluctantly, I gave the trooper all the information he asked for. Then Ricci said in his authoritative voice, "Be sure to get the registration changed on this car."

"We'll take care of that right away. Can I make arrangements to take the car?"

Ricci said, "We're about to close for the day. Maybe you should come back tomorrow."

He wanted to go through the vehicle more carefully, I could see. But he probably needed a warrant. He'd take a few hours to acquire one. I decided not to ask any more questions that might raise his suspicions any further.

He added, "Don't forget to bring some gas for the car."

I returned to Libby's minivan. Before opening the passenger door, I pulled the plastic tube out of my pocket.

Yep, it was a home pregnancy test.

And the results were positive. Which meant Porky and Rawlins weren't the only people who had been in the car lately.

Chapter 9

I asked Libby to drive me over to the high school in hopes of locating Rawlins before the police did. By the time we arrived, though, classes had been dismissed, and Rawlins was not to be found. He didn't answer his cell phone, either. So Libby drove me to her house.

Rawlins was not at home.

I wondered if he was with his girlfriend. Having a difficult discussion, maybe? Had he gotten someone pregnant?

I wanted to be there when Rawlins finally showed up, so I called Michael to tell him I'd stay at Libby's for a little while. He didn't answer, so I left a message. Monday night was my evening off from attending social events, so I helped Lucy with her homework while Libby drove the twins to their movement class, whatever that was. By the time Libby got back with the boys, I had fielded more invitations for work, and then I helped her make a batch of firehouse chili.

Still no Rawlins.

While I did the dishes, the twins tried to lure Lucy into a game in the basement, but she wasn't falling for that. Libby lost her patience with Harcourt and Hilton. "Go play outside in the dark," Libby told them. "Maybe you'll see a flying saucer."

They grabbed flashlights and disappeared. Max crawled

around at my feet and emptied a drawer of Tupperware containers onto the floor to play with. Lucy came into the kitchen, and I gave her the empty paper towel cylinder, which she proceeded to use as a light saber on invisible space invaders. She played all the roles, including a giant slug who liked to plot the gruesome executions of his enemies. I noticed one of his enemies had the same name as her current teacher.

I had to admit, Libby had her moments as a mother. She might go off on crazy karmic tangents and wild-goose chases, but she excelled at giving her children everything they needed to be creative. The windowsill was covered with art projects—snow globes made out of baby-food jars, Popsicle stick angels and macaroni snowflakes. Maybe the twins decapitated Cabbage Patch dolls, but they used them to make a movie. Even Rawlins was still writing.

I thought of Michael playing with the neighbors who had welcomed him into their home. His imaginary games with them were one of the few positive influences that shaped his life.

Libby took a phone call from Perry, the bug man. I thought she'd carry the phone into another room to speak privately, but she sat at the kitchen table instead. Her voice sounded businesslike as she dealt with him. I felt a tug of sympathy for the teddy-bearish exterminator.

Around eight, Libby piled Lucy and Max into the car and drove me home.

When we arrived at Blackbird Farm, the night was dark, and the driveway beside the barn was parked full of cars and SUVs.

"What's going on?" Libby asked.

For a second, I feared Michael had issued a summons for his whole posse to stage the penultimate assault on my furnace.

"Oh, it's poker night," I said with relief. No wonder Michael hadn't answered my earlier phone call. I'd forgotten that his usual once-a-month Wednesday night poker game had been switched to Monday this week.

Libby peered through the windshield at the lighted windows of the house. "Is That Man of Yours allowed to gamble? I mean, he's on house arrest. Isn't that kind of behavior forbidden?"

"His parole officer is part of the group." I got out of her minivan before I had to explain that particular irregularity. "G'night, Lib. Thanks for dinner and the lift."

I closed the door, then shouldered my bag and walked up the flagstone sidewalk. Ralphie grunted his usual cheerful greeting and came lumbering out of the darkness toward me. I gave him a scratch on his head. In the moonlight, I could see the leopardlike spots that ran down his back.

"Did you behave yourself today?"

He tipped his head to look up at me and seemed to smile.

"I didn't think so," I said.

I smelled a cigarette before I saw a figure on the porch, so I wasn't surprised when I went up the steps and found Jim Kuzik, Michael's parole officer, taking a smoke break. He was a watchful man with a serious face that probably posed a challenge to his poker opponents. I supposed men who dealt with criminals on a daily basis were prone to cynicism.

He said, "Good evening, Miss Blackbird."

"Hello," I said coolly. "Are you winning or losing?"

"Losing," he said with something that was almost a grin. "Good thing we don't play for big money, or I'd be looking for a second mortgage."

Usually, I avoided conversations with Kuzik, the court-appointed official assigned to making sure Michael stayed firmly within the restrictions of his parole. I figured that was business between the two of them in which I should not meddle. In addition to Michael's appointments in his office, Kuzik came to the farm at least once a month and sometimes stopped by oh, so casually on other days. Of course, his surprise visits weren't casual at all, but pop quizzes, so to speak. He wanted to make sure Michael didn't violate any rules.

So far, Kuzik hadn't found anything incriminating.

Normally, I would have been working on poker night, so I rarely bumped into him. Tonight, though, I lingered on the porch. I said, "Who's playing this evening?"

Perhaps surprised that I had initiated more conversation for once, he paused and flicked cigarette ash off the porch before speaking. "The usual crew. One of Mick's lawyers, and Ray, the bread-baking cousin. Ken, the guy from the fishing store. And the new kid, Dolph."

"Dolph?"

"He's one of Mick's guys. Not much of a player."

Card games usually bored Michael, and he didn't often win. Poker didn't bring out his competitive nature. I had long ago decided he played cards not for the money, but rather to learn something about his opponents. Sometimes he deliberately lost just to see what character flaw might show itself. His motivations for organizing the monthly poker game made me a little nervous, but I was also glad to see him enjoy the camaraderie of his male friends. He was always in a good mood when I came home after the game. Since Kuzik had joined the group, though, I wondered what Michael's agenda was. I felt pretty sure this kind of fraternizing was against the rules.

Carefully, I said, "Michael has a good time on these evenings."

"I brought some steaks. He did the cooking. They were great."

"He likes to cook."

We heard a roar of laughter from inside the house. Michael's lawyer, and his slippery cousin, along with one of his partners in the fly-fishing business were not the men from Michael's other life—the life I feared would suck him out of my arms and back into shady places where he could get into trouble. I felt moderately sure he was in safe company with this group.

Maybe I should have said good night to Kuzik and gone inside without further ado. I took a chance, however, and said, "I think Michael could benefit by having something else to do with himself."

Carefully, Kuzik extinguished his cigarette on the bottom of his boot, then turned his full attention to me. He possessed an air of professional intimidation that he could turn off and on—used, no doubt, to threaten his parolees into behaving themselves—and suddenly he switched it on, full force, aimed at me.

I stood my ground and met his gaze squarely. "I think Michael needs an outlet. Something that engages his mind, but maybe something physical, too. Normally, he'd go fishing or ride his motorcycle. But he can't do those things now, and I—I wish he had a way to blow off a little steam. He can't be cooped up like this without . . ."

"Without?"

"I don't know," I said, sure he was thinking of crime. "I just wish he had something else to do."

Kuzik didn't answer for a long time. Maybe he understood that I was asking for help. That I was worried about Michael's tendency to break the rules, if he could get away with it. That I was nervous about some of the people with whom Michael associated.

Finally, Kuzik said, "What did you have in mind?"

"If I knew, I'd have encouraged it already."

Kuzik frowned out into the darkness, considering the problem. "Does he like sports? Bowling, maybe?"

"He plays basketball."

Kuzik nodded. "Prison basketball, a dirty game. He ever get his teeth knocked out?"

"No," I said, testily.

Soothingly, Kuzik said, "All I'm saying is, I could get him into a game, couple of mornings a week, maybe. But it's with a doctor and a chiropractor and a university professor or two. Guys that don't want their smiles messed up."

"I can't vouch for his playing style, if that's what you're asking," I said. "I'm just saying Michael could really use an outlet."

Kuzik nodded again. "Okay, I get it. I'll see what I can do. And I won't mention we had this little talk."

"Thank you," I said, although I wasn't sure how I felt about making a secret pact with Kuzik. I reached for the door handle.

"Oh, there's another poker player here tonight," Kuzik said, as if it were an afterthought. "I forgot to mention. Your nephew. Is his name Rawlings?"

"Rawlins." I hoped my voice sounded normal.

I went into the house.

Kuzik followed.

The kitchen was a wreck of dirty dishes, the result of the feast Michael usually prepared for his friends now that the game was permanently at Blackbird Farm. Four empty wine bottles stood on the counter, no doubt a gift from Michael's lawyer friend, Cannoli. Several loaves of rich, crusty bread had come from Ray, Michael's cousin, who ran some kind of underground bakery that sold magnificent artisanal breads to the most discerning restaurants. I spotted a pastry box from a patisserie in New Hope—probably an offering from Ken, who managed the fly-fishing company Michael co-owned. Kuzik had said he'd brought the steaks. I wondered if he brought food to the homes of his other cases.

Was Michael drawing in Kuzik? Studying him the way he studied poker players? And if so, to what purpose? I felt certain their relationship was different from Kuzik's time spent with other parolees. But I wasn't sure how. Or why.

Kuzik followed me as I went through the butler's pantry and the dining room to the library where Michael's posse was gathered around an antique gaming table that had belonged to a long-dead Blackbird cardsharp. All of the players had just picked up their hands and were studying the cards. They had unlit cigars at the ready for the end-of-the-game ritual that now took place on the back porch since Michael and I had had a discussion concerning cigar smoke. And empty beer bottles were lined up on the floor around the table.

Michael put down his cards and got up to give me a kiss, which caused them all to stand and say hello like perfect gentlemen. Even the somewhat sullen newcomer, Dolph, I presumed, stood when Cannoli the Younger gave him a poke on the shoulder.

Michael introduced Dolph, and I shook his hand, which was the size of an iron skillet. He was a bodybuilder, I guessed, but short in stature. He clearly spent plenty of time in the gym or doing whatever manual labor Michael's family required. Not even as tall as me, he had the shoulders and chest of a much larger man. I recognized him for what he probably was—the latest in a line of interchangeable bodyguards from the Abruzzo family, albeit smaller than most. I wondered what had changed in the last day that required Michael to have protection in the house again. Dolph had one lone poker chip in front of his chair, while everybody else seemed to be sitting pretty.

"Don't let me interrupt," I said, feeling as if I were suddenly standing in a forest of big men. "Who's winning?"

"Not me," Dolph said dolefully.

"Cannoli," Michael said.

The lawyer smiled. When Michael got into legal trouble, he used the services of a law firm his family had dubbed, "Cannoli and Sons," because of their appreciation of sweet pastries. One of the sons was Michael's close friend as well as his attorney. He was tall and wore a bespoke dress shirt and a silk tie that had been selected by someone with very discerning taste.

To me, Cannoli said with his usual courtly courtesy, "You're looking lovely this evening, Miss Blackbird."

"Thank you," I said with a smile. "For that, I hope you win big tonight."

While they laughed jovially, I turned to Michael. "I heard Rawlins is here."

"He's waiting for you in the living room."

"Can I get anything for anyone?" I asked, feeling as if I should make an effort to play hostess.

"We're fine," Michael said. "Leave the dishes. The loser cleans up."

Dolph sighed.

I left them to their poker and went through the entry hall and into the living room. Shoulders hunched, Rawlins had his nose pointed at the screen of his cell phone as he lay on the sofa. His legs looked very long, his feet huge. He clicked off the screen when I bent over him, but he didn't meet my eye.

"Hi, Aunt Nora." His voice didn't have much enthusiasm.

I gave him a kiss on the forehead. "Come help me with the dishes."

I closed the door between the kitchen and the butler's

pantry to keep our conversation private. Rawlins followed me and made himself useful without being told what to do. Silent, he carried the wine bottles into the scullery to my recycling bin and scraped plates into the garbage. I wrapped up the leftover loaves of bread and rinsed the dishes before loading them into the dishwasher. Then I ran the sink full of soapy water to wash the glassware and pots. Rawlins pulled a clean dish towel from the drawer.

When I was elbow deep in the water, I said, "So tell me what's going on."

Rawlins sighed and accepted the first wineglass to dry. But he didn't respond.

"The police called. They towed your car."

"Mick told me. It was impounded, huh?"

"We took care of it. Your mother paid the fine, so you owe her. But when I showed up, a state trooper got a brainstorm about a connection between you and Michael—not in a good way. I'm afraid they are keeping the car so they can go through it more carefully." I put the second dripping glass on the counter. Seriously, I said, "Rawlins, you know you can tell me anything. We're not mad at you. We just want the best for you."

"I know." He avoided my gaze, looking miserable. "That's what Mick said."

I went back to washing dishes. It seemed easier to talk when we weren't looking at each other. "So what happened? You left the car out on Sheffield Road in the middle of the night? Why? Did you run out of gas?"

"That was part of it."

"Part of it? Were you with someone? A girlfriend? Or Porter Starr?"

My nephew's face turned stony, and he didn't answer.

"Rawlins, it's just me. I'm not the district attorney, but that's who's going to be asking questions next if we don't figure this out."

"I can't tell anybody. I promised."

I said, "Did you give Porter the keys to your car?" The boy's face twisted with discomfort, but he didn't answer, so I said, "I ask because I found the keys. Beside Swain Starr's body."

His eyes widened, but he said nothing.

"Start at the beginning," I said gently. "Where were you Saturday night?"

"I'd rather not—"

"You know Porter's father was killed, right? He was stabbed, Rawlins. Murdered in cold blood and left to die in a pigpen. I saw everything, and believe me, it was horrible. I haven't felt normal since the moment I found him. But the police are trying to discover who did it, and they're not going to give up until they do, honey. They're going to use sophisticated tests on your car, and they'll probably find DNA from every person who's ever been in it. So you might as well tell me now so we can figure out what to do. We can help you. But only if you tell the truth."

I thought Rawlins might burst into tears. His face turned dark, and his expression puckered. He didn't look seventeen anymore, but more like he had when he was eleven and I'd caught him playing with matches in the barn.

Michael let himself through the butler's pantry door and stuck his head into the kitchen. He said, "Don't do the dishes, Nora. I mean it. I'll take care of the mess later."

"It's okay," I replied. "Rawlins and I are just keeping our hands busy while we talk."

Michael's appearance stiffened Rawlins's spine. He said, "I can't tell you any more. You can't make me."

Michael had already turned and was on his way back to the game, but the words Rawlins spoke—although softly—made him change course and return to the kitchen, closing the door behind himself.

I glanced at Michael beseechingly, then said to my nephew, "Rawlins, we can help, but you have to tell us what happened."

Rawlins shook his head stubbornly. "I made a promise."

"You could get into terrible trouble! Michael, tell him."

But Michael was silent.

That silence seemed to encourage Rawlins. He said to me, "I can't go back on my word."

"Honey, are you involved in this murder somehow? How did your keys end up beside a dead man? And your car—if you didn't use it that night, did Porter? What for?"

"I can't tell you."

"Michael," I said, exasperated, "can you make him understand?"

Michael had been watching Rawlins grow more adamant by the moment. He didn't try to convince Rawlins to talk. Instead, he said quietly, "Sometimes your word is more important than the truth."

Rawlins flashed him a look of relief.

"What is this?" I demanded. "Some kind of misguided code of honor? It's a bad situation, and Rawlins needs to come clean or risk—"

Rawlins said, "I know what I have to do."

He met Michael's gaze, and the two of them exchanged a look I did not understand.

"So what happens next?" I asked. "Am I supposed to tell the police I found the keys?"

"If they ask," Rawlins said steadily, "you should tell them the truth."

"But—"

"Nora," Michael said.

"This is ridiculous! I don't want to get Rawlins in trouble. We should get everything out in the open so we can help."

Before I could ask more questions, Michael said, "You ready to go home, kid?"

Rawlins nodded.

Michael pushed open the pantry door and barked, "Dolph!"

The bodyguard appeared as promptly as a summoned dog, and Michael said, "Take Rawlins home. Come straight back."

Dolph took the order with a nod and went to the door. He opened it and held it wide, waiting.

Rawlins came over and gave me a kiss. "Thanks for understanding, Aunt Nora. I mean it."

I didn't understand. Not remotely. But I gave him a hug and was surprised to find how tall and substantial my nephew had become. He had a scratchy cheek, too. He had grown up fast, and now the world was getting complicated for him. Maybe he had to become an adult, but this felt like a hard way to do it. Tears stung my eyes as I held him tight and whispered good night. Before he went out the door, Rawlins grabbed a baseball cap off the hook by the door. He put it on, and they went out. Dolph slammed the back door so hard, the windows rattled. The concussion seemed to reverberate in my chest, too. Seeing Rawlins in a hat gave me a terrible thought.

Michael said, "Okay, then." And he turned to leave.

As steadily as I could manage, I said, "What are you doing? Rawlins needs to come clean."

"Rawlins has to do what he thinks is right."

"Do you know what's going on with him?"

"I don't know any more than you do, except he's trying to act in an honorable way."

"Michael, you should have explained to him that—"

"You don't explain to a guy, Nora. And Rawlins isn't a baby anymore. A messy, emotional, convoluted argument isn't going to work with him." Michael spoke quietly, but firmly. He set his jaw, too, exactly as Rawlins had done. "He has to think it through for himself."

"Are you condoning his behavior?"

"You gotta let a kid fall down on the playground once in a while. Maybe he gets his knees scraped, but he gets up by himself."

"This isn't a playground! We're not talking about scraped knees. He's not being honorable if he's lying!"

"He's not lying. That's the point. You were right with the code of honor crack. He needs to decide what kind of man he is."

"And if it's a misguided choice?" I asked, struggling with my composure. "If he gets into bad trouble? He could end up in jail."

Michael had been that boy once—playing games with the neighbors one day and hurting his brother the next. And paying a dear price. Eventually he moved on to stealing motorcycles and probably other crimes he hadn't told me about—but crimes that had landed him in big trouble. Nine years in prison had eaten up his young adulthood and set up the house of cards that was the rest of his life now. I ached with the thought that Rawlins might get washed into the same kind of quagmire.

"Jail isn't the worst that can happen," Michael said, keeping his voice down. "The kid has to figure out who he is."

I walked away from Michael and found myself splashing into a new puddle on the kitchen floor. Dolph's door slam had somehow triggered another leak, dammit.

Maybe the puddle on the floor was the last straw, I don't know, but like an idiot, I burst into tears.

At once, Michael came over and gathered me up in his arms. "Hey," he said. "It'll be okay. Take it easy."

I pushed out of his embrace and choked on my words. "I know who he's protecting, and that person isn't worth the sacrifice. Or maybe it's something totally different. Look at this."

I pulled the pregnancy test from my pocket. I'd meant to discuss it with Rawlins, but he'd left before I had the chance. I showed Michael.

He went still. "Is that—?"

"A pregnancy test, yes. And it's positive. See the pink lines?"

"Nora," he said.

"The girlfriend Rawlins was last seeing is away at college, and now he must be dating other girls, so who this belongs to I can't imagine. He's keeping a lot of secrets. If this is his doing, his mother is going to kill him."

"Oh," Michael said. "This came from one of Rawlins's girlfriends?"

"It must have! I was working up to talking with him about it, but I didn't get a chance before—I just can't—Libby's going to throw a fit." I could hear myself getting hysterical. "I can't stand it that a man is dead—a very nice man, who had a family who loved him and—and—Rawlins of all people is in the thick of it somehow. But a pregnant teenager, too, is just more than I—more than I—"

Michael caught me close again. "Calm down. You don't usually lose your head like this. What's the matter tonight?"

"I don't know!" I put my face against his shoulder and tried to steady myself. "Ever since finding Swain, I've been a mess. I'm just—I'm angry and scared for Rawlins. Plus I don't understand this male posturing."

"It's not posturing. It's life."

"Rawlins thinks he's doing the right thing, but I—" Without thinking, I blurted out, "Today my editor—he gave me an assignment that makes me feel slimy."

"What assignment? The Starr murder?"

"He wants me to find out everything I can about all the people in Swain's life. Especially Zephyr."

Michael petted my hair. "That doesn't sound so wrong."

No, it didn't. Except for the way Gus wanted me to dig out the information—by exploiting my friends. And there was more, of course. Eventually I would have to tell Michael that Gus had heard us in the scullery. But I couldn't explain all of that now. Not with the poker game several rooms away. Already, it had gone quiet back there, and I guessed they couldn't hear my exact words, but they certainly knew I was having a female meltdown.

So I snuffled up my tears and wiped my eyes. "I need a good night's sleep."

He held me snug again. "This is a delayed reaction, isn't it? From finding the dead guy. We should have talked it through last night. Want me to take you upstairs? Get you settled?"

"No, that's silly." I swiped off the last of my tears, feeling foolish. I sucked in a deep breath and let it out slowly. "I'll be okay."

He kissed me on the forehead. "I'll get rid of these guys and come up with you."

"No, don't do that. They'll think I'm a ninny."

"They think you're anything but," Michael said. "Don't worry. Rawlins will be okay. We'll make sure of it."

Chapter 10

I gave Michael a kiss and slipped up the stairs. Under the covers twenty minutes later, I conked out as if the Sandman hadn't just dusted my eyes with magic sand, but hit me over the head with his shovel, too.

In the morning, Michael let me sleep late and had the coffee made long before I went downstairs. The kitchen was immaculate, no signs of last night's bacchanal. And I could hear Michael on the telephone in the library, doing business already. He had hit the ground running.

I felt a little queasy after Libby's chili dinner, so I put a thin slice of the fabulous leftover bread into the toaster and poured two cups of coffee. To the noise of morning rain pounding on the roof, I carried them into the library while the bread toasted. Michael had a fire going in the fireplace. I noticed he had pulled on a warm black sweatshirt and jeans—a sign he wasn't planning on going to Mass this morning. Instead, he paced the floor, his face set while he spoke firmly to someone about the price of gasoline.

Somehow during the last year, Michael had become a self-taught commodities broker.

He accepted my good-morning kiss and squeezed my hand, but he didn't interrupt his call. I exchanged his empty coffee cup for a fresh one, and he mouthed, "Thanks."

Dolph was sitting on the windowsill, absently picking his ear while the rain streamed down the glass behind him.

I went back to the kitchen and ate my toast while opening my laptop. The profile of Zephyr—I had to come up with something.

Michael had left a note on my laptop. *Zeffer,* it read. *Chicken farm, Mingo County.*

He must have gotten in touch with whatever underworld kingpin ran the crime in far-flung parts of West Virginia. I was intrigued. I tried tapping out a few sentences on my Zephyr story, but all I could manage was how she seemed like a good person—kind to animals, concerned about the environment and sources of food. She'd been sweet to her husband, who may have gone behind her back to raise animals for slaughter.

On the stroke of nine, Gus Hardwicke called. "Where are you?" he demanded.

"At home," I said calmly. I had decided to keep my cool with him. "Why do you ask?"

"What have you learned about the murder?"

"Nothing since yesterday."

"And the profile of Zephyr?"

I looked at the screen of my laptop. I'd written a grand total of three paragraphs. "Do you have the research your assistant was going to gather?"

"I'll e-mail it to you. When do I get the finished profile?"

"Today."

He hung up.

Trouble was, I wasn't up to the task of writing the profile because I had no new information. All I had were the things I'd observed while interviewing her now-dead husband. And none of it seemed particularly newsworthy. She liked chai tea. That wasn't the kind of tidbit that would make Gus happy.

A minute later, the e-mail from Gus's researcher came through and I skimmed it—just the typical press release information about Zephyr's career.

Except there was a tiny piece in a New York gossip column about Zephyr bouncing checks two years ago. The columnist wondered why a model worth millions couldn't hire an accountant to keep her finances straight. I wondered if the columnist had missed the point. Had Zephyr bounced checks because she was broke?

Had she married Swain for his money?

I needed more, and Google was no help. Screwing up my courage, I telephoned Swain's house, hoping Zephyr might pick up. I could offer my condolences, I told myself. I would ask if I could drop in to see her. As a young widow myself, I could at least offer to be a listening ear when she needed it. And maybe face-to-face I'd get some ideas for the profile.

I felt like a parasite just entertaining the idea, but . . . my paycheck hung in the balance.

Their phone rang until the voice mail kicked in, and then I heard Swain's voice give the standard "leave a message" line. Spooked by hearing a dead man talk, I hastily hung up and immediately felt relieved. Truth be told, I hadn't really wanted to interview a vulnerable young woman just after her husband had died. Another avenue would surely come along.

I clicked my computer over to the *Intelligencer* Web site and scanned the headlines.

And gasped in horror.

A standard headshot of Porky Starr smirking in his hat was topped by the headline: STARR HEIR CAUGHT WITH SEXY STEPMOM.

The article detailed how the hotel security cameras had caught Porky sneaking out of the hotel in the middle of the night and how Zephyr had been removed from the same hotel by police a few hours later. The breathless prose hinted that the two had been involved in a tryst on the night of Swain's murder. A slightly fuzzy photo of Zephyr on the sidewalk outside the hotel must have been taken by someone with a cell phone camera. She looked gorgeous and sexy, indeed. Except her bare feet didn't look very clean.

The byline: Gilda Greygoose.

I seized the phone and tried calling Gus. How had he confirmed the information about Porky? Had somebody actually seen him in the hotel? Or had Gus made the assumption that the young man in the hat seen by Fred, the hotel security man, had been Porky, not somebody else?

Somebody like Rawlins in a baseball cap.

Gus's phone rang, but he didn't pick up. I decided not to leave a message.

My problem remained. I needed information. Whom among my acquaintances could I ask about Zephyr?

I had other items on my day's agenda, though. One, in particular, I had been dreading. While rinsing my plate, I had a flash of inspiration. Maybe I could kill two birds. I called my friend Crewe Dearborne, the restaurant critic for Philadelphia's most prestigious newspaper, who picked up on the first ring.

Crewe sounded out of breath. "Nora! It's good to hear your voice. I heard you found Swain Starr's body. Are you all right?"

"I've been better," I said. My toast hadn't quite settled my stomach, and I wondered if I was even more upset about Swain's death than I first thought. "Why are you panting?"

"I'm on the treadmill in my den," Crewe reported. "A restaurant critic is either eating or exercising all the food off."

"Could you take a break this morning?" I asked.

"Are you thinking of going to the art auction?"

"Yes, but I don't want to go alone. I was hoping you could hold my hand."

"You can hold mine, too," he said. "This is going to be tough."

"I need some other information, too. Can I pick your brain?"

"Of course."

A couple of hours later, I shook out my wet umbrella in the Philadelphia auction house that specialized in liquidating the estates of Old Money families who either died out or went bust. The lobby was decorated with beautifully lighted photographs of past triumphs—paintings that sold for millions and furniture that had been purchased by museums. In one of the frames, I spotted a silver tea set that had once belonged to my grandmother. She had hocked it to pay for my parents' extravagant honeymoon, and now I saw that it had filled the pockets of its new owners with several hundred thousand dollars.

Crewe Dearborne came into the lobby just a moment later, winding up his umbrella and wiping his brogues on the carpet. He gave me a hug, then held me away from himself to admire my outfit. "Who said the most beautiful thing about a dress is the woman in it?"

"Yves Saint Laurent, I think."

"He was talking about you."

I laughed. "Considering who I'm wearing, that's a staggering compliment."

"Who are you wearing?" he asked indulgently.

"The coat is Valentino." I flashed open the perfectly

cut raincoat with its oversized buttons and mandarin collar to reveal the red-and-white-striped wrap dress beneath—one item in my closet that hadn't felt too snug this morning. "The dress is TJ Maxx."

"Whoever the Maxx designer is, he's a genius. Sexy boots, too."

I frowned down at myself. "There's a fine line between sexy and slutty where boots are concerned." Especially thigh-high black leather.

"Those are not slutty. Just enough sexy." Crewe gave me a kiss on the cheek. "You look pale, though. You've had a bad shock with this murder thing. Really, are you okay?"

"Much better now that I've seen you. We should have gotten together sooner." I clasped my friend's hand in mine. "Have you heard from Lexie lately?"

My BFF had gone to prison in the fall after a terrible ordeal. At that time, Lexie had just tentatively started seeing Crewe, and he'd been devastated by her guilty plea and incarceration. Even today, I thought his face looked drawn, and perhaps his hairline had receded just another few centimeters. His eyes, turned down at the corners, had a melancholy cast that concerned me. Otherwise, he was his handsome self in a suit and tie, with a damp Burberry raincoat flying around him like a cape.

He continued to hold my hand as we started up the grand marble staircase together. "I got a letter from her yesterday. She sounds upbeat, but that doesn't mean anything. She's only superficial with me. How about you?"

"I'm going to see her on Saturday." Our first reunion since my dear friend's imprisonment had been a happy one, and I was glad to be seeing her again soon. "But she's upset about today."

"I'm sure she is. The collection of her lifetime is going on the block, and she can't even say good-bye."

I said, "I wish I could buy something—anything—and give it back to her. She loves very few things in life, but her paintings are dear to her. I hope the collection makes enough money to solve all the problems with the Paine Investment Group."

"That," Crewe said, "would be a miracle. If the economy were better right now, I'd have more hope. But the bidders with the deepest pockets are still running scared. At least, that's what my broker says. How's Mick?"

"Bored," I said.

Crewe took a closer look at my face. "That makes you nervous."

"He's allowed to go to Mass. So he goes a lot."

"Mass? Is that a euphemism for something a little more sinful?"

"I hope not," I said. "I think he just wants to get in his car and roll down the windows, drive fast and breathe fresh air. But I'm not sure."

Crewe's brows gathered in a sympathetic frown. "I heard the guys at our news desk talking. They say there's some kind of mob disagreement starting. Over the gambling business."

A gangland rumble would explain the arrival of Dolph in our house. A dispute within the Abruzzo family usually resulted in extra protection for Michael. I knew there were violent people in Michael's world. Very violent. And the gambling operation—their primary source of income—was worth fighting for.

I could trust Crewe with some of what I knew, so I said, "Michael's trying to get out of the gambling business. I think he wants to walk away from the rest of his family and let them fight over it, but . . . it's not that easy. There is pressure from all sides."

Crewe put his arm around my shoulders and squeezed. "What can I do to help?"

I pasted on a smile. "Come for dinner? Play chess with him? In no time, I think he'd be unbeatable at chess."

"Not if I'm the teacher. But I'll come. Maybe next week?"

One person from my world who had gotten past Michael's shields was Crewe. Perhaps because Crewe was so easygoing and Michael didn't sense any male bristling from him. So I looked forward to seeing them together. I said, "Sunday or Monday?"

"Monday. It's a date. I'll bring a salmon. There's a guy who's promised to fly me one from Alaska."

Upstairs, the auction house was mobbed. We made our way through the humming throng before slipping into the back of the main salon—a large auditorium packed to the rafters with well-dressed art lovers who clutched numbered paddles in their manicured hands and spoke excitedly with one another. Crewe and I had hoped to arrive just late enough not to be noticed, but no luck. The seats at the back of the auditorium were already full, which forced us to walk down the center aisle to the third row.

We might as well have been in a parade. Several friends called to me, and Crewe was just as busy acknowledging many acquaintances. The majority of the crowd, though, was older—men over sixty and their fortysomething wives—well-dressed "farts and their tarts," as my father would say. It seemed as if half the city's rich and once powerful had taken the day off to watch Lexie Paine's art collection go under the gavel.

In an aisle seat, halfway back in the auditorium, sat Heywood Kidd, the city's most renowned art collector. Beside him was a new curator in town who had probably been assigned the job of wooing Heywood into donating his collection after his death. Good luck with that, I thought. I suspected Heywood would be buried with his pictures. Dozens of curators had used their wiles with Heywood, and he had resisted them all. But he loved being fawned over.

We found seats against the wall, and Crewe helped me off with my coat. We sat. Then Crewe put his shoulder against mine and leaned close. "How's your job?"

"Not exactly great."

"The newspaper business never is anymore. Be glad you still have a column. And that your online edition wants so much content from you."

"There's no danger your column will be cut, is there?"

Crewe had been writing restaurant reviews for his paper since college, and he had a loyal following. But he said, "All the papers are slashing staff. I'm hanging on for the moment. But I've got a book proposal almost ready to send to a publisher friend in New York."

"Good thinking. A fun book?"

He smiled. "A food memoir, if that makes sense. I think it's fun. Restaurant catastrophes and best meals around the world. That kind of thing. What about you? Are you making alternate plans in case the *Intelligencer* decides to stop covering the social scene?"

I shook my head. "What am I trained for? Writing thank-you notes and planning dinner parties? That's not exactly a skill set. At the moment, Gus Hardwicke has me working on celebrity profiles. I don't like it, but I'll take what I can get."

"You didn't write that hatchet job in today's *Intelligencer*, did you? About Swain Starr's son and his wife having a rendezvous on the night he was killed? It made Zephyr sound like a stepmother from a porn movie."

I couldn't hide my dismay. "Gus took my notes and said he was going to rewrite a piece."

"I've heard about his reputation. Gus Hardwicke got

into some real trouble in Australia. Pushing the envelope so hard, his own father had to fire him. Is he making things tough for you?"

"He's not the ideal boss," I admitted.

Crewe looked sympathetic. "But you can't quit, can you?"

"I don't have a choice. I need the salary," I said.

"What celebrity are you supposed to write about next?"

"You can guess, I'm sure. Zephyr."

"She's used to the limelight and can probably take it. I was afraid you were going to say Marybeth, the grieving ex."

"Do you know Marybeth?"

"I know her kids better—the older ones, that is, not Porky. Our families both belonged to the Longhill Club for years. They always supplied the hot dogs for the annual Fourth of July party. Boy, those were great hot dogs." One of the best things about Crewe was his egalitarian attitude about food. He liked caviar and truffles, but he applied the same connoisseur's appreciation to pizza and hot dogs, too. "Too bad the family sold out to a corporation. The quality hasn't been the same since. Have you seen her since the murder? Is she happy or sad about Swain's death?"

"I'd call her feelings mixed," I said.

"If Swain had been killed on the night they broke up, I'd have said Marybeth did it. Nobody gets angry faster than Marybeth, especially when she's drinking. And her husband leaving, after four children? No jury on earth would have convicted her." He caught himself. "Well, that's an exaggeration. This is off the record, right?"

"Sure. Did Marybeth's money really get Swain's fashion house off the ground? I'd heard as much but never knew for sure."

Crewe nodded. "Funny to think one of the great fashion houses of the world got started thanks to a hot dog. He'd still be Sam Schulman, cutting men's suits in a sweatshop if not for Marybeth. I kind of admire her, though. She could have spent her life blowing his money, plus what she inherited from her family. But she used that capital to build her own career in genetics. She was driven to succeed, just like her grandfather."

The prototype pig was important to her, I thought.

We couldn't continue our conversation because the auctioneer came out on the stage. As the crowd broke into polite applause, Crewe handed me his list and I glanced at it. I found myself thinking about Swain Starr and his wives. If he had married Marybeth only for the money she could bring to the marriage, had he finally thrown her over when he found true love with Zephyr? Had he been secretly so needy that he sought the kind of geisha-like attention she gave him?

As those in the crowd found their seats, the auctioneer called the event to order. He was the senior partner in the firm, and his appearance indicated the high esteem they held for the art in Lexie's collection. He made opening remarks, smiling smugly that such a well-heeled group had turned out for the auction.

The first painting was wheeled onstage on a portable easel, covered with a dark cloth. As the lights dimmed in the auditorium, the audience murmured with anticipation. On the stage, a pinprick of light glowed on the dark cloth over the painting.

Crewe leaned close to me again. "Now that we're here, this is just painful."

"I feel the same way," I murmured, rubbing the goose bumps that had broken out on my arms. "But I wanted to come for Lexie's sake. She might actually have enjoyed it, you know."

It seemed impossible that a woman of Lexie's pedigree might find herself suddenly penniless, but it had happened fast and furiously. She had inherited her father's financial firm and built it to even greater heights. But a partner's hubris—and his stealing from their clients—led to tragedy, and now Lexie was serving a sentence for manslaughter. From prison, she was trying to make things right for the clients who'd lost their investments.

The auctioneer told his runner to remove the cloth from the easel, and the first painting was revealed.

It was the Gauguin that Lexie had inherited from an aunt. Not one of the artist's masterworks, the canvas was nevertheless lively with bare-breasted native women gathered under palm trees in a slanted evening sunlight. Hot tropical colors seemed to leap off the cool greens of the background. Lexie had boldly hung the painting in our college dorm room, for heaven's sake, and I could almost hear her roaring laugh as she set it on a nail and stood back to see how the fabulous painting looked in our untidy room. How many nights had I drifted off to sleep while gazing at the hot, romantic Tahitian sunset?

I reached for Crewe's hand, and he took it. He didn't look down at me, though. I think he was struggling to keep his own composure, too.

The bidding started. I saw paddles flash in the crowd, and the beautiful young women who sat at the bank of telephones were also busily signaling the auctioneer. The numbers escalated quickly—by the millions.

Whoever was bidding didn't know what a spell the painting cast in an otherwise dingy dormitory. The Gauguin had brought out the spirit of travel and adventure in Lexie and me. It had presided over our late-night talks and our sometimes less-than-earnest studying. When we threw parties, the frame had been decorated with Christmas twinkle lights and feather boas. I felt sure the painting would never again be loved as intensely as we had loved it back then.

Crewe handed me his handkerchief just as I managed to wrestle my own out of my handbag. I dabbed my nose. He put his arm across my shoulders. We didn't speak as the auctioneer pounded down his gavel. Thirty-nine million, paid by a bidder on the telephone.

The runner stepped back so photographers could snap pictures of the painting. In the flash of cameras, the colors suddenly seemed to fade away.

Four pieces were sold before I realized I was feeling light-headed. Perhaps the stress of the auction or the fact that I hadn't eaten anything since my slice of dry toast earlier—I wasn't sure which to blame.

I touched Crewe's arm. "I think I've had as much as I can take."

"Me, too," he said—glad to focus on me, not his own overflowing emotions. "As soon as there's a break, let's blow this joint and get some lunch. I've thought of somebody who might know Zephyr."

He whisked me out of the building, and we were soon seated in a small bistro Crewe claimed served the best mussels in town. I forgot about my struggle that morning to fit into the Dior that matched my coat and fighting back frustration when I belted myself into my cheap wrap dress instead. I dug into the mussels meunière as if I hadn't eaten in a week. Over lunch, Crewe and I talked about the auction and whether or not it might earn Lexie enough money to ease her firm's financial crisis.

Our waiter must have told the chef that Crewe was in the house, because as soon as the lunch rush was over, he came out and sat at our table. For all of Crewe's self-deprecation, he was perhaps the leading food expert in the city, and people came to pay homage. The chef was a heavyset young man with a shiny pink face and his hair contained in a traditional toque. He set a dish of ice cream in front of Crewe and passed a spoon to me, too.

Crewe introduced us. "Nora, this is Carlo Pinto, one of my favorite chefs in town."

"One of many?" Carlo protested with mock umbrage. "Give me back my ice cream!"

But Crewe pulled the dish closer, laughing. "What have you brought us, Chef?"

With a grin, Carlo hunkered down on the table with both meaty elbows. "A bacon hot-fudge sundae."

I put down my spoon. I could see the bacon bits floating on top of the dense ice cream, and I suddenly lost my appetite.

But Crewe laughed with delight and grabbed his spoon. "Now, this is a man's dessert!"

"Give it a try."

Crewe dug in and popped a creamy spoonful. He rolled the treat around in his mouth and began nodding even before he'd swallowed. "Excellent," he pronounced. "A hint of smoke, a suggestion of maple. Savory, yet slightly sweet. The mouth-feel is rich. Is it on the menu yet?"

"We're refining it."

I said, "Who'd have thought that pork would become the hot new ingredient in this age of healthy eating?"

"Pork is king," the chef agreed.

"I wonder," I said, "if you planned on buying any pork from Swain Starr?"

Carlo shook his head. "It's a shame he was killed, right? I hoped to get some of his product. He was going to have top-notch hogs."

Crewe looked intrigued. "What kind of hogs?"

Carlo said, "He said he was raising his own special cross. He told me it was going to be the perfect pig—a blend of all the best qualities of an American commercial hog that was the brainchild of the Howie's Hotties people, and a lean and mean feral pig found only in the wilds of rural Louisiana, known for its really great fork tenderness. Plus a dash of a Siberian wild boar, for some reason. Cross-breeding like that often results in sterile animals, though, which means the genetic line ends. But I'll tell you, if he pulled off what he claimed he was working on, we were all going to be enjoying bacon in wonderful new ways. He was very secretive, though. He didn't share any samples of the meat."

I said, "The Rattigan family thinks the credit—and the breeding stock—belongs to them."

The chef shook his head. "Maybe the Howie's Hotties hogs were the beginning. But as far as I knew, the final product was all Starr. That's what he said, anyway."

As far as I could tell, Marybeth thought the credit belonged to her alone. It sounded to me as if Swain had been grabbing the limelight that was due to his ex-wife. If Marybeth was angry enough, might she have killed her ex for that? But I remembered my orders from Gus and said, "Did Zephyr come along when Swain spoke with you?"

Carlo got a sappy grin on his face. "Zephyr? You bet. I just wanted to look at her while Swain did all the talking. With her standing beside him, he was very persuasive. But her thing was organic milk and vegetables."

"Did you buy milk and vegetables from her?"

"I was going to, as soon as her harvest came in. Who could say no to that face? And that body?"

Crewe said, "I knew Swain Starr as a fashion designer. But you make his death sound like a great loss for foodies everywhere."

Carlo nodded. "That's about the size of it. Are you writing a column about him?"

"I might," Crewe replied, already pulling out his note-book.

I tried again. "I thought Tommy Rattigan was going to be Swain's partner in pigs."

"I never heard anything about a partner," the chef said. "My only contact was with Swain himself. And Zephyr. Man, she's something to look at."

"Hmm." Had Swain Starr commandeered the pig-breeding venture from Marybeth and Tommy? "Is there a chance somebody might have wanted to stop this perfect pig from coming to market?"

Both Crewe and Carlo looked startled by such a question.

Quickly, I said, "I'm just wondering because Swain died under terrible circumstances. Unless the killing was a random act, it takes a big reason to kill somebody."

"I don't know who might have wanted to stop his pork operation," Carlo said. "I guess you'd have to ask the police."

Crewe went on studying me as the chef changed the subject back to his ice cream. The two men continued their conversation.

But I thought about pigs a little more. I had planned on serving Ralphie all winter long, but once we'd gotten to understand and enjoy his personality, I couldn't send him to the butcher. Since adopting him as a pet, I'd learned how personable he was. Still, hogs were big business.

I interrupted Crewe and Carlo again. "How much does a pig sell for?"

"One like the kind Swain was raising? Several thousand dollars."

"Per pig?" I asked, surprised.

"They were going to be really special pigs."

I had seen only one litter of piglets at the farm. How

many babies had there been? Eight? Ten? And he had planned on a whole pasture full of them. More than a hundred sows, he had told me. If every mother pig gave birth to eight piglets, that was—I did the math—a lot of money.

Carlo saw where my thoughts had gone. "I'm telling you, it wasn't chump change. Swain had a gold mine on his hands."

"I think what Nora's wondering," Crewe said, "is whether somebody might have killed Swain for starting this venture in pork."

Carlo shrugged. "I deal with a lot of farmers. A few of them have screws loose. I suppose one of them might have felt his livelihood was being threatened. But killing Swain? I doubt it."

"Maybe the Rattigans wanted their valuable Howie's Hotties breeding stock back again?" Crewe suggested.

"That would make one of the Rattigans . . . a murderer?" the chef asked, aghast.

Instead of worried farmers or angry hot dog heirs, though, I found myself thinking about Zephyr again. Carlo said she hadn't spoken much. But Swain brought her along when he pitched his pork to the restaurant owners. How had she felt about her beauty being used in an oblique way to help kill and sell animals? Remembering the way she had wept over chickens, I could guess how Zephyr felt about raising thousands of pigs destined to be slaughtered. She might have been happy to keep dairy cows—no animals were hurt in the production of organic milk. But if she thought her husband was going to start killing large numbers of specially bred pigs, perhaps she might have wanted to find a way to stop him.

I saw Crewe looking at me with concern. I managed a smile. "Don't mind me. I'm just daydreaming. Finish your ice cream."

"It's been a tough couple of days for you," he said gently.

"Yes." I gathered up my handbag and gave him what I hoped felt like a jaunty kiss on the cheek. "And this one isn't over yet. I must get to my office. Thank you for lunch, Chef. Your food was delicious. Just what I needed."

I couldn't put it off any longer. Stiffening my spine, I went to see Gus Hardwicke.

Chapter 11

The rain had given way to overcast skies, so I walked across town and thought about what I could write about the hillbilly supermodel.

I tried phoning Michael first.

"Yeah," he said when I asked about the note he'd left on my laptop. "Sorry I forgot to tell you before you left. Things got busy. My guy in West Virginia had all kinds of information."

Trying to decide how reliable the information might be, I asked, "How do you know this friend?"

"He's not a friend, just a guy. I met him inside. He ran a small-time racket, riding around remote mountains on an ATV to buy prescription painkillers from grandmas, then turning around to sell the stuff to the grandkids. Got caught when he drove over a ravine, and the rescue crew found him with enough Oxy to sedate a herd of elephants, plus enough cash to buy the herd, too. Hell of a way to make a living, but it paid for his vacation home in Belize. I hear it's a nice place."

I should not ask questions about Michael's prison acquaintances, I told myself. I never liked the answers.

I said, "What did he have to say about Zephyr?"

"Not the kind of stuff that gets printed in *People* magazine. She grew up pretty rough—big family, isolated cabin, no central heat. It was a low-rent chicken farm that went bust. She was the middle kid of, like, five sisters. When the chicken business went south, Dad started cooking meth. Mom died young—likely beaten to death by her husband."

I must have made a squeak of dismay because Michael said, "It gets worse. Zephyr took care of the younger kids. Her real name, by the way, is spelled with two *f*s. Zeffer. Eventually, two sisters went to jail for solicitation, one died of an overdose, the last one's getting rich in the meth business. At sixteen, Zephyr got into some kind of small-time pageant thing with the help of a local, like, wedding store that gave her dresses for free, and she won, and that was how she got out and started modeling. Anyway, word is," Michael said, summing up, "before Zephyr got off the mountain, she killed her father."

My breath stopped. "She—?"

"Yeah. Plugged him with a shotgun during a family dispute in the middle of the night. You don't want to think about why that went down. Or what kind of a mess a shotgun makes at close range."

No, I didn't. "Why hasn't anybody heard about this before?"

"She was never arrested. Dad was a shit everybody hated. One of the daughters—fourteen years old—was pregnant at the time of his death, so the local cop figured the shooting was justifiable. And once Zephyr got famous, the community rallied behind her. Proud of the hometown girl, they kept her secret."

"How does your guy know all this?" I asked, hoping the story couldn't possibly be true. "Why is he talking now?"

"He's known it for a long time, but I guess the surviving sister made a move on his territory, cutting into his profit, so he's taking his revenge. Swears on a stack it's all true."

"Why punish Zephyr for her sister's drug dealing?"

"That's the way it goes with those crazy drug people. No scruples."

I let that judgment call slide. Instead, I thought about Zephyr killing her father. Whatever the horrible circumstances were, she had pulled a trigger once. Did that mean she was capable of killing her husband, too? Would committing murder be easier the second time around?

"Thank you," I said. "Anything else?"

"That's as much as I could stomach."

Far more than I could. I was feeling nauseated all over again. But I said, "Michael, Crewe says his newspaper is working on a story about a gangland war."

"Oh yeah?" He sounded relaxed. "What gang?"

"Yours."

"Oh hell," he said, "there's no war going on. Just a few pissed-off cousins making threats. If things get bad enough, somebody will tell Nonna, and she'll make us all come for lasagna and a lecture about going to confession more often."

He made it sound so benign. And I wanted to believe him.

He added, "In your whole life, you never tasted lasagna worse than Nonna's. So nobody wants to risk the heartburn. This will blow over."

"Okay," I said uneasily.

"Gotta go," he said. "Another call."

I put away my phone and walked a little farther, thinking about Zephyr. I'd had no clue she had come from such a hardscrabble background. Yes, everybody had heard the barefoot-holler story, but maybe nobody realized how true it was. That blank face she wore on runways—so chic as she strutted before cameras wearing fabulous gowns—had hidden some very unglamorous secrets.

But I couldn't write about it in the newspaper. I didn't have the right ruthless streak.

By the time I got to the Pendergast Building, it was late afternoon and the big newsroom was almost empty. The few reporters who remained on the staff were either in meetings somewhere or on their way home. Only Skip Malone, one of three sports reporters who still worked for the *Intelligencer*, sat at his desk. He had a phone pinned to one shoulder, and he was typing madly on his computer. Like the rest of us who remained at the newspaper, he was doing the work of two reporters. He glanced up when I walked past, though, and gave my red coat and boots a raised thumb of approval.

The intern guarding Gus's lair cheerfully told me he'd gone out, so with the feeling I'd just earned a reprieve, I went to my desk. Before settling in to write the profile of Zephyr with the thin set of facts I felt comfortable sharing, I sorted through my mail. The mound of invitations that had arrived told me that the social season was building once again. Two invitations held gifts meant to entice me to attend the events—a helium balloon and a box of chocolates.

Although I wasn't supposed to accept bribes, I wrote a quick thank-you note to the chocolate giver—an old friend who wanted me to attend her brother's early-retirement cocktail party, which I had planned to attend anyway. And I wrote a regretful note to the balloon person who was trying to drum up guests for a clown-themed party for a disease of the week. Clowns tended to unnerve me. What was really behind that icky makeup? And if I wrote about every disease fund-raiser, as worthy as they were, I'd never have room for anything else. Clown pictures didn't play well in print anyway. But I carried the balloon across the floor to the desk of my friend Mary Jude, the food page writer, whose son Trevor might get a kick out of it.

Back at my desk, I tried doing a search through the *Intelligencer*'s archive for information about Zephyr's financial health. I found more gossip-column snarking about her bouncing checks, but nothing else. Then I saw an item about the prenup Zephyr had signed before marrying Swain Starr. The amount of money she inherited upon his death was tied to the number of years she remained married to him. If they were married less than five years, she got zip. I wasn't sure how long they had been married, but I could look that up.

I assumed Zephyr had money of her own—modeling was a lucrative line of work, for sure—so the five-year thing seemed only prudent. Or was it hiding something else?

Swain's vasectomy. I remembered Marybeth's rude crack about him spending weeks sitting on ice packs. He had no doubt been enduring the discomfort so he could create more children with Zephyr.

Before I could look up their wedding date, my phone rang.

"Nora? It's Sam."

My friend from the hotel didn't sound happy. I said, "Hi, Sammy, what's up? Do you need those Hermès scarves sooner than you thought?"

"Forget the scarves. I'll be lucky if they keep me in the show."

"What?" I finally heard the tone of his voice. "Sam, what's wrong?"

"I got fired this morning," he snapped. "The hotel told me to take a hike. Because of what you wrote in the newspaper."

"What?"

"You can't hide behind that stupid fake name, Nora. Gilda Greygoose? Who do you think you're fooling with that? I know you wrote that stuff about the hotel—about Zephyr getting escorted out by the police and her husband's son getting himself featured on the hotel security cam. Well, thanks to your blabbing, I'm out of a job."

"The hotel fired you?"

"*And* Freddy. The manager needed about two seconds to figure out where you got the information. I never said it was Porter Starr on the tapes. And now Porter says he's going to sue the hotel. I saw him on the noon news on TV."

I felt the bottom drop out of my stomach. Gus had taken my meager information and turned it into something bad enough to get my friend fired from his job.

"Sam, I'm so sorry. It's not what you think."

"It isn't? Can you honestly tell me you didn't run straight back to your desk to write what I told you—in confidence?"

"I told you I was working for the paper. Look, I'm sorry." Making excuses wasn't going to help either one of us. I said, "I take full responsibility. I'll talk to your manager. Maybe there's some way I can—"

"Forget it," he said, his voice catching in what sounded like a sob. "I don't want you making things worse. You, of all people! I thought I could trust you, Nora. Just— please stay away from me, okay?"

He banged down the phone.

I sat for a horrible minute, hands shaking, trying to think of something—anything—I could do to make it right. I had screwed up. I had hurt a friend—someone who had been kind to me when I really needed help.

I felt like crying. Or kicking myself.

I'd done it. I had blabbed to Gus, just as Sammy said. It was my fault he had lost his job. And I knew how awful that would feel. Unemployment sounded like a fate worse than death. How would Sammy pay his rent? Pay for food? I had to help him somehow.

But I didn't have any spare cash, either. I'd have rushed across the city to press a few months' worth of grocery money into his hand—but I didn't have it to give.

Slowly, I put my phone back into my handbag.

And became aware of a person standing next to my desk.

Gus said, "Bad news, luv?"

He slid his hands into the pockets of his trousers and lounged against the side of my desk, smiling down at me with something distasteful lurking in his eyes.

I said, "Now's not a good time to talk to me."

He laughed. "You think you have a choice?"

He used one foot to hook the swivel chair from the next desk and scoot it over to mine. "Let's see your Zephyr piece."

"It's not written yet."

"Okay." He sat in the swivel chair and wheeled it closer—so close that I had to scoot my chair out of his way before he practically pulled me into his lap. He fired up my computer with a flip of the button. "Give me what you have in dictation, and I'll type."

"I don't work that way," I said. "I need time to form my thoughts."

He gave me a raised eyebrow. "Time to form your thoughts? Who are you, Charlotte Brontë?"

I could barely hold back a scream. "I can't believe you took my words and twisted them around for today's story. All I said was a young man in a hat—and you turned it into libel about a lovely woman with principles and a boy who doesn't deserve bad treatment from the press."

He leaned back in his chair and linked his hands behind his head. "What's got the dingo in your knickers?"

"A friend of mine—the hotel employee who talked to me, who told me about Zephyr—he was fired today. Fired for telling me what I asked—what he thought was in confidence—"

"He talked to a reporter and thought his golden words were protected by—what? A magic force field of confidentiality?"

"I'm his friend!"

"You're a reporter," Gus snapped.

"You assumed the man in the hat was Porky."

"It wasn't?"

I got out of my chair and tried to walk away, but I was trembling with anger and shame and fear for Rawlins in his baseball cap. I had to stop beside the desk to catch my balance.

I said, "I can't do this."

"Of course you can."

"I can't rat on my friends."

"Then be more careful."

I glared at him, but he gave me a steady, challenging stare in return.

Calmly, he said, "You can't resign. You don't have that luxury. You have to stick with the job."

"Right now," I said over the slam of my pounding heart, "I can't think of a person I despise more than you."

"Get in line." He noodled with the computer's keyboard, frowning at the screen. "Now tell me what you know about Zephyr."

"Are you kidding?" My voice went up a notch. "You want me to compound my mistake by telling you—"

"We'll call her the hillbilly supermodel," he said, already typing as he ignored my outrage. "Born in a West Virginia holler to a barefoot baby mama and—"

"Don't say that. Any of it. It's insulting."

He kept typing. "That's where she was born, right?

And she is universally known as the hillbilly supermodel, isn't she? And her mother was fifteen when she was conceived? That's public record. So that language is dead set. In your notes about her husband, you said she cried over a bunch of dead chickens. We can use that to—"

"Are you going to twist everything into something lurid and sensational?"

"That's what sells papers." His fingers stopped moving on the keyboard, and he finally looked up at me. His face was hard, his green eyes searing. "Get down from your high horse and get with the times, Miss Blackbird. Or you'll turn to moldering dust like all your high-society pals."

"How can you—"

"We're in a new era, Nora. Everybody has money, not just the people who came to this fertile land two hundred years ago with their noblesse oblige and the rest of their paternalistic, slave-owning, feudal-lord crap. In fact, if you want to get really rich and powerful today, you get down in the dirt and fling it at as many people as you can. That nong Porky Starr isn't going to sue the newspaper. He's going to ride the publicity like a surfboard. Face it. You are a dinosaur, young lady. A dying breed. You just haven't noticed, because you're too busy trying to keep up appearances."

"I don't care how I appear," I said. "I care about honor and integrity. And you've taken mine and walked all over it."

"I'm teaching you how to do your job. You're bloody lucky, too. The rest of the idiots around here I fired."

I almost said something vile. The words were in my mouth. I spun away from the desk and headed for the ladies' room. I had to pull myself together before I said something that would humiliate me more than he had already done in print. Skip Malone looked up from his computer as I passed, but I hurried on, determined not to break into tears or shrieks of rage in public.

I banged the door behind me and went straight to the sink. I wrenched the faucet handle, and a gush of cold water splashed out. I bent down and cupped water in my hands. In the mirror, my face looked white.

The next second, the door swung open, and Gus barged into the ladies' room.

He said, "Don't walk away from a fight. Not unless you're admitting defeat."

"You can't come in here."

But he marched in, turned off the water and banged on the towel dispenser. He shoved a paper towel into my hand. "I expected more from you."

"I don't know what I expected from you, but I see an ethical bone in your body is not among your—"

"My ethics are fine. I know exactly what I will and will not print. But I also know how to write a story that will sell papers, so hustle yourself out to your desk and let's have a lesson, shall we?"

"I'm not going to sit still while you type a lot of lies about Zephyr."

"Do you even know her? Why do you care so much about her precious feelings? She was the last person to see her husband alive, so she probably killed him!"

"We don't know that. And we're not going to insinuate so in the newspaper—not with my name in any way attached to the story."

"We'll lay out the facts and let the public decide."

"We should allow the *police* to collect the facts, and a *court* will decide."

For a second, I thought the argument was over.

Gus didn't speak. But he was angry—I could see it. He glared at me. A vein throbbed in his forehead, and his hands were tightly fisted. I thought he might explode from the tension inside.

Instead, he seized my wrist, pulled me close and kissed me.

His mouth was hot, his body tense. He said something against my lips— I don't know what. And his other arm came around me, holding me like a band of steel.

I twisted, pulled back and slapped him. Hard. Across the cheek.

It was instinct—a bad one. Incredibly stupid, but heaven knew I didn't have a single sensible thought in my head at that moment.

I stepped back and collided with the sink, holding my breath. I had the back of my hand against my mouth as I stared at him.

He stepped back and cleared his throat, his palm against his cheek where I had clobbered him. He said, "I suppose right now stand-up sex with me is off the menu."

"Don't," I said. "Don't try to joke your way out of this."

"You have a powerful arm. Did you learn it from your thug boyfriend? Do you hit each other on a regular basis?"

I shouldn't have struck Gus, I knew that. I never did that kind of thing. Once again, he'd pushed me far out of my comfort zone.

He took his hand away from his lip and discovered a fleck of blood on his palm. I had hit him hard enough to cut the inside of his cheek against his teeth. As he looked at the blood, he said, "I guess I've given you reason to sue me for harassment, haven't I? You Yanks are a litigious lot."

I could, I realized. I had a case.

Someone knocked on the outside of the bathroom

door. From the hallway, I heard Skip Malone's voice. "Nora? You okay in there?"

I held Gus's gaze as I said, "I'm finished. I quit. You'll have my letter of resignation before the end of the day."

Gus didn't argue with me. He stepped aside, allowing me space to walk past him.

I did. I left the bathroom and almost collided with Skip in the hallway. He already had one hand on the door, coming inside to rescue me. To him, I said, "Thank you, Skip. I'm fine."

I didn't look fine. I saw it in Skip's face.

I picked up my coat and my bag and left the building.

Out on the sidewalk, rush hour had started. People were filing out of their workplaces, heading for home in a wave of anonymous humanity. A bus lurched past, followed by a surge of traffic. Head down, I walked quickly, feeling a thousand emotions, none of them good. Already, the adrenaline in my system was thinning out. I felt my legs trembling. My mouth tasted awful. I remembered how Gus had felt against me—strong and impulsive.

I hadn't expected such a move. It came out of the blue.

Or had it? I was part of a generation that—still, after all the politically correct training—felt guilty when a man came on strong. Had I given him any signs? What about me made him feel he could grab me? Kiss me? Was it some Australian thing I didn't understand? Or had it been the tiniest bit my fault?

While I wrestled with guilt and outrage, my cell phone rang. I was crossing the street at the time, so it wasn't until I stepped onto the curb and stopped that I took a look at my phone's screen.

Gus.

I let the call go to voice mail. Standing still for a moment, I tried to calm myself.

Pedestrians brushed past me. People going home

from work at the end of the day. I was out of a job, though. As broke as ever, but now without a paycheck, too. I wasn't sure how I could afford to pay any of my bills, but it had been the only thing I could do. I told myself that over and over. I'd had no choice. I'd had to resign.

But it was scary as hell. Standing on the corner, I got the shakes. Unemployment. Now what was I going to do? How would we manage? Michael was on house arrest. My family would be no help. What if I couldn't get a job waitressing?

My phone rang again. This time, when I checked the screen, it was Libby's name on the caller ID.

I answered.

"Nora, Nora," she cried. The rest of her sentence was so garbled with hysteria that I couldn't understand a word.

"Lib? Slow down." I plugged my other ear to hear her better. "I can't understand what you're saying."

She shrieked in my ear. I could hear the frantic emotion in her voice.

"Take it easy," I snapped. "Is it Max? Is something wrong with the baby? Or Lucy? Libby, I can't understand—"

"Rawlins," she managed to say clearly. "It's Rawlins!"

But she burst into tears and hung up on me.

I called Michael, my hands shaking almost too hard to dial.

He said, "You better come home."

"What's wrong?" I cried. "Libby just called. She was hysterical."

"It's Rawlins."

"Oh God," I prayed, thinking the worst.

"Libby says he's been arrested," Michael said. "For the murder of Swain Starr."

Chapter 12

I telephoned Emma next.

Emma said, "Libby just called me. She says the cops arrested Rawlins. For murder!"

"I know, I know. Is she okay?"

"She's out of her gourd. They took him out of school a couple of hours ago. She asked me to pick up the twins. What's with you?"

"I don't know. I—I—" I rubbed my forehead, trying to massage some sensible thoughts into my brain. "I just quit my job."

Emma cursed again. "Lousy timing, Sis. Libby is going to need cash. If Rawlins really is arrested, she'll need money for bail, money for lawyers. This is going to be expensive. I've got a few bucks, but—hell," she said on a sigh. "What's this going to cost?"

"Surely Libby has some savings?"

"You're kidding, right? Let's remember who we're talking about."

Of course Libby would have no savings. After her husband died, she took the last of their bank account and flew the kids to Disney World. The rest of the time she lived on carefully spaced payments from the life insurance policies of her dead husbands.

"Why'd you quit your job?" Emma demanded. "The

boss finally get to you? Can you afford to be prissy about him?"

Gus's behavior had been one deciding factor, but not the primary reason. I didn't want to admit my ethical failings or that I felt pushed into overlooking my personal values. And I certainly didn't want my sister thinking I was too feeble to handle a little job pressure.

When I didn't respond, Emma said, "What do you want to do?"

I wasn't thinking straight. Rushing to Libby's side to comfort her was my first instinct. Or going home to Michael to strategize. But he didn't need my help for that. My first move should be to help Rawlins.

So I said, "Can you swing by and get me before you pick up the twins?"

"Sure. Where are you?"

I told her, and she said, "I can probably get there in half an hour, depending on traffic. Sit tight."

"Thanks."

I stood on the corner for about ten minutes, trying to decide what to do. I was having major second thoughts. I could hear Crewe's voice saying I should hang on to my job by my fingernails. I shouldn't have quit. I should have been more professional. Rather than clobbering Gus for kissing me, I should have called a lawyer, then buckled down to work. Other people stuck with jobs plenty worse than mine.

My phone jingled again, and I looked at the screen. Gus.

I didn't answer.

A minute later, the phone rang again. Gus again. And again. And again. He was going to keep calling until I picked up.

Finally, in exasperation, I answered.

"Yes?"

In my ear, he said, "I can see you from my office window. Shall I come down there to hash this out, or will you come back up here so we can discuss it in private?"

I hung up.

But I felt ridiculous standing there, knowing he could see me, so I shouldered my bag, walked back to the Pendergast Building and went up to his office. I went past his assistant without speaking and pushed through the door.

Standing in the middle of the office, he said with perfect sincerity, "I'm sorry. That kind of thing isn't in my repertoire, and I don't know what got into me. That's no excuse, of course. But I'm sorry for my behavior."

I closed the door, knowing the assistant had probably heard every word, but she didn't need to hear any more.

He added, "I don't usually apologize, either, so I hope you appreciate that this is a first."

"I'm sorry, too," I said. "Quitting my job was also a first."

"So why did you come back?" he asked, staying on his side of the office. "Which do you want? More kissing or your job?"

Although I felt as if I were standing on top of a violent earthquake, I said calmly, "I'd like my job, please."

"Ah." He didn't look disappointed.

I said, "Believe me, I'd walk out of here immediately if I didn't need the money, but I do."

"Any demands?"

He took me by surprise. "Am I in a position to make demands?"

"You could have my head on a pike," he said. "You could get me fired and splash my name in headlines worldwide. My father will be annoyed, but he can't kick me any farther from home than I am now, so what does it matter? Still, the humiliation will be annoying."

The idea that I had such power startled me. And by something in the back of his gaze, I suddenly knew he very much minded being banished so far from his home and family. He pretended not to care what his father thought, but I knew it was a lie. The enraging Gus Hardwicke had feelings, too.

He continued. "I am genuinely sorry, Nora. I was overcome. And I'm not usually knocked for a loop by women. I enjoy the fairer sex, but I follow the mantra of get in, get off, get out—and nobody gets hurt. But there's something about you."

"Let's not get into that, please."

"I can't help it," he said, unable to suppress a smile. "You're attractive enough, but it's the look in your eye that compels me. You know you're headed down a mountain on a runaway toboggan with your mob boyfriend, don't you? But you like the thrill of it, despite your polite, ladylike ways. That's very appealing."

"I have no idea what you're talking about," I said. "My only demand is that we remain completely professional from now on."

"Done," he said.

"And although I recognize I am practically an amateur at this profession, there are lines I will not cross. I'll do the job, but I must do it my way."

"Your way?"

"Yes." Gathering momentum, I said, "The only reason I'm good at my work—the society reporting, that is—is because of who I am. People open their doors to me, talk to me, share their secrets with me. I speak their language. I know the rules. But if I start turning into somebody else, my access will be denied. You need my society page. Advertisers like what I bring to the newspaper, and they support the *Intelligencer*."

"Your column is very lucrative for the paper," he

agreed. "And your online social reporting more than pays for itself."

"So I have to protect my reputation," I said. "I have to be true to who I am. If someone is going to write about these people, it has to be me, who understands them from the inside."

"Rightio," he agreed, composing his face into solemnity.

"I'll write the piece about Zephyr, but not today. I won't write anything about her until I have new information—information I can confirm and stand behind."

"Okay," Gus said.

I turned to go.

"Nora," he said. When I paused, hand on the doorknob, he went on. "You can learn from me. You need to start thinking like a reporter, and I can help you with that."

He was right, and I knew it. But it felt good to leave the office without acknowledging his offer.

I met Emma a few minutes earlier than she had guessed. The traffic must have worked in her favor.

When I climbed into her pickup, I had to move a six-pack cooler off the seat to make room for myself. She snatched the beer cooler from me as if it were a jewel case loaded down with precious stones.

Carefully stowing the cooler behind her seat while horns blew around us, Emma said, "Why are you looking so smug?"

The six-pack cooler gave me pause. I was dismayed to think she was drinking again, but she seemed sober enough. Her question distracted me from giving her the third degree. "I got my job back. On my terms, in fact."

"No more digging up scandals?"

I fastened my seat belt. "Oh, I think there will be plenty of scandals to dig, but I'll do the excavating with

my own spade now. And I think it's going to help Rawlins."

"How?" She pulled into traffic.

I told her my new information about Zephyr—that
she'd killed her father and maybe it wasn't such a big
leap to killing her husband, too.

"I thought you were on her side," Emma said.

"I am! She's a nice person. But she killed her father.
That's a game changer."

"I dunno," Emma said as she drove. "I'm still on Team
Zephyr in this."

I looked at her with surprise. "How do you figure?"

"Everybody wants to demonize the second wife. Okay,
she's younger and prettier than the first wife, but is that
her fault? It's easy to think of her as the villain, the home
wrecker, but hey, maybe she was just in the wrong place
at the wrong time, and a powerful guy fell in love with
her. He was the one who decided to chuck it all to be
with Zephyr, not the other way around."

"Some people would say she broke up a marriage,
Em," I said, knowing full well my little sister occasionally
dallied with married men. "That she broke up a family."

She shook her head. "That marriage was already broken."

"What makes you so sure?"

"Doesn't matter. Truth is? In this kind of story, the
guy is usually the asshole."

I wondered if Emma was changing her opinion of
Hart Jones, her baby's father. "Are you saying Zephyr
didn't kill her husband?"

"Oh, she could have killed him. But if she did, I bet it
wasn't because she was a low-down, dirty home wrecker."

I saw Emma's point. There was no earthly reason to
suspect Zephyr. My own observation was that she had
devoted herself to her husband. She appeared to be a

paragon of high principles and gentle ways. She had absolutely no motive to kill Swain. I had to stay objective.

I finally realized Emma wasn't dressed in horsey clothes, but instead wore a short skirt with ballet flats and a clean sweater that managed to look feminine and rather pretty. I said, "Where have you been?" Something was up. My sexpot sister Emma didn't dress like a Main Line soccer mom for no reason. "Have you been shopping for Filly Vanilli?"

She groaned with frustration. "Do you know how hard it is to find one of those damn things? I went to a dozen toy stores! I wore my best jeans, my lowest-cut shirt—and I couldn't get a second look from the dweebs who run those places. So I switched tactics. I can play sweet and nice."

"Really?" I said.

I must have sounded astonished, because she snapped, "I pretended I was you. Please and thank you, the whole nine yards. But still, no dice. I'm gonna have to stake out a Walmart and hold up the joint when they get their next delivery."

"The racehorse trainer must really want that toy."

"Who?"

"You said the trainer who gave you a job—that he wanted the Filly Vanilli for his son."

"Oh, right," Emma said. "Yeah, him."

She was keeping a lot of secrets these days. But we had a more pressing problem on our hands, so I let it go.

The suburb of Manayunk hung on a curve of the Schuylkill River, bolstered by railroad tracks on one side and a jam of working-class housing on the other. It had long been a neighborhood crowded with hard-working immigrant families, but in recent years the usual signs of gentrification had taken over. Young hipsters sat at tables in front of coffee shops. Funky galleries beckoned with clever signs. The low rents drew the artistic class, and tourists followed. In a few years, though, the real estate values would rise and drive artists elsewhere, leaving a strong middle class behind again. Such was the ebb and flow of urban neighborhoods.

Emma parked down the block, and we walked up toward a former hardware store that had been converted into a fragrant shop that sold spices from barrels. On the second floor, the windows were painted with the name of a dance studio. But when we got to the top of the stairs, the dance studio's sign had been covered over by a sheet of lined notebook paper onto which someone had scrawled *Starr Hollywood Academy.*

We arrived on the landing at the same instant the door burst open and released a flood of chattering children. Emma and I flattened ourselves against the wall to let the tide roll past us and down the stairs. The kids were mostly girls, mostly in colorful dance and workout clothes. Their hair seemed to have been done by the same hand—topknots embellished with sparkly accessories. They were all bright-eyed and pink-cheeked—some singing snippets of a familiar tune from a Broadway musical. I heard a chorus of them yelping about living a hard-knock life, but I had seen the parental vehicles waiting in the street below: expensive SUVs and fancy cars with bumper stickers advertising beach vacations and prestigious colleges.

When the last of the singing poppets had brushed past us, Emma grabbed the door and held it open. "Ew," she said, looking at her hand. "This handle is sticky."

"I guess the Starr Academy doesn't hire a cleaning crew."

We walked into a large open space with a polished wood floor and a wall of mirrors behind a ballet barre. Although his name was on the sign outside, Porky Starr was nowhere to be seen.

At the far end of the studio, a young man in tights and a snug T-shirt was calling a handful of lanky teenage boys into a circle. I spotted Libby's twins among them — both hanging back and grinning with evil purpose. If they were attending the class, they had not come willingly. Their instructor was encouraging them to close their eyes and breathe.

To me, Emma muttered, "You close your eyes around those two at your own risk."

"The twins might benefit from some relaxation techniques." I saw an open door, and I elbowed my sister. "Let's look around before we take them home."

She followed me to the doorway, and we went into a short corridor. Through an open door, we could hear a voice.

When I turned the corner, I came upon Porky Starr himself sitting at a wobbly card table in a makeshift office and counting money. For once, he wasn't wearing his little hat. It sat on the edge of the table. I realized why he wore it, though. At twenty-something, he was nearly bald. Beside his elbow sat a stack of checks. He didn't look up from his task but continued to laboriously count cash in large and small bills.

"Seven-eighty, seven-ninety, forty-eight hundred!" He sat back in triumph.

But when he looked up and saw Emma and me, he quickly masked his pleasure. "Parents aren't allowed upstairs, yo," he said. "It interferes with the learning process. You can pick up your kids outside."

"It's me, Porter," I said. "Nora Blackbird. This is my sister Emma. We thought we'd stop in and give you our condolences."

"Huh? Oh, yeah, hi. Thanks."

His disinterested gaze went past me and sharpened on Emma. Maybe her soccer-mom look wasn't quite as wholesome as I'd first thought. Her hair was slicked back from the perfect features of her face, and her mouth, untouched by lipstick, was sensuously full. Her snug skirt made no secret of her slim legs and narrow hips, and her formfitting sweater didn't hide the fact that her bust size hadn't diminished since her pregnancy.

Porky scrambled to his feet and slapped his hat onto his head. "Yo," he said, tipping the hat to a rakish angle before extending his hand to her. "I'm Porter."

"Yo?" she said. "What are you, a reject from the Backstreet Boys?"

He seized her hand, raised it to his lips and kissed it.

Emma snatched it back. "Hey, cut that out, kid! Before I kick your ass."

"Porter," I intervened, "we're very sorry about your father. It must have been a terrible shock."

"Yeah," he said without tearing his gaze from my sister. "A shock. Even worse, we heard who did it to him. A kid whose twerpy little brothers are here in the program."

One look at Emma had emptied his head. He had forgotten who I was, forgotten my connection to Rawlins.

"The program?" Emma said, likewise choosing not to identify herself as the aunt of the twerpy brothers or his father's alleged killer. "You running some kind of rehab here?"

"No, no, this is the Starr Hollywood Academy. I'm a talent scout. And I gotta say, even before I've heard you sing, you've got what it takes, baby."

Nothing pushed Emma's hot button like being called "baby," but before the steam began gushing from her ears, I said, "The murder must have been so upsetting to you and everyone else in the family."

For a second I thought I might have to get out my handkerchief and wipe drool from Porter's chin. He responded to my condolence as though Emma had spoken it. "Yeah, everybody's all broken up. But the arrest should calm them down a little."

"This arrest," Emma said. "Who was the perp?"

"Nobody important. And his kid brothers are total dipwads. They can hardly walk and talk at the same time. Besides, I think there's something wrong with those two."

"So why keep them in your program?" Emma asked.

Porky jerked his head to indicate the stack of money and checks on the table. "Man's gotta make a living, baby."

Emma said, "The killer. He in your program, too?"

"Naw, he's just a hanger-on. You know, a fan. Nothing cool about that."

"So why'd he kill your dad?"

"Who knows? There's a lot of crazy stuff that goes on in our world. Fans can turn into stalkers in the wink of an eye, yo. Goes with the territory."

"Sounds like a pain in the ass, having fans."

"Yeah, it can be a drag. That's why I'm looking to make a change."

"What kind of change?"

"I got a call this afternoon, after my headshot ran in a newspaper. I might be up for another TV show. Hosting." He couldn't hide his pleasure. "You know, wear a suit, talk to the camera, introduce the talent. How hard can it be? I have an audition next week. You want to come along? Watch me work?"

While Emma engaged Porky—and she did it effortlessly, edging toward the door and leading him out into the hallway and beyond—I leaned over the table and got a closer look at the checks. With one finger, I fanned them out to read the amounts. A hundred dollars, two hundred. Different amounts, but they all added up to considerable money. I knew what Porky was selling. Each of the kids who had gone rushing down the stairs wasn't getting any real education or even the skills it might take to make a career in show business. But it was a chance to fantasize a life standing in the footlights.

Beside the checks, the sheaf of papers appeared to be a stack of posters that advertised more Hollywood programs in other cities—Pittsburgh, Cleveland, St. Louis. The dates were only weeks away. Porky was taking his make-dreams-come-true show on the road. His face—a headshot from his younger days—decorated the top of the poster.

But his office was as low rent as it got. His folding chair had a dent in it. Across the small space was a dusty beaded curtain that separated the room from a storage closet. Through the beads I could see a few boxes stacked there. The top one had been cut open. T-shirts lay in the box. I could see Porter's face on those, too.

His siblings must have been making millions working for their father. Why had Porky struck out on his own? Had he not been welcomed into the family business?

There was one more check on the desk, facedown. With Emma practically hypnotizing Porky, I flipped over the check and took a look.

And blinked.

Half a million dollars.

The recipient was Porky. The flourished signature on the check was none other than his father's, Swain Starr.

A day before his death, Swain had written a check for five hundred thousand dollars.

I sent Emma a glance and edged toward the storage room. She got the message and eased out into the small hallway, practically leading Porky by his nose. He followed her like a kitten eager for catnip.

I slipped through the beaded curtain.

And nearly tripped over Zephyr Starr.

In the ten square feet of floor space, she was stretched out in a yoga pose in front of an open window. Her face was blank. Her arms and legs looked unnaturally long. Barefoot, she wore a boat-necked T-shirt and capri-length yoga pants with her hair in a tangled but chic knot at the back of her head.

"Zephyr," I said, unable to stop myself.

She finished another ten seconds of stretching before acknowledging my presence. Her eyes were empty, though, and her face bare of makeup.

Seeing her like that, I realized that all of her features were a bit exaggerated—a nose too long, a chin too prominent, eyes sunk deep—and yet she was still undeniably beautiful. Perfect skin. Limber body. Without makeup, she was not as astonishingly gorgeous as when I had encountered her during my interviews with her husband—but certainly she was a showstopper of a woman. It was incongruous seeing her sitting cross-legged on the dusty floor.

She reached for a string of red licorice lying on one of the cardboard boxes. "What are you doing here?"

"I—my sister's children take a class from Pork—er, Porter." Before she could ask for details, I said, "Zephyr, I'm so sorry about Swain. You must have had a terrible shock."

If she was in shock, she didn't acknowledge it. In fact, she seemed perfectly composed, if maybe a little dreamy.

But she said, "Can you get me out of here?"

Chapter 13

I must have blinked at her. The words she spoke made no sense to me.

She shook her hair out of its bun, then gathered it up again and redid her hairdo. "Can you get me past Porky? Do you have a car?"

"Is he holding you prisoner?"

"Something like that."

"Should I call the police?"

She shook her head. "Just walk me out of here, would you?"

"Sure."

She stood up tall, slipped her feet into a pair of muddy gardening boots and gathered up a bundle—a coat wrapped around a few lumpy items. If she had stuck the bundle on the end of a stick, she'd have looked like a kid running off to join the circus. Except she walked out using the runway strut that had taken her all over the world.

I followed her from the storage room and down the hall to the dance studio where Emma kept Porky glued to attention alongside the mirrored wall and where the teenage boys were just finishing their relaxation lesson.

"Let's get in touch with our bodies," the instructor encouraged, eyes rapturously closed as he extended his arms over his head and stood on tiptoe.

The twins snickered. Harcourt pretended to pleasure himself, and Hilton cracked up laughing.

The other boys in the class turned to watch Zephyr make her entrance. The twins forgot about being obnoxious and stared, too.

"Hey," Porky said, tearing his gaze away from my sister at last. He registered Zephyr's speed and the bundle in her hands. "Where are you going?"

Zephyr kept moving toward the door. "This isn't going to work, Porky."

The instructor intoned, "Feel your feet, boys."

Porky made a lunge to grab Zephyr's hand and missed. "The hell it isn't. You're not going anywhere."

"Porky," I said, trying to head him off. But he rushed past me.

The instructor said, "Now feel your knees."

None of his students were feeling anything except astonishment. Their mouths sagged open as a flesh-and-bone supermodel said, "You're a nice guy, Porky. But the timing—don't you see how wrong it is? And our age difference is—"

"The age difference didn't bother you with my father." Porky skidded to a stop in front of Zephyr and blocked the door by flinging his chubby arms wide.

Zephyr stopped in her tracks, half a foot taller than Porky and looking down on him as if he were a gnome. "That was another story."

"You bet your ass it was! He was way too old for you. Too old for what you want."

"Feel your arms," said the instructor, oblivious to the fact that his pupils were agog at the unfolding spectacle.

"You deserve somebody young and exciting," Porky pleaded. He made himself into a human shield against the door. His voice rose an octave as he dropped the tough-guy routine. "Somebody willing to share everything with you. You can't go!" His face began to pucker with tears. "Don't leave, Zephyr. Give me a chance! I have money now. I can do anything—anything you want!"

Zephyr sighed. "Get away from the door, Porky."

"I want to make you happy."

With the scene turning maudlin, I said to Emma, "Think there's a back exit?"

"Either that or the fire escape."

"Fire escape," I said firmly. "It's quicker."

"This was never going to work between us," Zephyr said to Porky. "We knew that, even when your father was alive. But now it's worse."

"It can only get better! I have enough dough for both of us."

At that moment, someone shoved on the door from out on the landing, knocking Porky forward and into my arms. Through the door came a large, red-faced woman who gripped the hand of her young daughter and dragged her inside the studio. Behind her, we could hear the low rumble of more mothers—like a herd of angry elephants charging a fortress.

In a booming voice, the woman said, "Who's in charge here? I demand to speak to Porter Starr!"

"Uh," Porky said from under the shadow of her large bosom.

She stepped back and pointed a long, manicured forefinger down at Porky. It trembled with rage. "How dare you speak to my daughter the way you did! Madison is devastated! I demand an apology!"

Madison blew a halfhearted bubble of gum, as if accustomed to her mother's outrage.

With the noise of imminent pandemonium coming up the stairs, the class instructor belatedly opened his eyes. He gasped and made a futile attempt to gather his students out of range. The boys were having none of it. They continued to stare at Zephyr.

Porky regained some of his bombast and stood his ground against the maternal onslaught. "Mediocrity will not be tolerated in the Starr Academy."

The mother thrust out her jaw and glared down into Porky's face. "Mediocrity! Do you know who I am? Do you know who Madison is? She won the semi-regional Baby Girl dance competition two years in a row!"

More mothers boiled through the door. Any second, Porky was going to get bulldozed by more estrogen than he could handle.

Emma muttered, "He's toast. Let's get out of here."

I was already headed across the studio with Zephyr. I shot the twins a searing laser glance, and instantly they swiped the smirks from their faces. Obedient at last, they started after us. It took Emma and both twins shoving at the stuck window to finally get the sash up. One at a time, we clambered out the window onto a shaky metal platform.

I kicked the lever, and the ladder rattled down to the sidewalk in a shower of rust. I went first, balancing precariously on the clanging ladder as it swung wildly beneath me. Overhead, Emma cupped her hands and yelled, "Hurry it up! Any minute Porky's going to need an escape route, too!"

Which was how Emma and I ended up shuttling not only the twins, but also supermodel Zephyr Starr back to Bucks County.

"Anybody have a cigarette?" Zephyr asked, crammed into the middle of the front seat.

"Fresh out," Emma said.

"I need to quit," the ex-model said.

"You don't get off this easy, sister," Emma said. "What's going on? What the hell was that all about?"

Trust Emma to be blunt when the situation called for it.

Zephyr said, "Oh, it's all such a mess."

"It sure looked that way. You and Porky?"

"I know it looks funny. But I have a thing for small men."

"A thing?" I said.

"You know. An attraction. Don't get me wrong, Swain's size wasn't the big reason I fell in love with him. He was the first designer to make me feel like a contributor. A collaborator. Of course, that was before we went to China and I figured out what the score was, but he was nice."

"The score?" Emma asked.

"He wasn't perfect," Zephyr went on, ignoring Emma's question. "But he was one of the few men who could see I was a person inside the clothes." I must have looked puzzled, because she said, "To most designers, the model isn't really there. We're just a hanger with legs, you know? With Swain, though, things were different. He didn't treat me like a blow-up doll."

That didn't exactly sound like a compliment to me. "A—?"

"Give me a small man any day," she said on a fond sigh. "Once I was working with this big-time hetero fashion designer, and we were standing around talking—just talking—and he shoved two fingers up my—oh," she said, remembering the twins, crammed behind us in the jump seat and listening to every word. With more composure, she concluded, "Not everybody is nice in the fashion business. That's the life of a model. One minute, you think you're having an intelligent conversation, and the next minute—inappropriate touching. I mean, seriously inappropriate."

Emma was shaking her head. "Why would you put up with that?"

Zephyr smiled a little. "Most models grow up thinking we're weird—too tall, freaks of nature. We're ugly kids, right? And when somebody decides you're beautiful, you're still the ugly kid inside—the kid who will do anything to be accepted."

"Nobody deserves to be treated that way," I said.

She shrugged. "Tall men? Good-looking guys? They're the worst. They think they can take advantage. But little guys—they're . . . nicer. Safer. That's why I married Swain. He was always a gentleman." She sighed again. "But . . ."

"But?" Emma prompted.

"I'm not getting any younger."

With disgust Emma said, "Don't tell me. Your biological clock started ticking?"

"I think I want a family," Zephyr said, not exactly sounding convinced. "But Swain couldn't."

"Vasectomy?" Emma guessed. "All those rich and randy old guys are the same."

I thought of Marybeth and said, "Someone told me he had gotten his vasectomy reversed."

"I bet Marybitch told you. Well, we didn't know if it worked—not yet, anyway. Before we got married, he told me he didn't want any more kids. But I deserve a family of my own, right? That's what all the magazines say. So Swain said he'd get the operation to fix his vasectomy. But his recovery was taking forever. I started looking into other ways of having a baby, looking at different guys. And that's when Porky came along."

"Hold the phone," Emma ordered. "Gross me out! You slept with Porky? To have a baby?"

"Well," Zephyr began.

I thought of the check I'd seen among Porky's other financial windfalls. Before Zephyr could explain, I said, "Swain paid Porky."

"Jeez! To father a kid for you?" Emma demanded.

"That's not—Swain heard me and Porky talking about having a baby together, and—well, he paid Porky to go away. Again."

"Again?"

"Back when Porky was a kid, Swain gave him money to go to Hollywood."

"That was nice," I said uncertainly. "Helping his son get started as an actor—"

"No, Porky isn't really Swain's son." Zephyr used one fingernail to pick at her teeth, unaware of the megaton bombshell she was dropping. "He came along after Swain had his vasectomy. Marybitch was fooling around. Swain agreed to pretend Porky was his kid to avoid the bad press. Paying for him to go to Hollywood was supposed to get him out of Swain's life for good."

"Who is Porky's real father?"

"Just some random guy. Marybitch wanted another kid, but Swain didn't. So while he was out of the country, she got mad at him and made it happen. Swain couldn't forgive her for cheating on him, though, so he took it out on Porky. The money got Porky out to Hollywood, out of Swain's life. But only for the time being."

Emma and I exchanged wide-eyed glances.

"So, I couldn't resist being nice to Porky," Zephyr said. "I felt sorry for him. He's so small and cuddly and cute. And, y'know, needy. His genes were kinda not very attractive, though, so I kept looking around for a better donor. I mean, if Marybitch can do it, why not me? But Porky got the wrong idea. And then Swain got the wrong idea. All the jealousy, it got really unpleasant."

Emma came up with another direct question. "Think he killed his dad? Over you?"

"Little Porky? Oh, no, no, no, he'd never do a thing like that. It had to be Swain's ex. Who else, right? That's what I told the police." Zephyr leaned forward to turn on the truck's radio. "Marybitch came in the afternoon with a gun, and she'd have killed him then, but everybody stopped her."

"But Swain wasn't shot." Emma snapped off the radio. "He was stabbed. That would take a person with more strength than Marybeth has, don't you think?"

"Rage," Zephyr said sagely. "It gives you superstrength. And now his kids will get enough of his money to rescue the company before it sinks. I'm not getting a cent, either. That's everything Marybitch wanted, right? Me with nothing from Swain, and her kids getting the cash?"

So Zephyr knew the terms of Swain's last will. And from the sounds of it, all the children had a financial motive to kill their father, if they were trying to save Starr Industries from its downward spiral. I asked, "Even Porky gets something from Swain?"

"Yeah, Porky, too. He gets a share of Starr Industries, but he doesn't know it yet," she said. "I'm supposed to get the farm, but—well, I don't feel much like living in the place where my husband was killed."

"It would be creepy," Emma agreed.

Zephyr turned to me. "Mind if I stay with you for a little while?"

I felt the wave of nausea again, plus my head gave a dizzy whirl. But what could I do? Say no to the widow?

When we arrived at Blackbird Farm, I was dismayed to see that Michael's whole crew was back on duty at the bottom of the driveway. They had set up another security checkpoint—standard operating procedure when the threat level reached whatever DefCon circumstances triggered all-out alarm. The checkpoint consisted of two dark SUVs parked nose to nose to prevent anyone arriving at the farm without a thorough inquisition by the posse.

Emma said, "Looks like all the Corleones are back. What's up?"

I waved at Dolph through the windshield. "I don't want to know."

The checkpoint crew stared at Zephyr through the windshield as Emma drove past.

At the back of the house, a tow truck was depositing one of Michael's muscle cars in the barn. He stood outside, directing its placement. Beside him, Ralphie appeared to approve of the job, too. When Michael saw us arrive, he came over and helped me down out of Emma's truck.

"New car?" I asked.

"Now that the weather's warmer, it's something to work on in my spare time," he said. "What's up?" He got a look at Emma in her skirt as she came around the hood of the truck. "Jeez, Em, where have you been? Court appearance?"

She made a rude suggestion.

Michael turned. "And this must be Zephyr."

In an extraordinary moment, Zephyr uncurled herself from the truck and stood tall, squaring her shoulders and thrusting her heretofore unspectacular bosom into an eye-popping display of female sexuality. The tow truck driver slipped a gear and stalled his engine. Zephyr transformed herself from a gawky, somewhat mousey young woman into a stunning supermodel with a gaze that had probably pierced the skulls of mortal men and scrambled their brains. Even Ralphie was struck motionless.

"She's going to stay with us for a little while," I explained to Michael.

"Sure," he said, unable to stop smiling at Zephyr.

I didn't have time to kick him in the shins, because Libby's red minivan came barreling around the corner of the house, barely missing the departing tow truck. She slid to a stop in the gravel beside Emma's pickup.

Libby bailed out and quickly unfastened little Max from his car seat. We could hear him wailing over her shouted words.

"I can't believe this is happening!" she cried, carrying the red-faced baby around the minivan to us. "Rawlins is in *jail*! They won't let me *see* him! And now there are friends calling me every ten minutes, even *girlfriends* asking about him! What am I supposed to *say* to them? That my son is a convicted *killer*?"

"He hasn't even been arrested," Michael soothed. "He's just there for questions. Big difference. He's a long way from being convicted. Didn't Cannoli and Sons show up?"

Instead of answering, Libby burst into tears. The floodgate of her emotional state burst like the Hoover Dam, and she wept with all the pent-up sorrow and outrage of a mother whose promising eldest child had crushed her parental hopes and dreams. She threw back her head, and her howls matched Max's in volume. "My son has *lawyers* now!"

Michael gently pried a stunned-into-silence Max from her arms. I gathered up Libby in a comforting hug. She collapsed into me, weeping. I felt sympathetic tears well up inside me, too. Poor Rawlins. It was all too awful. Lucy climbed out of the minivan, also bawling, and joined us.

"Jesus," Emma said. "It's not like Rawlins is dead."

Whereupon Zephyr burst into tears, too, and there we were, a female group sob-fest, observed uneasily by Michael, his crew, Max, the twins and Ralphie. They all kept a safe distance while mascara flowed.

"C'mon, Luce," Michael said finally. "Let's you and me and Max go inside. I think you left your Candy Land game here last time. You wanna play?"

Digging her fist into her eyes, Lucy hiccoughed and nodded and reached for Michael's hand. With the baby in the other arm, he ambled both of the younger children into the house. The twins headed for the barn, whispering deviously, with an inquisitive Ralphie in hot pursuit. The security crew turned back to its duties, leaving the rest of us to bawl our hearts out. Even Emma wiped a tear from her eye.

"This is contagious," she grumbled. "Like yawning."

Perhaps the crying was a delayed reaction for Zephyr, too. In the middle of the group hug, she sobbed as if she'd lost a husband who meant more to her than she'd revealed in the truck. Libby clasped her to a heaving bosom, and they wept together, seeming ready to throw themselves onto a pyre.

Finally Emma said, "C'mon, you guys, this is embarrassing. Pull yourselves together."

Libby dried her eyes with her sleeve. "You have no idea how traumatic it is, Emma, to have your child snatched from your arms. No idea at all."

That thoughtless remark caused Emma to tell Libby where to stick her parental advice, after which she climbed into her truck and slammed the door. She gunned the engine with a roar and spun her tires in the gravel. She departed in a cloud of dust.

"That wasn't very thoughtful, Lib," I said.

"Oh." Libby blinked. Her nose was pink. "Well, I'll apologize tomorrow." She turned to Zephyr. "Do I know you? You look familiar. Are you one of Nora's friends? Or are you with the Mafia?"

"Hello." Zephyr shook Libby's hand. "Your son killed my husband."

"No, he didn't," Libby said. "But you must be Zephyr. Tell me, do you think fashion magazines are instruments of oppression?"

"I don't play any instruments," Zephyr said.

There wasn't much I could do after that except herd the two of them toward the house.

We had enough leftover bread and a chunk of cheddar to make grilled cheese sandwiches for everyone. I tended the griddle while Michael played Candy Land on the floor with Lucy, and Max crawled on his back. Lucy, intent on winning, held the cards and paid close attention to the action on the board. Max pretended Michael was a pony.

Libby and Zephyr—two women with no filters between their first thought and what came out of their mouths—had a heart-to-heart at the kitchen table with a bottle of wine left over from poker night.

Libby said, "I need to slim down just a little, but I can't seem to shave off the baby weight. You must know everything about the right foods. I mean, you're so skinny!"

Zephyr glanced down at Max, perhaps calculating how much dieting time had elapsed since his birth. He was walking now, and he wrestled with Michael like a pro. She said, "I don't really worry about dieting. I'm just naturally thin."

Libby sighed. "I was standing in the wrong line when thin was handed out. But I have an adventurous spirit. The trouble is, men are sometimes apprehensive around spirited women."

"Men apprehend thin women, too," Zephyr said, slugging back wine. "In my opinion, most men are disappointments."

"Yes," Libby said. "In books, men are wonderful, but in real life they spray poison to kill bugs."

On the floor, Michael glanced up from Candy Land. I shot him a firm look and shook my head. Moving his marker to Gum Drop Mountain, he wasn't in the best position to defend his gender at the moment.

"But you married your husband." Libby refilled Zephyr's glass. "He must have had redeeming qualities."

Zephyr shrugged. "He was a nice guy. And rich."

"Was he exciting in bed?"

"Average."

"Well, I'm very sorry he's dead," Libby said. "I hope you understand my son had nothing to do with it."

"Uh-huh."

"I thought he was arrested, but it turns out they're just asking questions. The police found his car, you see," Libby said. "Abandoned on a back road near your farm. The police want to find out why it was there the night your husband was murdered. And I'm sure they're keeping an eye on him because he's a flight risk."

"Flight risk?" I asked.

"He has a passport," Libby informed me. "From that vacation we had in Mexico. And the police probably think we're loaded and could afford to send him out of the country."

Zephyr looked around the kitchen. "You don't look loaded to me."

"This is my sister's house," Libby said. "She's not much for home improvements."

Michael grabbed my ankle to stop me from clonking Libby over the head with a skillet.

Zephyr got up and went to the refrigerator. She opened it and peered into the emptiness.

"I'd like to find out who really killed your husband," Libby said, pouring more wine. "I'd give that person a piece of my mind!"

Zephyr found our last spears of asparagus in the vegetable drawer. "I'm betting it was his ex."

"Marybeth Rattigan? Oh, no, darling. She's too nice a person to want to kill her former husband. Now, I'd believe it in a heartbeat if I heard she killed *you*, maybe, but not someone she shared a life with. Why, she bore his children! Surely a woman always has a bond with the father of her offspring."

"That bond fell apart when she went broke." Zephyr took the asparagus to the sink and washed it.

"Marybeth can't be broke. That's impossible. She inherited half of Howie's Hotties! They sold the company for millions!"

"She spent it all."

"On what?" Libby demanded. "How could any woman unload that much money? Does she have five hundred pairs of shoes?"

"She bought pigs. She built some fancy laboratory to breed them. You know, vegetarians will eventually convince carnivores that it's wrong to eat meat. And it costs too much to feed animals for food. So her thinking that creating a new breed of pig was a great idea just shows she isn't so smart after all. Marybitch spent all her money on a really dumb idea."

Libby said, "She had money from her husband!"

Zephyr took a crunch of raw asparagus and shook her head. "Her prenup was worse than mine. She didn't get a nickel in the divorce. Swain paid for the house and all the kid stuff during the marriage, but she had to use all her own money to research pigs."

"What about you?" I asked, concerned. "Zephyr, I hope you had some legal advice before you married Swain. You're not left high and dry now that he's gone?" I thought of my own position after Todd's death—down to the last of our savings because of his drug use, then plunged into debt when my parents gave me Blackbird Farm.

Zephyr avoided my inquiring gaze and shrugged. "I'm doing okay."

Confidently, Libby said, "Models are all rich."

"Well," Zephyr said, "not all. There are plenty of people out there who take advantage, y'know."

"Let me guess," Michael said from the floor. "Your accountant embezzled from you."

She sat bolt upright. "How do you know that?"

"There's a lot of it going around," Michael replied. "Are you broke?"

"I had some expenses," she began feebly. "And then — well, yeah, I'm kinda broke."

"Is that why you married Swain?" Libby asked, tactless as ever. "For his money?"

"No! Well, not completely."

Libby said, "It's easier to fall in love with a rich man than a poor one. Everything depends on what happens after you divorce him. I think Jane Austen said that."

"According to the prenup, I couldn't divorce him for five years," Zephyr said. "Not if I wanted to get some money when I left."

"Now that he's dead, what happens?"

"Not much," she said glumly. "I get the farm, but that's about it."

There went Zephyr's motive for murdering her husband, I thought. If she stood to receive money upon his death, she'd have had a reason to stab him with a pitchfork. Of course, the farm was worth a pretty penny, so she wouldn't be destitute. Now, though, I couldn't see why Zephyr might kill Swain.

And if she had, she obviously did it with a clear conscience. The rest of us watched while she blithely ate the last of our asparagus, raw spear by raw spear. She had kicked off her shoes and revealed ragged toenails and a spectacular bunion. Then she lounged inelegantly on the chair, lazily tracing wet circles of condensation on the table with her finger as if she didn't have a care in the world.

My cell phone rang in my handbag. I dug it out and looked at the screen. Gus.

I handed the spatula to Libby and went through the butler's pantry to the dining room to take the call.

He said, "What have you got?"

I had plenty more than he knew, but I wasn't talking. "I'll call you when I'm ready."

"You might be interested in what I dug up today."

"Don't you have a newspaper to edit?"

"I got out my little black book of contacts and made some calls. To Italy and Dubai. My father has newspapers in those countries, perhaps you knew?"

Of course I knew. But I said, "Fascinating. What did you learn?"

"I asked about Zephyr. Are you sitting down? Five years ago, rumor has it, she killed her boyfriend."

I sank into the chair at the head of the table. "What boyfriend?"

"A guy she met in Rome. Another model."

"Was he tall?"

"What does that have to do with anything?"

"Never mind." I put my hand around the phone to muffle my words. "She *killed* him? Are you sure?"

"Pretty sure. The bloke was loaded with money and good looks. They had a few laughs. Then she shot him in an argument on a yacht. The police were totally on her side, said she was getting knocked around by him and had every right to blow his brains out. So they took her name out of their report."

"How does that happen?"

"Hasn't your thug taken you to Italy yet? To see the corruption firsthand?"

I ignored the insult. I tried and failed to imagine the young woman in my kitchen holding a gun, pulling a trigger. Killing both her father and a boyfriend. I could, however, picture her convincing the police that she was as innocent as a lamb. She had told us some appalling things in the truck, but I had fallen for her charms enough to bring her into my home.

"And to top that," Gus went on when I didn't respond, "there's a rumor she also offed a bloke in Dubai, too, but my little black book doesn't have enough good contacts there—yet—to check the details."

"Dubai?" I said, trying to grasp what he was telling me.

"A member of the Saudi royal family mysteriously drowned in a hotel bathtub. He was last seen in her company."

"She got away with drowning him?"

"Word is, she paid the police to forget she was there."

That might explain the "expenses" Zephyr mentioned. I asked, "How big was the Saudi?"

"Why are you so interested in his size?"

"I just—how many women have the strength to drown a man?"

"Something to check," he acknowledged. "I can't help wondering if maybe there are more she might have finished off."

"There are," I said, and took a deep breath. "She killed her own father."

"Crikey!" Gus sounded truly surprised. "How did you find that out?"

"Sources I can't quote. She shot him back in West Virginia, before she got into modeling."

Gus let out a few Aussie curses of astonishment.

"Check your little black book for contacts in West Virginia. Maybe she's paying people to be quiet there, too. For me, though, the awkward thing is," I said, "right now she's here in my house."

"How did that happen?"

"I bumped into her today, and she ended up coming home with me. I think she wants to stay for a while."

"Make sure you lock your bedroom door."

We both fell silent, thinking. My mind raced through everything I knew about the hillbilly supermodel, trying to decide if perhaps killing three men before she married Swain made her the most likely suspect in his murder. If she had killed two boyfriends and convinced the police she was the victim, not a cold-blooded killer, had the sob story about her sexually abusive meth-cooking father been a cover-up, too?

But most of all, I was starting to develop a gut feeling that Zephyr wasn't exactly the lovely, thoughtful person she'd first led me to believe. The act she'd put on—waiting on her husband hand and foot, weeping as she spoke about the inhumane treatment of animals—it was starting to feel like an act, all right. In Emma's truck, she had been quite blunt about her relationship with Swain. And here at the house, we'd learned even more about the fairy-tale marriage of the fashion designer and his beautiful model. It hadn't been as "happily ever after" as everyone thought.

I said, "Zephyr said something peculiar about learning the score about her husband. Something happened when they were in China. Does your little black book reach that far?"

"You want somebody in the fashion business in China? That could be about a million people. Thin the herd for me."

"I'll see what I can find out."

Gus said, "We need to nail all this down before I print the story. I'll work on confirming what we've got on Zephyr's past. And you—"

"I have another angle I want to pursue," I said, thinking of the check Swain had written to his son. Zephyr said the money was paid to make Porky go away. Was that true? What exactly had Swain's relationship with Porky been? Had Porky harbored enough hostility against his so-called father to murder him?

Gus said, "A promising angle?"

"I'll tell you when I know more. Is my deadline extended?"

Gus let a frustrated moment of silence pass. We didn't have enough solid information to print yet. We had a lot of rumors to confirm first. He said, "Let's have a natter early tomorrow, see what else comes up between now and then."

"Here's one more idea. I heard Marybeth Starr was broke at the time of her divorce."

"Last I checked, that's not a motive for murder."

"Still, it keeps her on the list of suspects. We already know she was upset about the divorce and Swain's new marriage. And she wanted the missing pig back—probably to continue her genetic research. She has a temper. And she was, if you recall, drunkenly waving a gun in Swain's direction when they were last together."

"I don't think she's the one to focus on. She hasn't already killed three people."

I was surprised to hear him give up so easily on the person who might have had the most reason to kill Swain Starr. "So what should I do? Get Zephyr drunk and hope she confesses?"

"She might try to kill you first."

I pushed my hair off my forehead and tried to think. "We'll be all right. We have extra help at the moment."

"What kind of extra help?"

I hesitated, sorry I had let this detail about my personal life slip. I admitted, "Michael has people here."

"People, huh? You mean guys who put bullets into

skulls and dump bodies in swamps? I've seen all the movies, you know. Everything from *Al Capone* to *The Godfather*."

"We'll be fine," I said again. "Meanwhile, there's a lunch event I must attend tomorrow, and I just thought of somebody who will be there and could be helpful. I'll see what I can find out."

"All right," he said. "Just watch your step. I'd be sorry to lose you."

A moment stretched while I considered the best response to that sentiment. I decided to ignore it. Briskly, I said, "I'll call in the morning if I have anything new to tell you."

"Call me anyway," he replied. "I want to know if you survive the night. And, Nora?"

"Yes?"

"It wasn't a bad kiss, was it?"

I took a deep breath. And hung up.

I sat for a moment, stewing. I had left Gus's office thinking I had the upper hand with him. But now I was feeling at a disadvantage again.

I toyed with my phone and tried to put Gus Hardwicke out of my mind. I needed to think about Zephyr now. Specifically how to draw more information from her. Without driving her to murder. I heard sharp voices from the kitchen, so I hurried back.

I found Zephyr pointing a knife at Michael's chest.

Chapter 14

"I can cut a sandwich," she snapped. "You don't have to treat me like a child."

With his hands in the universal I-surrender position, Michael said, "It's just that Lucy likes her grilled cheese cut on the diagonal. It's the only way she'll eat it."

"With catsup," Lucy piped up from the table where she sat wearing a milk mustache. "Lots of catsup, Uncle Mick."

With a shrug, Zephyr relinquished the knife, and Michael cut Lucy's sandwich to my niece's specifications and set the plate in front of her. Max protested her special treatment, so Michael scooped up the baby and held him in one arm while preparing his sandwich, too.

Libby looked up at me from her seat at the table. "Zephyr says you were talking to Porky at his studio. Did he say anything about the twins? About their prospects?"

"Maybe we should be concentrating on Rawlins right now, Lib."

Busy at the stove, Michael said over his shoulder, "Cannoli and Sons should be calling me soon. We'll get an update."

"What could the police be doing to my son?" Libby cried. "Are they torturing him?"

"Only if he drank the soda they offered," Michael said. "It's the first trick in the book. If he drinks it and has to take a leak, he'll be miserable, and that's what they want."

"Rawlins wouldn't fall for that." I patted Libby's shoulder. "He watches plenty of *Law and Order.* He'll be fine. They're just asking him questions."

"For all this time?"

Unaware that I was trying to ease my sister's mind, Michael said, "They'll make him sweat first. Standard procedure. When he's tired and cranky, they'll start. But Cannoli will handle it. Nothing to worry about."

Libby got up and snatched Max from Michael's arm. "Except the damage to my family's reputation. I've always been grateful my children don't bear the Blackbird name. They don't need that kind of bad publicity. But this is too much."

Zephyr had been standing at the counter, picking a grilled cheese sandwich apart with her fingers to nibble the cheese inside. She dropped bits of bread into the sink. "What kind of bad publicity?"

Libby said, "Our parents borrowed money they couldn't repay, then fled the country two steps ahead of the police. It was very embarrassing. Thank heavens our grandparents didn't live to see the destruction of the family name. Then Nora took up with—"

"Libby," I said.

"Well," Libby said, "then there's the Blackbird curse."

Zephyr ate more cheese but looked intrigued. "What curse?"

"All Blackbird women are unlucky in love. We marry in haste, and our husbands die."

"How do they die?" Zephyr asked. "You mean you kill them?"

Libby let out a trilling laugh. "Of course not, darling. They just die. Accidents, mostly. My first husband died in the pursuit of whale hunters. He was harpooned and drowned. Of course, Nora's husband was shot. My second husband was, too. Or was Ralph my third? Emma's husband was killed in a car wreck. Our aunt Dorothy's third—"

Zephyr said to me, "Did you shoot your husband?"

"No," I replied. "He was shot in a drug deal."

"Bummer," she said. She jerked her head at Michael. "What about him?"

"I'm fine," Michael said. "I take my vitamins and stay out of trouble."

"He goes to church a lot, too," I said. "And prays."

He sent me a grin and slid a plate in front of me. Suddenly starved, I ate my grilled cheese in no time.

Zephyr said, "Maybe I'm cursed, too."

Libby's cell phone played a version of "It's Raining Men," and she grabbed it. A minute later, she seized her coat and headed for the door. "It's the lawyers! They need me now! I get to see Rawlins! I'll be back in the morning, Nora. Take care of my children overnight, will you?"

"Doesn't Lucy have school tomorrow?"

"She can be a little late."

"Why don't you take the twins with you?" I asked, trying not to beg too desperately. "Think how much they'd enjoy seeing the inside of a police station."

"They'll be happier here," she said, shouldering her handbag and reaching for the door. "They have a project going in the barn."

"What project?" I asked, my blood pressure spiking.

"Maybe they need to do some research," Michael suggested, sounding casual. "You know, in case they have to create a character for a whattayacallit, an audition."

Libby's face went through several contortions— consideration, rejection, rethinking, the dawn of hope for television stardom, then finally a decision. "You've got a point. I'll take the twins. See you in the morning!"

Michael and I barely held back our sighs of relief.

Then Michael said, "Nora, what happened to your sandwich?"

I couldn't remember what I'd done with my grilled cheese, although I seemed to be licking my fingers. I peeked up at him. "Uhm, do you mind making me another one?"

Later, when we'd found places for everybody to sleep and I had showed Zephyr the guest bedroom with its antique bed and extra blankets in case the furnace quit for good, I locked the door of our bedroom and slid under the heap of covers with Michael.

He gathered me up to warm me. "What's the matter with you? Lucy always sleeps on the couch downstairs so her imaginary friend can play the piano."

"Shh. She's perfectly happy with a sleeping bag in my closet."

He dropped his voice to a whisper, too. "We could put Max's crib across the hall."

"He'll be safer in here with us."

"Safer? What's got into you? I told Dolph he had to spend the night on the staircase because you asked. What's going on?"

Alone at last, I told him the information Gus had given to me about Zephyr and her various dead boyfriends. "We think she killed them all," I said as quietly as I could manage. "Starting with her father."

Michael rolled over onto his back and stared at the ceiling to absorb what I had told him. "Your editor thinks Zephyr is a serial killer? What do they drink down there in Australia? She's a perfectly nice girl. Not too smart, maybe, but she's kinda sweet."

"Are you listening to me? She probably killed at least three men. And you could be next!"

Michael rolled up on one elbow again and tried to

subdue me with a kiss. "Nora, sweetheart, you've had a bad couple of days."

"You were the one who said she shot her father!"

"Maybe I was wrong." Michael gave up trying to comfort me. The bedroom was dark, but I could see him forming an opinion. Finally, he shook his head. "She seems really nice."

"As soon as she flashes her chest and gives you the smoldering glance, you're suddenly an expert judge of character?"

"You're a little nuts tonight. Why don't I try calming you down?"

I settled into the bedclothes and pulled the sheet up to my chin. "Not with Max and Lucy right here."

"They're asleep." He slid his hand under the covers to touch me. "We could be really quiet."

I gave him a chaste kiss. "Good night."

It was the first time I had been alone with him to talk since my horrible scene with Gus. There was so much to tell him. How Gus had heard us in the scullery, how he'd manipulated me, how I'd caused Sammy to lose his job. How I'd quit, then gone back and asked for my job back. And that damned kiss. Eventually, I was going to have to tell Michael about all of that. But I was too tired to relate it all just then. In fact, I heard him say something more about Zephyr, but I was already half asleep. Before he finished, I heard myself exhale a little snore.

Michael tucked me against his frame and let me drift off to dreamland.

But in the middle of the night, something woke me. I lay still, aware that Michael was awake, too.

"Did you hear that?" I asked softly, still not sure what I had heard. A noise in the house? Or something outside?

"Yeah." Michael was already half out of bed and reaching for his cell phone.

I sat up, too. "What is it?"

"Sirens," he said, already dialing. As he punched the keypad, we heard a large vehicle pass by the farm, whooping. A red light flashed across the bedroom walls.

While Michael spoke to one of his men at the bottom of the driveway, I slipped out of bed and hurried into the closet to check on Lucy. She was snug in her sleeping bag, sound asleep. I slid my dressing gown off its hanger and put it on. When I came out of the closet, Michael was already zipping his jeans.

He spoke quietly, so as not to wake Max. "The guys think something's on fire up the road. Something big."

A fire at Blackbird Farm was my worst nightmare. Involuntarily, I put both hands over my mouth.

Michael touched my face. "There's nothing you can do. Stay here with the kids."

"Where are you going?" I whispered.

"Outside. I'll be back in a few minutes."

He let himself out of the bedroom, and of course I followed, fastening the satin belt on my elaborate vintage robe. Dolph was sitting on the top step, slurping from a coffee cup and leafing through a bodybuilder magazine. He barely looked up when Michael went down the staircase. But he stared up at me as if I had just walked off the set of a British costume drama on the arm of Prince William.

I said to him, "Stay here. Make sure nobody goes into the bedroom."

"Nobody, like who?" he asked.

I didn't respond but followed Michael down the stairs and through the dark house. I slid my bare feet into my gardening boots. The kitchen door was open, and I caught up with Michael on the back porch. In the moonlight, he stood still, looking north.

The sky glowed orange, and an eerie light flickered through the trees.

"What's up there?" Michael asked when I arrived at his side.

"That's Starr's Landing. Oh, Michael."

He put his arm around me, and we stood together, watching the fire light up the horizon. The night air was cold around us. He said, "Is anybody still staying in the house?"

"No, nobody. With Zephyr here, the house is empty. And they moved all the livestock off the property on Sunday. Emma helped." The first whiffs of smoke began to drift down. I felt an ache in my chest at the thought of the destruction of the beautiful landscape Swain Starr had created—his last masterpiece. I said, "I hope the firemen are safe."

In a cryptic tone, Michael said, "I hope the insurance was paid up."

"I should wake up Zephyr and tell her."

Michael caught my elbow as I turned. "What's she going to do? Help put out the fire? Let her sleep and tell her in the morning."

"Maybe you're right. She's not as attached to the place as I thought she'd be." Not the way I felt about Blackbird Farm, anyway. "She didn't want to go home to it."

"Y'know," Michael said, still thoughtfully watching the glow on the horizon, "it's a convenient night for the place to burn, isn't it?"

"What are you saying?"

But I knew. A modern house and that beautiful barn? I had seen the sprinklers myself, and I knew Swain had taken pains to make sure the place would survive a stray cigarette butt. The fire was no accident.

Michael's cell phone rang in his pocket, and he went back into the kitchen to take the call.

I stood for a while longer on the porch, watching the molten glow in the sky.

But I had already sensed something moving around in my barn. I waited until I knew Michael was engaged in his phone call. Then, in darkness, I slipped down the steps and went across the wet grass. A sliver of moon shone down through the still-leafless oak branches overhead, dappling the ground with meager light.

I caught my balance on the open door of the barn.

"Em?" I said.

Mr. Twinkles threw up his head and snorted. Emma turned from the act of pulling a saddle from his back.

I said, "What are you doing? It's three in the morning."

She had changed back into boots and jeans with a dark pullover buttoned up to her throat. Her face was white in the half-light.

Startled, she cursed. "How come you're awake?"

In the barn, I made my way around Michael's fix-up car parked beside a stack of hay bales. "I asked first. I thought you had a date."

"His water bed sprang a leak."

She had tied Toby to the stall door, and the spaniel lay quietly, listening to our voices. Mr. Twinkles was sweating, his eyes luminous, his nostrils distended. When she pulled the saddle off him, I could see his coat matted down from the saddle pad.

I said, "You've been out riding. In the dark."

"I took Sheffield Road." She threw the saddle over the stall bars and set about unfastening the cheek buckles on the horse's bridle.

"Em, what have you done?" I said, and my voice sounded hollow.

When she didn't answer, I said, "I can smell the gasoline."

"Then take care of Twinkles," she snapped, "while I change. Mick will be here looking for you any minute."

My fingers shook on the bridle, but I managed to get it off the horse and slide the bit from his mouth. He nuzzled my hair and gave me a shove with his nose, still full of energy. His legs were mud-spattered, but he was also wet up to his knees and hocks as if he'd splashed through a stream. I used a rag to rub the worst of the mud from him.

While I cleaned up the horse, Emma went to the back of the barn where she'd parked her truck to conceal it. She pulled her sweater over her head and threw it into the straw. I could see her shucking off her boots next, and then her jeans. She climbed into the truck and rummaged for something else to wear.

I gave Mr. Twinkles a slap on his haunch, and he swung willingly into his stall. I went with him and ran a brush over his damp coat while he munched on a mouthful of hay.

Emma came back, yanking a T-shirt over her head. Her buff riding breeches were clean. She had found a pair of sneakers, too. At the water trough, she dunked her head and swished her short hair around to rid herself of the last fumes of gasoline. When she came up for air, she shook her head like a dog coming out of a lake and reached for the beer that she had balanced on the rim of the trough. She snapped the top and took a long, thirsty slug.

I said, "Tell me you didn't do something terrible."

She drank a little more.

A rush of fury boiled up inside me, and I batted the can out of her hand. It landed in the straw off in the darkness.

"Screw you," she said.

I grabbed her by the arm. "What have you done, Emma?"

Matching my anger, she said, "On Sunday I found Rawlins's jacket in Starr's barn."

Still holding her arm, but frozen with dread, I listened.

She said, "I figured either he'd been there, or he was being set up. When I heard the police nabbed him, I figured somebody better do something in case he left any other evidence at the farm."

"My God." I had known Emma was on the brink of something bad, but this was far more than my imagination could conjure up.

She pulled out of my grasp and ran both hands through her short, wet hair. "Maybe it was a stupid thing to do. Or crazy. But if somebody's going to get caught helping Rawlins, it might as well be me. I got nothing left to lose, right?"

"Don't say that."

She had been drinking long before she'd left the barn on Mr. Twinkles and ridden the back road to Starr's Landing. I couldn't judge how drunk she was, but she certainly wasn't sober.

I said, "We love you, Em. We don't want you to go to jail any more than Rawlins. You can't run around in the middle of the night setting fire to—"

"Shut up," she said. "Forget I was here. Go back to bed. Go back to Mick and make a baby. Let me do what has to be done."

"You're not thinking straight. Giving your child to Hart has made you—"

"It hasn't done anything to me, so forget it. Get out of here. I'll sleep in the truck for a couple of hours and go to work before anyone—"

Behind me, Michael said, "Before anyone what?"

Both of us nearly jumped out of our skins. We spun around and faced him. He had pulled on a pair of boots and a jacket over his otherwise bare chest. Emma and I must have stared at him stupidly.

He laughed. "The two of you look like you just robbed a bank. What's going on?"

"We're having a fight," I said as calmly as I could manage. "I want Emma to come into the house and sleep in a bed. But she's determined to stay out here in the barn. Make her see reason, will you?"

He looked past me at my sister, no longer amused. "She knows what's best for herself."

Behind him, a set of headlights suddenly swept across the yard, and we heard the crunch of tires in the gravel. Michael glanced over his shoulder.

"State police are here," he reported. "So get your alibi in order, ladies."

He turned to intercept the cop who got out of the cruiser.

It was Ricci, the trooper I'd spoken to at the impound lot. Michael shook his hand, and they exchanged a sentence or two before Ricci came to the open barn door and directed a blazing flashlight in my face. He said, "Everything all right here?"

"We have a sick horse," I said. "My sister's taking care of him."

The flashlight illuminated Emma's face next, but she didn't flinch. She said calmly, "Don't scare him. He's a valuable animal."

Ricci paced into the barn and used the light to skim past Michael's parked car to Mr. Twinkles, now nervously eyeing the growing crowd and shifting his feet in the straw. He still looked hot and sweaty to me, but maybe Ricci had no experience with animals.

The trooper put his flashlight back on me, letting it slide down my figure. He said, "That's some getup you're wearing tonight."

There was no covering up the low décolletage of the vintage dressing gown I'd picked up in a Paris thrift shop years ago. The straps of my black silk nightie showed, too, making me look like an escapee from a French boudoir. For an instant, I thought Michael was going to step in front of the light to shield me, but he thought better of it and let the trooper take a long look.

I said, "I didn't plan on running around in public like this. What's going on? There's a fire?"

Ricci shut off the flashlight. "Yeah, the barn at Starr's Landing is burning. I thought I should stop here and make sure everybody's okay."

"Why?" I asked, a plausible note of fear in my voice. I didn't have to fake my shivering. I was suddenly very cold. "Is there a pyromaniac in the neighborhood?"

Michael said, "Nobody's going to light a match to this place, Nora. Not when we've got half a dozen guys watching the drive."

Ricci turned his attention to Michael then. "What's that all about? You expecting trouble?"

Michael shrugged. "I like knowing my family is safe."

"Which family?" Ricci asked.

Michael stiffened, but Emma spoke up before he could pop off an angry retort. She said, "Do you mind taking this conversation outside? I've got a sick animal here, and you're getting him all worked up again."

Ricci glanced in the direction of Mr. Twinkles, who gave a timely snort of annoyance.

I led the way out of the barn, and the two men followed, leaving Emma behind. I glanced back in time to see her gather up a blanket and throw it over the horse's back.

I hugged myself, suddenly shivering, and said to Ricci, "It was very nice of you to check on us. But if you don't mind, I'm freezing now. May we go back to bed?"

Ricci gave Michael and me another long, suspicious stare. Finally, he said, "Sure. Go to bed before you catch cold."

He tossed the flashlight into the cruiser and climbed

in behind the wheel. I heard Michael ask him a question, and the two of them spoke while I let myself back into the house.

Upstairs, I warmed up and rinsed off the smell of horse in a very hot shower before I put on a clean nightie. My dressing gown was going to need a trip to the dry cleaner. Michael came in as I slipped under the bed-clothes.

He checked on Lucy and Max before climbing in beside me. "I almost knocked that cop on his ass for looking at you with that damn flashlight."

"Thank heavens you didn't," I said, keeping my voice to a whisper so we wouldn't wake the children. "We already look like America's Most Wanted around here."

"I didn't punch him because you were putting on a hell of a distraction. You gonna tell me what you and Emma are keeping secret?"

Taking a line from Michael's own script, I said, "It's better if you don't know."

He said, "I can guess. I had some other stuff delivered when that car was put in the barn. Including a gas can. It wasn't there tonight."

I sank back against the pillows. "What about you?" I asked when Michael began rubbing my feet to warm them. "When do I get an explanation of what's going on between you and my sister?"

There wasn't any use ignoring it any longer. I'd sensed it for weeks—Emma making cryptic remarks and Michael changing the subject when Emma's name came up. They'd had a fight. And neither of them wanted me to know the details.

He shook his head. "It's over. Nothing to worry about."

"Michael," I said. "She's hormonal. Giving up her baby has been much harder than she thought it would be. She can't be held responsible for her behavior."

"The hell she can't," Michael shot back in a tone that surprised me.

I sat up in the bed and pulled my foot from his suddenly painful grasp. I whispered, "Something serious happened between you two, didn't it? Michael, she's my baby sister. As tough as she pretends to be, we have to give her some slack now and then."

"Maybe she's gotten too much slack over the years."

"You're mad at her," I said, amazed.

"Not mad," he replied. "But fed up."

"What happened between the two of you?"

He almost got out of bed, but I reached for his hand and pulled him back.

"Tell me," I said.

A bad moment ticked by before Michael admitted, "A couple of weeks ago, I threw her out of the house. Told her she couldn't live here anymore."

"Why?" I demanded, my voice rising. "You had no right to do that!"

He looked at me, his usually lazy-eyed gaze suddenly sharp. "Didn't I?"

"You did," I hastily corrected myself. "This is your house as much as mine now."

But that didn't settle the matter. I had said the wrong thing in the heat of the moment. Michael hauled me out of the bed and pulled me into the bathroom. He closed the door. In the dark, he said, "You were right just now. This isn't my house, Nora. It's yours."

"We're together," I insisted. "What's yours is mine. For better or for worse—"

"Bullshit." Michael loomed over me. "We may be together, but not the way I want it."

"Are we back to that?" I asked.

"We said some words in front of your family, but

we're not married. I want a license and a priest and everything else that comes with making it official."

I couldn't help myself. "Such as the right to toss my sister into the street?"

"If she comes climbing into my lap every time you leave the house, yes."

My legs loosened under me, and I sat down hard on the edge of the tub. I knew Emma was attracted to Michael, but I hadn't guessed she'd acted on those feelings. Not in my own home. "She—?"

Michael stayed on his feet and ran an exasperated hand through his hair, sorry he'd said it but determined to keep going. "She's good at hiding her drinking, Nora. She started again right after she gave away her baby, and she got plastered every day. Every damn day, she'd get numb and dumb. And as soon as you were out of sight—" Michael caught himself.

"She came on to you?"

He shrugged. "You know how she gets."

I did. When Emma really got loaded, she had no control. Numb and dumb, indeed. And Michael was her type—a bad boy with a powerful sexual presence.

He had something else she needed, too—an inner strength a woman could rely on, be comforted and protected by. I had been drawn to that quality in him perhaps more than anything else at first, when I needed it. To Emma, he probably appeared battle-tested and undaunted.

He said, "She knew it was wrong. But she couldn't stop, and after a few weeks I couldn't take it anymore. She was a pain in my ass. I don't want to be with two Blackbird sisters. I want to be with you."

"You did the right thing," I said softly. "But . . ."

"But what?"

"She said something tonight. That she has nothing left to lose. That worries me."

Michael sighed and leaned his back against the door, eyes closed.

I looked up at him. "I can't help wanting to do something for her."

"I know," he said harshly. "That's your specialty—helping lost causes."

A hard lump suddenly clogged my throat. "You think she's a lost cause?"

"No," he said swiftly, rubbing his face to wake himself up. "Sorry. I didn't mean it that way. It's your—I know you want to help all of us—Rawlins and Emma and me, too, but sometimes, Nora, you have to let people make their own choices. Make their own mistakes. People have to learn for themselves."

I thought about that for a moment. It made sense. But I couldn't make it work in the context of my own family. It was harsh—more harsh than I could stand. Maybe I was too exhausted to think straight. My head felt like a woolly mess.

"I'm sorry, too," I said at last. "I'm sorry you had to put up with Emma's behavior."

"It was pretty comical, her chasing me around the house."

I tried to smile.

Our gazes met, and we shared a complicated moment. I knew why he'd kept the secret—both to protect Emma and to spare me the hurt of her betrayal. Now that it was out in the open, however, neither one of us felt good about it.

He said, "I didn't want you to lose your sister."

"I know. But that might happen anyway."

"Did she set the fire tonight?"

"I think so. To protect Rawlins. I can't believe she'd be so reckless. So stupid."

"She's never been the sensible type," Michael agreed. "And lately? I've been expecting her to do something really wild."

"It's so wrong. Destroying property, defrauding the insurance people. Will she get caught?"

"Depends on what she left behind. Whether or not the cops can track a horse. I could send some of the guys to—"

"No, don't," I said at once. "I don't want you connected to the fire in any way whatsoever. Promise me you won't. If she goes down for this, let her do it alone. Please."

After a long moment, he said, "All right."

I put my hand up to him, and he pulled me to my feet. I stepped into his arms and touched the bristle of his cheek. I knew how much he wanted us to be married. But I was afraid. Afraid the Blackbird curse would strike as soon as we exchanged vows. And with Zephyr in the house, I was doubly concerned about his mortality. I gave Michael a kiss on the mouth. Lingering there, I murmured, "Please don't get yourself killed, okay? On top of everything else that's going on right now, I really couldn't handle that."

Chapter 15

In the morning, though, Zephyr tried to bash in Michael's skull.

First, Lucy woke us far too early by climbing into the bed and asking for cake for breakfast. A little bleary, I took her into the bathroom, and we brushed our teeth. By the time we were dressed and ready, Michael had crawled out of bed and changed Max's diaper. I switched places with Michael and buttoned Max into his clothes while Lucy used our bed as a trampoline.

We tiptoed past Zephyr's closed bedroom door and went downstairs while breaking the news to Lucy that there would be no cake for breakfast. While I made oatmeal and sliced bananas, Michael brewed a pot of coffee and strolled it down to the security detail to check in for the day.

While the kids ate, Libby telephoned, in tears.

I said, "Is there any word from Rawlins?"

"He's still with the police," she said with a sniffle. "They're keeping him a little longer. For more questions. But those lawyers of That Man of Yours—they were very solemn with me, Nora."

"I'm so sorry, Lib."

She gave a woeful wail. "The police won't tell me anything."

"What about bail?"

"He has to be charged with a crime first. And depending on the severity of the crime, the bail could be just a few thousand dollars or—or it could be something beyond my reach. Nora, I can't let Rawlins sit in jail! He's so young! So impressionable! What if some horrible person tries to hurt him? I can't stand it!"

"It's okay, Lib. We'll manage somehow." I had no idea how, though.

Sounding more composed, she said, "I'm going there in a few minutes. Can I leave Max with you for a few hours?"

"Sure. What about Lucy?"

"I'm sending someone to pick her up and take her to school."

"Someone? Who?"

"Oops, hang on, I just dropped an earring." She fumbled the phone, and I heard a muffled noise.

"Libby—?"

"If you must know," she said when she came back on the line, "I'm sending Perry."

"Perry? The bug man? Does Lucy even know him?"

"Yes, she knows him perfectly well. She follows him all over the house when he comes to spray. The only way he'll go into the twins' room is if she goes first."

Smart man, Perry. But I said, "Are you sure he's okay? Safe, I mean?"

"I'm giving him the opportunity to earn my trust," Libby said loftily.

Something sounded suspicious, but I couldn't figure out what. "I'm sure one of Michael's people could drive Lucy to school." No sooner were the words out of my mouth than I knew Libby would be appalled by the thought of her daughter being chauffeured to the local elementary school by a New Jersey wiseguy.

"Perry will do just fine, won't you, Perry?"

"He's there with you?" I demanded. "For heaven's sake, Libby, did the bug man spend the night?"

"I'll talk with you later," she said frostily, "as soon as I've seen Rawlins."

She hung up, leaving me to wonder if she'd had a fling with her exterminator.

Michael came back, and he had Zephyr with him. Both of them had smiles on their faces.

"Zephyr went running up to Starr's Landing," he told me as he ushered her into the kitchen. "My guys told her about the fire, so she went to look. I met her in the driveway."

"I hope you don't mind," she said to me, looking impossibly beautiful and as long-legged as a gazelle. She held out one foot. "I borrowed your sneakers."

Although I couldn't remember the last time I'd worn my sneakers, I suddenly minded very much. The fact that she seemed totally unfazed by the fire made me surprisingly angry. If Blackbird Farm had burned, I'd have been devastated. She seemed more concerned about her exercise program. And watching Michael go through the motions of making her toast and coffee, I started to feel more and more steamed for reasons beyond understanding. When I went running, I turned red and sweated through my shirt and sometimes threw up afterward. Which explained both why I rarely went running and why I couldn't fit into my clothes anymore. In fact, just looking at Zephyr was making me nauseated.

"I borrowed the rest of these clothes, too. I found them hanging on the hook in the bathroom. I should probably wash it all." She was wearing one of Emma's T-shirts and a pair of shorts I wore when I gardened in the summer months. It all looked a little limp.

"I'll show you where the laundry is," Michael volunteered. "It's back this way."

He led, and she followed him down the hallway past the scullery.

To Max, I said, "Beauty isn't everything."

Max gave me a big smile with banana leaking out of his mouth.

The next moment, we heard a resounding *thunk*, and Michael made a noise I had never heard before.

I called, "Everything okay?"

Michael returned, rubbing the back of his head. "An iron fell off the shelf in the laundry room."

Zephyr came back, looking innocent as she picked up her cup of coffee.

I gave Michael a bag of frozen peas and a stern look.

Zephyr continued to seem unaffected by the destruction of her property. "The farm is an awful mess. The fire marshal said the barn was a total loss. But everything else is pretty good. The house is fine. Maybe I'll go over later and get some clothes."

"Uh, how long are you planning to stay here?" I asked.

"I'm not sure."

"Stay as long as you like," Michael said, making me think of ker-blamming him with an iron all over again.

We heard a rumble in the driveway. I peeked out the window. Perry Delbert had arrived in his large van with the exterminator logo printed on the side. Above his name, a giant spider lay dead, all eight legs pointed sky-ward. On top of the cab, the model of a very large mosquito perched as if ready to spring into blood-sucking action. I took Lucy outside, and she bounded happily into the van's front seat.

While Perry buckled her in, I said, "You're so kind to help my sister in her time of need, Mr. Delbert."

He was a big, soft-spoken man with a tendency toward shy smiles. This morning he looked a little shaken, however. His nose was sweaty, causing his glasses to slide downward. "She's in need a lot, isn't she?"

"Libby's life is complicated," I said diplomatically.

"She sure is pretty, though." He spoke on a wistful sigh.

I waved good-bye to Lucy as they trundled down the driveway in the bugmobile. I told myself I was going to have a stern discussion with Libby as soon as the worst of our troubles blew over. She had no business toying with Perry Delbert's tender heart.

I checked my watch and dashed upstairs to change into work-suitable clothes. I flipped through my wardrobe very carefully. Not only did I have a tough fashion crowd to face today, but I wanted to be sure my clothes fit properly. And it wouldn't hurt to show Zephyr she wasn't the only woman in the house who could clean up nicely.

Finally dressed, combed and ready to face the day, I ran down the stairs. I heard the shower running in the guest bathroom, so Zephyr was safely off the radar screen. Michael was alive and doing business on the floor of the library with Max using him as a jungle gym. Michael had the phone to his ear and one eye on the futures market on his laptop computer, while Max crawled all over him. Dolph sat on the window seat, chin in one hand, his face mashed against the glass, sound asleep.

Michael ended his call within a minute. Without moving from the floor he said to me, "You look good today. Really good."

"Thank your countrymen, Dolce and Gabbana." I executed a little spin to show off the black suit—a narrow skirt with a slightly forgiving elastic waist and a hint of lace at the hem, topped by a ladylike jacket with a leather-trimmed shawl collar cut low enough to reveal a corset-style underlayer that suggested I wasn't perfectly well-mannered all the time. A professional look, I thought, with a hint of sex appeal. To offset the winter suit, I wore spring shoes—a pair of buff suede kitten heels with little black bows on the toes. I had listened to the weather forecast and heard no rain, so the shoes would be safe. The suit showed off my legs and gave me a nice bustline, while being forgiving about everything in between.

The look in Michael's eye boosted my confidence. He was a man, I told myself. He'd probably stop looking at other women when he was dead. But his expression also told me if I lingered very long, I'd be undressed all over again. Although he might look at others, I was the woman he really wanted—of that, I was sure.

I had to spoil the mood, though. "I may be dressed in a garment that cost thousands, but I don't have train fare to get to work. Have any spare change in your pocket?"

He dug into his jeans and came up with four dollars and a quarter. "Is that enough?"

"I might have a quarter or two in the bottom of my handbag."

He shook his head. "We can't keep going like this. Not if we have to feed other people. It's time to hit the pawn-shop. I'll see what I can get for the laptop."

"Then you won't be able to do your business. Don't worry. I'll go through my coat pockets. Maybe there's some change from my trip to the grocery last week. How's your head?"

He gave the back of his skull a tentative rub. "Sore. I'm still not sure what happened."

I gave him a raised eyebrow.

"It was an accident," he assured me. "No girl is going to bump me off that easily."

"Are you okay with taking care of Maximus for a few more hours?"

Max tried to climb over Michael's shoulder, but he slipped and nearly hit the floor. Michael caught him easily and hung him upside down by his ankles, which sent Max into a fit of gurgling laughter. Michael said, "We're good. Is Libby going to come here after checking on Rawlins?"

I tucked the money into my handbag. "Unless she scheduled a nooner with the bug man, yes."

Michael dropped Max into his lap and sat up with interest. "That's a new development."

"But not unexpected. Rawlins, though—"

"He's a smart kid. He won't say anything that will get him deeper into trouble."

While dressing, I had started worrying about Rawlins all over again. About how he was being treated. Whether he could keep calm in the face of intense questioning. And whether or not the police might decide he had a connection to the fire at Starr's Landing. But Rawlins didn't have the benefit of Michael's experience for getting through such an ordeal.

Michael guessed where my thoughts were and took my hand. "Try not to worry."

"Okay," I said. "I can't get back home until after dinner. I have to go to the office, and then I have a couple of events." And I wanted to learn more about Swain Starr's life. After Zephyr's revelations about him, I had some ideas about whom I could ask for information.

I leaned down and grabbed a handful of Michael's shirt. I pulled him until we were nose to nose, smiling. "If I come home and find you smelling like Zephyr's perfume or dead by her hand, I'm going to be annoyed, got it?"

"Me, too," he said with a grin. "Especially the dead part." He kissed me good-bye. "We'll be careful."

Put Michael in the middle of a swamp full of starving alligators, and I'd bet on his getting out alive. But Zephyr might have already murdered three men, and I had a right to be concerned about the nearest target in her range.

Dolph woke when Michael told him to, and he got up to drive me to the train station. On the back porch, I stopped, and he nearly collided with me.

"Have you seen Ralphie lately?"

"Huh? You mean the pig?"

"He's usually here on the porch. Come to think of it, I don't remember seeing him last night, either."

Dolph shrugged. "Maybe he went looking for a lady pig."

Dolph drove me the short distance to the train station. As I looked at him sitting behind the car's steering wheel, I realized how short-legged he was. He had to scrunch the seat forward until his chest almost touched the wheel. I wondered if Zephyr had noticed him.

I did not engage Michael's bodyguard in conversation. He seemed to appreciate the silence. I missed Reed, my usual driver. But Reed had decided to go to community college full-time this semester, and I knew he was better off studying hard to transfer into a four-year program. I wondered how Michael was going to continue paying his tuition.

I rode the train into the city while making a few notes about my schedule for the day. Then someone left a newspaper on a seat near mine, and I picked it up. It wasn't the *Intelligencer*, but a paper with a more dignified editorial policy. The fire at Starr's Landing hadn't made the front page yet, but the investigation into Swain Starr's death made a quiet below-the-fold headline. I didn't read anything I didn't already know. The good news was that Rawlins wasn't mentioned by name, only as "a juvenile from the neighborhood held for questioning."

Lunch was first on my schedule, a small affair called

Bow Ties and Bowwows to benefit an animal rescue organization. The men had been asked to wear bow ties, and many of the animals on leashes also sported clever collars and neckerchiefs. The lobby of an important bank was the venue, and the vast marble space was arranged with round luncheon tables, although most guests preferred to take a small plate from the buffet and circulate around the room to pat the dogs on display. For my column, I first snapped photos of the centerpieces—life-sized sculptures of dogs crafted out of carnations. But pictures of adorable live animals would do more good.

I remembered attending a much different event in the same bank when I first started attending charity events for the *Intelligencer*. Back in those days, the bank had been lavishly decorated with great, swooping swags of chiffon and twinkle lights. The tables had groaned under centerpieces of fresh flowers six feet tall, elaborate plates of exotic food, an impressive selection of wine, glowing candles and party favors for every guest. Today, though, the decor was austere by comparison. Bank executives had no doubt decided to tone down any hint of extravagance lest they be criticized. I suspected one of the organization's board members either worked for the bank or was married to someone who did.

I cruised around the lobby, greeting friends and patting the rescue dogs that were looking for forever homes.

"Nora," said English Hubble, a friend whose father owned two of the most popular tourist restaurants in the city. Normally a solemn sort of young woman, she seemed more outgoing today around all the animals. "Don't you need a nice pet?"

"I already have my hands full with a pig," I told her, ruffling the white fur of a blue-eyed husky mix. His tail wagged, and I could see he was the source of English's good mood.

"A pig! You mean, a potbellied pig?"

"No, a big pig. A hog, in fact. His name is Ralphie, and I have a terrible time keeping him out of the house."

She laughed. "You have such a wonderful sense of humor."

I doubted I could explain Ralphie's pushy personality to her in such a short time, so I said, "Can I take your photo for my column?"

English had an expressive face. She had trained as an actress, but she never hit the big time onstage. I'd heard she'd started working for her father in a business capacity, but she devoted her spare time to good causes like animal rescue and reading books for the blind. Maybe I imagined it, but she seemed to hesitate at my question. But her acting training took over. "Why don't you just take a picture of Chewie? He's much more photogenic."

"No, the two of you look great together. Do you mind?" I lifted my phone to snap a candid shot.

"Actually, I do." English raised her hand to protect her face. "I'm sorry, Nora. I know you've done wonderful work for many organizations with your column, but I— I'd rather not appear in the *Intelligencer*."

I tried not to lose my smile. "No problem. Smile, Chewie!"

The dog gave me a big lick when I bent to pat him after the photo, and I was glad I could hide my expression from English. This was a first. Somebody didn't want to be seen on the pages of the newspaper because it had become a disgraceful tabloid.

English seemed relieved that I didn't press her to explain her feelings. We parted friends, and I moved farther around the room to talk with the organizing committee. Three young women and a dapper elderly gentleman had no qualms about talking to me and were happy to explain the particulars of the party. They hoped to raise several thousand dollars with their luncheon, and the bank had agreed to match whatever funds were collected. The money would support one no-kill shelter for a short while.

"It's very difficult to raise money for animals during hard times," the committee chair told me. "Whatever you can do to help us will be much appreciated, Nora."

I went snooping among the tables. At last, I came upon the man I hoped to find.

Dilly Farquar sat grandly at a table by himself, one elegant hand balanced on the ebony handle of a handsome walking stick. He wore a natty blue jacket with a crisp white shirt, a sky blue bow tie and a checked pocket square. His gray flannel trousers held a sharp crease. The highly respected fashion columnist for the city's most prestigious newspaper also wore a clunky plaster cast on his left foot.

"Dilly, darling," I cried, "whatever have you done to yourself?"

He remained seated but pulled me down to give two kisses. "It's so boring, Nora, I can't bear to tell the story again. Would you believe I broke my foot fighting off a mugger? Or should I go with hiking the Andes? How about I was pitched off a pier in Venice by an irate gondolier?"

I slid into the chair beside his. The table was decorated with a poufy poodle made of pink and white carnations. It had jelly beans for eyes. "I'd believe all three stories," I said. "I know you've been an adventurer all your life."

"My adventuring days ended ten years ago," he replied. "To tell the truth, I fell off a ladder while taking down my Christmas tree. I broke eight glass dachshund ornaments and had to crawl out onto my balcony to shout for help. I was rescued by two teenage boys who were skipping school. Damian and Joe-rell."

"Lucky for you they were nearby."

Dilly was one of the city's truest aristocrats—an elderly gentleman of means who had devoted himself to the study of fashion. Every week in his newspaper column, he wrote beautiful prose in praise of fine tailoring. He kept his white hair combed straight back from a long, elegant face that looked rather French to me, but perhaps it was just his expression—always composed and slightly aloof, very discerning, not quick to smile—that gave him the look of a very sophisticated man who could hardly wait to get home to his collection of rare porcelain.

He said, "Damian and Joc-rell have become my good friends. Almost every day, they come to my house to check on me. Sometimes they walk my dogs, but I have to pay them considerable money because dachshunds, apparently, are unmanly if you're under the age of sixteen. They encouraged me to invest in World of Warcraft—do you know what that is?"

"Of course. My nephews play it all the time. A fantasy role-playing game on the computer."

A certain devilishness lurked around the edges of Dilly's smile. "My avatar is a swordsman. Damian thinks I have a brilliant mind for battle strategy. I'm their commanding officer. We have a wonderful time together."

"Perfect, since you can't get around very well at the moment."

He said, "I hate getting old."

"You're not old," I said firmly, although I was uneasy to see him looking more pale than usual. His injury must have taken more out of him than he pretended. "But," I continued, "you've reached the time in life when you should throw a party to undecorate your Christmas tree. It's more fun, among other things. And somebody else can take a tumble off the ladder."

"Good point." He smiled at me dotingly for a moment, eyes glimmering with appreciation for my suit with the hint of corset underneath. But he got serious fast. "Nora, dear heart, I've been hearing terrible things."

I put my hands in my lap and tried not to sigh. "I need your advice, Dilly."

"I read yesterday's *Intelligencer*. Tell me you didn't write that garbage."

"I did not. But . . . I supplied some of the information."

He shook his head in dismay.

"I know, I know. I was wrong, and it didn't take me ten minutes to figure that out. But I—I feel as if I'm groping through a dark cave, Dilly. The editor has me working on stories that are over my head."

"Don't complain. It's beneath you."

I straightened my shoulders. "Right. I have to take responsibility."

"You do," he agreed.

"Am I wrong to print the things people tell me?"

"No, of course not. That's your job. But you must be careful what you ask, Nora. And how you ask it. If information is off the record, you can't use it. And when people think they're speaking to you as a friend—you must be doubly cautious."

"My source was more candid than he should have been. And, unfortunately, he lost his job because of it. I feel terrible."

Gently, Dilly said, "You learned a lesson. Move on."

"But—my friend? Should I help him find another job?"

"That's up to you, dear heart. It would be a nice gesture, but maybe he would resent you for it, too?"

I blew a sigh. "I never thought this job would be easy for me, but I had started to enjoy it. Now, I feel . . . inadequate."

"I hear your new boss is a bit of a rogue."

I shook my head. "I'm not going to blame him. I need to figure out my own ethics."

"Everybody must carry his own moral compass. Perhaps his doesn't point true north?"

"It doesn't point the same direction I want to travel, that's for sure."

Dilly tapped the edge of the table with his walking stick. "I can see your newspaper is trying to dig up the story of Swain Starr's death."

"Yes. In fact, that's the other reason I hoped to find you today."

He raised an elegant eyebrow. "Are you going to use me in a despicable way?"

"No. I need—what do you call it? Deep background?"

He laughed a little. "I don't know anything about last night's fire."

"Deeper than that. Did you know Swain?"

"We were acquainted. Professionally. I must admit, his work did not interest me much. He used clichés. He had pedestrian color sense. His fabrics were often mediocre. His taste was erratic. Oh, I understood his popularity. But it was mimicry, not art."

"Wow," I said. "That sums him up very neatly."

"I wrote a scathing piece about him once. But I never used it. I am aware that I could damage a designer's livelihood with harsh words."

I reflected that Dilly could do more than damage a designer. He could have mopped the floor with Swain Starr, perhaps destroyed him. But he hadn't.

I said, "Did you know him personally?"

"We met many times. But Swain was not a man to get close to other men. He preferred the company of women."

"Yes."

"I know Marybeth a little better. After she raised her family, she developed the kind of drive I didn't see in the man she married. Her grandfather's life was an American success story. Marybeth and her brother had the good sense to be quiet about their money, and they worked hard. There was no New Money stink on the Rattigans."

Without mentioning to Dilly that I had learned Marybeth had spent all of her inheritance, I said, "You sound like a snob, Dilly."

"I *am* a snob. I'm a professional snob. I make judgments about people on the basis of their clothes, for heaven's sake. How much more ridiculous does that make me? I have money, too, but I love my work." The small smile again. "As you love your work, too, deep down."

Yes, I did love it. Despite the pressure from Gus, I loved getting out, meeting people, communicating their messages to readers with my own spin. Which made making a mistake so much more difficult to bear.

Dilly said, "I don't know who killed Swain. I can imagine the motive, though. Swain Starr loved women — perhaps too much. But he also alienated men."

"Why do you say that?"

"He never knew how to get along with his own gender. Not even his sons. He didn't talk sports. He didn't play cards. He didn't follow politics or have any interest in art or business," Dilly said. "My point is, he had no common language with other men. He was a poor friend, a bad father. He quit fashion, which proves to me he didn't have the fire in his belly anymore."

"What are you saying, Dilly? That a man killed him?"

Dilly lifted his shoulders eloquently. "I could be entirely wrong. But I wouldn't be surprised."

Dilly was being far more forthcoming than I had

hoped for. I was aware that he was demonstrating how much he trusted I wouldn't make the same mistake I had with Sammy. I said, "My other reason for seeking you out is to ask why Swain left the fashion business. To most of us, he seemed to be at the top of his career. Why did he quit?"

"I thought his new wife asked him to."

"I know, but . . . is that reason enough to give up a billion-dollar enterprise? His creative outlet? The work of his whole life?"

Dilly paused, frowning. "I can't be sure. . . ."

"Of what?"

Slowly, Dilly said, "I know some fashion designers. Kaiser Waldman for one. I gathered he had no respect for Swain."

"Artistic differences?"

Dilly shook his head. "It was more than that. I have a gut feeling. A suspicion Swain Starr didn't design anything more complicated than a T-shirt in his whole life."

My mouth opened, but I couldn't make my voice obey. At once, though, I remembered that Swain had not recognized the dress I wore to the party at Starr's Landing. It had been his own design—albeit twenty years old—but he'd had no recollection of having created it.

Dilly leaned closer to make sure our conversation could not be overheard. "I think Swain had others do all his design work. Oh, he may have had some creative input at the beginning of his career, and he certainly had an appreciation of beauty, but was he capable of complex designs? I have my doubts. He liked being with women, watching them, and fashion was the best place to indulge himself."

"But—if Swain didn't design his own clothes, who did?"

"He spent a lot of time in China, didn't he?"

"Yes." And I remembered how hastily Swain's daughter, Suzette, jetted off to China immediately after her father's death. To take care of business there, her mother had said. Or to ensure the silence of whoever really designed Swain's clothes, perhaps?

Dilly said, "There's still a lot of unscrupulous business being done in China. For the right price, a talented designer might be happy to have the Starr label go on his work. And people in the Western world might never know. Once he had the right contacts, it would be a simple matter to take credit for the creative work of others. Despicable as that might be."

Gus had smelled a rat. And Dilly's idea was stinky indeed. If Swain had pretended to do his own designing, someone who knew the truth might have blackmailed him out of the business. Or maybe Swain hastily retired before the truth came to light.

"Who else might have guessed Swain was a fake?"

Dilly lifted his shoulders. "Maybe a lot of people. If I suspected it, many others might have assumed, too. Family, certainly. Or very close confidants."

Marybeth, I thought. His ex-wife would have known whether her husband was truly a designer—or a phony.

I caught Dilly looking at me with concern on his face.

I squeezed his hand. "Thanks, Dilly. Not just for the insight into Swain Starr. I need a mentor. I appreciate your willingness to kick me in the head now and then."

He took both my hands in his. "No kicking. Call me anytime, dear heart. Are you going to the Farm-to-Table gala on Friday night?"

"Yes. I have to think about just the right dress to wear. Will I see you there?"

He laughed with delight at the prospect of seeing me in whatever dress I chose. "Let's have a drink together then. We'll review the week's news."

I gave him a kiss, very glad to have a father figure so willing to share his wisdom, and I went on my way.

I headed across town to a quick stop I hoped to make before going to my office. In addition to the celebrity profile I was working on, I still needed to fill my Sunday column with social events.

Outside a slightly down-at-heel ballroom in a hotel overdue for refurbishment, I dashed up to a registration table and gave my name to the young woman on duty. She checked off my name and found my name tag.

"I'm sorry, ma'am," she said, "but I think they've already served lunch. You might get some dessert and coffee."

"That's okay." I fastened the name tag to my jacket. "I only need to make an appearance and take a couple of photos. Do you know if Delilah Fairweather is here?"

The young woman wore her medium brown hair in a too-tight ponytail, and her clothes were equally nondescript. But she had a clear-eyed gaze that met mine directly. Her name tag said WEINER. No first name, which was unusual. She spoke with little evidence of social polish. "Yes, ma'am, Miss Fairweather's inside."

I smiled. "I don't suppose she saved me a seat?"

The event wasn't my usual kind of social scene. It was a solemn, civic lunch honoring soldiers returning from service in Afghanistan. I hadn't had time to pay attention to the information I'd been sent, and I was a little embarrassed about that. Usually, I brushed up diligently on the sponsoring organization so I knew whom to interview and photograph. But my friend Delilah had promised to be my guide.

The young woman came around the table. "I'll see if I can spot her for you, ma'am."

I hadn't realized Miss Weiner was handicapped in any way, but as she led me toward the closed ballroom door,

I realized she was wearing two prosthetic legs—curved metal blades, the "cheetah legs" so many injured veterans used now.

She peeked through the peephole in the door. "I see Miss Fairweather at the back of the room, ma'am. When I open the door, go to your left. You'll see her at the second table."

"Thanks," I said. "Are you one of the veterans we're honoring today?"

Miss Weiner kept her expression neutral. "I came back from Afghanistan last year. I said I'd help out today, but I didn't want to get up onstage."

"Why not?"

She almost shrugged, but remembered her military training. "It's not my way. My dad was a marine. He didn't like being paraded around, either. He'd be happier to see me out here, doing something useful."

I put out my hand to shake hers. "It sounds as if your family deserves a lot of thanks for your service."

She accepted my hand and opened the ballroom door for me. "Take a left. Second table."

"Thank you," I said, and slid into the ballroom.

The meal was long over, and the after-lunch speaker was already making his remarks. I eased into the empty chair beside my friend Delilah, perhaps the city's most accomplished party planner. Usually, Delilah organized fancy galas and lavish charitable events. But I knew her aunt had served two tours in Iraq a few years ago, so my friend donated her time and skills to make sure returning veterans were entertained just as professionally as big-spending donors might be.

I tried to peek through the centerpiece to see the speaker, but the tall flowers blocked my view. I suppressed a smile. I suspected the flowers had been recycled from whatever event Delilah had thrown the night before. They were magnificent—more lavish than was quite right for a luncheon—but nobody except me was probably the wiser.

As applause broke out for the speaker, Delilah leaned over and gave me a kiss. "You look like you mugged Madonna for that suit. It's killer."

"Coming from you, that's high praise." Delilah always looked great.

"I thought you weren't going to make it."

"Sorry," I whispered. "I ran into Dilly Farquar, and we had a heart-to-heart."

"You went to a dog party before this one?" Delilah scolded. "Honey, this is more your style."

It wasn't really, but I quickly figured out it should be. The tables around us were full of military personnel and their families. They were all intently focused on the speaker, a bluntly eloquent man who had run for president a few elections ago. I remembered his military record had been a big part of his résumé. Today, though, he spoke humbly of his service while the crowd nodded appreciatively.

As I listened, I couldn't help thinking about Carrie Hardaway, the young woman who had recently come into our lives. She had been serving in Afghanistan when her mother died. While Carrie was at home for the funeral, she had decided to find Michael, her long-lost father. He'd dated Carrie's mother back before he went to jail the first time, and Carrie was the daughter he'd never known. Their relationship was still iffy. From afar, I had watched their tentative efforts to get to know each other.

While listening to the luncheon speaker, I wondered if part of the problem was that Michael and I didn't entirely understand the military culture. I decided we had to start making a greater effort to do that.

After the luncheon broke up, I chatted with Delilah for a few minutes.

"Thanks for inviting me. You were right. This is a special organization."

Delilah grinned. "I figured you'd get it."

For once, my friend didn't seem in a hurry to dash to her next event. She probably had a little time to kill before her evening schedule heated up.

"Delilah, you organized a party for Marybeth Starr a couple of years ago, right?"

"Yeah, a dinner for her father before he passed. You were there, weren't you? No, that was before you got your job. At that huge house out in the burbs. We put up a tent in the backyard by their swimming pool. I had a couple of mermaids come and do a water ballet. The old man loved it."

"This was before Marybeth and Swain divorced?"

"Yeah," she said cautiously. "Why?"

"I'm looking for insight into Swain's life."

"To guess who might have killed him, I bet." Delilah slid her eyes at me. "This is between you and me, right?"

I felt a pang in my chest and knew she had read the *Intelligencer.* "I won't quote you."

She hesitated a moment longer before saying, "I think they were breaking up at the time. I went into the wine cellar to take a phone call, and they ... were having a fistfight."

"A fistfight?"

"She was beating on him pretty bad. From my perspective, it was like a couple of dwarves going at it. They were both so little compared to me. He didn't fight back, just let her punch and kick. Lemme tell you, she was furious. When she started smashing wine bottles, though, I let them know I was there, and they stopped right away."

"What were they fighting about?"

Delilah shook her head. "Something about one of their kids, I think. The youngest son, the one who had the TV show and then that big car wreck? From what I heard, Marybeth was trying to get Swain to give the kid some money. He didn't want to. Surprising, right? A guy that rich holding out on one of his kids?"

Swain and Porky had a complicated relationship, from what Zephyr had said. And it sounded as if Porky always needed cash.

I wanted to stay longer with Delilah, but I could see she had places to go. She rarely sat still for more than five minutes. It was one of the reasons she was so successful.

"We'll have a drink and get caught up," Delilah promised, giving me one of her bone-crushing hugs that said she cared about me no matter what mistakes I had made.

Together, we eased out at the tail end of the luncheon crowd. Outside the ballroom, I saw Miss Weiner cleaning up the registration table, and I went over to her again. I asked if she lived in the city, and she told me the name of her modest neighborhood.

"I wonder if you might have lunch with me sometime?" I asked.

She was suspicious, I could see, but reluctantly she said, "Okay."

I handed her my card. "My fiancé's daughter is serving in the army. I'm trying to find a way for them to have a closer relationship. I thought maybe you'd have some advice for us? Help us understand her better?"

Her face brightened, and she dug one of her own cards out of her wallet.

"Next week I'll have more free time," she said, handing it over with a friendly smile. "I'd be happy to help."

"Thank you very much. I'll be in touch."

I walked out of the hotel feeling better, but as soon as I hit the sidewalk I remembered where I had to go next.

To see Gus.

Chapter 16

The guys at the sports desk boosted my confidence by looking up from their computers in unison as I walked by and giving me a round of silent applause. I gave them a smiling salute in return. Maybe men weren't supposed to whistle anymore, but it was nice knowing I could still turn a head now and then. I blew a mental raspberry at Zephyr.

Gus's intern was not at her desk. Maybe she had finally decided working at the *Intelligencer* was not worth the aggravation. I could hear Gus storming around his office, shouting on his cell phone.

I knocked once and let myself in.

He scowled at me but kept shouting.

I left the door open and leaned against the windowsill, crossing my ankles to wait for the shouting to end. On his desk lay assorted mail. One large padded envelope had been torn open. A small framed photo stood on his desk. I peered closer and saw it was a picture of Gus in a brief bathing suit, water streaming off his broad shoulders, goggles perched on top of his head. He held a fishing spear aloft with a bright red fish skewered on it. Behind him, an outdoorsy blonde in a bikini raised a triumphant fist. She seemed to have a lot of very white teeth. A brilliant sun shone down on the transparent blue water around them.

Gus ended his call with a bellowed, "Bring me a story I can print, damn you, or I'll find somebody who will!"

When he shut off the phone, I said, "Have you considered yoga?"

"Are you suggesting I need to calm down?" He tossed his phone onto his desk. "This *is* calm for me, luv. Are you on your way to a funeral for a rock star in that outfit?"

"Is that supposed to be a compliment? Or a wisecrack?"

Gus didn't answer my question. "How's your houseguest? Have you learned anything about her?"

"She likes to exercise."

"A little target practice before breakfast?"

"I will admit, she seems overly interested in Michael."

Gus laughed. "That should keep him on his toes. Did you tell him about her record?"

"I warned him, yes. He seems to think he can handle her."

Gus closed the office door. "He's handled worse, from what I hear. And now he's breaking up the family. Causing a bit of a stir among the hoodlums."

"Is that your next headline?"

"Precisely how much do you know about the Abruzzo family? Enough to get you indicted?"

I glared in silence.

He said, "Big Frankie is safely tucked in jail, and so are his other sons. But the cousins are the violent ones, right? And what about your thug's missing brother? Little Frankie?"

"He's dead."

"Presumed dead. That's different from dead."

"What are you asking, exactly?"

Gus paced the office. "You've been holding out on me, Nora."

"I have less than nothing to say to you about Michael. Or his family."

"Not about him. Your nephew's been arrested for Starr's murder."

Once again, Gus had distracted me before thrusting his sword for the kill. It took me a second to collect myself. "He was not arrested. He's being questioned."

"When were you going to tell me about him?"

"I wasn't."

"That's honest. How long do they plan to question the kid? Until he cracks?"

"He's cooperating," I said. "He's trying to help the police get to the bottom of this terrible crime."

"Good spin," Gus commended me. "People might believe it for another day, but soon we're going to think you're covering up for the boy, and that he's guilty as sin."

"Rawlins is innocent," I said. "Let's move on."

"I'm thinking of running him as our headline in the morning. 'Blue Blood Boy Pitches Pitchfork.'"

"That would be doing a disservice to your readers," I snapped. "And you'd just have to retract it in the next edition. Why don't you use last night's fire for your headline?"

"People like to read about other people, not smoldering manure. The only thing that's happened in this damned case is your nephew. So I'm running with him."

I was on my feet then, too, circling Gus. "Is this your way of pushing me again? Forcing me to give more information before I'm ready to divulge? What about you, the seasoned newsman? Don't you have any new information?"

"Have you learned anything useful or not? Who are the other possible suspects in Swain Starr's death?"

"I've been thinking about Marybeth."

"The first wife? That's boring."

"She had motive. She was angry with her ex-husband about family issues, and the missing pig. Her genetic research was important to her, but Swain stole the pig before she was finished."

"She has an alibi."

"We don't know that for sure. She threatened Swain earlier in the day, and the bullet that whistled past my ear was the real thing. She had intent."

Gus picked up a red marker and went to the wall where the large sheets of newsprint had been haphazardly taped up. He scrawled, *Marybeth: Motive, but no opportunity.*

"All right, all right," I said. "You want to go with Zephyr."

In large, sweeping letters, he wrote Zephyr's name on the next sheet of paper, then looked at me expectantly.

I snatched the marker from his hand. "She had opportunity, right?"

"Right. The police report I acquired—without any help from you, by the way—says she checked into her hotel long after the murder happened, which gave her time to kill Swain before she dialed room service."

While Gus stood back, I scribbled the time factor on the paper. "Zephyr has a history of violence, too, obviously. But no motive. Why would she kill Swain?"

"Do you know any married couple that doesn't have at least one unresolved problem? Surely she gave you some insight into her marriage while cozily staying in your home?"

"She wanted a child," I said, throwing caution to the wind. "Swain didn't, but he recently had surgery to reverse a vasectomy."

"Ouch."

"His recovery was taking time, though, and she was impatient. If he had refused to reverse the vasectomy, I could see why she might have been angry. But he did it for her, so there goes her motive."

Gus took the marker from me and wrote, *Disagreed about children*. He said, "Anything else?"

We were standing uncomfortably close, so I stepped back two paces. I wasn't ready to tell him about Swain's paying his son to stay away from Zephyr. That story would make ideal tabloid headlines. Gus would jump on it faster than he could spear a sport fish. Instead, I said, "What about Porky? What information do we have on him?"

Gus wrote Porky's name and spoke as he continued to write. "We know Porky and his father didn't get along. I can vouch for the consequences of disagreeing with your father. Witness my exile in these distant lands. We're also not sure where Porky was at the time of the murder. And he's an unpleasant bloke, isn't he?"

Although I wanted to ask Gus more about his family situation, I tried to force myself to focus on Porky. But the father-son dynamic buzzed around in my head like a persistent bee. Not just Porky and Swain, but Michael and his violent father. Now Gus and his alienating dad. Rawlins and his lack of a father at all. It had to mean something.

I said, "I'm not so sure about Porky's unpleasantness anymore."

Gus swung on me, tall and very close. "Change of heart where Porky is concerned?"

"Oh, he's still an unpleasant person, but yesterday I saw a different side of him." I tried to remember something specific about Porky's desperate effort to keep Zephyr. "He was—well, pathetic, actually. He wants to be loved. And I don't think he's had much of that in his life."

Gus rolled his eyes. "Do I hear violins?"

"He was an unwanted child," I insisted. "His father made no secret of that all his life. Porky came back to

Philadelphia—not to be reunited with his family, but because his TV career died. He's desperately trying to make a living at what he knows—performing children. It's a distasteful career, yes, but he's doing something, not sitting around waiting to be pampered by his wealthy family. You must see something noble in that."

"Noble?" Gus tossed the marker up and down, eyeing me. "Don't tell me you admire the little pig now?"

"No," I admitted. "I don't admire him. But I do feel sorry for him."

"Could he play Oedipus in this family drama? Could he have killed his father?"

"My instinct says no. I don't see the rage in him."

"Rage," Gus said thoughtfully. "What would you know about rage?"

"I assume it takes rage to kill someone, that's all." Thinking about finding the keys at the crime scene, I added, "And this killer had to be composed enough after the murder to throw blame, too."

His interest sharpened. "What do you mean by that?"

"The police suspect my nephew. That didn't come from nowhere."

"Do you know something you're not telling me?"

"Quite a bit," I said frankly, and smiled. But I wasn't going to tell Gus any more just yet. "Another person I'd like to know more about is Tommy Rattigan."

Gus threw the red marker on his desk and grabbed his jacket. "Rattigan, the restaurant owner? I haven't had lunch yet. And I'd like an opportunity to study that outfit of yours in more detail. Let's go."

Which was how I found myself being ushered to a table by a young hostess who seemed charmed by Gus's Aussie accent.

"Did you play rugby?" she asked him as he pulled out a chair for me.

"Of course," he said, making an effort to be pleasant. "Why do you ask?"

She hugged the menus and released a besotted sigh. "I think of all Australian men without their shirts, playing with big sticks."

He laughed and chucked her under the chin with familiarity. "You mean lacrosse."

"Do I?" With a giggle, she presented him with a menu and as an afterthought dropped the other one in my lap. She drifted away with a starry-eyed smile on her face.

"Get your big stick under control," I said when we were seated and alone. "That girl is too young for you."

"I like older women anyway. Give me a woman with experience, perhaps one insecure enough to let me have what I want without too much fuss, and I'm a happy man."

Instantly, my annoyance with the hostess evaporated. I said, "Do they teach you how to be such a pig in Australia? Or is that an American misconception?"

"It's my gift. Speaking of pigs." He raised his gaze to the boar on the wall over my head. "Did Rattigan kill that one himself?"

"Worried for your own safety?"

"Not worried, but," he said, "now that you mention safety, there's something I've been meaning to ask you."

I waited while the server's assistant came and poured water into our glasses. When he went away, Gus said, "Has your gangster boyfriend got somebody following me?"

I couldn't help smiling. "I don't believe Michael has spent two minutes thinking about you, let alone having you followed. Why?"

Gus shrugged. "Nothing I can confidently say is evidence of fact. But I have a feeling there are a couple of goons with their eyes on me."

I glanced around the nearly empty restaurant. The lunch hour was long past. Only a few diners remained, and they were older ladies, none of whom looked more threatening than those in my grandmother's bridge club. "This minute?"

"No, but this morning when I came to the office. And last night, when I went out."

"Out?" I asked. "Not home?"

"Out," he repeated, then frowned at the menu. "What shall we have?"

I scanned the menu. I had missed lunch at both my earlier events, and suddenly my stomach gurgled. Everything on the list looked delicious to me. All that mattered was how soon it could appear on a plate and I could be attacking it with a fork.

The waiter came, and Gus ordered a beer. I requested an iced tea. Gus hummed while studying the menu with interest. The waiter came back a heartbeat later, drinks on a tray, and told us the lunch specials. Thinking of my waistline, I reluctantly ordered a salad of foraged greens with two grilled scallops on top and the lemon vinaigrette on the side.

Gus proceeded to cross-examine the waiter until I thought the poor man might cry. From what river had the trout come? How was the duck breast prepared? Where had the tomatoes been picked? Were the mushrooms imported, too? How long ago? And the fennel. Was it local? Gus displayed a gourmand's expertise by his questions, and I noted he wasn't a rugged adventurer from the outback who ate his mutton from a stick. He had grown up the son of a rich man. He was a gentleman of more refined taste than I had first assumed. I sipped my tea and listened to him.

In the end, he ordered a hanger steak, rare. He drank three inches off the top of his beer as if the task of ordering had made him thirsty. When the basket of rolls arrived, Gus pushed them aside.

"Back to the Starr murder," he said, getting down to business. "I'm still going with Zephyr."

I tried not to gaze longingly after the bread basket. "She grew up poor. As a teenager, she killed her father at their home in West Virginia. Other than—"

Gus nodded and twirled his finger for me to continue. "Tell me what else your boyfriend learned about her."

"What makes you think Michael had anything to do with that information?"

"You said you couldn't quote your source. You have a certain protective tone in your voice when you mention him. Ergo, he learned the details about Zephyr. Come on. There must be more."

I ticked off on my fingers what I knew. "Zephyr got into beauty pageants, then modeling. We know she traveled to Paris and Milan. You say she killed two boyfriends, which brings her victim count to three. You also say she was paying the Saudi police for silence, and I got the impression she had financial problems. Maybe she paid off more people to keep quiet? She wanted a child—maybe to ensure she'd get some child-support income if Swain died—and her husband was doing everything he could, even enduring surgery and an unpleasant recovery period, to give her the baby she wanted. But none of that adds up to a reason for her to kill Swain. So let's forget her for a moment. Let's talk about Tommy."

"You get a glow when you talk about murder. Did you know that? Maybe that's why you're attracted to your thug. Crime turns you on."

I ignored him. Since we were sitting in Tommy's restaurant, I kept my voice low. "Tommy had a serious disagreement with Swain Starr over the production of pigs. He thought Swain had betrayed and cheated him when their prototype pig went missing. As a sidebar, I believe things aren't quite on the up-and-up in Tommy's kitchen."

Gus groaned with exasperation. "The man's such a bore, he puts me to sleep. I'm only slightly heartened to think he has something interesting going on. Could he be a shady character underneath the dull facade?"

"Gus, Tommy and Swain thought they could raise a perfect pig from something Marybeth had bred. But instead of obtaining it in a civilized way, they stole it from her. At least, that's what I think happened. Tommy and Swain stood to make a lot of money from what they obtained from her, but also I think they both wanted credit for bringing this miraculously delicious pig to the table. When the lynchpin of the breeding stock disappeared, Tommy blamed Swain. Marybeth blamed Swain. I don't know who Swain blamed."

Gus had been frowning at me. "I'm with you so far. What's your point?"

"Maybe Tommy killed Swain over the pig disappearance. The pig was his big chance. His means to be famous and save his restaurant."

"His rescue was coming from a pig?"

"Your father has his newspaper empire, not exactly a pristine one. But I presume you'd be angry if somebody tried to steal it from your family. Or," I said, "would you rather just forget about working and go spearfishing instead?"

He smiled into my eyes. "I might spear the empire myself someday."

"Who's the blonde in the bikini?" I asked.

"My ex-stepmother," he replied coolly. "My father's third wife. She's great in bed."

I took another slug of iced tea, and we regarded each other. I wondered under what circumstances Gus had been chased out of Australia. I could probably find out by using my own little black book of contacts.

Meanwhile, he looked very attractive sitting in the restaurant with young hostesses staring dreamily at his broad shoulders. Even seated at a small table, he cut a manly figure. His hair looked burnished from the sun, and his smile had a devilish twist at the edges.

His gaze dropped appreciatively to my suit. "Does the jacket component of that outfit come off?"

"Not in public," I said.

If he was disappointed, he didn't let it show. He drank more beer and set the glass back on the table. "I notice you're better motivated to work on this case now. Protecting your nephew?"

I made a conscious effort to stop thinking about how attractive my editor was. "He's a good kid with a lot of potential. He doesn't deserve what's happening to him."

"Where there's smoke, there's fire."

"If there's smoke, somebody's blowing it in his direction."

"A conspiracy? To frame your poor, innocent nephew? That seems a little far-fetched, luv."

"Rawlins had no reason to kill Swain. At the moment, I think Tommy could be our man. He claimed he was out foraging when the murder happened, but can he prove it? And since he's a Rattigan, we know he can get angry. We need to find out how much of his life depended on the success of the pig."

"Hmm." Gus seemed to take my theory seriously. "You mentioned things aren't quite on the up-and-up with this restaurant. How well do you know your way around?"

"I've been in the kitchen area, if that's what you're asking."

Gus leaned forward, elbows on the table. Anyone watching probably thought he was about to share an intimate confidence. "That's exactly what I'm asking. You could find Rattigan back there? This afternoon? Now?"

"I suppose so, yes, if he's here." Uneasily, I asked, "Why?"

From the pocket of his jacket, Gus pulled a small cardboard box, the size in which a jeweler might package a ring. He popped the box open and upended it. Into his hand fell a small black object—something electronic, no bigger than a nickel.

"What is that?" I asked.

"A bug."

"A—?" I looked into his face and found him meeting my gaze directly, suddenly serious.

"It's a sophisticated electronic listening device. I want you to take it back to the kitchen and find Rattigan. I want you to put it in his pocket or somewhere—any-where—so we can listen to what he has to say."

"Are you kidding?" I demanded after a heartbeat.

"If we can listen in, we may hear what he has to say about Starr's death. If you're right, we might get a full confession."

"Is this legal?"

"Do you ask Abruzzo questions like that?"

"We can't do this!"

"It's not legal," he agreed.

"More important, it's wrong. We'll get caught. We'll go to jail."

"You won't get caught. And nobody goes to jail for this kind of thing anymore. Slap on the wrist, pay a fine, it's done. Besides," Gus said, "do you want to save your nephew's neck? Or not?"

Before I could speak, our waiter returned. Or, I thought it was our waiter. An instant later, I realized it was Tommy Rattigan who appeared beside us, buttoned into his chef's jacket, sweat on his dark face.

"Hardwicke?" he said.

Gus had palmed the bug before Tommy's shadow quite crossed our table. He glanced up, friendly. "Yes?"

"You son of a bitch. I want you to stay away from my sister!"

Tommy hauled back and slugged Gus across the jaw and sent him sprawling out of his chair. Before Gus could scramble up from the carpet, Tommy bent down and seized him by his lapels. He dragged Gus up to a half-sitting position and tried punching him again. He had powerful strength in his arms, but Gus's advantage could have been his greater size and quicker reflexes. But Gus couldn't get up off the floor. They struggled, grunting, and then Tommy let fly another blow that glanced off the side of Gus's head. I leaped to my feet and grabbed my iced tea, prepared to fling it on them as if they were a couple of snarling dogs. But Gus fell back on the carpet, no fight left.

Standing over him, Tommy pointed a trembling finger at Gus and snapped, "And get the hell out of my restaurant!"

He stormed off, red-faced and breathing hard.

I looked down at Gus. "Stay away from his sister?"

Gus stayed where he was, looking up at me and rubbing his jaw. "I guess I should have mentioned this earlier. The man with Marybeth Starr the night her husband was killed? That was me."

Chapter 17

We went outside. On the sidewalk, I spun on Gus. "You slept with Marybeth Starr? She's twenty years older than you are!"

"She's an attractive woman. Eager for male companionship. Divorcées and widows often are. Cuts down on tiresome preliminaries. She was a tigress in bed."

"You are," I snapped, "a total snake!"

"I blame you," he said. He had scooped the ice out of my iced tea and wrapped it in one of the restaurant's white linen napkins. He held the makeshift ice pack against his face. "Listening to you and your thug humping in the closet, then seeing you afterward—the look in your eyes and the well-shagged wobble in your usually ladylike walk—it gave me the urge. I left your house and drove down the road a couple of miles and saw the silver Mercedes parked outside a bar. So I went in, and she was having a drink. A big drink. She wasn't you, but she wasn't bad. We had a good time together. She is an experienced lover, just my type."

Boiling inside, I turned and walked half a block. He matched me stride for stride. I said, "You spent the whole night with her?"

"Why does that matter to you?"

"It doesn't matter one iota to me," I snapped. "But the

police are going to ask about your timetable. You're her alibi!"

"Our timetable wasn't as brief as yours in the closet."

"It's not a closet," I said, feeling completely ridiculous and knowing full well that he was goading me again. We were stopped at a traffic light, and two more pedestrians appeared around us. They glanced uneasily at the dripping napkin Gus held against his face. Then their expressions turned suspicious when they looked at me. I was almost sorry I hadn't punched him myself. At least I could have enjoyed the satisfaction. The light changed, and they both walked hastily across the street. I stayed where I was.

So did Gus. Still clasping the ice pack to his jaw, he said, "We didn't spend the whole night together. There's always a scene in the morning, and I'd rather get to work than try to make peace with a weeping woman."

"Spare me the details of your sex life."

"Are you jealous?"

"For heaven's sake!"

"Do you and the thug like sex in the morning?"

I almost told him Michael liked sex day and night, often both, but I had just enough presence of mind to hold back.

"Anyway," Gus said, "she needed a pick-me-up. The silly cow was upset about her husband's new farm, and she'd had some kind of career setback, so it was natural for her to turn to—"

"What kind of setback?"

"I wasn't interested enough to ask. It doesn't matter. She's not important. We're in good shape now."

I turned to look at him at last. "Who's in good shape?"

"You and me." He showed me the empty box. "You don't really think I'd let a weenie like Tommy Rattigan knock me down, do you? I faked it and slipped the bug into his pocket. If he says anything about the murder, it'll be recorded. We can start listening any minute."

I stared at him for a second, my mouth open. The ease with which he broke the law shouldn't have shocked me—I'd had plenty of time to get used to Michael's occasional walks on the wild side—but I was stunned just the same. In his handsome suit and tie, Gus hardly looked like a criminal, but that was exactly what he was—a low-down, dirty criminal who could have done his job by taking the ethical high ground, but didn't bother with that.

I snapped my mouth shut and swallowed the lump of disgust in my throat. "I'm going to walk away now, and I don't want you following me."

"Oh, enough with the outrage."

"I have an event to attend," I said with more calm than I was feeling. "And you need to go back into the restaurant. You need to tell Tommy that you accidentally dropped something into his pocket and you want it back."

I must have spoken with more ferocity than I thought.

"Okay," Gus said, nodding, full of contrition.

"You can't pull that kind of cowboy stunt here. This isn't some Third World town where you can make up your own rules. It's Philadelphia, the birthplace of the Constitution!"

"I know," he said.

"Go get that bug back."

"Right."

I left him on the corner holding the ice to his swelling face. I walked across town to my next event.

Since I was within walking distance of a place I'd learned about from Michael, I went a little farther and pushed through the door of a giant pawnshop on the edge of South Philly. A clerk looked up from a computer and nearly knocked over his own chair to get to me fast. When I asked after the proprietor, one of Michael's shady friends, I was told he was off the premises. The clerk stood behind glass cases full of glittering watches and abandoned jewelry, trying to look down the black lace of my cleavage.

It was time to do something about our financial situation, so I pawned the earrings Todd had given me. I walked out with two hundred dollars. I could have taken a cab with that money, but I decided a continued austerity plan was good for me, so I walked the rest of the way to my evening event.

Even though I'd made a detour along the way, I arrived fifteen minutes too early for the party and grabbed the first waiter who walked past. "Are there any appetizers?"

He must have seen I was as ravenous as a wolf, because he provided me with a plate. I took it out to the garden and ate while trying to put Gus out of my head. Maybe he wanted to sell newspapers, but bugging a suspect was way, way out of my comfort zone. I wanted nothing to do with it. I only hoped he was taking my advice at that very moment and returning to the restaurant to retrieve the listening device.

Somehow, I doubted it.

The party was a small cocktail affair in the magnificent home of a friend of mine, Angelica Gump, a pipeline heiress. Angelica championed a scholarship fund for foreign students who wanted to study in the United States. Any student who wanted to study American law could apply for a grant from her foundation. She gave considerable money to the fund every year, and she threw an elegant party on her patio to encourage other contributors.

I sat on a carved marble garden bench and brushed my fingers through the pink peonies that had been massed in twin flower pots on either side of the bench. Where must peonies be shipped from at this time of year? I wondered how many meals Michael could put on a table for the price of those peonies. But extravagances like flowers encouraged big donors to give more money. So I understood the strategy.

My phone rang.

When I answered, Emma said, "Where are you?"

I told her. Then I said, "I'm not feeling very kindly disposed to you at the moment."

But she had hung up and didn't hear me.

Within a few minutes, Angelica—six feet two in her towering Louboutin heels and a fire engine red cocktail dress—came out onto the flagstone patio and made a beeline for me. She was not exactly beautiful—her family's nose was a spectacular genetic specimen—but she elaborately made up her dark eyes and always looked exotic.

"Nora, somebody said you were here already. Is everything all right?"

I got up from the marble bench as I tried to swallow my mouthful of bruschetta with heirloom tomato and fresh basil. Apologetically, I said, "I missed lunch. I'm starving. I tackled one of your waiters and wrestled him to the ground to get some food. Is he traumatized?"

Angelica laughed. "He'll survive." She gave me a hug and steadied the plate in my hand when I bobbled it. "You look like you just walked out of a fashion magazine—as always. You're a peach to come, Nora. Thanks for plugging our cause in your column."

"I'm happy to do it. I wish more people saw the value in starting scholarship funds. Especially ones like yours that promote a healthy cultural exchange."

Angelica had loved education—we had met in boarding school—and she had earned her first PhD before she was twenty-two. She had hiked all over Kazakhstan in search of new oil fields and spent a summer living on an oil rig in the North Sea to study new seismic technologies. She married a Scotsman, a petroleum engineer, and they promptly had two children. But he continued to live in Scotland, and she kept her impressive house in Philadelphia. I'd heard that my friend had recently jumped into an executive position with a blue-chip company, so travel and a young family hadn't slowed her down.

She linked her arm through mine to pull me down to the raised beds that would soon be overflowing with colorful and fragrant flowers. A large swing set stood on a grassy spot above the rose bushes, and we could see her two beautiful children playing with their nanny.

Angelica waved. The kids—both under four—waved back, but they stayed with the nanny, a tall girl who clearly had the children eating out of her hand.

"That's Brooke," Angelica said. "Our fourth au pair in two years."

"Wow. Why the turnover? Your kids seem to be angels."

"Oh, my kids aren't the reason au pairs leave. They get better offers."

"What do you mean?"

"The competition for truly talented child care is incredible. Can you guess what we're paying Brooke? Almost two hundred thousand a year, plus her own investment account and a car. Not just any car, but the latest Lexus SUV. And I had to outbid three upwardly mobile acquaintances to get her. But she has a master's in early childhood education, speaks French and Italian *and* Arabic, and she makes bath time into a Broadway production, so my children adore her. She's a better mother to them than I could ever be. And she doesn't mind flying with the kids to see their papa every six weeks. So I'll pay the going rate to keep her. What do you think of that?"

"I think I should go back and get a degree in education and learn some languages."

Angelica laughed. "You're lucky you don't have kids, Nora. You can pursue your career as you please."

"Hmm," I said.

With a critical eye she watched her family clambering on the swing set. "I keep thinking I should have waited a little longer. I took almost three years out of my working life at a crucial time. I lost a lot of ground. If I'd waited until I was forty—well, maybe I'd be farther along the career path. Maybe I'd have reached some important goals by now."

I found myself at a loss for words. If I could have chosen, I'd have had children years ago—lots of them—but fate hadn't exactly worked in my favor. Maybe, I thought, I should focus on my work now. With Gus to push me and a friend like Dilly to act as a mentor, I could get ahead as Angelica said.

Briskly, Angelica turned to me. "Now, what's this I hear about sweet Nora Blackbird jumping the tracks? My mother called. She says you're writing outrageous stuff under a fake name in some ghastly newspaper?"

"The ghastly newspaper is my employer, the *Intelligencer*, but I didn't write the articles."

"Thank God. I told Mama it couldn't have been you."

"Well, I provided some of the information. I'm very embarrassed about that, Angie. I'm still learning the ropes. I screwed up this time."

She patted my arm. "At least nothing exploded. In my line of work, when things go bad, there's major destruction."

"I feel as though I lit a fuse, though. So I've got some fires to put out."

"Seeking redemption is good for the soul. You can start by telling your readers how terrific my scholarship fund is. But first, it looks as if you could use a little more food."

I looked down at my plate and realized I had demolished all the appetizers, including a sprig of parsley intended as a garnish. Blushing, I let Angelica lead me back into her home—a once-sedate Federal-style manse that had been splashed with electric colors of paint and Angelica's collection of tribal art. Even though the catering company had taken over some of the private areas, the rest of the house was open to guests, and I mingled.

But instead of making meaningful conversation, I found myself thinking maybe it was better for Michael and me to remain childless for a while. The financial responsibilities that Angelica had outlined were far beyond our means.

I rounded a corner and nearly ran slap into a couple sipping wine in front of Angelica's latest acquisition—a surprisingly ugly painting of the St. Andrews golf course.

I introduced myself and discovered they were Jorge Ramirez, a law professor visiting from Texas, and his new wife, Elizabeth Regner. He had a lively face with dark eyes and a fringe of black hair, while she was slender in a long, narrow skirt and a statement necklace that fell nearly to her waist.

"We're enjoying a few days in Philadelphia," Elizabeth explained, clasping her husband's hand with a smile. "Jorge and I haven't had a honeymoon yet, so we're soaking up the culture here—art museums and cheesesteaks."

"The cheesesteaks may be an acquired taste," Jorge said with a twinkle in his eye, making me laugh.

I gave them a rave review of the new Barnes collection. I had attended a gala there just a few weeks earlier. "I think you'll love the space as much as the art. It's an astonishing collection, and the ensembles Dr. Barnes created are beautiful. You'll be thinking about it for weeks after visiting."

"Thanks—it sounds like just my thing," Elizabeth said.

"Where are you staying?" I asked.

"The Rittenhouse."

I suggested they might enjoy afternoon tea in their hotel. "It's one of my favorites. The restaurant is so pretty. That is, if Jorge doesn't mind tea sandwiches instead of cheesesteaks."

They laughed easily. As a passing waiter offered us appetizers, Elizabeth said to me, "Have one of the figs. They're stuffed with some kind of cheese. Delicious."

I ate one and immediately asked the waiter for another. "I don't know why I'm so ravenous," I said to Elizabeth.

Jorge indulgently watched us chat, but his arm was jostled by a burly oil executive who pushed past, saying he'd played the Scottish course recently and wanted to see the painting. Politely, we listened to him brag about his score and the awful weather and which club he'd chosen for an important shot. Inside, I winced at the idea that the visiting Texans were forced to listen to a typical Philadelphia bore—a very successful businessman who thought his own experiences were far superior to anyone else's. He had obviously forgotten I had already met him, but I introduced Jorge and Elizabeth anyway. He didn't get the hint and proceeded to regale them with more golf.

Which was when I noticed his wife.

I remembered Chen Dan Dan had been a model in Hong Kong before she met her husband. He had whisked her out of the fashion world to become his high-profile spouse. Tonight she looked bored out of her wits, her beautiful face smooth but barely hiding the frantic darting of her dark, wide-set eyes. She held a glass of scotch in her slender hand. Thinking nobody watched her, she drained the glass and looked around for a waiter.

Abandoning Jorge and Elizabeth to their unfortunate fate, I approached her and introduced myself. In my nearly forgotten Mandarin, I said, "I traveled in China many years ago. You must miss your beautiful country."

Her smile bloomed like the sun, and she immediately burst into a flood of language that I barely understood.

I laughed and apologized for my shortcomings, but I had won her over with my attempt to communicate in her native tongue.

She said, "That's okay. It's nice to hear a friendly word. Hardly anyone knows any languages in this country."

"We're terribly provincial," I agreed, glad that her English was far better than my Mandarin. "Everyone I met in Beijing knew two languages. I love your dress."

Dan Dan wore a simple draped frock of black chiffon that swooped around her slim curves, yet managed to flatter her petite height. Somehow, the sharp angles of her short, chin-cupping haircut seemed to echo the shape of the dress. She plucked at one of the pleats and said with a proud smile, "Valentino. He gave it to me after a shoot a few years ago."

"It must have been a thrill to work with him."

"He's a genius," Dan Dan agreed. "And your suit? Dolce and Gabbana?"

"But very old," I said. "It belonged to my grandmother."

"She had style, your *nainai*. Are you in fashion?"

"No, actually, I'm a reporter. I'm taking a few pictures for my newspaper's social column. May I take yours?"

Dan Dan agreed and struck an effortlessly chic pose for my phone camera, one hand on her hip, the other limp at her side, shoulder back. But she projected a lively energy into the lens, and I took the liberty of snapping several photos of her.

Finishing up, I said, "Do you keep in touch with your friends back in China?"

"A few. Most of my family has moved here, though."

"How nice. It must have been hard to be separated by such a great distance."

"Very hard," she agreed. "When growing up, my sisters and I used to fight like—how do you say it?—dogs and kittens? But I missed them so much, so we helped them move to the United States."

"I have sisters, too, and we still fight," I said again, trying to ease her back into the topic I wanted to ask her about. "You knew a lot of designers in China?"

"Yes, but it's hard for the Chinese to make international reputations in fashion. We must look back into our culture, back to find Chinese ideas that translate to the global market. Not many have found the right path yet."

"So if they can't create their own designs, what do they do?"

She lifted her elegant shoulders. "Work for other designers, foreign designers, doing piecework, not whole collections. Learning, making contacts, growing as artists."

I gave up trying to be subtle. "Dan Dan, did you know Swain Starr?"

She blinked at me, dimple gone. "I did not work for Starr. Not that I know of."

"Not that you—?"

"Starr has studios all over China. Many cities. Sometimes many designers use the same facilities, especially in ready-to-wear, so it's a mix-up."

"I see."

She looked around for a waiter. Or maybe for a way to escape our conversation.

Before she fled, I blurted out, "Did he design his own clothes? Or did somebody else do the creative work?"

Dan Dan gave me a cold look. "He's dead now. What does that matter?"

It might matter a lot, I thought. But I decided honesty was the best tactic. "My nephew is in trouble. My sister's son." In a few sentences, I sketched out Rawlins's problem. "I need to know, Dan Dan."

Dan Dan glanced cautiously around again, then lowered her voice. "Swain might have designed some of his sportswear. But not all. It was a well-guarded secret. Many designers work for Starr. He was generous with them, to keep them quiet. Not long ago, though, he stopped paying, and people were resentful."

That might help explain why Starr Industries had faltered in recent years. And why Swain's daughter felt compelled to rush off to China when he died. Had she gone to rehire the many designers who had created the Starr look?

I thanked Dan Dan. I tried to give her my card and agree to lunch sometime soon, but she was eager to forget she'd ever met me. She walked over to her husband and interrupted his epic golf tale by putting her hand meaningfully on his arm. Jorge and Elizabeth didn't miss a beat but wished him good sport in the future.

To Elizabeth, I said, "Sorry to abandon you."

She laughed. "I can handle the occasional bore. Thanks for the museum suggestion. We'll go tomorrow."

I shook both their hands and wished them a happy honeymoon.

Someone grabbed my arm then, and I turned to find myself confronted by one of my father's drinking pals.

"How's the old man?" he demanded, breathing fumes of booze in my face.

While Jorge and Elizabeth eased away, I told him my parents were fine, but I soon found myself trapped into listening about a recent change in the rules of croquet, which I was assured my father needed to know about the next time he was in touch. I was relieved when the front door opened and my little sister blew in as if she owned the place.

Emma spotted me and came over. She was wearing a Versace cocktail dress from Grandmama's collection—a dress I would never wear in a million years, so I'd given it to Em, thinking she might someday have an occasion to zip into it. Like maybe a Halloween party. In typical Versace style, the hot purply pink silk number was cut down to eye-popping depths and slit from her knee up to show the color of Emma's panties if she wasn't careful. The fabric had been slashed and looked as if it had been attacked with a weed whacker. Emma's long legs were spectacular, her cleavage the envy of any pole dancer within five states. Her buff arms showed the results of her recent return to physical training.

In short, she looked like a dominatrix on her way to the senior prom.

Our father's droning friend dropped his glass, and it smashed to bits on the floor. In the resulting flurry of waiters to clean up the mess, Emma pulled me into the foyer.

I said, "Where are you going in that dress? Is Hooters hiring?"

"Never mind," she said. "You gotta come outside."

"Right now I'm not feeling very cooperative, Emma." Michael's description of how she'd chased him around my house was still fresh in my mind. And burning Starr's barn was a crime I couldn't ignore.

She said, "I've got Porky Starr in my truck."

I had been prepared to knock her on her gorgeous butt at the first opportunity, but she took me by surprise. "Porky's in your—? What's going on?"

In the gathering dusk, she hauled me down the brick steps and across the street. Our high heels clattered on the pavement. A taxi screeched to a halt at the sight of Emma. The headlights illuminated the two of us in the middle of the street. Emma was a neon vision of hot pink sex. A man hung out the taxi's window and yelled, "C'mon, baby, light my fire!"

She flipped him a universal hand signal and kept going. To me, she said, "Yesterday after I dropped you off, I went out to Starr's Landing to make sure the farm animals were off the property. While I was there in the afternoon, who shows up at the farm but Porky?"

"What was he doing there?"

"He crashed a car through the gate, but I don't think that was intentional. He's a maniac behind the wheel. Anyway, I think his plan was to tamper with the crime scene."

"Gee, there's a lot of that going around."

"Shut up." She yanked open the door of her pickup, and there was Porky Starr, lolling in the passenger seat, sweaty-faced, half conscious, his bald head shining in the light of the streetlamp. If not for his seat belt, he'd have toppled out onto the pavement at our feet.

I stood in the street, tapping my foot. "What's wrong with him?"

"He's drunk. Loaded. Smashed out of his gourd."

I faced her. "And you?"

"I'm fine."

"Have you been drinking?"

She exploded, saying, "I've got the guy who might be able to clear Rawlins, and all you're worried about is if I've had a beer?"

She looked sober. I just couldn't imagine her putting on that Versace unless she'd knocked back a few strong drinks. She even wore a pair of very fashionable strappy heels. I squinted more closely. Yep. Earrings, too. Maybe even lipstick.

"That's not the only thing on my mind at the moment," I said. "But I'll put everything else aside for the time being. What have you learned from Porky?"

"That he's terrible in the sack."

"Oh, Em! You didn't!"

"No, I didn't," she snapped, voice dripping with disgust. "But he tried. This kid has learned all he knows about sex from watching porn. I don't put up with that shit. Shove him over and get in."

I unbuckled Porky and tried to push him to the center of the seat. Emma went around to the driver's side and pulled him from her angle. Porky groaned. Between the two of us, we got him into position and fastened the belt around him.

I said, "If he upchucks on this suit, I'm going to be furious."

"He hasn't had anything to eat since yesterday."

"Where was he last night when you took your midnight ride?"

"Handcuffed to a bed."

I didn't want to imagine what had transpired between the former child actor and my little sister. I hoped she was kidding. We got into the truck and buckled up. Emma pulled away from the curb.

I said, "Where are we going?"

"Just listen." While she drove, Emma lit a cigarette. "After I found Porky sneaking onto Starr's Landing, I rode Twinkles back to your place; then I drove up the road and found Porky hiding in some bushes, watching the farm. I took him to a bar and got him liquored up.

And we talked. We talked a lot. I know more than any human being should have to know about how to con suburban mothers out of thousands of dollars in the hope of making their kids famous. I mean, what the hell? Would you want your kids earning a living by doing kitty litter commercials? Making asses of themselves on reality TV? Not to mention a whole other world of degradation. Do you have any idea what Porky has in mind for the twins?"

"Advertising chewing gum?"

"No. Twins are the hot new thing in X-rated movies. First chance he gets, Porky wants to measure their dicks."

"Oh my God!" Appalled, I said, "They're not even fourteen! I don't want to think about my nephews without their clothes on, let alone—"

"I know, I know. We gotta get Libby off this kick, and fast."

Porky tried to speak. He managed a couple of disjointed syllables and dozed off to sleep again. His head lolled against my shoulder. I tried not to shudder.

Emma said, "And I found out who invited Rawlins to the party at Starr's Landing."

"Porky?"

"Nope. Zephyr."

Again, I was surprised. "Why would she invite Rawlins? Does she even know him?"

"Porky introduced them. He got all squirrelly when he told me about that."

Emma found her destination, and she pulled into a parking lot. She shut off the engine and pulled her six-pack cooler out from behind her seat. She said, "Hand me that bag on the floor, will you?"

"Why are we here?" I looked out the windshield at a hotel sign. We had come a little more than a mile out of the city, I guessed. The hotel was nothing fancy, the kind of place where salesmen stayed for a night while on business. Emma had pulled into the only check-in parking space. Through glass doors, I could see people wheeling suitcases around a brightly lit lobby.

I hefted a backpack off the floor. It felt lumpy inside and gave a clink of metal. But instead of giving it to Emma, I hugged it against me. I said, "I'm not cooperating yet."

Emma's expression hardened. "Hand me the bag, Nora."

"Tell me what's in it first."

She cranked down her window and pitched her cigarette out into the darkness. Then she made a swipe for the bag, but Porky slumped between us and hampered her effort.

I unzipped the bag and peeked inside. Even more thoroughly confused, I lifted out a piece of equipment—plastic and metal with a cone at one end and something like a trigger at the other. A medical device. Or an instrument of torture.

I gasped. "Em, what in the world have you been doing to him?"

"I haven't done a damn thing to him! It's a breast pump!"

"A—? What are you doing with a breast pump?"

"What do you think?" With both hands, she indicated her substantial cleavage. "I've been pumping!"

"You—? Why?"

"For the baby, of course! Hart and his idiot wife were feeding him formula, but he has a—like, a delicate stomach. So the real thing, you know, makes him feel better. And I thought the kid ought to have the extra nutrition from breast milk. It has all kinds of good, like, benefits."

"So that's what's in the cooler? Breast milk?"

"Well, yeah." Emma was starting to look sheepish. "I

pump, then bottle it and freeze it at the Rusty Sabre. They've got a big freezer there, and Jay keeps an eye on it for me. A couple times a week I drop off a supply so the kid can, you know, drink it."

"Em, that's—I'm surprised." Flabbergasted was more like it. "I thought you didn't want to have anything to do with your baby."

"I don't. I'm not. I just—twice a day I have to pump myself like a dairy cow or I feel like I'm going to explode. And I'm already starting to leak." She pressed her forearms to her breasts and held her breath to stem the tide of what surely must have been a substantial flow. "So you have to wait here with Porky while I go into the bathroom and take care of it."

I put the pump back into the backpack. "The toy you've been looking for. The Filly Vanilli thing. Is that for your baby, too?"

"He's not my baby."

"Is the toy for Hart's baby?"

"Yeah," she said. "He likes music. I thought the Filly Vanilli would be a nice, you know, going-away present."

I was glad to be sitting down, because I probably would have fallen over otherwise. I held out the backpack. "Okay, go. I'll babysit your passenger. Then we're going to have a discussion."

She eyed me with a gratifying amount of trepidation. "I can guess what that's about."

"Yes, you can," I said dangerously. "Michael told me what happened between you two. But first, go pump. Here."

"Thanks," she said, grabbing a strap. "Just one more thing."

"Yes?"

"If you tell Libby about any of this, I'm gonna kill you."

The last thing either of us wanted was a weakness that Libby could jump on the way a night owl comes screaming out of the darkness to sink its talons into a helpless field mouse. She would be relentless with Emma—giving advice, offering unwanted opinions, the works. I didn't envy Emma the difficulty of keeping her secret from our pushy older sister.

She slammed out of the truck and disappeared into the hotel, leaving me with a softly snoring Porter Starr.

So Emma hadn't been able to give up her child as easily as she pretended. Three months later, she was still pumping—and delivering milk to the home of Hart, her lover, and his new wife.

I tried to put myself in Emma's shoes. I found myself remembering the long months of her pregnancy. Her hormones had made her überemotional. She had spent months constantly hungry, and eating day and night. She had lost her waistline early and developed an enormous belly fast.

As I counted up her list of symptoms, suddenly the sky opened up over my head, and a bright light penetrated my thick skull. The illumination electrified every nerve ending in my brain, and the angels sang. I put both hands on my stomach as the shock dissipated into woozy amazement.

When Emma returned and got behind the wheel, she took one look at my face and said, "What's wrong?"

"Em, we need to find a drugstore."

"Sure." She started the engine. "Now?"

"Right now."

"What for?"

I swallowed hard. "I'm pretty sure I need a pregnancy test."

Chapter 18

I felt foolish for having missed the signs. But I'd spent nearly a year after a heartbreaking miscarriage trying to get pregnant, with no results. Every month, I'd dreaded the recurrence of my period. Eventually, it had gotten so depressing that I stopped keeping track of the dates. For the last few weeks I must have been firmly in denial. When I started gaining a little weight, I assumed it was because I couldn't resist all the food Michael had lovingly made for me. Lately, when I hadn't felt great in the morning, I'd assumed I was suffering the aftereffects of discovering a dead body.

But now I suspected otherwise.

And the possibility made me giddy. Elated. Also a little scared. But definitely eager to find out for sure if I was carrying a baby at long last.

Unfortunately, when I came out of the drugstore with my plastic bag, Porky Starr had begun to regain consciousness.

"Yo," he said woozily when I climbed in beside him. "Who're you?"

"Doesn't matter," I said. "We're not a long-term thing."

While struggling with my seat belt, I fumbled the bag, and it upended. Into his lap dropped the box containing the home pregnancy test.

His grabbed it, and his eyes widened. "Yo! Not you, too? Did we do it, baby? How were you?"

"Me, *too*?" I repeated, holding the box up so he could see exactly what it was. "Do you know who else needed one of these things?"

He tried to collect his wits by shaking his head adamantly. "No way I'm talking, yo."

Curious, Em said to me, "What's up?"

To Emma, I said, "I found a pregnancy test in the car Rawlins was driving. And the test was positive."

"You've been holding out on me, Sis."

"I thought if anyone had information that shouldn't be mentioned to the police, it was better if I kept it to myself."

"So? Who's pregnant? Besides maybe you?"

"I assumed Rawlins. Libby said he had a girlfriend."

She looked surprised. "Hasn't Libby had the Talk with him yet?"

"Of course she has. And she started giving him condoms before he hit junior high. He must have made a mistake."

"A very big mistake." Emma wasted no time grabbing Porky by his ear.

"Hey!" he cried.

"Shut up, nimrod. You're in no position to deny us anything at the moment. Who's pregnant?"

"Nuh-uh," he said. "That's nobody's business but ours, yo."

"Yours?" I asked. "Not Rawlins's?"

"Rawlins? You mean the kid with the cool car?"

"You don't even know his name?" I cried. "He's under suspicion of murdering your father!"

Blearily, Porter rubbed his face with both hands. "I could use something to get my buzz back, yo. You girls have any good stuff on you?"

"Listen, Yo Yo," Emma said. "I'm gonna stuff something down your throat in a minute, like maybe my fist. Who's pregnant?"

He let out a whine of frustration and finally said, "Zephyr."

"Zephyr?" Emma and I said in unison.

Em said, "Who's the father?"

Porky began to turn green before our eyes. "Yo, I think I'm gonna be sick."

"Tell us who the father is. You? Or her husband?"

"C'mon, I'm gonna blow!"

I bailed out of the truck and helped Porky to the pavement. He staggered over to some bushes at the edge of the parking lot, and the next minute we could hear him dry heaving.

Emma stayed in the truck, but she was shaking her head. "He's a moron. But a stubborn moron."

"I don't think we're going to get any more information out of him," I said. "Zephyr's hold on him is too strong, and she's dangerous."

"Huh?"

"Zephyr has a surprisingly long record when it comes to murder." The idea that the black widow might be pregnant gave me the willies. "I say we go to Blackbird Farm and regroup."

"You got it," Emma said. "Climb in. He can find his own way home, yo."

Emma spun the wheel and pointed the truck toward Blackbird Farm. I said, "Or maybe we should be going to Hart's house first? To drop off the contents of your cooler? You put on that dress just for the occasion, didn't you?"

She grinned at the road ahead. "Yeah, maybe I did. To show him what he's missing."

I didn't like Emma's habit of dating married men. It had come too close to home for me when she tried to seduce Michael. I knew that kind of behavior suited her—good sex without commitment or the risk of intimacy that she found so difficult after the death of her much-loved husband.

But I said, "Did you ever think to try the opposite tactic?"

"What tactic?"

"Show Hart what you've got on the inside, Em." As she stayed silent, I said, "Michael told me. About asking you to leave the farm."

"He didn't exactly ask," Emma said. "And, okay, I deserved it."

"You did. But I know what you were doing. And it wasn't just looking for quick sex."

"Mick's a sexy guy."

"Don't be flippant," I said. "I'm being serious here. He may come from the wrong side of the tracks, and he may have done some bad things, but Michael is surprisingly dependable."

"He's a good guy," Emma agreed quietly.

"Yes," I said. "So I know why you wanted to turn to him. You need someone in your life who doesn't run away when things get difficult. Is Hart that kind of man?"

Emma's jaw was tight as she drove, as if she didn't trust herself to answer.

"When you find someone you really want, Em, you have to open up first. You have to show your tender side, too."

She snorted. "I don't have a tender side, Sis. What you see is what you get."

"I see a woman who's pumping milk for a baby she gave away. A baby she hoped to forget about."

"The alternative is sore tits."

I shook my head. "Part of you can't let go of that child. Part of you wants to be with Hart and your baby. But you haven't told him that, have you?"

"He doesn't want to hear it. He's with Penny now."

"Is he really?"

"He married her! He made his choice. And he has the kid, too, so what else is there?"

I heard the anger in her voice. Also a note of vulnerability. More gently, I said, "You had something wonderful with Jake, Em, and now you're afraid to try again. I know exactly how scary it feels to throw yourself off that cliff again and wonder if somebody's going to catch you."

"Hart's not the type to catch anybody." The acid was back.

"Then why do you like him so much?"

"I dunno. Maybe I don't." She slammed the steering wheel with her fist. "I hate the mess in my head!"

In the resulting quiet, I said, "I'm worried about you, Em. About what you said last night. About not having anything left to lose."

She let out a bitter laugh but didn't answer.

"Setting fire to Swain Starr's barn Em, that was a terrible thing to do."

"Not if it protects Rawlins."

"We could have found another way," I insisted. "A way that didn't include committing a crime. We know Rawlins didn't kill Swain Starr. Eventually the police are going to figure that out, too. But destroying property was wrong."

"Nobody was there. Not so much as a piglet. Besides, if Zephyr wants to rebuild the barn, she has more money than God to do it, and she'll employ half the county again to make it perfect."

"That doesn't make what you did—"

"Nobody would have known it was me if you hadn't come traipsing out to talk to me last night."

"You're off the rails," I said. "You're taking bigger and

bigger risks. First it was riding dangerous horses, and now it's lighting a match to gasoline. You're breaking the law! What's next?"

"I can take care of myself. It's Rawlins I'm worried about. Do you think he was at the farm the night Swain was killed?"

At last, I told her about the keys I had found near Swain's body.

The news made her curse. "You found his keys, and I found his jacket? I was right to guess there might have been more of his stuff at Starr's Landing. What the hell was Rawlins doing?"

"I hope he wasn't there at all. I think Porky was there. I think Rawlins lent him the car—there was a new scrape on the bumper, and Rawlins would never have put a tiny scratch on that vehicle. That's why I think Porky had the car that night. Maybe Porky killed Swain and left the keys and the jacket to implicate Rawlins. And I think Porky was the one who went to the hotel with Zephyr. At least, I hope so. The other option is that Rawlins was with her that night, but that doesn't seem likely. Does it?"

"I dunno. Maybe. Back up. Porky doesn't seem smart enough to throw blame and plant evidence."

"I know." I slumped in the seat and rubbed my forehead. I hoped my hormones hadn't scrambled my wits. "There's another possibility."

"I'm listening."

"Maybe Zephyr killed Swain."

I filled in Emma on Zephyr, the serial killer supermodel.

"Holy shit!" Emma barely kept her truck on the road. "And you left her alone with Mick?"

"Michael has half his father's crew stationed at the house, plus a new bodyguard. I don't know why, but they're prepared for D-Day."

"Yeah, things are hot in Mob Land. Down at the gas station, all the guys are pissed off about Mick shutting down the gambling. With the March Madness basketball tournament coming up, he's making a big dent in everybody's income. There's a turf war going on. One dude shot another one outside the Dairy Queen."

"Oh, Em!" This news horrified me.

"He's alive. Took a bullet in the butt, nothing serious, which shows they're probably amateurs. But there's something big brewing. If all the bad guys settle their differences and unite to push Mick to do what they want, it could get ugly." She caught sight of my face. Hastily, she said, "But hey, don't worry. You and Mick, you're out on the farm, surrounded by the hired muscle. You'll be fine."

I fervently hoped she was right.

At Blackbird Farm, there were extra cars parked behind the house. I didn't recognize most of them, except a state police cruiser. Emma was right. Something big was definitely stirring in the underworld.

"Another poker night?" Emma asked, pulling up next to a plain black sedan that had to be government owned.

"I don't think so."

She rolled down her window and lit a cigarette. "About changing tactics," she began, blowing smoke away from me. "With Hart."

"Yes?"

"You really think that's . . . worth a try? Tonight?"

"It depends on what you want from Hart," I said. "If you're hoping for something besides sex, maybe leaving the triple X duds at home would be a worthwhile change of pace. For once, you could talk to him instead of getting naked."

She eyed my Dolce and Gabbana—sexy, but more sedate than anything in her closet. I could see her weighing her options.

I said, "Want to switch?"

"You serious?"

"C'mon," I told her. "I will if you will."

In the darkness, we unzipped and undressed. I helped her into the black suit with the pencil skirt, and she looked great. Her shoes were all wrong, so I gave up my kitten heels, too. It was more of a struggle getting me into the hot pink Versace, but we managed.

Emma gave my décolletage a long look. "Wow. You really must be pregnant."

My head spun again, and I laughed. Grabbing my drugstore bag, I said, "I'll let you know what I find out. Meanwhile, good luck with Hart—if that's what you want."

I jumped out, and she put the engine in gear. I barely had time to close the passenger door before she pulled away and tooted her horn. I watched her go, wondering if I was aiding and abetting adultery. Or helping her decide one way or the other if Hart was a man worth fighting for.

I went up the flagstone walk in Emma's shoes, which, a size too big, were making me a little wobbly. I let myself in the back door. Zephyr and Dolph sat on either side of the kitchen table, staring deeply into each other's eyes, as if trying to make a psychic connection. He was munching on an apple. She was picking raspberries out of a bowl and eating them one by one. But the thing that hit me was his size—a good four inches shorter than Zephyr.

When I closed the door a little too hard, she tore her attention from Dolph and blinked at me, docile as a cat.

She said, "That's not your usual look."

I wasn't the only transformation. The kitchen was overflowing with fresh groceries. There were bananas on the counter, fruit in the bowl, a basket full of onions. The canned goods hadn't been put away yet. Three more paper bags of supplies sat on the counter, as yet unpacked. On the floor sat a fifty-pound sack of something labeled PREMIUM SWINE FEED. Even Ralphie was going to eat well tonight.

"Who went shopping?" I asked.

Dolph dragged his gaze from Zephyr's, and he finally looked at me. What he saw made his eyes pop. Unable to speak for a second, he jerked his head toward the living room. "The boss."

Where had Michael gotten the money to splurge like this? Had he gone to a pawnshop, too?

I didn't bother asking Dolph. I could hear male voices in the living room. I followed the noise, and when I teetered into the room, I found myself in a crowd of men: Cannoli the Younger, Ricci the cop, Michael's parole officer and more—including one stern-faced person in a state trooper's uniform who turned out to be a sour-faced woman. I stopped dead in the doorway.

Conversation ceased, and all heads swung my way.

Everybody gaped at me as if I had grown—well, not two heads, but definitely two ginormous breasts. If anyone in the room had any doubt that I might have married into the mob, my entrance must have convinced him. I was spilling out of the top of the dress, and the slit up my thigh threatened to expose Brazil. I must have looked like an exaggerated Hollywood version of a good fella's gun moll. All I needed was some chewing gum to crack and a pistol to wave around.

Michael was the first to regain his wits. He headed toward me, an expression on his face I didn't recognize— astonishment, but something else, too. There was bad news to hear.

He tried to sound soothing as he touched my bare shoulders. "Hey."

"Is Rawlins okay?"

"He's fine." But there was something very wrong, wrong, wrong, and everybody in the room was waiting for him to tell me. Michael said, "Nora—"

As long as they all pegged me for some kind of New Jersey floozy, I interrupted him, raising my voice and glaring up at him as if ready to flay him alive. "Then just what the hell is going on between you and my sister?"

Everybody froze all over again.

Michael said, "What?"

"You heard me. I want to know how long you've been playing around with my sister." I braced my fists on my hips and let the pink dress do the rest of the talking.

Michael cleared his throat and turned to the group of people who were now staring at us with a mixture of trepidation and amusement. Michael said to them all, "Mind if I have a minute alone with Nora?"

The woman in uniform shook her head. "Sorry. Not now. I've got orders to—"

"Oh, come now, Officer," Cannoli said. "I could argue a case for spousal immunity, so you might as well give them a few minutes to—er—settle a domestic matter."

I grabbed Michael by his shirt. "Let's go."

Half a minute later, we were alone in the scullery.

He took me in his arms. "I think they bought it. Good thinking, sweetheart." He was distracted by my dress, though, and his hands traveled instinctively down my curves. "You look fantastic. But this wasn't what you were wearing this morning."

"It's Emma's. We switched."

His eyes widened. "You saw her? Talked to her?"

"Yes, and although we haven't settled anything where you're concerned, at least we're speaking. And I think your virtue is safe for a little while."

"Whew." He pulled me into a quick hug but said with more urgency, "Listen, we don't have much time. Here."

From inside his shirt, he pulled a fat envelope. He pressed it into my hands.

"What's this?"

"Cash. A couple thousand. It should be enough to—"

"Where did you get this kind of money?" My own recent experience with a pawnshop told me he'd have had to part with something very large to get such a vast sum in return. If he had pawned an item, it was far more than a mere laptop computer.

"I caught a break today," he said, trying to smile. "I made payroll, too."

"What kind of break?"

Something hardened in his blue eyes. "Do you want to cross-examine me?"

"If it's none of my business," I said, just as firmly, "just say so."

He relented. "The night when the leak started under the sink again, you cried about it, and I just couldn't stand—I borrowed it. From my family."

I frowned. I hadn't been crying about the leak, but I supposed that was the way he saw it. I said, "Your father's in jail. So are your brothers. Did the money come from your Pescara cousins?"

"No. C'mon, I had to do something. We couldn't keep going the way we were. For one thing, we need money to pay lawyers."

His talk of lawyers frightened me. I was also unnerved by what borrowing from the Abruzzo family might mean.

I said, "I took my diamond earrings to Uncle Sam today. There's two hundred dollars in my handbag."

He closed his eyes and cursed. "I don't want you hocking your stuff."

"They weren't important. Parting with them was easier than—Michael, what have you done? Tell me."

My expression made him gentle his grasp on me. "It's not that bad. Complicated, that's all. It killed me to ask people getting minimum wage to wait for their paychecks, but putting everybody out of work by closing the gas stations was worse—and then you crying over a little more water on the floor. It was the last straw. So I worked it."

He "worked it." I knew the phrase. He used it when he spoke on the phone when he thought I couldn't hear.

"Will you have enough to pay everybody again next week?"

"Yes."

So he had borrowed a lot of money—not just enough to help us through until my paycheck arrived, but enough to keep his business afloat for a while. Holding the envelope, I searched his face and knew he was holding back more.

"Don't be upset," he said quietly, cupping my shoulders. He couldn't meet my gaze. Or maybe my cleavage was just too astonishing to ignore.

I laid the envelope against his chest. "There's talk in town that people are ganging up against you. Emma says one man has already been shot at the Dairy Queen."

"He was an idiot, a small-time punk, nothing to worry about. That won't happen here, not with the guys out front." He pushed the envelope back at me. "This is a short-term solution, but at least we've got enough cash to get us through what's coming. Kiss me. Because it's going to be a while before we can be together again."

He pulled me close. I felt his mouth brush mine, but I turned my head away to avoid a real kiss. The walls of the scullery seemed to press in around us. I said, "Not here."

"What? Why not?"

I tried to laugh. "I may never be able to kiss you in this room again."

"What's wrong with it?"

I sighed. "There's so much to tell you. But—Gus Hardwicke heard us."

"What do you mean he heard us?"

"When we were in here on Saturday. After the party. He knew what we did. He told me about it Monday morning. Held it over my head, actually. Got me off balance and then . . ."

Michael's voice sounded hard. "Then what?"

"He pushed me into investigating this stupid murder. He wants to make it a big publicity thing for the *Intelligencer*. He thinks it can be his Watergate. And he's pushing me hard."

Michael's face darkened. "What the hell are you talking about?"

Someone knocked on the other side of the door and called to Michael.

I said, "It doesn't matter. He's been a jerk for the last couple of days, and I—I just don't want to think about it. Not now. When will I see you again?"

"I don't know. This may take a couple of days. You just have to keep your head, okay? Don't get emotional, or they'll use it against you. If you can, try to make an ally. Use your sense of humor, but don't be a smart-ass. And Cannoli will stay with you. Do whatever he says."

"Cannoli is staying here? Why? Why won't he be with you?"

Another knock—more insistent this time.

"They're not arresting me, Nora," Michael said. "The cops are here for you."

Chapter 19

The state trooper took me outside to the cruiser, holding my arm in her clammy hand.

"Don't I have time to pack an overnight bag?"

The trooper opened the door of the cruiser and gave me a pitying look. "Honey, you won't need a suitcase where you're going."

As she eased me into the backseat of the car, I suddenly said, "Where's Ralphie?"

"Who?"

"Our pig. Michael, where's Ralphie?"

There was a crowd watching—more police and Michael's posse, half of them ogling me in Emma's weed-whacked Versace. Michael was trying to muscle his way past Cannoli, who held him back. He called, "Don't worry. Ralphie's around here somewhere."

Panic started to rise up from inside me. There was too much happening too fast, and I was rushed by humiliation and fear for Ralphie. I said, "I think he's missing. He wasn't here this morning. Wait," I begged the cop. I knew it was my hormones talking—my panic was misplaced—but I couldn't stop myself. "Please let me look in the barn for our pig."

"Lady, you're certifiable."

She slammed the back door of the car, and I met Michael's tortured gaze through the window. He was angry

and sorry and worried—all the emotions that overwhelmed me every time he was arrested. My heart
twisted as Cannoli blocked him. Otherwise, he looked as
if he might storm the cruiser.

At the state police barracks, they ushered me into a small
room with a table and four battered folding chairs. One wall
was mirrors, just like on television. I presumed they were
one-way windows with stone-faced detectives lurking on
the other side. The woman asked me if I'd like a soda.

"Diet Coke? Maybe a Sprite?"

"No, thank you."

"Sure?"

The thought that she was setting me up to suffer made
me mad. But I told her I'd be fine, and they left me alone
for two hours. Probably to wear down my resistance before asking questions. I tried to remember Michael's advice. What had he said? Stay calm. Find an ally. Was there
something else? About being a smart-ass?

Problem was, the room was cold, and I was inade-
quately dressed to say the least. I paced to keep myself
warm. I kept hearing doors open and close, and I wondered if the police were taking turns looking at the idi-
otic woman in the skimpy dress.

I tried to think, tried to imagine what questions they
intended to ask me. I tried to come up with reasonable
answers, too—especially to inquiries that involved Rawlins. I wasn't going to lie. But I had to be careful.

Eventually, Cannoli was permitted in the interroga-
tion room with me. The first thing he did was take off his
suit coat and sling it around my shoulders. It smelled of
sandalwood and felt blissfully warm.

He avoided looking at my cleavage and said kindly,
"Let's sit down, Miss Blackbird."

"I think we've reached the stage where you should
call me Nora."

He put his hand out and smiled. "I'm Armand."

Armand? Really?

His hand was very warm, and I shook it gratefully.

He said, "Keep in mind you're only here to answer questions. You're not in any trouble. And I have lodged appropriate objections to the treatment you've endured already."

"I'm fine. Just—cold."

"Please sit down. We'll talk."

I perched on a freezing metal chair while he explained things to me, but I will admit I didn't have the wits to process much of what he said. I had been invited to answer questions regarding Swain Starr's murder, he told me. The state police claimed they wanted to know more about what I had observed at the crime scene before it burned, but Cannoli felt they were on the hunt for other information. Perhaps something that would incriminate Rawlins.

Or Emma, I thought.

"So I'm working it," he said.

There was that phrase again. "Working it." To me, the words had nefarious overtones.

He said, "They have to charge Rawlins within another hour or let him go. They're questioning him again in a few minutes, and then they want to talk to you."

"Rawlins didn't do anything wrong. I'm sure of that."

"Can you prove it?"

"No," I said quietly. "But I know more about other people. People in Swain's family."

"Like who? You can tell me. I'm your lawyer and I'm on your side."

"I've been researching Zephyr for a story. We have—my editor and I have uncovered information that Zephyr may have killed three people before. Her father in West Virginia and a boyfriend in Italy and somebody else in Dubai."

Cannoli's brows rose. "Do you want me to tell the police?"

"I can't prove that information, not unless my editor has learned more since I last spoke with him. But I think we should take it seriously."

"We should." He considered it all, then said, "Sharing it with the police would be an act of good faith they might appreciate. I'm sure they would have discovered it eventually, but this particular jurisdiction is hampered by a lack of manpower and resources."

"Then you'll tell them for me?"

"I'll give them the basics, but the details will be better coming from you. Right now I need to go listen while they question the boy. I'll get back here as soon as I can. Meanwhile, can you sit tight?" he asked.

"How much longer?" I said, still shivering.

He tried to mask his concern with a neutral expression. "I'll see what I can do."

"Have you talked to Michael?"

Cannoli smiled a little. "Only every ten minutes."

Of course Michael would be worried. "Tell him I'm fine, please? I don't want him getting upset enough to leave the farm. Not while he's wearing his monitor."

"Don't worry about him," Cannoli assured me. "Taking care of your own mental health is the best thing you can do for the both of you."

He knocked on the mirrored window, and a moment later someone opened the door for him. They left me alone again. Another agonizing half hour or more elapsed before I heard more noise out in the hallway. Raised voices this time. Someone shouting with anger. With my heart in my throat, I backed against the wall just as the door burst open.

Libby launched herself into the room, crying, "They're torturing you! Police brutality! Your civil rights have been violated!"

My sister was dressed in one of her running suits.

Printed on the T-shirt were the words STAY HUNGRY. She had taken the time to blow-dry her hair so that it curled seductively around her shoulders. Her lipstick was fresh, her mascara lavish.

"Libby—"

"Ma'am," said the harried female state trooper. "Ma'am, I have to ask you to step outside, please."

"Excessive force!" Libby shouted, flinging her hands in the air. "Psychological abuse! Verbal intimidation! It's un-American!"

"Lib, I'm fine."

My sister swept me up in a hug and crushed me against her bosom until I couldn't help but inhale the vapors of her most seductive perfume. "They've brainwashed you, poor darling!"

Two more uniformed troopers crowded into the small space. Libby released me and spun around. She flung herself at the nearest trooper—a male, I noted—and cried, "You can't torture my sister this way! I insist you release her immediately!"

Their struggle didn't last long, but there was a lot more shouting, and Libby's clothing went askew until her maroon lace bra made an appearance. The male state trooper backed up against the wall, hands in the air. I caught a glimpse of Cannoli in the hallway, one hand clapped over his eyes.

In a few minutes I found myself locked in a cell.

With Libby.

"This wasn't the outcome I intended at all," she fumed. "I thought we'd sit down with some of those charming policemen for a discussion, but they aren't charming at all, are they? How am I supposed to find an escort for the Farm-to-Table dinner if I'm locked up?"

"You came here looking for a dinner date?" I demanded.

"Well, naturally my first goal was to take Rawlins home. And to rescue you, too, Nora. But I—what on earth are you wearing?" She blinked at the Versace.

I hugged Cannoli's jacket closer around me. "It's Emma's dress."

"Why are you wearing it?"

I must have been more addled than I thought. The words popped out in a long, shuddering burst before I remembered I wasn't supposed to tell. "Because Emma's delivering breast milk to Hart's house, but I thought she was looking a little trashy, so I suggested she switch dresses with me, and she ran off to talk to Hart." I knew I wasn't making any sense. I felt the pressures of the day start to boil up inside me like molten lava. "Now—now *I'm* the one looking trashy, and there's a gangland war starting, so I've got rejects from *The Sopranos* hanging around my door, plus a serial killer in my house, and besides all that I might—I might be—" Okay, I was on the brink of hysteria, but I blurted out the rest anyway. "I might be pregnant!"

"Oh, darling!" Libby gathered me up in another comforting hug. "What wonderful news! Not the gangland part or the serial killer thing, either, but a new baby! Nora, you must be overjoyed!"

"Overwhelmed is more like it." I sniveled against her bosom.

She held on tight and patted my back. "You've had a hard time ever since losing your baby last spring. You probably gave up hope, didn't you? And you want a family so very badly. Well, here's proof that everything turns out right in the end, don't you think?"

"I'm in *jail*!" I cried.

"Well, yes, that's a small glitch," Libby agreed.

"I haven't even taken a test yet. And Michael—Michael might be *dead* in front of the Dairy Queen before I get out of this hellhole!"

As if I were talking perfect sense, Libby said soothingly, "It's not a hellhole, is it? Why, it's actually quite
comfortable. Here, sit down on this bed. It's kind of like
camp, don't you think? Shall we think of a camp song to
sing? What was that one about friends being silver and
gold? I always thought it was about jewelry, but it wasn't
exactly, was it? Or the dog named Ringo."

"Bingo," I said with a sniff. "Which reminds me, Ralphie is missing."

"Ralphie?"

"Michael's pig. Libby, I'm afraid somebody's going
to—to *eat* Ralphie!"

I burst into tears all over again.

Libby patted my back a while longer. "I don't think
you need to bother taking the test, Nora. You're definitely pregnant."

She settled me on the bunk and sat beside me until I
pulled myself together.

Finally Libby asked with exaggerated calm, "Emma's
pumping her breast milk?"

I wiped my eyes with a crumpled tissue pulled from
Libby's handbag. "I wasn't supposed to tell you. Emma's
going to tear me limb from limb for blabbing. But, yes.
For her baby."

"Well, we should have guessed. I mean, no woman
could have her figure without some major hormone imbalance. And what about her situation with Hart?"

Her steely gaze worked more efficiently than a lie de-
tector. "She doesn't know where she stands. And I'm not
sure we should be encouraging them, Lib. I mean, he's
married."

"Happily?"

"How do we know? He could be deliriously happy,
and maybe Emma's causing a problem by interfering.

Besides, I'm not convinced Hart is good for her. He's been a bit of a rat."

Libby wagged her head in dismay. "Emma should never have given up that baby. She needed more time to think it through."

"She had nine months!"

"Well, she needed more than that. She should have given the baby to you and That Man of Yours."

I felt another wave of hormonal hysteria rise up. "If she had, the baby would have starved by now. We're totally broke, and if I'm pregnant, it's the absolute worst timing. How can we raise a baby if we can't even afford cheese sandwiches? There will be diapers to buy and vitamins and—and—my God, Libby, people are paying nannies these days in *stock options*!"

I lost my self-control again and blubbered.

Finally, Libby said, "In the first place, you don't need a nanny. With That Man of Yours stuck in the house all the time, he'll be the perfect father. You can be the breadwinner."

"If I don't get *fired*! I'm supposed to be writing a profile tonight, and instead I'm *incarcerated*!"

It wasn't like me to fall apart, but a demonic hurricane of estrogen seemed to well up from inside.

Libby sighed. "Nothing wrecks a woman's health and mental well-being like pregnancy."

From the next cell, a voice said, "Tell me about it."

Libby and I sat up and looked around.

She was young—somewhere between sixteen and twenty—with badly highlighted blond hair whooshed on top of her head and popping out of a plastic clip. She had more eye makeup than a fortune-teller and bitten-down fingernails painted bright blue. She was not very tall, slender of limb and pouty of lip, wearing a T-shirt stretched to its limit over a pregnant belly big enough to hold triplets.

She stopped chewing her gum long enough to say, "Who's the serial killer?"

"My houseguest," I said. "She's trying to kill my fiancé."

The girl nodded, as if it all made sense. "Anybody got a cigarette?"

Libby said, "How about a Tic Tac instead?"

The girl blinked her crusty black eyelashes as languidly as a cow and said, "Yeah, sure, why not?"

Libby dug into her handbag and handed the plastic container through the bars to the other cell. She said, "I'm Libby, by the way, and this is Nora, my sister."

"Yeah, hi." She lazed up from her bunk and took the container without thanks. She snapped open the Tic Tacs with her thumbnail. "I'm LinZee. L-i-n, capital z-e-e."

With a bored kind of concentration, she poured Tic Tacs into her palm, then proceeded to line them up on the gigantic curve of her belly. "You're not under arrest, y'know. This is just the drunk tank."

"We're not drunk," Libby said firmly.

"Me neither," LinZee said. "This is where they put girls when we get outta hand. They let you have your purse, see? So you're not arrested. You're supposed to cool off, that's all."

"You seem to know the drill," I said.

"Oh, I'm a regular." She gave her belly a long rub, frowning. "I'm just not sure . . ."

"Are you okay?" I asked.

"Oh yeah. I'm just wondering if maybe, y'know, I'm in labor."

Libby and I stared at her. Judging by the size of her belly, when her water broke, it was going to gush like a fire hydrant.

But after a moment of contemplation about labor, she shrugged, unfazed. "Nah, I don't think so."

Libby cleared her throat. "How long have you been here? I'm just wondering if you know anything about my son? Rawlins Kintswell? Is he still being held?"

"The tall, skinny guy with the Mohawk?"

"Uh, no," Libby said. "No Mohawk."

"The short, fat guy wearing the Flogging Molly T-shirt?"

"No," Libby said. "The clean-cut boy with blue eyes and a sweet face."

"Sorry," LinZee said. "Haven't seen that one. Is he cute?"

"Very cute. But he's not looking for a girlfriend right now," Libby said firmly. "And he's innocent. Whatever anybody said about him, he had nothing to do with anything bad. He was a victim of circumstance."

"That's a good line," LinZee said. "Victim of circumstance. In fact, that could be a really good name for our band." She lay back down on her bunk and massaged her mountainous belly. "I'm the lead singer."

"Libby," I whispered, tugging my sister back down on our bunk, "maybe it's time you faced the reality that Rawlins could actually have some connection to—" I caught myself, aware that LinZee was listening to every word. I lowered my voice. "He could have some connection to the unfortunate business on Saturday."

Libby paused in the act of pulling a lipstick out of her bag. "Why would you say such a thing? You know, Rawlins was a perfectly nice boy before he became associated with That Man of Yours."

I experienced a sizzle of temper. "He was flunking school and had more piercings than a carnival sideshow before Michael came along. Without Michael's influence he might have a bone in his nose by now."

Reminded of reality, Libby dropped her lipstick, and her voice wavered. "My poor baby. A fatherless child. He never really had a chance, you know. None of my husbands paid him enough attention."

LinZee asked, "What color is that lipstick?"

Libby consulted the cap. "Virgin Rose."

LinZee laughed. "Lemme see it." She screwed out the lipstick and was studying the color with disappointment. "Do you guys have a lawyer? One that does those *bono* cases? I mean, does he do any cases for free? They have to do that, right?"

Libby said, "What have you been arrested for, dear?"

"I wasn't arrested. I might have been disturbing the peace a little. But it was a mix-up. My boyfriend got a little out of hand at rehearsal. Like he has perfect pitch?" She snorted.

I eyed LinZee's belly and thought he hadn't been the only one who got out of hand.

"He won't get married," LinZee said. "Do you know how hard it is being a single mom?"

"Yes, I do," Libby said. "I'm raising five children by myself."

"The statistics are against us." LinZee pointed at her unborn child. "I mean, this is my second. Unmarried mothers have, like, no chance of getting on *The Voice* or *America's Got Talent*. Or finding a decent job. I'll be lucky to get a shift at the dry cleaner."

"You shouldn't be breathing those fumes anyway," Libby counseled.

"Yeah, well, Declan doesn't want to get married. He said as much when I blew the lyrics on 'Another Bag of Bricks.' He pissed me off. You know how dangerous it is to piss off a pregnant girl? So I kicked him. Well, I knocked him down with the mike stand first, but then I kicked him. But it wasn't really my fault, was it? He—

what do you call it? He coerced me. The good news is his brother is a bail bondsman. Here."

LinZee dug into the pocket of her unsnapped jeans and passed me a grubby business card. On it was printed the slogan of her friend the bail bondsman: YOU RING, WE SPRING.

LinZee said, "What time is it?"

Libby consulted her watch. "Almost eleven."

LinZee handed back the lipstick. "Okay, good, because Declan's gonna bust me out of here. He said he'd wait until I slept it off, and that should be about now."

"You really shouldn't drink alcohol," Libby said. "Not if you're expecting."

LinZee laughed again. Then her expression changed, and her hand went instinctively to her belly. "Hot damn. Maybe I'm in labor after all."

We heard an alarm go off somewhere in the building. It sounded like an insistent timer on an oven.

LinZee gathered up her belongings. "That'll be Declan. He always finds a way to pull the fire alarm."

"I'm pretty sure that's illegal," Libby said.

"Yeah, but it works. Wait and see."

Several police officers came into the hallway outside the drunk tank, and one of them unlocked our door. She said, "Ladies, we're having an alarm malfunction. As a precaution, we're going to evacuate you."

By the time Libby and I gathered up the contents of her handbag, LinZee was already smugly leading the way to freedom.

In the lobby, we came upon Rawlins, who looked paper white and exhausted, but otherwise healthy. Most important, he looked free. His mother threw herself at him with a wail, and I had to content myself with putting my arm across his shoulders and giving him a kiss on the cheek.

He gave me a tired smile. "Hi, Aunt Nora. You look pretty wild. Mardi Gras party?"

To the continued beeping of the fire alarm, Cannoli appeared with a sheaf of papers in hand and announced that we were all free to go due to a minor emergency in the building, but the police requested that we all be open for more cordial questioning at a later time. They were currently engaged in arresting someone for tampering with a fire alarm. He ushered us all outside where Libby gave the keys to her minivan to Rawlins, declaring she was too upset to drive.

Outside, Libby said, "Do you need a ride, or can you find your own way home, Nora?"

She had already observed my lawyer holding the door for me. Ever the gentleman, Cannoli immediately offered to take me back to Blackbird Farm, but said, "There's someone else here for you, however, so if you don't mind me running off, I have to check my son's algebra homework before I go to bed."

"Thank you very much, Armand. For everything, but maybe most of all for your coat." I gave it back to him.

"Think nothing of it," he said as politely as a courtier.

And he left me with the man who waited beside his convertible. It felt surreal, seeing him there in the cold.

Gus Hardwicke allowed his gaze to rest on my barely contained nipples for about half a second and said, "If I'd known you had frocks like that, I'd have tried to kiss you sooner."

I hugged myself. "I'm in no mood for this. Can you drive me home without hassling me? Or shall I hitchhike?"

He opened the passenger door and handed me into the car. When he came around and got in behind the wheel, he said, "I see they released your nephew. For lack of evidence?"

"He wasn't arrested in the first place. He was being questioned. Why are you here? How did you know to come for me?"

He started the car and thumbed the heater on for my benefit. "The police called. Apparently, you decided to tell them what we know about Zephyr. They asked me a few questions on the phone, and I learned you were here, so I toddled along."

"That was a quick trip from the city," I observed.

"Actually, I was a little closer. Why did you spill the beans?"

"If Zephyr is dangerous, she shouldn't be roaming around," I said. "So, yes, I told the police. I'm sorry if that ruined your Watergate plan."

"We're running the Zephyr story tomorrow. How she's under suspicion for killing three men. If the police are going to blab about her past, why wait? I used some of your notes and a lot of my own and sent it to print. Call it a collaborative effort."

"Is my name on the story?"

"Not your name or even a phony name. One of the other reporters did some of the research, so I let him have the credit. I thought you'd want it that way."

"Thank you," I said.

He pulled out onto the road and headed toward Blackbird Farm. "When I heard you were being held here, I thought I might as well come over and see what an aristocrat looks like in handcuffs."

"There were no handcuffs."

"Don't spoil my fantasy."

In no mood for banter, I said, "I think I know why Swain got out of the fashion business. Turns out, he didn't design his own clothes. Maybe never did."

Gus thought fast. "Swain left his business because someone was going to expose him as a fraud?"

"Makes sense, right? He had to get out before the world heard he'd been taking advantage of other designers."

"Or he was blackmailed?" Gus suggested.

"Maybe. Or perhaps the family asked him to leave, hoping to cut down on negative publicity if *Vogue* magazine got wind of the fraud story. I bet his daughter, Suzette, feels it's very important to quiet the rumors before they get started."

"That would explain why Swain retired early, but not why he was murdered."

I had already reached the same annoying conclusion, so I said, "Exactly what were you doing in my neighborhood?"

"I was out for a run in the car."

"Liar. You had another assignation with Marybeth, didn't you?"

"I'm a grown man with healthy urges," he said. "She's willing and not unattractive. She told me all about Starr's vasectomy, as a matter of fact. How he had one back when they were married because he didn't want any more children. How he recently had it reversed, but the outcome was iffy. Not to mention exceedingly painful. The gruesome details were enough to put me off my stride for a few minutes."

"What is it with you and older women?"

"Shy virgins bore me," he said, and glanced my way. "That dress is anything but boring, by the way. But hardly in your usual good taste."

"It's my sister's. Long story."

"Maybe I should meet your sister."

I tried to put Gus and Emma into the same mental picture, but my brain rejected the idea as about as safe as a nuclear blast. I said, "What else did you learn from Marybeth about her ex-husband?"

Promptly, Gus said, "That he resented her having a fourth child after he adamantly informed her he was finished with children. Marybeth has probably run interference between father and Porky all their lives. She rhapsodized about the boy's wonderful qualities to me. Lately Swain and his youngest had some kind of reconciliation. At least, that was her impression."

I thought of the half-million-dollar check sitting on Porky's table—probably bon voyage money from Swain. They hadn't reconciled. They had agreed to disagree again and parted ways. I was too tired to explain it all. Suddenly I wanted to sleep more than breathe the air.

Gus pulled up to a stop sign and braked. He sat for a moment, looking into the rearview mirror. "Do you recognize the vehicle behind us?"

I craned around in my seat, but all I could see was a pair of headlights and the dark, looming shape of an approaching SUV.

"I didn't mean you should turn around and tip them off," he said with some impatience. "I just—well, let's see if they follow us."

He pulled away from the intersection, and the SUV paused briefly before turning another way.

I watched the SUV disappear. "Still feeling paranoid?"

"About your boyfriend putting a tail on me? Just a little."

I wouldn't have been surprised to hear Michael had decided to keep a close watch on Gus Hardwicke. But I said, "Well, obviously, they're not following you now."

"With you in the car, they must know I'm delivering you safely home. Or risking my life by taking you elsewhere for a tryst."

"Home, please," I said on a yawn.

"You don't have to sound quite so unenthusiastic.

What would your boyfriend do if I made a concentrated effort to seduce you?"

"I can fend off a seduction attempt all by myself."

"But what would he do?"

I took the question seriously and thought for a minute about the way Michael's mind worked. Finally I said, "He'd probably have you ambushed when you least expected it. I'm not sure about how much bodily harm would be involved, but it would be a terrifying incident forever seared into your mind. And I'd never hear a single detail about it."

"So you keep secrets from each other?"

"Yes," I said.

"Will you tell him about you and me?"

"There is no you and me."

"Does he tell you everything?"

"There are no other women, if that's what you're asking."

"You seem very sure about that. But I meant about his business. Does the pillow talk include mob secrets?"

"He doesn't have to tell me about his business if I don't ask about it."

Into a short silence, Gus said, "That's interesting, isn't it? A version of don't ask, don't tell. And here I thought all you Americans set great store by truth and honesty."

"Truth isn't always in Michael's repertoire. So I don't push."

"And you can live with that?"

"Yes," I replied, having come to terms with the way things were. To have Michael in my life meant reaching an uneasy impasse on many touchy subjects. I understood that now. His fidelity was faultless. But there were issues—business issues, family issues—that he would always keep close to the vest. And with a child on the way, it was perhaps even more important than ever that I trust him to make the right choices.

"What's this?" Gus said when his headlights lit up the roadblock beside my mailbox. Two gigantic SUVs were parked nose to nose, and a band of dangerous customers hung around in the cool air, smoking cigarettes. When it became apparent that Gus wanted to turn into the lane, they backed off, taking up positions that could best defend the house against invaders.

I said, "Heightened security measures."

"Bloody hell, what for? The zombie apocalypse? Are they armed?"

They weren't supposed to be armed—that was all I knew. I rolled down my window. The man who came over to my side of the convertible was one of the part-time mechanics in Michael's motorcycle shop. I suspected he was the full-time leader of a marauding biker gang. He wore a chain for a belt and had a long, crooked scar on his cheek. If the zombie apocalypse was coming, I wanted this one on my team. I leaned out the window and said to him, "It's just me."

He waved us through, giving Gus the evil eye through the windshield.

Sedately, Gus drove up the lane and around the house. He parked and turned sideways in his seat as I unfastened my seat belt. "Nora," he said.

"Thank you for bringing me home. And for behaving yourself. I'm really not up to fighting with you tonight. I'll be in touch in the morning." I reached for the door handle.

He put his hand around the back of my neck. "Nora."

I turned my head to look him straight in the eye, one brow raised. "Do you have a death wish?"

He kept his hand where it was, gentle, with his thumb extending up into my hair. Quietly, he said, "I was only going to say that you've held up admirably through all this. You've worked hard on the story, and I know you

have learned more than you've told me so far. I'm trusting you to come clean eventually, though, right?"

"Don't ask, don't tell," I said. "Try it on for size."

He leaned a little closer. "Have you ever been to Australia?"

"I get sunburned."

"We have beautiful moonlit nights."

"Good night, Gus. Don't walk me to the door."

I climbed out of the car and walked to the back porch
in the too-high, loose shoes and the skimpy dress with as
much dignity as I could muster. Gus made a spin in the
gravel. I wondered if he was heading back to finish what
he'd started with Marybeth Starr. I didn't think he was
going home to his own bed.

I was just about to go into the house, when another
vehicle roared up the drive and narrowly missed nailing
Gus's car to the pasture fence. Emma's truck.

She braked and climbed out, leaving the engine running. Still wearing my black suit, she ran around to the
passenger door and opened it. She was fumbling with
something inside, so I went to investigate.

"Em, what are you doing back here?"

Over her shoulder, she said, "My conversation with
Hart was short."

"How short?"

"Like, he was having a fight with his wife, so we didn't
have much time for pleasantries."

"What happened? Did you talk? Did you reach any
conclusions about—"

She turned around to face me. In her arms, she held a
baby in a blue blanket.

"Oh my God." I could barely remain standing. "Is
that—?"

"His name is Noah." She had a funny grin on her
face—half giddy, half terrified.

"Emma!"

"Quiet, Sis. You'll wake him up. Although I think he's a champion sleeper."

"What are you *doing*?"

"I took him. Why the hell not, right? His parents don't want him."

"They don't *want* him?" I realized I was holding my hair with both hands, as if to rip it out of my head if one more disaster showed up on my doorstep. Setting fire to Starr's barn was bad. But this was the big one—the colossal explosion at the end of the sizzling fuse that was my little sister.

"With all the shouting, it was hard to tell. Look. Doesn't he have a cute nose?" She tilted her bundle toward me.

I looked at the little boy in her arms, and my panic melted into something almost like sanity. I tried to speak calmly. "Em, do they know you have him? Hart and Penny?"

"I'm not sure," she said. "Maybe. Kind of. Things were a little dicey. So, look, I need some help."

"I just sent our lawyer home."

She dug back into the front seat of the truck and came up with a huge bag. She looped the strap over my shoulder. "Here's the diaper bag. There are diapers and wipes and a change of clothes. And some of my milk, too. It's frozen, but all you do is thaw it out, and you're good to go. I don't know how the bottles work, but I figured you'd know. He's got stomach trouble, so take it easy when you feed him."

"Have you gone completely crazy?"

"And he needs some special kind of vitamin, but I'll have to pick those up tomorrow. I think he can go a day without them."

"Em," I cried, not caring if I woke every baby from here to Siberia. "You can't do this!"

"Yes, I can. I'm leaving him here with you."

She dumped the baby into my arms, and I made an instinctive grab to hold him tight.

Emma had tears in her eyes, but she was laughing, looking both completely insane and delighted with herself. "I gotta go," she said. "I've got a lead on a Filly Vanilli. Black market. It'll cost me a bundle, but you'll see—he's gonna love it. I'll be back in the morning."

"You're going back to see Hart, aren't you?"

She started back around the truck, but she turned. Instead of responding to my question, she said, "How are you? Pregnant?"

"I don't know yet," I managed to say. "Maybe."

She gave a howl of delight. "Way to go, Sis! See you tomorrow!"

"Em!" I called before she jumped behind the wheel.

"Yeah?"

I had a zillion questions to ask her. I wanted to wrestle her to the ground and ask them all—or maybe beat her senseless. But I said, "What's his name again?"

"Noah!"

I watched her go tearing out the driveway. Then I stood for a long time in the darkness, cold in the Versace dress, but somehow hot inside, too. I held the sleeping baby and looked down into his moonlit face, wondering if the day could possibly get any more bizarre. But also thinking there was nothing, but nothing more amazing than a perfect child held close to the heart.

I went into the darkened house and found Michael asleep on the sofa in the dark living room, wrapped in the cashmere throw, his face buried in a throw pillow. The dying embers of the fireplace flickered across his sleeping frame, and nothing had ever looked so comfortable and tempting to me in my life. In that moment, I was overwhelmed by a tsunami of exhaustion, and all I

wanted was to be held in his arms and told that everything would work out soon.

I dropped the diaper bag on the coffee table and put
Noah down in the middle of the big armchair across the
room where he would be safe. Then I kicked off Emma's
shoes and stripped off the Versace, leaving it on the floor.
In my bra and undies, I climbed onto the sofa to wake
Michael as gently as I knew how.

I slid under the throw and wrapped my arms around
his neck. I kissed his bristled cheek and snuggled my
breasts against his chest. He woke up a little and gathered me closer, murmuring something against my hair.
At once I felt him ready to make sweet, hot love with me,
and there was nothing I wanted more at that moment.

But first I whispered, "I brought a surprise home."

Over my head in the gloom, Michael said, "I think it's
you who's gonna get a surprise."

I looked up at him standing over me in the dark, but
at the same time I felt his arms around me, his legs tangled with mine and his hands on my bare back. My brain
couldn't quite make the jump to understanding why he
was both beneath me and standing beside the sofa. It
took a second before the right synapses kicked in.

I gave a shriek and leaped off the sofa in a single
bound. I grabbed Michael and spun around to see who
was the man on the sofa.

A complete stranger sat up with a bleary grin. "You
must be Nora."

Michael eased me behind him and said, "Nora, this is
my brother."

I peeked out from behind Michael at our newest
houseguest. "I—I—I thought he was in jail!"

"Not that brother," Michael said. "This is Frank. Little
Frankie. My dead brother."

"Not so dead." Little Frankie lazed on the sofa, one

arm cradling his head as he smiled up at the two of us. He had Michael's curly dark hair and the same shape to his face. The same lazy-eyed grin, except his eyes were dark, not blue. He wasn't quite as substantial as Michael, not quite as broad through the shoulders and chest. Clutching Michael from behind, I couldn't fathom how I could possibly have mistaken them.

Michael yanked the cashmere throw off his brother and calmly passed it to me. "He's not staying. He'd be out of here by now except for a transportation problem. He'll be gone in the morning."

"Probably," Little Frankie said.

I wrapped the throw around myself. "Why are you here in the first place?"

"I made the drop." Pleased with himself, he stretched like a cat. "I brought the cash, saved the day."

I looked up at Michael. "You borrowed money from your dead brother?"

Grimly, Michael said, "It seemed like a good idea at the time. Stay away from him. He's trouble."

His phone rang in his pocket, and he walked down the dark hallway to answer it.

While I hugged the throw around my body, his brother continued to smile at me with a lazy-lidded, secretive Abruzzo attitude. He said, "Mick didn't tell me you were a babe."

Chapter 20

While Michael muttered to someone on the phone, I hastily gathered up my dress and the diaper bag and the sleeping baby and endeavored to make a dignified exit.

"G'night!" Little Frankie called after me. The throw slipped off me, and he laughed.

From the beginning of my relationship with Michael, I knew he had two living brothers who rotated in and out of jail. But Little Frankie had disappeared a few years ago and was presumed to have been killed by an enemy of the family. I had tried reading through newspaper archives to learn more because Michael certainly hadn't welcomed any discussion of the subject. The details of Little Frankie's disappearance had been hazy.

I guessed his reappearance was supposed to be equally hazy.

When I got upstairs and put Noah in the middle of our bed, the baby gave a yawn and a burp, but didn't wake—a champion sleeper, Emma had said. He rubbed his nose with his tiny fist and relaxed back into sleep. I put a fresh pillowcase down in the Pack 'n Play where Max sometimes slept. Then I changed Noah's diaper. He woke up for that but seemed content to take a long, solemn look at me while I dressed him warmly in a pair of Humpty Dumpty socks and a sleep sack from the diaper bag. The room was already cold and would be colder by morning. When I put him down into the portable crib and covered him loosely with his blue blanket, he dozed off again. I turned off the bedroom lamp, and the crib disappeared into the shadows.

I sat down on the bed, got out my cell phone and called Hart Jones.

When he answered, I was all business. "Hart, it's Nora Blackbird. Please don't worry. I have Noah here with me."

"Hi," he said, sounding rushed. "Can I call you back?"

"Of course, but—well, I just want you to know that he's fine."

"Okay, great. I'll call you."

He hung up on me, and I stared at the phone for a long moment.

"For heaven's sake."

I put the phone down and took a quick shower. I had just pulled my nightie over my head when Michael let himself in the dark bedroom.

He dropped his cell phone on the bedside table and turned to me. Because he hadn't shaved in hours, he had a criminal sort of bristle on his face, but his gaze was warm with concern. "Are you okay?"

"Fine," I said, brushing out my hair. "Armand was wonderful."

Michael looked blank. "Who?"

"Cannoli. That's his name. Armand."

"Really?"

"He's been your friend for years, and you don't know his name?"

"I guess I forgot it." Michael was starting to look a little punchy. "He's been Cannoli since we were kids when his dad was my father's lawyer. Did the cops ask you questions?"

"No, there was a fire alarm that disrupted everything.

I have to go back sometime. But I told them about Zephyr's track record, so they're going to be busy for a while."

"And Rawlins?"

"They let Rawlins go tonight, too. They still don't know who killed Swain Starr. Libby was there, and a girl whose boyfriend pulled a fire alarm—but that can all wait. Michael, why is your brother here?"

He sat down on the bed. "Because Dolph took my car and ran off with Zephyr."

My hairbrush hit the floor with a clatter. "He did what?"

"Dolph quit and left with the supermodel. She said he was just her type and she couldn't wait to be alone with him." Dazed, Michael said, "They stole my car. I imagine they went off to find a hotel to consummate whatever they forged in the last twenty-four hours of staring across the kitchen table at each other. Personally, I think it's only going to last until she sees what he eats for breakfast."

In shock, I stood in the middle of the bedroom floor. "Dolph and Zephyr are an item? Did you warn him about her?"

"I did. He thought I was kidding. The cops showed up about half an hour ago, looking for her. Little Frankie had to hide under a bed while I reported my car stolen. The cops have escalated a full-blown manhunt for Zephyr. Dolph, too, now. Me, I just want my car back. Ironic, huh? Me getting my car stolen."

"Michael." I was dizzy, keeping it all straight. "Dolph and Zephyr?"

"Hey, I couldn't stop them. There was lust in the air. Speaking of which—" He made a grab for my waist and pulled me to the bed. "Every time I saw you today, you seemed to be wearing less than the time before."

"Your brother certainly got an eyeful."

"My turn," he said, tugging at my nightie while pulling me down onto the bed. "Right now I want to stop thinking about everything and just be with you."

I managed to deflect his hands. "Michael, we have a lot to talk about."

"Can it wait until morning? All I want is—"

His plan was interrupted by a little squall from the portable crib.

Michael sat up. "Max is back?"

"No," I said. "This is someone new."

I went to the crib and picked up the baby. He was wide-awake this time, kicking his way out of his blue blanket. He put his fist in his mouth and frowned when it wasn't what he wanted. He had feathery fair eyelashes and the Blackbird dark blue eyes.

Michael stayed where he was, his face slack with surprise. "What the hell is this?"

"Emma's baby."

Michael couldn't speak.

"His name is Noah."

I sat beside Michael and showed him the little boy. "Emma gave him to me in the driveway. I called Hart to say his son was here with us, but he hung up on me. He said he'd call back, but I—well, he sounded very distracted."

Michael still hadn't touched the baby. He said, "Emma kidnapped him?"

"That's what I thought at first, but now I don't think so. Hart was abrupt on the phone just now, but he didn't seem surprised or concerned really, just in a rush. There's something going on, but I don't know what."

"Call him back. Call him now."

"Okay, but—look, I think Noah must be hungry. Emma brought some milk. He has a delicate tummy, so we probably shouldn't let it get too empty. Here, take him, will you? And I'll make him a bottle."

Noah was kicking up a fuss and gave a full-throated yell.

Michael didn't take the baby from me. Instead, he said coldly, "Call the kid's dad."

"I will, but I can't do everything at once. Take him, please?"

Michael moved back on the bed. He shook his head. "He doesn't belong here, Nora. We need to get rid of him. Tonight."

"It's after midnight. We can keep him for a few hours."

"No. Get him out of here."

"Michael—"

"I mean it, Nora. For one thing, the police will have a field day. But more important, it's not good for us having him here, even for a night. It's going to get complicated—you know that."

"It's all right to have your brother downstairs, but not an innocent child? What's wrong with you?"

He made a grab for his phone. "What's Hart's number? I'll call him myself."

I checked and gave him the number, but when Michael punched the keys and listened, Hart didn't pick up.

"I'll try Penny," I said. "Hold the baby."

"I don't want to hold him." Michael got up and backed himself against the dresser.

"What has gotten into you? You play with Max and Lucy all the time."

"Max and Lucy are family."

Noah might have been family, too. Maybe I hadn't realized how hard the decision had been on Michael. His face was stormy.

"Okay, I'll call Penny," I said. "But I'm going to feed him first. I can't talk to her on the phone with her baby crying in the background."

One-handed, I found the milk in the diaper bag and carried it into the bathroom. I ran one of the half-frozen bottles under the hot tap until it was warm enough. By the time I managed to assemble the bottle, Noah was howling. Finally, I got everything right, and he seized onto the bottle as if he'd been starved for days. I carried him back into the bedroom and found my phone again. Michael paced the room while I tried searching for a number for Penny. But I couldn't manage the baby and the phone at the same time. The cell phone slipped from my hand and fell on the floor.

Without a word, Michael finally took the child from me.

Unencumbered, I rapidly went through my phone and flipped through my old day planner before I found a viable number for Penny. I dialed.

She picked up on the fourth ring, sounding sleepy.

I gave her the same quick explanation I had given Hart. "I have Noah here," I said. "He's safe and sound."

"Oh," she said. "Okay."

"Would you like to come get him?"

She yawned. "No. Not right now."

Whatever was going on in her household, I couldn't imagine. I must have said something about talking again in the morning, but she only sighed and hung up.

I tried Emma's cell phone. She didn't answer.

I sat down on the bed. "I think Emma's with Hart."

Michael didn't argue with my theory. "Where?"

"I don't know." I looked over. Michael had Noah in the crook of his arm, and the baby was still sucking down milk like a pro. I said, "I don't know what's going on. I can't imagine what anybody is thinking."

"They're not thinking," Michael said. "They're certainly not thinking about this kid."

He still hadn't called Noah by his name.

Michael's cell phone jingled.

Sounding a little chilly myself, I asked, "What's going on that you're getting phone calls at this time of night?"

"It's a thing," he said, easing Noah into my arms. "A thing I have to do for Little Frankie."

"Because he lent you money?"

Michael didn't answer me. He went down the hall before he took the call.

By the time he came back, I had fed and burped Noah and put him back down to sleep. I brushed my teeth and crawled into bed. I could have crept downstairs and found the shopping bag from the drugstore. I wanted to take the pregnancy test. But I'd have to make my way past Little Frankie. And tonight really didn't feel like a night for celebrating anything.

And I wondered if Michael would welcome the news of a baby. His reaction to Noah's appearance in our home worried me.

I put my phone on the night table in case Hart should call. Or Penny. Or Emma. Anyone who could explain what was going on with the baby in our midst. I turned off the lamp. I was half asleep when Michael slid into the bed and pulled me close.

"You okay?" he murmured.

I sighed, unable to express how many ways I wasn't okay.

He kissed the back of my neck. "I'm sorry about the kid," he said in my ear. "It's just—it's dangerous, him being here."

"Dangerous?"

Gently, Michael said, "I don't want you getting your heart broken, Nora."

I turned into his arms, grateful to hear his words. He kissed my mouth and found a warm spot with his fingertips, and I felt my whole body grow languid at his touch. In a while, he rolled me onto my back and whispered that he loved me. I let him have what he wanted, felt his mouth on me until I gasped, both of us forgetting the complications, the tensions. For a while, we were slow and quiet with each other.

"Better?" he asked when he had finished.

"Yes," I whispered in his arms. "And no. In the morning, we'll talk. Can we talk?"

But Michael was already asleep.

It occurred to me that he had been using sex to try to make everything better, to make me happy. It was his way, like cooking me enormous quantities of comfort food, I thought fleetingly as I drifted off to dreamland. It was easier for him than talking things through.

Noah did not turn out to be a champion sleeper, after all. He woke us up at five, wanting breakfast. I slid out of bed and made him a bottle, but he wasn't satisfied with food alone. He wanted to be entertained, so I took him down the hallway to another bedroom to rock him. He knew my face wasn't familiar, but he studied me and listened to my voice. Finally, when I was singing "Little Bunny Foo Foo," he rewarded me with a big, toothless smile that melted my heart, and I knew what Michael had meant. I was getting attached already.

So I put Noah down in the portable crib and tried to go back to sleep. But he was soon crying again, and this time Michael got up and walked him around while I zonked out for another hour. Eventually I figured it was time to give up on sleep. I dressed, tucked my phone into the pocket of my jeans and took Noah downstairs, tiptoeing past Little Frankie snoring on the sofa.

While I warmed a bottle and toasted the last of the artisan bread, I tried to find the drugstore bag with the pregnancy test inside. I couldn't locate the bag anywhere in the kitchen or the scullery or the laundry room. I began to think somebody had thrown it away. Noah was happy to be carried around, though, and eager for his breakfast. I tried to feed him slowly and burped him twice to ease his digestion. After we ate, I put on the old jacket I kept on a peg at the back door. I wrapped Noah up in a towel from the laundry room and grabbed the jar of maraschino cherries from the fridge. Then we went outside to look for Ralphie.

The pig was nowhere to be found. I left a trail of his favorite treat on the ground, hoping to draw him out of the woods, if that was where he'd gone.

I even walked to the back of the pasture. Emma's ponies, curious about where I was going, followed me along the fence, butting one another, and I fed them each a cherry, too. At the back of the property—where Blackbird Farm's border ran along Sheffield Road—I came upon a muddy set of tire tracks. A vehicle had parked there, I thought, while people walked around. I could see many footprints in the mud, none of them distinct. The scene worried me.

I walked Noah back to the farm and left the empty cherry jar on a fence post before walking down to the end of the driveway where Michael's crew was making a shift change. The new guys came armed with coffee and bagels. A couple of them wandered over and made goo-goo sounds at the baby while their less-social compatriot spat on the road. Noah was fascinated. I asked them if they'd seen Ralphie. They expressed so much concern that I felt reassured they hadn't whisked him off to be barbecued.

As I was starting to walk back to the house, a state police cruiser pulled up next to the mailbox. I went over just as the driver's-side window rolled down. I recognized Ricci.

Almost friendly, he said, "Whattaya got there?"

"My sister's son."

I showed him Noah, and Ricci took off his sunglasses to get a better look. "He's a cute little bugger. I have three boys. With a daughter on the way."

The idea that Ricci could have a home and a family— including a pregnant wife who must worry every time he went to work—hadn't really been a thought that took root in my head before, but it did now. It was a nice change of pace to think of him as a human being.

"Congratulations," I said.

"You don't have any kids of your own yet?"

My heart gave a flutter of hope. "Not yet."

Ricci nodded and resumed his cop face, devoid of animation. "Well, be careful what you wish for."

Where had I heard that before? The words sounded prophetic.

I said, "Did you solve the problem with the fire alarm?"

He made a grimace but didn't apologize for inconveniencing me. "Yeah. It was a bozo. He's in custody now."

With a pang in my heart, I thought of a young mother going into labor without the support of the child's father.

Ricci didn't notice my reaction. "Look, I just stopped by to say thanks for the information about Zephyr Starr."

"Have you found her? Or Michael's stolen car?"

"Not yet. But we did some checking. Her history is certainly interesting. And the arson investigation team has been looking at Starr's Landing. They found a gas can and plenty of accelerant evidence."

I hadn't decided what to do if directly questioned about the fire. I knew I couldn't protect Emma from what she'd done, but technically, Ricci hadn't posed a question. Feebly, I said, "Everything on a farm burns quickly. Hay, straw."

"Yeah. But somebody took the time to make sure the animals were all safely somewhere else before splashing around the gasoline and lighting it up. We're thinking that sounds like Zephyr. She's a big animal lover, right?"

Carefully, I said, "I know she's a vegetarian."

Ricci wagged his head. "Crackpots. You never know what they'll do. Anyway, thanks for your information. The other thing is, we've had complaints about a kid driving erratically in this neighborhood. He was stopped once, so we know who he is. Porter Starr. Has he been harassing you?"

I felt harassed from a lot of sources, but not particularly from Porky. I shook my head. "I know him slightly. He hasn't bothered me."

"Well, he's around. Neighbors have seen him acting suspicious, but we haven't been able to spot him a second time. I guess your security team will keep him out of your hair, but just in case. Be aware."

"Thank you."

We hesitated, neither one of us quite ready to say good-bye. Ricci was taking a good squint at Michael's crew of misfits, as if trying to match descriptions with known criminals.

"Do you have a minute?" I finally asked.

Ricci switched his attention back to me. "What's up?"

"We're missing a pig. He's a pet, actually, but I—I can't help remembering that at the Starr's Landing party, Swain Starr and his former brother-in-law, Tommy Rattigan, argued about another pig that had disappeared. They were partners in raising hogs for restaurants, and Tommy—no, it was his sister, Marybeth, who accused Swain of stealing an important animal."

Ricci considered that tangle of information for a moment. I thought he was going to laugh me off, but at last he said, "So in addition to a stolen car, we now we have two missing pigs? What are you thinking—bacon rustlers in the neighborhood?"

"I know it sounds silly, but—"

"I'm not really pulling your leg," Ricci said with kindness. "Got any evidence?"

I pointed. "Back on Sheffield Road, I found some tire tracks and footprints. Maybe—"

He cut me off at the mention of Sheffield Road. "Hop in. We'll take a drive." He popped the lock on the passenger door.

I got into the front seat with the baby. "I suppose we need a car seat."

Kind again, Ricci said, "We'll be careful."

He was true to his word, driving very slowly as I directed him up the lane, past the house. We got out of the cruiser and walked the rest of the way across the pasture. I showed him the muddy mess I had discovered on the back road.

He crouched down to examine the footprints. He pointed. "Is this what a pig footprint looks like? Or is this a deer?"

I bent over his shoulder. "I think that's a pig. A deer's hoofprint is more rounded and doesn't have these little impressions behind the big ones."

"Lots of boots were here, too. Plus these tire tracks." Ricci frowned at the scene for a long time. When he finally got to his feet, he nodded. "Well, I think your pig has been stolen, all right. And if I had to guess, I'd say he put up a fight. How much did he weigh?"

"A lot," I said, dismayed to hear the trooper use the past tense. "He's a pet, but he's big. His name is Ralphie."

Ricci looked into my face and must have seen the distress I was trying to tamp down. He said, "I'll make a report, start a search. We're busy looking for the model, but I'll check the rendering plants, butchers, meat processors. They don't do much business except during hunting season, so—hey, look, I didn't mean he's, you know, dead or anything."

I wiped a big tear from my cheek. "I'm okay. Just a little emotional. I didn't get much sleep last night."

"That'll happen with kids. Does Porter Starr have any interest in pigs?"

"I doubt he has anything to do with Ralphie's disappearance."

Ricci opened the door to the cruiser for me and drove us back to the back driveway. As I got out with Noah in my arms, he said, "If you think of anything else that might help us . . ."

"If I do, I'll call you."

"Take care of that little guy. Maybe he'll grow up to pitch on my Little League team."

As Ricci drove away, I sat on the back porch steps and balanced Noah on my thighs. I pulled out my cell phone. I showed it to him and let him listen to the beeps as I dialed. I said, "I'm going to call your mama. Both of them, if that's what it takes."

I telephoned Emma first. No answer. I tried Hart with similar results. For some reason, I hesitated to call Penny. Instead, I sang to Noah, wondering what his various parents thought they were doing.

Michael came outside about fifteen minutes later with a gym bag in hand. He was looking annoyed. But he leaned down and gave me a kiss. "Get enough sleep?"

"Nope. How about you?"

"I'll survive." He spoke to me, but he was looking down at Noah. The baby looked back, his eyes wide.

I tipped sideways so the two of them could get a clear view of each other, but I said to Michael, "Where are you going? Church?"

He showed me the gym bag. "I've got a date with

Kuzik. No idea what he wants, but he said to bring sneakers. I overslept, no thanks to that little guy. So I'm running late. With my car stolen, I gotta get one of my guys to take me into town."

I guessed the parole officer had found a basketball game for Michael to join, but I decided to let Kuzik do all the explaining. Instead, I said, "I just talked to the state police. We think Ralphie has been stolen."

Michael gave up being late and sat down beside me. "Stolen? What the hell happened?"

I told him about the crime scene I had discovered at the back of the property, and Ricci's conclusion about what all the tire tracks and footprints meant.

"How the hell did anybody get past my guys?" Michael cursed and said dangerously, "It's time I laid down the law with those mutts. And who would steal Ralphie?"

"Somebody who wants pork chops, I guess."

He put a gentle arm around me. "Don't cry. The cops will find him. That's the kind of crime they're good at solving."

Michael's opinion of police and their crime-busting skills was skewed by personal experience. I wiped my face again and said, "What if it's too late?"

"It's not too late," he said firmly. "I'm gonna put some of my guys on it right now. The A Team, not these idiots."

"I hear Porky Starr has been driving around the neighborhood, too. The police think he's behaving suspiciously."

"You worried about him?"

"He's probably looking for Zephyr."

"Time for the A Team for sure. I need to put a stop to the coffee klatch anyway. Don't worry. We'll have Ralphie back, I promise."

"How can you promise?" I asked.

He kissed the top of my head. "Wait and see. Have you reached Emma yet? Or her married boyfriend?"

"They're not answering their phones. And I'm afraid to call his wife."

"Why?"

"Because last night Penny sounded ... drugged or something."

"You woke her up, right?"

"Yes. She was groggy. Not just a little groggy."

Noah had been watching us intently, and he suddenly gave a yowl for attention. We looked down at him, and his little face split into a grin of pure delight. Michael and I laughed.

Michael sobered first. He said, "Call the mother. Get this kid back where he belongs."

He got up to leave.

I said, "Is your brother awake?"

Michael jerked his head toward the house. "He's coming with me. I don't trust him here with you. Or the kid, for that matter."

I held Noah close. "What does that mean?"

"Little Frankie's always working something." He opened the back door and shouted for his brother.

Little Frankie appeared, rubbing his face and carrying a cup of coffee. The cup was one from the perfect Limoges china collection from the glass-fronted cupboard in the butler's pantry, which meant he'd been snooping in the house. He said, "What's the rush?"

Michael took the cup from him and set it on the porch railing. "You can wait at the diner while I have my meeting." He gave me another kiss. "See you at lunch."

"We have some things to discuss."

He caught something in my eyes. "Good things?"

I smiled. "Maybe so."

He smiled, too, and touched my chin. "It's a date. Meanwhile, be careful. If Zephyr shows up again, the crew is supposed to defend you with their lives. But call 911."

Little Frankie tagged along after Michael, but he shot me a grin over his shoulder.

When they had headed down the driveway to talk to the crew, my phone rang. I checked the screen first. Emma. When I answered, she said her ETA was ten minutes. While I waited, I made myself another piece of toast. I was starving again.

So was Noah. But I realized I had allowed all the frozen milk to thaw, and it was probably not fit for his consumption. I had no formula in the house.

When Emma showed up, I said, "Take off your shirt and feed this child. He's hungry."

Chapter 21

Emma came over and gave her son a cautious inspection. Perhaps involuntarily, she folded her arms over her breasts. "I'll pump, but I'm not gonna feed him directly from the source."

"Why not?"

She gave me a glower. "Because, that's why."

"He's hungry, Em."

"He can wait five minutes." She went out to her truck and came back with her equipment. She disappeared into the bathroom, leaving me to jiggle a fussy baby on my shoulder while I tried to do the dishes.

When she came out of the bathroom, she had enough milk for two feedings. I gave Noah a bottle while she put the rest of the milk in the fridge. Then she came over and sat beside me at the kitchen table to watch from a safe distance.

I was about to ask if she'd had any luck finding a Filly Vanilli, but she spoke first. She said, "Penny's addicted to prescription painkillers."

I almost dropped the baby. "She's what?"

Emma shrugged. "She broke her ankle on the golf course last year and started taking some strong stuff. It got out of hand, and now she's hooked pretty bad. Her family didn't know, and neither did Hart until they moved in together. When I gave Noah to them, it became obvious really fast that she couldn't handle herself and a baby, too."

"Oh no."

"They've been through a string of nannies, but Penny kept firing them when they found out about her drug problem. So she's out of control in a lot of ways."

I tried to absorb this new wrinkle in Emma's life. "What's Hart going to do?"

"He's pushing Penny to try rehab. She doesn't want to go, doesn't see the problem. But he can't be a dad day and night, not with his job. He's up for partner at his firm."

"Which is more important? Becoming a partner or being a father to his son?"

Emma got up and poured herself a tall glass of orange juice from the refrigerator. She drank it down and said, "He told me to take the kid last night. So I did. But after five minutes in the truck, I knew it was a stupid idea." She began to pace the kitchen. "Hell, Nora, I'm in no position to be this kid's mother. Not even for the short term. I'm less mature than he is!"

"You could stop drinking."

"I could, sure. Easy as pie." Barely holding on to her exasperation, she said, "Look, we both know I'm not cut out for this."

I felt a typhoon building over my head, gathering momentum, growing in size like a storm surge.

"Emma," I said when I could make my throat work, "you're not asking me to take this baby. Are you?"

She finally looked straight at me. "Until Penny gets through this addiction thing."

"You know as well as I do that it might never happen. Todd's addiction got him killed."

"You gotta keep Noah at least until Hart figures out something."

"Like whether or not he really wants to be a parent?"

Emma had the grace to look unhappy. "Yeah, maybe so."

I shook my head. "Michael won't do it."

"What d'you mean? He's a natural!"

"He's upset about this, Em. He wants Noah out of the house before he gets back for lunch."

Emma checked the clock on the wall. "That's not gonna happen."

"It's not like Noah is a puppy." I heard my own exasperation and tried to hold on to my temper. "You can't just pass him around until things settle down at home."

"It happens all the time in the real world," she snapped at me, "Maybe it's harsh, Sis, but that's the way a lot of kids live these days. The girl who was in the delivery room next to mine? Remember her? She was seventeen and living in a foster home herself. Social Services took her baby six hours after it was born. I don't know if she's seen it since. Two parents under one roof with three meals a day? That's not the way things work much anymore."

I thought about LinZee, the pregnant girl in the drunk tank. I held Noah and looked down at his downy head. He was sucking on the bottle blissfully, but his gaze locked on mine, full of trust. I felt a tug under my ribs.

"Please," Emma said.

We heard a car in the drive, and a minute later Libby blew into the kitchen, Max on her hip. "You won't believe it!" she crowed with delight. "The twins have an audition! They're up for their first modeling job! And I think they're honestly going to get it! My karma hasn't been compromised after all! I just—oh, look how darling! Who is this?"

Libby bent over the bundle in my arms. Noah spat out the nipple and stared up at her with astonishment that quickly morphed into delight. He gave her his widest grin and began to wiggle all over.

"Oh, you little dear!" she cried. She practically dumped Max into my lap as she snatched Noah from my arms.

Libby wore a lime green velour running suit, and today's T-shirt read, IRONY, THE OPPOSITE OF WRINKLY. She danced around the kitchen, swinging the baby over her head. "Is he yours, Emma? What a sweet baby boy! A little charmer! A lady killer! Oh, how I love the way babies smell! And look at all this hair!"

Max struggled down from my lap and followed his mother jealously around the kitchen. "Da! Da!"

Emma introduced Libby to her nephew and explained about Penny's drug problem. Libby sat down at the table with a plunk, appropriately horrified. "What's going to happen?"

"That's up in the air," I said.

Libby heard my tone. She hugged the baby close and glared at Emma. "You can't leave him here. That would be too cruel."

"For who?" Em demanded, her second glass of orange juice almost gone.

"For Nora, of course! And That Man of Hers isn't made of stone! Emma, you can't be so obtuse. You're toying with their worst fears and deepest emotions—at a time when they're just setting the course of their relationship. Do you want to tear them apart?"

"So what the hell am I supposed to do with him?" Emma cried. "*I'm* certainly not going to take the kid home. I don't even have a home at the moment! I'm living in a bunkhouse."

"Then he must go back with his father," Libby said firmly. "Hart has to grow up sometime, and this is it."

"Da!" Max flung himself at his mother and hung on to her legs. His gaze implored Libby to love him. He was full of need and hope. He just wanted one glance of reassurance from his mom. "Da!"

Libby leaned down and smilingly rubbed her nose against Max's. "It's a baby! See, Maximus? Just like you! Only little! You're a big boy now!"

Max smiled uncertainly.

My throat had tightened with excruciating pressure. But I managed to say, "I think we should all go to the farmers' market in New Hope."

My sisters stared at me as if I'd lost the final smidgen of sanity I had left.

"We need a change of scenery. And I'm starving. I'd like some of that jam those nice Amish ladies make."

Libby stood up. "Cravings! You're obviously pregnant! Eventually, you'll move on to a big bowl of ice cream with sweet pickles. You see, Emma, this would be the worst possible time to inflict added conflict on Nora's relationship with That Man of Hers. They need time to experience the miracle they've created. Here, hold your son. He won't bite. Do you think the farmers' market will have doughnuts? Last October, they had the most divine spice doughnuts. That's probably a seasonal flavor, darn it."

Within a few minutes we were speeding into town in Libby's minivan, Max and Noah strapped into their car seats in the middle, Emma in the back. Libby drove, and I asked about Rawlins.

"How is he doing? Is he traumatized by his brush with the law?"

"He tried to shrug it off, but when we got home, he was a little teary. Which is a good thing. I wanted him to be terrified. He says he needs to sleep for three days, and then he wants to figure out how to become a police officer. Which is not exactly the reaction I had in mind. Honestly, Nora, I could strangle that boy with his own jockstrap. He claims he's clueless about why he was taken into custody for so long, but I know he's lying. If he wants to be a good police officer, he should become a parent first. Now that's training for law enforcement!"

I thought of the pregnancy test I'd found in his car

and remembered Ricci's words: Be careful what you wish for.

Libby nattered on. "I didn't raise that boy to skip college and go directly to some kind of police boot camp."

"He'll change his mind," I said. "He gets a new idea every month. It's probably a good thing to keep reimagining what you want to do with your life."

"Exactly! I'm still doing it myself!"

"And what's the job the twins might get? You said it was a modeling job?"

"Feet!"

"What?"

"A company that makes a cream for athlete's foot! They want a set of teenage twins who have nice feet. They won't have to dance or sing or do anything except wiggle their toes. Harcourt and Hilton have their quirks, but you must admit they have perfect toes."

I couldn't remember anything about their toes, but I said, "That sounds very promising. Did Porky set up that audition for them?"

"Porky!" Libby said with scorn. "Do you know how much I paid that young man? More than a thousand dollars! And for what? No, I was the one who saw the ad about feet, so I did it all on my own. Do you know, I have half a mind to turn him in to the Better Business Bureau. Trouble is, he has up and disappeared."

"He disappeared, huh?" Emma said.

"He doesn't answer his phone." Libby checked her lipstick in the rearview mirror. "But he's probably going to the Farm-to-Table dinner tomorrow—I advanced him the cash to buy his ticket, if you can imagine—so I plan on giving him a piece of my mind then."

"Not to mention getting your money back," I said.

"Oh, I assume that's long gone," Libby replied with more savvy than I expected of her.

From the back of the minivan, Emma spoke up. She had obviously been watching her son, because she suddenly said, "How come he's not sleeping? He's wide-awake. Doesn't every kid fall asleep in a moving vehicle?"

Libby said, "Noah's obviously very bright. He's curious about the world around him. He looks a little like Daddy, doesn't he? Something about his smile. It would serve Hart right if the baby turned out to look just like a Blackbird."

Slightly disgruntled about my lack of rest, I said, "I was told he was a great sleeper, but he was awake half the night, and he's clearly not sleepy now." Noah was fascinated by his cousin in the adjoining car seat. The two of them stared at each other with interest.

Emma said, "Every time I've ever seen him, he's been zonked out."

We arrived at the site of an old flea market, and Libby parked the minivan in the grassy area roped off for vehicles. She pulled a stroller out of the back, and we buckled Max into the seat. We walked up to the farmers' market. Libby carried Noah. I pushed the stroller.

"I didn't think the market opened so early in the year," Libby said.

"It's a special event," I told her. "In conjunction with the Farm-to-Table gala. This early in the season, I don't suppose there will be much in the way of local produce. But I'd really like to pick up some jam."

We made our way through the tented tables of the farmers' market. The path was crowded with locals from every walk of life. Some women with expensive jewelry and recyclable bags on their arms purposefully hustled from booth to booth to pick up exactly what they wanted without socializing. But there were also elderly couples, young families and tourists who meandered more slowly from booth to booth, gathering in small knots to exchange pleasantries.

I waved at the young couple who had bought a dilapidated ranch house just down the road from Blackbird Farm. They had spent the winter working on the inside, I'd heard. Lately, I had seen them on ladders outside, trying to repair their own roof. I couldn't help noticing the young wife paying for a loaf of Amish bread with food stamps.

At once, I thought of the small field of Blackbird Farm nearest their house. It hadn't been cultivated in years, but perhaps my neighbors would like to put in a garden. The idea grew in my head. Maybe other neighbors would like a patch of the farm to grow vegetables. I could knock on doors in the next week or so to invite them to join a kind of community garden.

The booths didn't have any local produce except for one table that featured bundles of fresh asparagus. The supply was dwindling fast, so I bought some for dinner, thinking if we were lucky, Michael and I might be alone together this evening. I hoped we'd have celebrating to do.

Other tables featured a kaleidoscope of local offerings. Honey in decorative jars, baked goods sold by shy Amish girls, canned vegetables of every description—salsas and hot pepper jams along with beautifully jarred tomatoes, green peppers, even potatoes. Platoons of colorful jellies and pie fillings lined a checkered tablecloth beside a booth that sold varieties of homemade bread. One farmer had brought along a live goat for the children to pet while he encouraged parents to try his goat's milk cheeses and fudge. Max was intrigued by the goat.

I bought two jars of jam—strawberry and blackberry. Libby bought raisin bread and a shoofly pie.

At the end of the alley between the booths, a crew

was setting up an outdoor kitchen. We saw a couple of chefs in white coats readying their ingredients for a demonstration.

"Is that Tommy Rattigan?" Emma asked.

I glanced around and thought I spotted Tommy, too, but the crowd shifted and I lost sight of him.

"I'm not sure," I said. "I was hoping he'd be here to promote the Farm-to-Table gala. His restaurant will be one of the featured locations tomorrow night."

Emma stopped short at the last booth. "Jesus," she said, looking at the hand-lettered sign on the display table. "Breast milk cheese? Is this what I think it is?"

The smiling gentleman behind the table leaned forward. He had a bald head with white fringe, and the pink complexion of a well-fed baby. With a twinkle in his eyes, he offered Emma his tray of cheese samples. "What do you think it is?"

I made sure Libby had a hand on the stroller before I went across the walkway to a tent that was advertising fresh, home-raised meat. The proprietor had set up a small electric grill, and he was cooking a steak. He had a scruffy beard and wore a baseball cap with the logo of his company emblazoned on it—a crowing rooster. A young, ponytailed woman from the vegan group that had been selling dried blueberries just a few booths away was engaging him in an argument.

"It's disgusting," she said. "You're polluting the whole market with that stink."

"Lady, take a hike." He used his long fork to gesture her away. "I've got a right to be here, same as you."

"If I cut up your mother and cooked her, you wouldn't say that."

"Go away," he said.

I leaned in. "Do you butcher your own meat?"

He seemed relieved to have a potential customer on the hook. "Yeah. Hi. We got a shop over near Doylestown, fresh meat daily. Beef, lamb, anything you want."

"Pork," I said. "To tell you the truth, I've lost my pig."

He rolled his eyes. "Is everybody nuts around here today?"

"I'm serious. Somebody stole a pig off my property, and I'm afraid he's going to be killed before the police find him."

"I buy everything I sell from local farms, okay? Guys I've known for years. I don't know anything about your pig."

"Does anybody try to sell you animals from other sources?"

"What are you talking about? Stolen pigs? Of course I don't buy stolen pigs! Now go away. I got a living to make."

I turned around to see Emma spitting out a mouthful of cheese. She was saying, "That's the grossest thing I've ever put in my mouth."

"It's an acquired taste," the cheese salesman admitted. "A specialty market. But lots of people love it. Guys especially."

Libby was frowning. "Where do you get your main ingredient?"

His twinkly smile got brighter. "Funny you should ask. I see you ladies have a couple of youngsters. I can't help wondering if you might be interested in a simple business transaction. I mean, I might have to watch to make sure you're giving me the real thing. Not pulling some kind of switcheroo on me. I'm always looking to expand my supply chain."

My cell phone rang, and I gratefully walked away to check the screen. I didn't want to hear my sisters becoming part of a breast milk supply chain.

My caller was Gus.

I let it ring four times, hoping he'd give up, but when I finally answered, he said, "Why aren't you here in the office?"

"Because," I said, "I deserve a day off."

"Shouldn't you ask your boss when you want to take a day off?"

"My boss would probably refuse my request, so I didn't ask."

Gus said, "Your boss is not as unreasonable as you think. I hear you're missing a pig."

I walked farther away from the booths of the market and found a grassy spot where I could speak privately. "How do you know about that?"

"We have reporters who listen to police scanners. How do you think we follow the news? Normally, our blokes don't pay attention to lost and found or a kitten up a tree, but when they heard the name Abruzzo, they started listening more closely. They hoped for more exciting updates than missing livestock. Actually, they were quite amused."

Michael made headlines no matter what he did. I expected the pig story had just moved from the petty-crime report to the front page. I hoped the hardened criminals in his family wouldn't think less of him for keeping a pig for a pet. He had enough troubles with them already.

Gus said, "I may have news for you concerning your animal."

I forgot about Michael's tough-guy reputation. "What news?"

"Tommy Rattigan is hosting the artisanal butchery demonstration at tomorrow night's gala. It's not my idea of a good evening out, you understand, but apparently a lot of people are interested in seeing their dinner cut from a carcass before they eat it. Really, do you Americans ever sit down for a normal meal? I just received a tutorial from the food reporter about deep-fried fair food. Did you know it's possible to fry a Snickers bar? How revolting is that?"

"This from a man who probably eats Vegemite?"

"Don't knock it, luv," Gus said. "It's the ambrosia of my youth. I think Rattigan has your pig."

"What? Where?" I clutched the phone closer to my ear. "Oh my God, they're not going to eat Ralphie, are they?"

"Ralphie? I had a dog named Laver once, after Rod Laver, the tennis player."

"Dammit, Gus, you're trying to distract me, and right now I just can't stand—" My brain might have been side-tracked last night, but now I could think quite clearly. "How do you know about this? You didn't get all that information from the police scanner."

Gus hummed into the phone, hesitating.

"Did you go back to see Marybeth last night? After you dropped me off, you played slap and tickle with her again? Did she tell you?"

"There was no slapping. Rather a nice amount of tickling, though."

"Spare me," I snapped.

"What? You and the gangster didn't make hot love after I delivered you home last night? I underestimated your libido?"

I couldn't come up with a retort fast enough, and Gus laughed. He said, "Rattigan doesn't quite know what to do with your porker. He says—well, that doesn't matter, I suppose, but I think you could—"

"Hang on," I said. "You're listening to Tommy, aren't you? You're listening to that damned bug!"

"You don't need to know where I get my intelligence. I simply—"

"Intelligence? That's what you call it? Eavesdropping on people?"

"Will you lower your voice?" he asked. "I don't want anyone overhearing this conversation. Not even your thug."

My turn to laugh. "I don't believe you. How many laws are you breaking by planting a listening device on a chef?"

"I heard him talking about your pig, didn't I?"

I hung up on Gus. Not because I was necessarily finished chewing him out, but because I caught another glimpse of Tommy Rattigan himself. He was standing behind a demonstration table, sharpening a long, thin knife with broad, dramatic strokes. Around him, two sous chefs bustled with bowls and cutting boards. One of them fired up a flame under an iron skillet. A group of spectators had begun to fill the folding chairs set up in front of the white tent. Two elderly ladies were settling into the back row with an overweight Labrador retriever wearing a red neckerchief.

I stuffed my phone into my pocket and headed for Tommy.

Behind me, Em called, "Nora?"

Libby said, "Where's she going? Nora, be careful! In your condition—"

I pushed past the elderly ladies—one gave a cry of outrage—and I managed to put a foot wrong and step on the Labrador's paw. He yelped, and the crowd in the folding chairs looked around at the commotion. I plowed ahead, climbing over a box of candles left in the aisle by a couple of young hippies.

Tommy looked up from his knife to see me headed straight down the aisle in his direction. My expression must have tipped him off, because a flicker of fright crossed his face. Then he turned, knocked over his pudgy assistant and bolted out the back of the tent.

Like a bullet, I went after him.

I jumped over the fallen sous chef and shoved through the back of the tent. I nearly fell over a waiting crate of vegetables, but I caught my balance on the open tailgate of a pickup truck. I saw Tommy disappear around some parked cars. I took off running after him.

I must have shouted. He threw a terrified look over his shoulder at me and kept going through the makeshift parking lot, his green clogs flapping. I ran around the parked cars and thought I'd caught up with him, but I stopped, panting. He'd disappeared.

Emma charged up next to me, barely out of breath. "What's going on?"

"Tommy Rattigan—he stole Ralphie! Go that way! I'll run around this way and—"

"And we'll nab him," Emma said. "Gotcha."

We bolted in opposite directions.

I dodged between a minivan and a Prius and ran down the row, hurdling a basset hound on a leash and barely missing a man with an armload of bread loaves. I saw Tommy zigzag between two cars that were simultaneously pulling out of opposite parking spaces. I leaped over a rope and almost cut him off, but he plunged down a ditch and emerged on the other side, running hard. Emma appeared out of nowhere and nearly blindsided him, but he saw her coming and made an about-face.

"Tommy!" I shouted.

He stumbled into traffic, and for a horrible moment I thought an oncoming car was going to flatten him.

But the car braked, a horn blew and Tommy caught his balance on the hood of the vehicle. He blundered around it, grabbed the passenger door and hopped inside. The driver hit the gas.

Emma yanked me out of the path of the car, and it blew past me with only inches to spare.

It was a silver Mercedes, a grim-faced Marybeth Starr behind the wheel. Her brother ducked his head and fastened his seat belt as the car accelerated away from us.

"What a douchetard," Emma said. "Does he think we don't know who he is?"

"Why was his first instinct to run?" I panted. "He has a guilty conscience. For stealing Ralphie? Or killing Swain Starr?"

Libby arrived, pushing the stroller and laden with children and shopping bags. She said, "Why on earth are you two making such spectacles of yourselves? Everybody back at the farmers' market thinks you're chasing down a nonorganic carnivore."

"That's about the size of it," Emma said.

"Ready to go home?" I asked, suddenly overcome with exhaustion. "I could use a nap."

Emma checked me for other signs of injury and decided I was A-okay. But she said, "Maybe we'd better stop at another drugstore? Get you another test?"

"Oh yes!" Libby cried. "Let's go home and watch Nora pee on a stick!"

Chapter 22

We made a detour to a Walgreens, and I dashed inside to grab a pregnancy test off the shelves. With the money from my stop at the pawnshop, I got a two-pack just in case the first results were iffy. I purchased some diapers for Noah, as well as some formula and other supplies.

On the way home, my cell phone rang while Libby was regaling us with stories about auditions for television commercials—mostly how people misunderstood the mothers of auditioning kids.

When I answered my phone, Michael said with suspicious cheer, "Hi. How you doing?"

"Fine. We think we figured out who rustled Ralphie."

"Oh yeah? Tell me, and I'll send a hit squad."

Sometimes it was downright delightful to be cohabitating with a kingpin of organized crime. Smiling, I said, "Tommy Rattigan. He owns a restaurant in the city."

"The one you told me about before?"

"Yes. He's—Michael, Tommy is putting on some kind of butchering demonstration tomorrow night. I'm so afraid—"

"I'm on it. Anything else?"

"A little something else. But we can talk about it when I get home. Are you at the farm now?"

"Uh," he said. "No. And it looks like I may not be there for a while."

My stomach took a cold plunge. "What's wrong?"

"So, the thing this morning? Kuzik wanted me to play basketball with some guys he knows. Nice guys. Good game."

I sensed he wasn't calling me to report a basketball score. "But?"

"Kuzik's not exactly a great player himself. He's a little slow, and his grasp of strategy is—anyway, the bottom line is I kinda knocked him on his ass. Not his ass so much as his head."

"Oh, Michael!"

"It was an accident. He knows it. Everybody knows it. He was bumbling around, and somebody was going to hit him eventually, but it was my fault that it was me. I was driving the ball around him, but he stepped wrong and—anyway, I brought him over here to the emergency room. He's getting some kind of head scan at the moment."

"He has a concussion?"

"Maybe it's just a bump. But his nose is looking a little funny."

I could hear the regret in Michael's voice. I said, "I'm sorry he's hurt."

"Yeah, me, too. Thing is, the police are here for other business, and they got interested."

"Oh no." I suddenly knew where this conversation was going.

"Right. I think they're gonna arrest me for assaulting Kuzik. At the very least, they're going to take me in for a bunch of questions. And until Kuzik can explain his side of things, it doesn't look great for you and me having lunch together. Or dinner, either."

"Please don't say you're going back to jail."

"Hell, no, not for this. But until Kuzik can talk to the cops, I'm in limbo."

"Have you called Armand?"

"Who?"

"Cannoli!"

"Oh, right. Yeah, I called him. He's on his way. Between your family and mine, we're going to pay college tuition for a lot of little Cannolis." He was trying to make light of the situation, but I knew he was annoyed. He said, "Listen, when you get back to the farm, you'll see I fired the old crew. I told the new guys to keep a close watch while I'm gone, especially for Zephyr and the Starr kid who's looking for her. I shoulda made sure we were better covered before. I didn't know about the road in the back. I'm gonna think about that, and we'll fix it when I get home. Meanwhile, there will be a couple of extra guys around today."

"Are we in danger?"

"Don't worry. Mostly, I don't want my brother coming back to surprise you. Don't let him in if he shows his face, okay? I told him to keep his distance, and I meant it." Michael's tone changed, turning brisk. "I gotta go now. I'll call you when I know more."

"I love you," I said.

But he was already gone.

"Trouble?" Emma asked from the backseat.

"Nothing unusual," I said on a sigh.

"You need a diversion," Libby said, having overheard most of our conversation and no doubt sensing my plummeting spirits. "Why don't we go out for lunch? While we wait for our food, Nora, you can take the test. We'll have champagne! It'll be fun! And when That Man of Yours finally gets home, you can have a celebration all ready — something romantic with candles and lingerie. And maybe cake. Who doesn't like cake?"

She was already making a U-turn and pulling into the parking lot of the Rusty Sabre.

Emma took a cell phone call while Libby and I managed to get the children into the restaurant and seated at a window table overlooking a picturesque stretch of the canal that ran through New Hope. Our waiter seemed willing to cope with a table that included two little ones, which was a relief. Sometimes the mere presence of Max discouraged good service. Libby opened a plastic container of Cheerios and scattered a supply on the tray of Max's high chair. He immediately started throwing cereal at Noah, who looked mystified about being the object of Max's jealousy.

Libby had rummaged through my shopping bags while in the minivan, and she handed over the pregnancy test.

"Now?" I asked.

"Why wait?"

"Maybe I should do it in the privacy of my own home."

"Nonsense." Libby saw my fear, and she said, "If the news is negative, wouldn't you rather be with your sisters instead of home alone to wallow in disappointment? Go take the test now, Nora. We'll cope with the results, no matter what they are."

With mixed feelings, I headed into the ladies' room of the Rusty Sabre.

I opened the box with trembling fingers. The Rusty Sabre had been the setting of many a Blackbird family turning point. My sisters and I had wept over our dead husbands here. We had discussed Libby's election to the presidency of the Erotic Yoga Society and Emma's opportunity to train with the Olympic Grand Prix team. I'd broken the news to them of my decision to sell a couple of ancestral acres of Blackbird Farm to a stranger named Michael Abruzzo. We had engaged in petty squabbles and made monumental decisions here.

I could barely get my eyes to focus as I read the directions on the box.

I took the test.

Within a few minutes, I returned to the table. Libby and Emma turned their faces to me. Even Max looked up with anticipation.

"Well?" Emma demanded, holding her son awkwardly.

"Oh, Nora," Libby said, seeing my tears.

I wobbled into my chair and took a deep breath.

"It's positive. We're having a baby."

Emma cheered. Libby squealed and leaped to her feet. She did a little fertility dance, then hurried around the table to hug me. Max burst into wails of jealousy. I saw stars and felt the universe at long last tilting in my direction.

The waiter brought champagne.

"I took the liberty of ordering it," Libby explained as the waiter filled glasses. "Either way, we were going to need it. You can have a sip, Nora. Go ahead. If you can go tearing around the farmers' market without endangering your unborn child, you can certainly withstand a sip of champagne."

We toasted the newest member of the family, and I ate an enormous, satisfying lunch—even stealing a couple of French fries from Emma's plate—and didn't care what my waistline was going to look like at tomorrow night's gala. We babbled and made plans and talked about my due date and whether or not it's best to find out the sex of a baby before it's born or at the moment of delivery. And I don't know when I'd been happier. Sharing the moment with my sisters was the right thing to do.

I'd have another kind of moment with Michael later.

Over dessert—one apple crumble with ice cream that

we shared—Libby had taken possession of Noah again, but she turned to Emma. "Who was on the phone when we arrived?"

Emma took time to finish her champagne before answering. "Hart."

Libby and I put down our forks, suddenly all ears. "Well?"

She avoided our attentive gazes. "Things are still up in the air with him."

"What does that mean?" Libby demanded.

"Penny's family staged an intervention. She agreed to treatment for the pill thing. So he's taking her to a rehab place this weekend. He has to stay a couple of days, too. It's part of the program."

Libby held Noah protectively close. "What about their child?"

Emma took a deep breath. "Look, you guys, I can't handle this. Hart says Noah can go into foster care where he'll be well—"

"No!" I cried. "Can't someone in Penny's family take him?"

Emma shook her head. "Not an option. This weekend, they have plans to go to Paris."

Libby said a rude word.

I reached and grasped my sister's hand. "You can do this, Em. You can take care of him."

She shook her head firmly. "I can't. What's more? I don't want to. I gave him up for a lot of reasons, and I'm not going to change my mind."

"But—"

"I mean it, Nora. I'm not turning into Nanny McPhee with the wave of a magic wand. I'll provide his milk. But that's as far as I'm willing to go. Help me out here, will you?"

Emma asked for help . . . well, never. She had a stubborn set to her face, but there was something trembling underneath that expression.

Into the tense silence that followed, Libby said, "I'll look after him this weekend. I have a sitter coming tomorrow night for the Farm-to-Table dinner, and she's excellent—completely capable and trustworthy. The rest of the weekend, I'll be in charge. We'll have fun, won't we, Noah?" She held up the baby and smiled into his sleeping face.

Max let out a squawk of objection.

Emma was frowning at the baby. "He finally fell asleep."

"He's had a busy day," Libby said.

"Thing is," Emma said, "he normally sleeps all the time. Really, I don't know when I've seen him awake since he was born."

"What are you saying?" I asked.

"Well, Penny takes all those pills. Do you suppose she . . . slips Noah something, too? To keep him quiet?"

Libby and I recoiled with horror.

"Maybe I'm imagining it," Emma said quickly. "It's just weird seeing him so awake."

Libby vowed to take good care of him over the weekend. Then she dropped me at Blackbird Farm and gave me a joyous kiss. Emma even gave me a hug and congratulated me before taking off in her truck.

I noted the arrival of new members of the wiseguy patrol. The one on the porch—an older gentleman in a tracksuit very much like Libby's, minus the T-shirt— even tipped his invisible hat and gave me a smile that revealed two gold-capped teeth. I shook his hand and introduced myself.

"Yeah," he said. "The boss said to make sure you're okay, Mrs. Boss."

"What's your name?" I asked.

He grinned even wider. "I'm Road Kill. But you can call me Rocco."

"I will," I said. "Thank you, Rocco."

"There was a kid here earlier, driving a rental. He tried to get through the guys. Almost ran over Jimbo."

"My God, is anyone hurt?"

"Naw, kid hit the fence instead, bashed up his car but good."

Porky, I thought. "Did you speak with him?"

Rocco wagged his head. "He jammed the car into reverse, almost hit the mailbox and peeled out of here fast. Don't know what his problem was. He comes back, though, we'll take care of him."

"Call for the police," I advised.

"Yeah, maybe." Rocco flashed his gold teeth again.

It was some comfort knowing that the terms of Michael's parole included no association with any convicted criminal. I could trust that the crew was made up of relatively upstanding citizens. Sort of I went upstairs. Feeling safe and wonderfully pregnant, I fell across the bed and dropped into the deepest, most peaceful sleep I had ever experienced.

I woke up at six when the phone rang.

Cannoli told me with regret that the police would be keeping Michael overnight.

Resigned to spending the night alone, I made myself a slice of peanut butter toast for dinner and went back upstairs to bed. I thought I might be able to read for a few hours—my book club would meet in a week, and I hadn't made a dent in the book yet—but my pillow called again.

In the middle of the night, I woke when the phone rang. I rolled over and fumbled for it on the bedside table. "Michael?"

A male voice said, "I need to talk to Zephyr."

"What? Who is this?" I couldn't quite drag myself into full wakefulness. I groped for the switch on the lamp.

"Put Zephyr on the phone. I know she's there, yo."

"Porky?"

"I have to talk to her," he insisted, adding a few curses.

"I'm sorry, but she's not here. She left yesterday. I don't know where she went. The police are looking for her."

"You're lying."

"She left with one of—she left, that's all." I snapped the lamp on and flinched from the light. "Porky, I know you're upset. First your father, and now Zephyr is—well, not what we thought she was, but—"

"Where did she go? I have to find her! I can help her." I thought I heard him sniffle. "We can be together."

The panic in his voice put a terrible thought in my head. "Porky, you didn't—? When your father gave you money, that was to help with your business, right?"

He made a noise that might have been a sob. "He was supposed to give me more. A lot more."

"He shortchanged you?"

"He promised. Said he'd give me a couple mil if I went away. But he cheated me." Miserably, he pleaded, "I need to talk to Zephyr and make her understand it's enough for both of us. I'll give her all of it, if that's what it takes."

"I'm sorry. She's not here."

He began to rant in a strangled yell, but he snapped off his phone before I could make out his words.

I lay back in the bed, staring up at the ceiling. What did it mean? Swain had given his son a substantial amount of walking money. I had seen the half-million-dollar check myself. Porky had hoped to run away with Zephyr, I guessed. But . . . had Porky killed his father when Swain "shortchanged" him?

I got out of bed and went into the bathroom for a drink of water. I stood on the rug, my feet freezing, and looked at my shadowy face in the mirror. My reflection frowned back at me while I tried to imagine the relationship between Porky and Zephyr. She seemed curiously distant with people—unemotional and bland. Beautifully bland, but still bland. By comparison, Porky had temper in spades. Had one of them killed Swain with a pitchfork?

I thought about LinZee in the drunk tank. What had she said? Don't piss off a pregnant woman? Had Zephyr's pregnancy put her mentally over the edge?

I got a pair of socks from a drawer and went back to bed to put them on. I turned off the light, fervently wishing Michael were at home to talk to. He could imagine what went on in dark hearts much more clearly than I could.

I had slept too long earlier in the evening, so I lay awake for a long time. I found myself picturing Swain Starr lying dead in the pigpen, his chest punctured by someone enraged enough to stab him over and over. Who had been strong enough? Angry enough? Tommy? Marybeth? Zephyr? Porky?

My sleepy mind began to turn over the various combinations of fathers and sons I knew, and Michael's upbringing swam into focus. He had said there was violence in his home, and although I felt safe with him now, I knew he was still capable of it. And what might drive him to kill his own father?

With sudden clarity, I figured it out. He'd do it to protect me. Or his children, when the time came. Had Porky needed to protect someone he loved? Zephyr, maybe?

Finally, I became aware of a weird flickering light outside. I sat up in bed. "What in the world—?"

I grabbed my dressing gown and slippers, then hurried down the stairs. The whole house seemed to glow and throb from a light source outside. With my heart pounding, I ran across the dining room, through the butler's pantry, across the kitchen floor to the back door. My hands fumbled with the locks, my breath coming in gasps. "Please, no," I begged.

I yanked open the back door and ran out onto the porch. What I saw was the barn. On fire.

I shrieked.

Michael's crew was all there—some of them running, one using the garden hose, another one, blessedly, holding Mr. Twinkles by his halter. The horse danced around on the grass, throwing his weight against his captor and dragging the man like a rag doll. The fire illuminated the animal, turning him into a magical beast on my lawn. I saw flames licking around the door of the barn, flickering brightly.

A fire truck came around the curve in the drive and blasted its horn. Everyone scattered to make room for the truck.

One of Michael's men—the one with the gold teeth— came to me and slung his jacket around my shoulders. "Go back inside, Mrs. Boss. We got this under control."

"What happened?"

"That kid came back. The kid who was around earlier. Said you were hiding somebody here. We chased him off, but he musta come back somehow."

"Why would he do this?"

"I dunno, but he was plenty upset."

Then I was too dizzy to stand. The man with the gold teeth sat me down on the porch steps and brought me a long coat from inside the house. I wrapped myself in it, hugging my arms and watching the firemen work. They had brought a tanker truck, and they sluiced water through the open barn door to fight back the licking flames, then advanced inside to wash all the hay and woodwork.

Ricci arrived in his police cruiser with red lights flashing. He came over to the porch, and I felt my faculties return sufficiently to explain how I'd been awakened by a phone call and that perhaps Porky had come back and set fire to the barn. Ricci radioed for backup, and when his counterpart arrived, they drew their weapons and went inside to search the house.

Road Kill came over and sat with me, awkwardly patting me on the shoulder. Together, we watched the firemen put out the fire.

Chapter 23

"No," I told Emma when she arrived the next morning. "The police didn't find Porky in the house."

Emma kicked the porch railing with frustration. "They checked everywhere, right? Even the cellar? He's not hiding somewhere in this mausoleum?"

"The police made a thorough search," I said. "Ricci told me he thought he was permanently lost in the attic. He thinks there's a cannon up there. Do you know anything about that?"

She shook her head, and we stood on the porch, looking at the mess left by the firemen. The barn still stood, but the front door was a gaping black hole, and the interior would need shoring up before the structure could be used again. Emma said, "It's lucky the whole barn didn't burn down to the foundation."

"I know. The original timbers are so old, they could have burned like tinder." I was still in shock, looking at what remained. The task of repairing it all felt very daunting. I sat down on the top step. "I'm sorry, Em. Mr. Twinkles—"

"He's okay. I checked. He'll be fine in the pasture. The ponies are good, too. They're indestructible. But the barn. Is your insurance paid up?"

"Yes, barely." My damaged barn felt like some kind of karmic response to Emma setting the fire at Starr's Landing.

Standing on the step below me, she put a steadying hand on my shoulder. "This will turn out okay."

I hoped she was right. I put my chin in my hands and stared at the rubble of junk the firemen had dragged outside before dousing it with water—old barrels, an antique travel trunk used for hauling tack, bales of straw. I presumed what was left inside—hay and feed and more—had been ruined by smoke and would need to be disposed of. But that work was beyond me at the moment. I said, "The police think Porky came from Sheffield Road and lit a match to the straw. He's crazy to find Zephyr. Maybe he thought a fire would draw her outside."

"Well, he didn't find her." Emma shook her head. "Mick's really gonna get worked up when he sees this. Those wiseguys are probably in fear for their lives for letting this happen with you at home."

"They're all embarrassed that Porky got past them. And worried about what Michael will do when he gets back. The good news is this humiliation has made them doubly determined to find Ralphie. Except for the skeleton crew here, every good fella in three states is in Philadelphia right now, combing the streets for Michael's pig. I should be doing something, too."

She swung on me, shaking her head firmly. "You're in a delicate condition, Sis. You have a tendency to miscarry, and that would be—look, just let the police handle the investigation from now on."

I eyed her. "I certainly can't tell them what I know, can I? Or you'll go to jail for arson, and God knows what will happen to Rawlins."

"Rawlins is in the clear. There's no evidence that can be used against him. The cops turned him loose."

But I had reached another conclusion.

"Em," I said quietly. "What if our nephew is the father of Zephyr's baby?"

My little sister sat down hard on the porch steps. "Holy leaky condom! You think that's possible?"

"I have a bad feeling that it might be."

"Just a month ago Rawlins was picking his nose and playing that game with the hobbits! Now he's all grown-up and banging a supermodel?"

I had reviewed every memory of Starr's Landing of the afternoon the party took place. I could still see Rawlins in his blue jacket, holding a drink and trying to look grown-up. He'd been watching Zephyr, I realized now. It was Zephyr who had invited him to the party. He could have been the one in the car with Zephyr when they abandoned it. She probably took the pregnancy test and showed him the results. Whatever happened after that included leaving the car behind and perhaps the two of them going separate ways—Zephyr to a hotel in Philadelphia.

But might Rawlins have gone straight back to Starr's Landing to confront Zephyr's husband? Had things gone horribly wrong?

Emma listened to my theory with growing horror. "No. No, that's not possible. The kid wouldn't hurt anybody. He couldn't have killed Swain Starr."

"I don't want this to be true any more than you do," I said. "I'm trying to make sense of what we know. There are a lot of missing pieces. But something's not right, Em. That's why we have to keep a few things from the police just a little longer."

She considered it all and finally blew a gusty sigh. "I get it. I don't like it, but I get it. But if Libby hears she might be a grandmother, she's gonna blow like Vesuvius. I don't want to be around when the molten rock starts flying."

"That's the best reason to keep her in the dark as long as possible," I said, trying not to imagine the meltdown Libby was going to have. "So you'll stay here tonight?

Until I get back or Michael gets home? Checkpoint Charlie has been doubled. There's a crew watching Sheffield Road now, too. But I'd be relieved to know you were here keeping an eye on things."

Emma agreed. She pumped more milk while I dressed for the Farm-to-Table gala.

I had planned to wear a pink Givenchy from Grandmama's collection, but the waistline didn't fit me anymore. Although I had been dismayed to see how my clothes were looking on me lately, today I felt considerably happier about my thickening figure. I dug into my closet and found a very forgiving Carolina Herrera gown with an empire silhouette of flowing silk. The light fabric was a print of pale blue with streams of darker colors that brought out the new glow in my eyes. And the halter-style neckline showcased parts of my body in a whole new way. The slit up past my knee gave it youth and a little informality. Open-toed slingbacks, a sequined clutch and my diamond ring were all the accessories I needed to make a sophisticated appearance.

Besides, if you want to feel feminine, there's nothing like a Herrera dress.

"Va-va-voom," Emma said when I twirled before her in the kitchen where she was making herself some eggs and bacon. "You look sexy in that getup. Hardly like a pregnant lady at all. I hope Mick gets back tonight."

"He will. Cannoli said they'd have to either arrest him or release him soon. If he gets here before I do, tell him I'll be back before eleven."

"I'll tell him," Emma said. "And then I'll be leaving. Just so you know."

I gave her a kiss. "I know."

We had both heard my ride arrive in the back of the house. We could also hear Libby's shrieks of horror at the sight of the damaged barn.

But she didn't cry.

"That would ruin my makeup," she said, pulling herself together with an effort. "How do I look?"

She wore layers of red chiffon, gathered fetchingly under her prodigious bosom and flowing loosely around her hips so that she looked like an escapee from a Renaissance fair. Every curve in her full figure looked luscious. She had swept her dark hair to one side with a flounce over one eye and a tumble of curls on the opposite shoulder.

Meaning every word, I said, "You look completely fabulous."

"Red always boosts my confidence." She struck a proud pose that nearly popped her breasts out of their minimal containment. "I got the dress on eBay. It once belonged to Kirstie Alley."

Emma said, "I hope you have some double-stick tape in your bag. If you sneeze, you'll get arrested for indecent exposure."

"Of course I have tape," Libby replied. "Do you think I'm a rookie when it comes to boobs?"

From the driveway came a tall figure wearing a dark suit and a silk tie. It was Rawlins, looking as if he'd rather be anywhere but in the company of his mother.

Libby said, "I bought a ticket for Rawlins, too. After his ordeal with the police, I decided it was high time he associated with some nice people for one evening."

Emma said, "I hear he's been doing a lot of associating with his evenings."

Rawlins gave her a double take and turned pale.

"You look really great, Rawlins. Everybody does," I said, shooting Emma a look that told her to shut up. "And thanks for giving me a lift, Lib."

"Well," she said uncertainly, looking at our ride for the evening.

The rest of us turned to examine the vehicle idling in my driveway. Perry Delbert's exterminator van had been freshly washed and waxed, so the image of the giant dead spider gleamed in the failing sunlight. On top of the cab, a mosquito the size of Ralphie had blinking lights in its eyes.

Perry stood attentively by the passenger door, buttoned into a very snug rented tuxedo like a footman ready to help Cinderella into her magic coach. He had flattened his usually bushy brown hair into damp curls, and his beard looked freshly trimmed. He gazed at Libby as if she were the most beautiful princess in the world.

Libby sighed. "He volunteered to drive. I didn't have the heart to tell him I'd rather take the minivan."

I patted her arm. "It's okay. The valet parking will only take a moment, and after that, nobody will remember what chariot we arrived in."

Shortly, we were on our way to the Farm-to-Table gala in the bugmobile. Rawlins and I sat in the backseat. He kept his face turned to the window. While Libby chattered in the front seat, I patted his knee.

As we neared Philadelphia, I asked Libby, "How's Noah? Is he eating all right?"

"He's fine," she assured me, and she deftly changed the subject.

Several Philadelphia restaurants had agreed to share their venues for the gala, and the evening was pleasant enough for guests to wander up and down the street to visit all of the parties. But a grand entrance had been set up in front of one of the city's premier hotels, and we settled into the line of traffic as it inched toward the point of disembarkation. Someone took a photo of the bugmobile with a camera phone that flashed, and pretty soon dozens of people were laughing and snapping our picture.

"What's going on?" Libby peered through the windshield at the throng on the sidewalk.

"Guess this is a pretty popular party," Perry said.

"Why isn't everybody in the restaurants?" she asked.

I spotted Crewe Dearborne in the crowd on the sidewalk. Wearing a sharp dinner jacket, my restaurant-critic friend cut an unmistakably aristocratic figure.

With my hand already on the door handle, I said, "Perry, would you mind if I bailed out here?"

"Sure, but—"

"I'll catch up with you later," I said, halfway out of the van. "Call me on my cell if you decide to leave early!"

Eager to escape his mother and her dubious date, Rawlins hastily unsnapped his seat belt and followed me.

The decorated van had already caused a stir among the people, but it was Crewe who burst out laughing as Rawlins and I scampered toward the sidewalk.

He caught my hand and steadied me as I stepped up over the curb. "You always know how to make an entrance, Nora. But this time you've outdone yourself. Is that a tsetse fly on top of that truck?"

"A mosquito. If you want to have your house sprayed for West Nile virus, I can hook you up. This is Rawlins, my nephew. Rawlins, have you met Crewe Dearborne?"

They shook hands, and Crewe said, "I met you at a birthday party for somebody. You had cotton candy stuck in your hair."

"That was a while ago," Rawlins said.

I was looking at the crowd. "What's going on here?"

Crewe hooked his thumb past the crowd at the restaurant behind us. "This restaurant was just evacuated. They say a wild boar got loose in the kitchen."

My heart leaped into my throat. "Just now?"

"Yes. In the dining room we heard a commotion, and suddenly—"

"What kind of commotion?"

"Screaming from the kitchen. And something crashing around—"

Crewe was cut off when a city police squad car pulled to the curb and two officers jumped out. Two more foot patrolmen pushed through the well-dressed mob, heading for the front door of the restaurant. They drew their guns.

At once, I knew it was Ralphie—and his life was at stake. I grabbed Rawlins by the hand. "Come with me!"

I hitched up my long skirt with my other hand and ran for the corner, Rawlins and Crewe dodging behind me. Crewe called, "Nora, what has gotten into you?"

We hustled around the block and into the alley behind the restaurant. A large metal structure had been rigged over a drain in the cobblestoned street. Portable lights were aimed at the gleaming metal, and a stainless steel table was laid with glitteringly sharp knives. Chains hung from the crossbar of the structure, heavy enough to hold a large animal for a gruesome butchering demonstration.

At that moment, a motley crew of wiseguys bolted out the kitchen door. They scattered into the night like the Three Stooges, probably flushed out the back door as the policemen barged through the front.

I recognized Road Kill, "Rocco!"

He headed my way, out of breath. "Mrs. Boss! What are you doing here?"

"Have you found Ralphie?"

"We found the pig," Rocco panted. "They were trying to get him trussed up here, but a crazy lady cut him loose. Trouble is, he went wild. Instead of running away, he ran straight into the kitchen. Now he's breaking up the whole restaurant."

We heard more shouts and high-pitched screams from inside.

"He's gonna hurt somebody in there," Rocco said, already heading for freedom. "Unless the cops shoot him first."

My pregnant-lady hormones kicked in, filling me with estrogen-laced purpose. I yanked open the back door and led the way inside. "Rawlins, come with me! Crewe, see if you can find some maraschino cherries!"

"Some *what*?" he cried.

With my heart in my throat, I ran down the hallway toward the dining room.

But I caught my balance on the doorjamb of Tommy's office in time to see Tommy haul off and slap his sister, Marybeth.

"You moron," she shouted at her brother. "I told you not to use that pig! If you serve the meat, you'll spoil everything our family worked for!"

"You're no scientist!" Tommy shot back. "You're incompetent!"

"You never understood," Marybeth said. "You never understood the importance of Grandpa's work."

"He made *hot dogs*!" Then Tommy cursed. He had seen me, and he pointed a shaking finger in my direction. "It's her," he said to his sister. "That Blackbird woman who stole your pig in the first place!"

I turned to run, but it was too late. Tommy seized me by the wrist. He whirled me around and dragged me into his office.

"Hey!" Rawlins cried.

From his desk Tommy grabbed an enormous knife. There was blood on the blade.

"Tommy!" Marybeth cried. "You can't!"

But he hauled me close and put the knife to my throat. I found my voice. "Don't make this situation worse for yourselves. Maybe you killed Swain, Tommy, but you had good reason if he was going behind your back to—"

"I didn't kill him!" Tommy pointed the knife at his sister. "She did!"

Marybeth recoiled with horror. "I did not! I tried to get the pig back, that's all. I knew he was going to ruin everything—all of our reputations."

"Why?" I asked. "What's wrong with Ralphie?"

"Who?" Marybeth asked.

"The pig," Tommy snapped. "He tastes bad flavor-wise, that's what's wrong with him! The almighty super-pig that was supposed to be God's gift to bacon turns out to taste like crap! There's nothing we can do to fix the flavor of his meat. No sauce, no rub, no process—"

"He tastes bad?" I asked.

Marybeth said, "Something went wrong with the breeding. We thought we were getting something special, but there's a liver problem I can't breed out of them. The meat is inedible. I was keeping him to study, but Swain and my genius brother stole him from me—"

"You should have told me he was worthless!" Tommy cried. "You had all that security on him—I figured he was the right one."

"I didn't want anybody to find out about the liver problem!"

"Wait," I said, trying to make sense of it all. "So you tried to steal him back, Marybeth? Before anybody found out he was worthless?"

"I wanted to get him back last fall," she said. "But he disappeared. Zephyr set him free! But a few days ago, Porky told us he saw the pig at your place, so Tommy got him back. He wasn't supposed to butcher the animal!"

"Thank God we tasted the tail first," Tommy said. "It was revolting. If I had served the rest of the meat, my reputation would have been ruined for good!"

As he lamented his career, I felt Tommy's grip slacken. In that instant, I raised my foot and jammed the heel of my shoe down on his green rubber clog. He yelped and dropped me. Rawlins seized my hand, and together we rushed down the hall.

A tall person in a white chef's jacket and toque was the only person left in the kitchen.

Rawlins said on a gasp, "Zephyr?"

I blinked and realized the chef wasn't a man, but Zephyr, who had tried to disguise herself with the kitchen whites.

She came around the counter, peeling off the toque. She gave Rawlins a kiss on the mouth that lingered long enough to knock him back on his heels.

Kiss over, she looked him in the eyes and said, "I'm sorry about everything."

Rawlins swallowed convulsively and shook his head as if he'd been sucker punched. "Hey, I'm not."

She cupped his young face in her hand. "You sure, Rascal?"

He nodded, turning pink.

Zephyr swung on me. "We got your pig loose. Take care of him. I have to go."

"Zephyr, wait. It was you, wasn't it? You killed Swain."

"I have to run," she said. "Before the police arrest me."

"We can help," Rawlins said. "We can get you a lawyer."

"No lawyer has ever been able to help," she said. "And this time I don't have the money to make it all go away. Bye, Rascal."

Another crash and more screams. I left Rawlins to say good-bye to his lover, and I ran down the hall for the dining room. Before I got close, I could hear shouts, thunderous noises and the shattering of glass. I skidded to a stop in the doorway and saw the once-serene dining room was in shambles. A mob of shrieking diners was still trying to cram through the front door to escape, while the tables and chairs lay overturned as if by a tornado. The floor was littered with dishes, centerpieces, broken glassware. Candles from several tables had ignited tablecloths, giving the otherwise darkened restaurant the look of a tribal ritual in progress. Two waiters knelt on top of the bar, clinging to each other as if bracing for a human sacrifice.

Below them, Ralphie rampaged around the floor, knocking over a busboy's stand and sending another load of dishes crashing into a heap of wreckage.

"Ralphie!" I cried.

But he didn't hear me. Grunting in a rage or a panic, he charged the escaping customers and drove half a dozen beautifully dressed people around the hostess stand. Behind the bar, I saw Crewe bobble a jar of maraschino cherries as the mob jostled past him for safety. He leaped for the bar and climbed up just in time to avoid Ralphie's lethal tusks.

Ralphie rounded the bar and charged another group of people, snorting maniacally.

"Ralphie, please!" I shouted.

The pig swerved from his path of destruction, and for an instant I thought he heard me. But no, he had spied Marybeth as she came into the dining room. Lowering his head, he made a run at her, grunting like a mad beast.

"Crewe!" I cried. "The cherries!"

Marybeth screamed. Crewe tossed me the jar of cherries, and I almost caught it in midair. But I was distracted, and the jar barely grazed my fingertips before sailing past me. It hit the wall and shattered, sending pink liquid into a spray that hit Marybeth across her chest. Perhaps mistaking it for blood, she looked down at herself and let out an earsplitting screech.

Ralphie must have caught the scent of sweet cherries in the last instant before he could gore Marybeth. He jammed his piggy forefeet into the carpet and slid to a stop, wild-eyed and drooling.

"Ralphie," I called.

At that instant, however, Tommy came running from the kitchen with a huge empty stockpot in one hand and a ladle in the other. He pounded the ladle onto the pot, and it rang like a gong.

Startled by the noise, Ralphie spun around and headed for the front door just as Tommy intended. Before him, people scattered like pigeons.

"No!" I cried. "Keep him inside!"

But of course nobody wanted the pig in the restaurant, so they gave him all the room he needed to escape out the door and into the street.

I hiked up my skirt and ran after him.

Outside, the line of traffic had evaporated. Libby and her bug man had just arrived on the sidewalk. To avoid the charging pig, Libby threw herself into Perry's waiting arms. Ralphie blew past them, heading for the street. He zigged and he zagged through the panicked Farm-to-Table guests.

Two more police cars squealed to a stop in front of the restaurant. Ralphie dashed between them and jumped into the street. I cried out. Any second he was going to be struck down and flattened by a passing bus.

But a tall figure bailed out of the passenger seat of one of the police cars. He put two fingers between his teeth and blew a piercing whistle. Michael.

Ralphie's maddened gallop checked, he turned.

In that instant, a taxi sped around the corner and headed straight for the pig.

Michael put out a commanding hand and stepped in front of the cab. I watched it happen, and I couldn't cry out, couldn't call his name. Time slowed down, and every detail of what was going to unfold was crystal clear to me in the flashing red strobe of the police lights. The Black-bird curse. I was pregnant at last, poised on the edge of our happy ending, but Michael was going to die.

In slow motion, he walked out into the street in front of the oncoming vehicle, oblivious to everything but saving a pig.

As if from miles away came the shriek of brakes. The crowd screamed. My heart stopped. Stars burst in front of my eyes as a life without Michael flashed before me.

But the taxi rocked to a stop, just inches from him.

Ralphie trotted over to Michael and leaned lovingly against his leg. My pulse gave a painful *thunk*, restarting my brain, and I tottered for the street. I made it to Michael's side and threw myself against him, too. He caught me close and held on.

"Hey," he said. "What happened to Ralphie's tail?"

The pig had a bloody wound where his tail had been.

The police officer who climbed out from behind the wheel of the cruiser was Ricci. He came around the hood of the car, shaking his head. He said, "Which one were you so determined to find, Abruzzo? The girl or the pig?"

To Ricci, I said, "Zephyr is pregnant. It's not her husband's baby. She ran away with Dolph, but he's not the father, either. And Swain wasn't murdered because of the pig. It was the baby. He didn't want another man's baby again. Zephyr killed him over it. But Michael's alive."

"Nora," Michael said, "you're not making any sense."

Crewe arrived, breathless, his hands cupped to hold a dripping mess. "I brought the cherries."

Ricci shook his head. "You people are all crazy."

Chapter 24

Gus said, "My point is, Nora, when you're a reporter, you're supposed to tell the story to your editor before you tell the police."

"I'm sorry." I tried to appear contrite. "It all happened on the spur of the moment. I had to tell the police what I knew before Zephyr escaped. I'll try to do better in the future. That is, if I still have a job?"

We were standing under the oak trees at Blackbird Farm, a safe distance from Ralphie, who eyed Gus from the shade of one of Michael's muscle cars while he chomped meaningfully on a snack. His backside was decorated with a large white bandage where his tail had been, and his expression made me think he might blame Gus for his recent amputation. So I stayed between Gus and the pig in case Ralphie decided to charge him.

Behind us, the ponies grazed in the pasture, and Mr. Twinkles watched us from the fence, his tail swishing.

Beside his convertible and keeping a wary eye on Ralphie, Gus had his arms folded across his chest, looking stern even though the spring breeze charmingly ruffled his hair.

Frowning, he said, "At least you got a photo of Zephyr's arrest when they dragged her out of the restaurant. It made a great front page, even with the blurry bits."

"Thank you," I said.

"We still need to teach you some basic photography," he said darkly.

"So . . . I still have a job?"

He hesitated. Then finally he said, "Yes."

"With the raise you promised? Thirty percent?"

"Thirty—! Get real. I reckon you misunderstood."

"Plus, you promised to hire my friend Sammy to be your new assistant instead of those interns. He'll do a good job for you, I'm sure of it. And you don't need to tell him I asked you to hire him."

"Are these demands of yours going to go on forever?"

"I wonder if the police will misunderstand when I tell them about the bug you planted on Tommy Rattigan?"

Gus stared. "Are you blackmailing me?"

I tried to muster some outrage about his illegal methods, but I had to admit it was Gus who'd learned where we could find Ralphie before he was butchered. For better or worse, my time with Michael had taught me that gray areas existed and should be tolerated on occasion. So I said, "Are you going to promise you'll never do such a thing again?"

Gus raised a skeptical eyebrow. "What do you care about the way I do my job?"

"I care about the integrity of the newspaper."

"Is that all? Would you care if I got myself deported?"

"I don't know what you mean, Mr. Hardwicke," I said.

We eyed each other from a safe distance, both aware that Michael might very well be watching from one of the windows in the house. I saw Gus's expression soften, and something in his gaze hinted he was resisting the temptation to say more. But he refrained.

Finally, he put out his hand. "A thirty percent raise."

"With that," I said, while his hand remained poised to accept mine, "I hope to be treated as the rest of the reporters are. Without having to worry about being chased around the desk. I may have things to learn, but I won't put up with any more unwelcome behavior from you."

After a moment's hesitation that was suddenly electric with a dozen comebacks, he said with dignity, "Agreed. And to mangle a quote, I hope this is the beginning of an interesting friendship."

I accepted his handshake, and we stood for a second too long, perhaps, under the trees, steadily meeting each other's gaze.

"Thank you," I said graciously.

I did not invite him for dinner. Gus drove off, waving at the wiseguys who were helping the fencing company install a large fence that would soon wrap the whole way around Blackbird Farm. Against the house, a security company crew had leaned an assortment of ladders while they tinkered with all the new electronic gadgetry Michael had ordered for all the windows. He had gone overboard, perhaps, but I knew how he felt. Where the money had come from to pay for all the improvements—that part worried me. There would be more to that story, I was sure.

I went into the kitchen and found my sisters squabbling about feet.

"The twins refuse to get pedicures," Libby said, "so I need help getting them into the salon. And you're elected, Emma. You owe me for all the babysitting."

"You enjoyed every minute of babysitting Noah," Emma snapped. "I'm not risking my life so those boys can get one lousy athlete's foot commercial. Nora, do you have any batteries? I need four C batteries to get Filly Vanilli to work."

"Check the second drawer," I said. "But good grief, that's an ugly toy."

Emma held up the misshapen horse with its googly

eyes and shaggy mane. "I think it's kinda cute." She pulled a string, and the animal began kicking its gangly legs and making squawking noises.

With delight, Max pointed at the singing horse. "Mama!"

"Mama?" Libby cried. "Did you hear him? He said his first word!"

"Yeah," Emma said. "He's also got you confused with a horse. How much bug spray is he inhaling these days?"

I decided to avoid the coming argument and went through the butler's pantry and the dining room to my grandfather's study, now Michael's office.

But the door was closed. I hesitated in the gloomy hallway, listening. From inside the room, I could hear Rawlins speaking slowly, his words muffled. Michael asked him a question in an equally low voice, and there was a long pause before Rawlins replied. I didn't interrupt. I wondered if my nephew had reached any important decisions yet—decisions he was ready to share with his mother, that is.

Quietly, I turned to go.

But the door opened from inside, and Rawlins said, "Aunt Nora?"

He'd been crying. I gave him a hug, holding him tight while I looked past him at Michael, who leaned on the edge of the desk, looking solemn, too.

"You both are very serious," I said, trying to make my voice light. "What's going on?"

Rawlins said, "I guess I have to tell my mom."

"Yes," I said. I rubbed his arms to bolster his resolve.

To me, Michael said, "We thought maybe you could soften the blow."

I shook my head. "Learning that Rawlins is going to be a father is bad enough, but Libby is going to flip out when she realizes she's going to be a grandmother. Nothing I say is going to help."

Rawlins glanced at Michael and seemed to gather his strength. "I didn't know most of what was going on, Aunt Nora. You know that, right? I mean, I was—Zephyr and I, we hooked up in January, but I didn't know anything about the pig stuff. I didn't know she killed her husband, either. That night when she told me about—you know, about being pregnant, we were in my car. We sat and talked until the car ran out of gas. She was all worried about telling her husband."

"Because she was pregnant with your child, not his?"

Rawlins flushed. "Yeah. She was afraid he'd get mad because he'd already raised one kid that wasn't his. I said I'd stand by her while she told him, but she wanted to do it herself. She took my keys so I couldn't follow her. I gave her my coat because she was cold. That's how come you and Aunt Emma found my stuff at Starr's Landing. Anyway, when she told him about the baby, her husband went apeshit. He said he'd gone through a bad operation just for her, but she went behind his back with me and—anyway, he said he would divorce her. He wouldn't raise another kid that wasn't his. He was gonna leave her broke, with a kid coming. So . . . she went nuts and killed him."

"Thinking she'd be better off financially," Michael guessed, "if she wasn't divorced, but a widow instead."

"If she was thinking at all," Rawlins said. "She's really pretty, but kinda impulsive and—well, a little strange, I guess."

I took Rawlins's hand and gave it a squeeze, very glad that he was alive. With Zephyr's past history, it might have just as easily been my nephew whom she tried to kill. I said, "I'm sorry you had this experience, Rawlins."

He nodded. "Yeah, well, it's not over yet. Here's the thing, Aunt Nora. Zephyr's probably going to go to jail for a long time. Killing her husband—that was crazy bad, and Mick doesn't think she's going to get out any time soon, not with her record. She knows that. So she says the baby doesn't matter now and—well, it's mine after it's born."

"Oh, Rawlins," I said.

"Hey, I know I was stupid," he went on, unable to drag his gaze up from the floor. "My mom's been talking to me about taking precautions since I was, like, ten years old, so I should have been smarter, even in the, you know, heat of the moment. Mick says that was probably Zephyr's plan. So now I have a—a kid coming."

"Or not," Michael said.

Rawlins nodded. "Talking to Mick got me thinking about college again. About my future. That maybe the best thing for me and for the—the baby—is that I decide not to be a dad right now. I mean, Aunt Emma gave up her kid, right? And that's the best thing for him?"

"I hope so," I said gently.

"So maybe you would take Zephyr's baby. You and Mick."

I met Michael's gaze. He tried to wipe all expression from his face, letting me make the decision.

Which was impossible, of course. Neither one of us could make a choice of this magnitude alone.

I gave my nephew another hug. "Rawlins, how about if you let Michael and me talk about it?"

"Okay." He sighed as if his heart were too heavy to budge off the floor. "I guess this is the right time to tell my mom about Zephyr and me."

"It won't be too bad," I said. "She's not going to be happy to hear she'll soon be a grandmother. But she'll get used to it. She loves babies, you know." So much that I already worried she might make a rash decision where Perry Delbert was concerned. "You'll be okay."

Rawlins didn't look as though he believed me. He turned and said, "Thanks, Mick. I mean it."

Michael shrugged, making light of his contribution. "Anything you need, kid. I can always listen."

Rawlins walked over and shook his hand, then gave me a kiss on the cheek before going out the door. He closed it behind him.

I went to Michael, and he gathered me up tight.

Holding him close, feeling his heart beat against mine, I whispered, "This is so not the way I expected things to turn out."

"Me neither," he said. "Lemme tell you right now, I'm not buying a minivan. I don't care how many kids we have—a minivan is out of the question."

"Any other fatherly demands?"

His embrace turned gentler. "Nora, when you told me we were going to have a baby, I was happier than I've ever thought I could be." He smiled at the memory of our private interlude when we got home from the evening's excitement in the city. His voice turning husky, he said, "I know a lot of guys whose lives are behind them. But with you, now, I feel like I've got the whole world ahead of me. Ahead of us."

"We do, Michael."

He pulled back enough to cup my face and look into my eyes. "This thing with Little Frankie. I'll be honest. It's not over yet. I've got business to take care of. But I'll work it, I promise."

I tried to quell the anxiety that fluttered inside me. I knew the money Michael had received from his brother had come at a price. I just hoped it wasn't too dear. I took a deep breath and said, "You'll be careful."

"Sure. I'm not worried about that problem. I gotta admit, though, this development with Rawlins has me a little . . ."

I smiled. "Overwhelmed?"

"Overwhelmed in a good way. This is big, Nora. You're going to have to marry me now for sure. We can't provide a half-assed life for these kids. They make things forever between you and me."

Yes, it was forever. I felt as if we were rowing out into the swift and turbulent river of life together, only now our little boat had children in it—with all the joy and heartbreak, the memories and the future that came with a family of our own. Michael and I each had an oar in our hands, but our course was plotted and steady, together. I needed to find a way to make marriage a part of our journey.

A noise came from the old Blackbird family cradle. Noah gave his usual sigh before he woke up and decided he was starving. Michael and I turned to look down at him—the little boy who didn't quite have a home yet, but who had come to live with us for the time being. He seemed to become more and more a part of our household with every passing day in our care. With his little fists, he rubbed his nose, then opened his eyes and looked up at us with happy trust.

In recent days I had spent a lot of time thinking about boys—about sons and fathers and the consequences of wrecked families. I knew it had all weighed on Michael's mind, too. Neither one of us wanted Noah to grow up wondering if he was somebody's consolation prize. Maybe because of that, we already loved him. Perhaps too fiercely for a child who wasn't really ours. Not yet, anyway.

I said, "Hart and Penny and Emma are still fighting about Noah. I don't know how that's going to turn out."

"Until they decide," Michael said in his most no-nonsense tone, "he's better off here, at home with us, than anywhere else."

"Are you sure?"

"Yeah. You and me, we'll handle it somehow. But . . . three kids? All coming at the same time?"

I smiled up at him, my love, my heart, the man with whom I had decided to set sail into the eternal adventure of life. I said, "Be careful what you wish for."

Nora is eight weeks away from giving birth when the antics of her two sisters, the unpredictability of her Aussie boss, and the questionable dealings of her baby's father, Michael Abruzzo, make her life *really* complicated. Oh, and then there's a murder....

Turn the page for an excerpt from

A Little Night Murder

Available now from Obsidian in
hardcover and e-book,
and in paperback beginning in August 2014.

As I waited in the frigid backseat of a limousine, watching the front gate of a women's prison on an otherwise beautiful July afternoon, I wondered if I could tap politely on the door and ask the warden to please incarcerate my sister. Just for a few days of peace and quiet.

She was sitting beside me, skimming the newspaper and driving me crazy. Which I could do nothing about, because I had asked her to do me a favor, and as usual she'd agreed faster than she could touch up her lipstick.

"Why on earth," Libby demanded, "are some men so infatuated with their man parts that they take pictures?" She rattled the offending newspaper. "Really, Nora, here's another story in your paper about a fellow who photographed himself and sent the picture to fourteen women in his workplace. His colleagues called him Thunder Dick. I think that probably just encouraged him. Don't you?"

Distracted, I said, "Uh-huh."

"If Mr. Dick truly wanted to arouse the interest of a woman, he should have photographed himself washing dishes. Now, *that's* sexy! These days, a picture of a man lathered up with Palmolive suds would make me faint with desire."

"Uhm," I said.

"But maybe he could be pictured without his shirt."

She began to stare off into the distance, her eyes going dreamy, her lips turning slack. "Bare-chested. With a splash of lotion on his skin to catch the candlelight. Because—"

I finally began paying attention. "Are you having a stroke?"

"—let's face it," she said, as if I had not spoken, "the right lighting can conceal a lull in a person's gym routine or a temporary overindulgence in burritos. What is it about men and burritos? I find it puzzling. Don't you? I mean, why have a burrito when you could have chocolate? Does That Man of Yours use lotion?"

I blinked, pretty sure I'd missed something important. "What?"

Libby finally folded up the paper and sighed. "Nora, your hormones have addled your brain. By the time your baby is born, you won't be able to keep two thoughts in your head at the same time."

During the last several months, she had repeatedly volunteered to help guide me through my pregnancy. So far, her most practical advice had been for me to scrub my nipples to toughen them up for nursing.

"I'm a little distracted at the moment, Libby."

She pointed out the front-page article that had started her rant. "Why is your newspaper on such a penis kick this summer? I liked it better when journalists got obsessed with fun things like movie stars and shoes. Why don't you write a nice article about summer sandals?"

I love my sister—both of them, that is—but sometimes I wish we were back in the days when I could lure Libby into a closet with a Butterfinger bar and lock her up for ten minutes of solitude. My solitude, that is.

In the front seat, the chauffeur had been studiously ignoring my sister's rambling discussion of male anatomy. But suddenly he said, "There she is, Miss Blackbird."

The door of the stark prison building opened from the inside, and my best friend stepped out into the sunlight. If her first instinct was to wince at the searing sunlight, she suppressed it. But then, Lexie Paine, as close to royalty as anyone in Philadelphia got, was all about self-control. She put on a pair of very dark glasses and squared her shoulders. Then, wearing the same black Armani suit she had worn in court the day she'd confessed to manslaughter, she walked briskly toward the fence that separated the free world from the prison where she'd been incarcerated for nine and a half months. She carried a ragged manila envelope, which I presumed contained all that remained of her considerable fortune.

"She doesn't look fat at all." Libby leaned over me to peer out the window. "I hear they serve white bread at every meal in prison. I might as well glue white bread directly to my thighs. One jaywalking citation and I'd be a poster girl for Jenny Craig."

I opened the car door and bailed out onto the hot, cracked asphalt of the parking lot. "Stay here," I said to Libby. "And remember what I told you. No reporter can find out where Lexie is going, okay? Don't tell a soul."

"What do you take me for? I am perfectly capable of keeping a secret when it's—"

I closed the door on my sister's next volley of claptrap.

For the last several days since I'd heard of my friend's upcoming release, surprising Lexie had seemed like a good idea. Now, though, I had every expectation she might slap my face and hitchhike out of there. For my role in her incarceration, I might have deserved that.

She walked straight through the gate, and from behind her sunglasses, she said coolly, "Nora, I knew you were pregnant, but isn't this overdoing things just a bit?"

"Maybe a little." Noting that she did not hug me, I said, "Lex, we need to get in a car right away."

Lexie did not obey my request. She stood still, back stiff, head high. I could not see her eyes behind the glasses. Back when she was young, after a blue-blooded cousin broke her bones and assaulted her, Lexie had reinvented herself into the girl who'd never be a victim again. She became the smartest student in her Ivy League class. Then a powerful woman who crushed the competition on Wall Street. Now that she'd been to prison, I wondered how she planned to reinvent herself one more time.

She said, "Why should I get into your car?"

"Because you're going to be the hottest news story of the summer," I said, "and you'd hate that. We're trying to protect you from the reporters. Lex, please get into the car."

A long, awful moment stretched, and I wondered if the most important friendship of my life had ended.

"No," she said. "No, just for a minute, let me breathe."

With her face tilted to the sunlight, she reached out and took my hand. Clutched it, really, and her chilly facade crumbled. "Thank you, sweetie. I was afraid my mother might show up today, and there are times when you just can't face your mother. You're such a welcome relief. I can't tell you."

I felt the bubble of tension break in my throat. She had stuck by me during the worst time of my life, and I intended to do the same for her.

For now, I said, "I brought Oreos."

She laughed unsteadily and let me go. "You're a lifesaver. But you shouldn't be doing this. It's not going to be easy being my friend now."

"You think I'm a stranger to scandal?" I asked with a smile.

"Good point." She removed her sunglasses and brushed something that might have been a tear from the corner of her eye. "Your tribulations have made you stronger, haven't they? All right, let's go—but why three limos?" She gave the three idling black cars and two hired taxis a composed inspection.

"Television trucks are waiting out on the street, and so are about a dozen print journalists. There's even one man with a camera on a motorcycle. We're going to do our best to lose all of them before they can figure out where we're going. And Libby's going to stage a scene to attract their attention."

Libby chose that moment to rap her knuckles on the car window and wave brightly at Lexie.

Lexie waved back, trying to conceal her trepidation. "What kind of scene?"

"I thought it best to leave the details to her. But I'm sure whatever she dreams up will do the trick. This way."

Lexie followed me to the second limousine. "Has your beau plotted all this?"

"It was a team effort. Ready now?" I opened the rear passenger door for her.

Our escape was touch-and-go. I thought the reporters spotted us. But in the rearview mirror we saw Libby bail out at a traffic light and feign a shrieking meltdown—scattering the contents of her handbag, which might have included several rubber snakes. Later she told us reporters called an ambulance because they thought the chauffeur was having a heart attack. I also learned that my sister scored a date with a traffic cop who had stopped to help.

A few days after that, Lexie was still successfully concealed from the press, although lounging around the pool at her mother's summerhouse felt more like a vacation at a luxury spa.

"Who knew you had such a cunning side?" Lexie said, seated in her bathing suit at a glass-topped patio table under a striped umbrella.

I was drifting in the cool bliss of the swimming pool on a large pink noodle. "It's a recessive gene I inherited from my parents."

"They certainly know how to live the good life," Lexie said. "So does my mother. She's an enthusiastic wife, but mothering never suited her. Does that worry you, sweetie? The possibility of evolving into a terrible mother now that you're hatching one of your own?"

"Most of the time I'm too hungry to worry," I said. "Tell the truth. Do I look like a manatee?"

She tilted down her sunglasses to make a better examination of me wallowing in the water in all my pregnant splendor. Diplomatically, she said, "That swimsuit is very flattering, sweetie."

She looked elegant in a black bathing suit with a black lace cover-up designed by an artist who knew how to make a woman's nearly naked body look chic, not tarty. I, on the other hand, was simply glad there were no harpoons handy, since it would have been easy to mistake me for the great white whale.

I said, "I have eight weeks to go. We Blackbird women get big early."

"Well, you look happy," she said.

She slipped off her cover-up and waded down the steps of the shallow end. With the seemingly unshakable composure of her Mayflower forebears, she inhaled a deep, cleansing breath of fresh air and let it out on a sigh.

She said, "The press continues to be baffled about my whereabouts?"

"So far, so good." I didn't want to bother her with the

details, but there was a full-scale hunt going on—complete with baying hounds and irate letters to editors from former clients whose fortunes had been ruined by the millionaire investment whiz who'd gotten out of jail thanks to a team of mobbed-up lawyers.

"I'm grateful for your help, Nora," she said. "I'll probably have to sell my house, you know. To help with the Cause."

"I hope not, Lex."

She shrugged. She had taken to making light of her effort to repay all the clients who'd been swindled by her former partner at the Paine Investment Group. I knew she was obsessed with getting the hundreds of stolen millions back into the hands of the investors who had trusted her firm with their life savings. After all, she said, it was her name on the brass plate that still hung on the building in the center of Philadelphia, not her larcenous partner's. But it was going to take time. And sacrifice.

Meanwhile, she admitted to feeling guilty about her luxurious hiding place.

Indoors, the great house's many gracious amenities included a billiards room with cigar burns courtesy of J.P. Morgan, a salon where polo teams could be plied with cocktails and a servant's wing with forty numbered bells in the hallway. That wing was currently empty, since Lexie couldn't afford more than the services of her longtime houseman, Samir, who had taken a deep pay cut to continue to loyally shop, cook and keep house. Lexie confided in me that he had accepted the job offer because he was writing a book in his spare time—subject unknown so far—and he was glad to have his own sprawling suite in the essentially empty house for staring glumly at his computer screen. To our tremendous gratitude, Samir made our lunch every day and regularly appeared with frosty pitchers of herbal tea.

It was not Samir, however, who came through the diaphanous curtains of the French doors and stepped onto the bluestone terrace of the pool, carrying our refreshed iced tea pitcher in one hand and pinning a portfolio under his other arm. Rather, it was a tall, hulking man with an infamous reputation.

He said to Lexie, "I think I just scared the bejesus out of your butler."

"Don't worry, darling," Lexie called to him. "He recovers quickly. Michael, is Nora expecting twins, do you think?"

The father of my baby put the fresh pitcher on the table. "Doctor says just one. Last month, she showed us the pictures to prove it, 'cause I had my doubts." He ambled to the edge of the pool and smiled down at me. "How was yoga class?"

I paddled over to the stairs. "Great. Baby Girl loved it, too. She was very peaceful." I put my wet hand up to him.

Michael Abruzzo, who had sworn he was getting out of organized crime, was still frequently mistaken for a wanted criminal. He had big shoulders and a broken face, and in public he often kept up a kind of benign menace that could scatter a crowd. But he helped me out of the pool as if I were precious glass. From a nearby lounge chair, he pulled a towel and clasped it around as much of me as it could cover.

I stretched up on tiptoe and gave him a kiss. "Did anyone follow you?"

He raised one eyebrow. "You're kidding, right?"

"After that masterful display of evasive driving during last week's escape," I said, referring to Michael's command of the lead car in our prison-escape plan, "I don't mean to cast any doubt on your criminal expertise, but—"

"I didn't have any reporters on my tail today. Lexie's

undisclosed location is still a secret." He kissed me again. "Did you tell her?"

I smiled up into his blue eyes. "I was waiting for you to get here."

Lexie perked up. "Tell me what? Are you two keeping secrets?"

I clasped his hand, and he squeezed mine back. I took a deep breath and faced my friend. "We're getting married."

The Bestselling
Blackbird Sisters Mystery Series
by
Nancy Martin

Don't miss a single adventure of the Blackbird sisters,
a trio of Philadelphia-born, hot-blooded bluebloods
with a flair for fashion—and for solving crimes!

How to Murder a Millionaire
Dead Girls Don't Wear Diamonds
Some Like It Lethal
Cross Your Heart and Hope to Die
Have Your Cake and Kill Him Too
A Crazy Little Thing Called Death
Murder Melts in Your Mouth
No Way to Kill a Lady

Available wherever books are sold or at
penguin.com

facebook.com/TheCrimeSceneBooks

OM0052